The Devon Bookshop

The
Devon
Bookshop

V. E. HALL

Matador
Unit E2 Airfield Business Park,
Harrison Road, Market Harborough,
Leicestershire. LE16 7UL
Tel: 0116 279 2299
Email: books@troubador.co.uk
Web: www.troubador.co.uk/matador
Twitter: @matadorbooks

ISBN 978 1 80313 538 0

British Library Cataloguing in Publication Data.
A catalogue record for this book is available from the British Library.

Typeset in 11pt Minion Pro by Troubador Publishing Ltd, Leicester, UK

Matador is an imprint of Troubador Publishing Ltd

This book is dedicated to Angie Wells
with thanks for her support and encouragement.

ONE

The presence wasn't sinister. She could tell that much. Why was it there? What did it want?

Matt interrupted Acacia's thoughts, 'I've done as much as I can. If you're ready to call it an evening, let's go upstairs.'

'Okay. I'm ready.'

Matt switched off his office light, and walked over to his wife. He smiled at her. 'Thanks for helping.'

Acacia kissed him lightly on the cheek.

They made their way to the door that led up to their flat above the bookshop. The presence had gone as soon as Matt had spoken. Acacia knew she wouldn't be able to rest now until she found out who the presence was and what it wanted. She'd have to wait in the bookshop one evening while Matt was out playing darts.

*

Acacia seemed to radiate light everywhere she went, and people she talked to felt happier after seeing her.

Walking to the supermarket, she stopped to talk to an elderly man with a Labrador. He gave her chapter and verse of the dog's morning. 'He's a very handsome dog,' she said, stroking the dog's head. 'It's a bit nippy this morning. Are you going to stop for coffee?' Acacia pointed to a small coffee shop over the road. 'He has a great selection of homemade cakes, and the coffee's very good.'

'I don't think he'll let me in with the dog,' the man said.

Acacia saw the way he looked longingly towards the shop and could sense the man was lonely. Time in a coffee shop, surrounded by people, with his dog safely by his side, would probably make a big difference to this man's day. She'd lived alone for a few years. She knew what it was like. 'It's a dog-friendly place. He'll be pleased to see you both.'

'Really? Are you sure?'

Acacia nodded. 'He likes dogs.'

A smile on his face, the man said, 'It'd be great to have a coffee and be able to take Milo in with me. We usually just go home after our walk.'

'Give it a go,' Acacia said, giving the dog one last pat as owner and dog headed across the road.

The man and his dog reached the coffee shop, pushed the door open and paused. Acacia could see he was asking if it was alright to go in with the dog. Then the man turned back to Acacia, and gave her the thumbs-up sign. She smiled and waved in return, then walked on.

Inside the supermarket, there was a flustered woman struggling with a wheeled shopping trolley. Acacia helped her out, the woman stuttering her thanks. Acacia made her way round the grocery aisles until she came to the milk, grabbed a pack, made the girl on the checkout laugh about something and stood outside watching the town as it got ready for the day. She said a cheery, 'Good morning,' to the road sweeper, who waved at her.

Acacia's last port of call was the thirteenth-century church. The grey stone tower stood tall, a symbol of permanence and stability. It clearly said *I'm here for the long haul.* The people of Holsworthy had been attending services here for hundreds of years. Acacia walked past the tidy burial plots and headstones of the cemetery, opened the heavy wooden door and chose a seat on one of the benches, breathing in the sense of peace, the calm reassurance that all was well.

Looking at the stained glass windows she tried to find a message from the colourfully depicted scenes. But what she got was reassurance. No answers. She sighed.

Acacia was a Christian, in stark contrast to her parents, who had been what they called *charmers.* They refused to be called witches, hating the word, saying they only harnessed nature's power. They did nothing negative. She knew that was true, but still it was at odds with her beliefs, wasn't it?

She bowed her head in prayer and asked for guidance. She knew there was a ghost, or maybe ghosts, in the bookshop where she lived. She'd known it the moment she'd walked in. Being psychic and a Christian was an unusual mix, but life was full of contradictions. Should she try to communicate with the ghost? Did it need help to move on? She was hoping to get answers.

Acacia heard the heavy wooden door open and close, and the sound of someone walking to the row of benches opposite. She watched as a man bowed his head in prayer, hearing his voice but unable to catch the words. Acacia's sense of peace remained. She bowed her head again, asking what she should do. Should she ignore the ghost? Should she try and help it? Then, as always, she got the answer in her mind.

'The ghost you sense is no threat. He's there because he wants to be there. He'd like you to talk to him. Follow your instincts.'

She said a quiet thank you. Then she got up and walked out of the church, pausing in the graveyard to read some of the headstones, always interested in how those around her lived – and had lived – their lives. She could smell the damp earth, still mingled with the fallen leaves of last autumn. Its compost was good, and flowers and grasses thrived. Not many flowers there at the moment, winter was still holding sway. It was that damp cold that seemed to seep through your clothes, but she knew once spring arrived many of the graves would be adorned by daffodils, tulips and other happy reminders that life goes on, and loved ones are remembered.

She walked back to the bookshop, heard the 'ding-a-ling' of the doorbell as she entered.

'You were up and out early this morning,' her husband, Matt, said. 'Everything okay?'

She went over to Matt and kissed him. 'Everything's fine. I'll make fresh coffee.'

Acacia was still thinking about the ghost as she approached the coffee area. She couldn't mention it to Matt. He didn't believe in anything supernatural, but she found that reassuring about him. He knew exactly what he believed. There were no grey areas in Matt's life. Things were ordered, everything in its place. Acacia was the *flaky* one. She smiled to herself. *Flaky* was what Matt and his granddad called anyone who held views other than theirs. What would Matt say if she told him there was a ghost in his bookshop?

'Did you mention coffee?' Matt prompted.

'Sorry, I was miles away. I'll get some going.'

*

What was that?

Outside, the rain hammered on the bookshop windows, but Matt had tuned that out.

No. There was someone or something in the bookshop other than him. He knew it.

Matt's fingers itched to turn on the light. But if it was an intruder, the light would alert him. Matt was sure he'd seen movement, and could smell cigarette smoke. He peered through the gloom, and thought he could make out a figure sitting on the sofa in the coffee area.

'I've called the police. They'll be here soon,' Matt blurted out, but he got no answer. He edged around the first bookshelf, and narrowed his eyes trying to see in the dark. There was a faint glimmer ahead, but he couldn't see what it was. Was it a torch? He listened for movement of any kind but heard nothing. He felt his way to the next bookshelf. The blinds were drawn, but he could see a faint glimmer from the street light outside. He made his way to the coffee area and peered round the bookshelf. There was a light coming from the sofa and a blurred shape, but he couldn't make sense of what he was seeing. It didn't seem solid.

He took a deep breath, and flicked the light switch, flooding the shop with light, revealing the opened box of new books he'd left by the poetry section. He saw it just in time and stopped himself tripping over it. He could still smell the cigarette smoke. He checked the windows and doors. All was secure. Where was the smoke coming from? He checked the sofa. Yes, the smell of smoke seemed stronger there. Was it from earlier in the day? Customers weren't supposed to smoke in the shop. He thought he must have imagined the image on the sofa, but the smell of smoke was still there. That was real.

Matt heard someone at the front door, and he froze.

His wife Acacia's smiling face appeared, peering through the glass. She was carrying a lot of parcels and looked happy, if rather wet, rain dripping off her hood.

'Good shopping trip?' he asked, unlocking the door, eager to put some normality back into his day, and forcing his breathing to slow down.

'It was crazy busy, but I got some lovely curtains for the living room,' said Acacia, handing some parcels to Matt. She crinkled her nose. 'You haven't taken up smoking, have you?'

'Not in this lifetime,' he smiled. 'I think a customer must've had a crafty ciggy when we weren't looking.'

'Smells quite fresh to me,' she said. 'Maybe we should put another No Smoking sign by the coffee machine?'

'Good idea. Let's get this stuff upstairs,' Matt said, kissing his wife briefly on the cheek, and opening the door that led upstairs to their flat.

Matt walked up the stairs as normally as he could, but his mind was racing. What had just happened in the bookshop? Maybe the cigarette smoke had been there from earlier and he hadn't noticed? But it smelt recent. And what was that image he'd seen on the sofa? Had he really seen something, or had he imagined it?

His grandfather had told him his mother was *unhinged*. Was it hereditary? Was he starting to see things that weren't there? He frowned, unsure what to make of what had happened.

*

After breakfast, Matt went down to the bookshop. He was pleased there was no sign of cigarette smoke now.

Since he'd taken the bookshop over from his granddad, he'd changed things slightly. He'd had the wooden floor sanded and painted a light blue and the same with the window frames and sills. He was pleased with the effect. Modern furnishings had helped, including the new coffee area for staff and customers, and a natural-flame fireplace encouraging customers to sit on the sofa and read a little, either before or after purchasing their books. Acacia had a good eye for decorating, and the bookshop was welcoming and comfortable while maintaining its Georgian character. And he'd enlarged the book selection, creating a couple of new sections and thinking of adding more. His grandparents seemed pleased he'd made the shop his own with these alterations. Custom had increased too.

He made fresh coffee for customers and staff, poured himself some, then headed to his office. Justin, his assistant, wouldn't be here for over an hour so there was plenty of time to sort out the invoices. He attacked his in-tray enthusiastically. He loved creating order out of chaos. It seemed barely two minutes later that Justin knocked at his office door and said, 'Morning, Boss.'

'Hey, Justin,' Matt said. 'Let's hope the weather drives some serious booklovers in this morning. Cold but dry usually means people wandering in. Could you have a look at the mystery section today? Have a good think about how you can make it eye-catching, and run it by me before doing anything drastic. Okay?'

'Right. I'll put my thinking cap on,' Justin said. He wandered over to the back of the shop, thinking about possibilities. He went to the storeroom to pick up a box of new books, then put it on the trolley and wheeled it to the mystery section. He was going through the box, his serious grey eyes focused on the box content list, when Matt came over later.

'Have you thought of any ideas for the display?' Matt asked.

'What I thought was…' Justin stopped, and his nose twitched. 'Is someone smoking in the shop?'

Matt put down his mug and went round the bookshelves. No one was there. He could smell it too though. Again.

'Nobody there, Justin. Maybe it's coming from next door?' Matt said. 'What were you saying before?' Matt was distracted by the smell of smoke. Was there an electrical problem? Or was it really cigarette smoke?

'I thought we could do a specifically British mystery authors thing,' Justin said. 'Get some posters from the publishers, put them on the wall behind the customer's sofa, and right next to the coffee area have a selection of mystery books. Maybe we could get a new author to come in and sign books? What do you think?'

Before Matt could answer, Justin added. 'Matt, that cigarette smell is quite strong. We don't have any customers in here at the moment. It seems to be right in the coffee area.'

'I'll go to the shops either side to see if they have anyone smoking in there,' Matt said. 'I think it must be coming from next door.'

*

Justin went over to the sofa, where the smell was strongest, and closed his eyes. He could sense something or someone. He opened his eyes but couldn't see anyone there. He closed his eyes again. Yes, he could definitely sense someone. He opened his eyes to see Acacia standing there smiling at him. Startled, he gave a nervous laugh.

'You can smell it too, eh?' Acacia asked. 'Where do you think it's coming from?'

'I didn't hear you come in,' Justin frowned. 'Matt's gone to the shops either side to see if it's coming from one of them.'

'What do *you* think?' Acacia asked. She'd seen him standing there with his eyes closed. She'd noticed little things about Justin before. She was pretty sure he was psychic.

'I'm not sure what to think.'

'Well, give it your best shot.'

'I think it might be a ghost trying to communicate with us, trying to get our attention for some reason,' Justin said, avoiding her eyes.

'There now, that wasn't so difficult was it?' Acacia said. 'I've been thinking about it and come up with the same thing you have, Justin. Let's see what Matt says when he comes back in.'

'You believe in ghosts?' Justin said. 'But Matt doesn't believe in anything like that.'

'Well, I'm not Matt. And I've seen a fair few ghosts myself, Justin, so I know they exist. Matt and I don't talk about it though of course.'

'Wow. Does Matt know you're psychic?'

'We've never discussed it, Justin,' Acacia said. 'He made it clear anything supernatural was *nonsense,* and so we just never talk about it.'

*

Matt came back into the bookshop and shook his head at them both. 'No one in either shop is smoking,' he said. 'Neither of them allows smoking on their premises. I don't know what it is or where it's coming from.'

Justin took a deep breath, then blurted out, 'Matt, do you think maybe it's a ghost trying to get our attention?'

'Ghosts? Come on, Justin, you know there's no such thing. Maybe I should ask you to do a display for a supernatural section rather than the mystery section?' Matt laughed, and Justin's head sagged.

'Matt, can I have a word?' Acacia said, taking Matt's elbow and steering him away.

Matt look surprised, but went into his office with his wife.

'That was rather unkind, Matt, speaking to Justin like that,' Acacia said.

Matt's eyebrows went up, and he was about to say something smart when Acacia continued before he could. 'You should apologise to Justin, Matt. It took courage for him to suggest a ghost to you. He knows your views on the supernatural, but he felt he had to suggest an alternative to the scenario you came up with, and frankly, I agree with him.'

'You agree with him? You think there is a ghost in the bookshop?' Matt asked.

Acacia knew her husband's thoughts on the subject, so she continued with caution. 'Matt, Justin and I know your convictions,' she said, 'but we think differently, and we don't deserve to be dismissed out of hand just because our beliefs conflict with yours.'

Matt sat down behind his desk, and stared at an invoice.

Acacia went over to him, and put her hand on his shoulder. 'Justin looks up to you, Matt. He loves working here, and he's very loyal. But, things aren't always black and white, sometimes there's some grey in there.'

'You really believe in ghosts?' Matt asked, fidgeting on his chair.

'I've had dealings with ghosts before,' Acacia said. 'The cigarette smoke does have the hallmark of a ghost trying to get our attention, and I'm going to look into it further in my own way. You've done your bit, and it didn't work. Now it's my turn, and I might ask Justin to help as he obviously shares my views. Do I have your blessing?'

Matt contemplated his wife's face. She was serious. He shuffled some paper on his desk, but said nothing.

'Matt,' Acacia continued, seeing his eyes had glazed over and needing him to take in what she was saying. She reached over and took Matt's hand in hers, holding it firmly. 'Please, Matt, hear what I'm saying.' Her usually smiling green eyes held steely determination.

Matt met his wife's gaze. The edges of his mouth came up in a rueful smile, and their eyes met. Matt would listen.

Acacia hesitated, but she knew what had to be said, so she took a deep breath. 'I know what your granddad said about your mum, but it's not true. She was not unhinged, and neither am I. You know I'm not. I know this is a bit of a shock, and I've never discussed it with you because of your beliefs. But, I think it's time you realised there's more to the world than you think, Matt. Someone is trying to tell us something, and we owe it to them to find out what it is. I'm going to look into it.'

Matt swallowed. He looked down at the desk again.

Acacia watched her husband. She knew his world was out of kilter. He didn't know how to handle it.

'I'm going to get some coffee,' he said. 'I'll think about what you've said. I didn't mean to upset Justin. You're right, I'll apologise to him. See you later,' said Matt, getting up and moving towards the smell of freshly brewed coffee.

Acacia watched as her husband walked to the seating area, and poured a mug of the coffee that always made him feel better. He sipped it, and she saw the tension ease out of his body. He then made his way to where Justin was unpacking some new books. She saw him speak to Justin, put his hand on his shoulder, and smile.

Justin's face lit up, and then he and Matt tackled a new box of books together.

TWO

Acacia closed the transcription programme and looked out of the window. She could hear the sounds down in the square as people went about their day. The Wednesday market stalls were bustling, stallholders wrapping up goods and customers chatting. Delivery vans were unloading. Somewhere a dog was barking.

Acacia had started transcribing reports at 5.30am and stopped at nine to bake a cake. It was now cool enough to ice. She breathed in the freshly baked cake smell appreciatively. She loved the freedom working from home gave her, and she loved the creative act of baking. Matt always appreciated it too. As her aunt had once said, 'If there's cake in the tin, everyone's happy.' She put it on a plate, and headed downstairs to the bookshop.

'Ooh,' Justin said. 'Freshly baked lemon cake. It smells yummy.' He took a piece, and put fresh coffee on to brew.

'How's it going?' Acacia asked Matt, handing him a slice.

'Alright,' Matt said. 'Busy. The weather's fine, and that always brings people out. That new author we decided to feature is selling well. It's great to have an author from this area.'

Acacia heard the doorbell jingle and looked over. What she saw was a very handsome man, six feet tall, blue eyes, blond hair and wearing very smart, expensive looking clothes. He moved quickly, like he was on a mission. She watched as he came over to them.

'Hi, Matt. Lovely blue skies today,' he said. 'Could we have a chat, do you think?' He looked at Acacia and then back at Matt.

'This is my wife, Acacia,' Matt said.

Morgan put his hand out. 'Morgan,' he said. 'Pleased to meet you.'

Acacia shook hands with Morgan and smiled at him. He smelt good, and was certainly attractive. She mentally reprimanded herself for thinking these thoughts, then turned her attention back to her husband, giving him a dazzling smile.

'Like to join us, Acacia?' Matt said. 'Morgan and I are going to take some coffee to the seating area.'

'Oh, no,' Acacia said, 'I have to get back to my reports.' She smiled at Morgan. 'Nice to have met you.' She put the cake next to the coffee machine, then turned back to Morgan. 'Please have a piece of cake with your coffee. It's fresh.'

*

Morgan accepted a slice of cake and watched her go, appreciating the way she moved in her jeans and loose blue top. And she baked too. And those eyes! Deep green. Highly unusual.

He mentally slapped himself. She was Matt's wife.

'What's up?' asked Matt in his usual open manner.

Morgan was struggling a bit. He quite liked Matt, at least the couple of times he'd seen him so far. Yet his mother had told him that Matt was a spoiled, arrogant liar and had told Morgan to have nothing to do with him or his sister. Morgan's mother had hated *her* sister, Eliza, Matt's mother, with a vengeance and ever since Morgan could remember she'd gone on and on about how Eliza had ruined her life, how she'd mistreated her, lied about her, turned their parents against her. Morgan had never met his Aunt Eliza or his cousins, Matt and Sarah, but ever since his mother died he'd wanted to meet his family. He had no one, other than some friends – and were they really friends, he wondered?

'Thanks,' Morgan said, accepting the coffee Matt offered him and taking a seat on the sofa.

Matt, sitting in the armchair the other side of the coffee table, leaned forward, and waited. Morgan said nothing, so Matt spoke again. 'Do you have a particular book you'd like me to order for you? You don't live around here, do you?'

'No thanks. It's nothing to do with books really, although I must admit whenever I come in here I find books I want to buy,' Morgan smiled. 'I live in London. I'm here for a few days.'

'What is it then?' Matt asked. 'There's nothing wrong, is there?'

'No, nothing's wrong,' Morgan said. 'The fact is, I've been looking for you, and I found you here in this bookshop.' Morgan paused, weighing his words.

Matt frowned, clearly puzzled.

'You see, I'm pretty sure you're my cousin, Matt,' Morgan said after another sip of his coffee. He put the cup down and looked at Matt, waiting for his reaction. The coffee really was exceptionally good. Not what he'd expect to be given away to customers at all.

Matt's mouth opened and closed, but no words came out. He took a sip of coffee. Morgan noticed it seemed to stabilise him.

'I thought my mum was an only child,' Matt said.

'Well, our mothers didn't get on, as I understand it,' Morgan said, 'and their parents are dead, so the rift was complete. My mother died recently, and I have no siblings, so that's why I wanted to find you. You have a sister, Sarah, I believe?'

'Yes, I do. She lives up north now. But this is a complete mystery to me. It's going to take some time to sink in. Are you sure about this?' Matt gulped some more coffee. Morgan could almost see Matt's brain starting to react to it. He thought it was the comforting heat of it, the flavour, not just the caffeine.

'Yes, I've done some research,' Morgan said, watching Matt's reaction with concern. 'Here's our family tree, Matt. See? There's Eliza and her sister, Wiladelle.' Morgan laid the documents on the coffee table, and they both studied them.

Cigarette smoke wafted over them both, and Matt looked up.

'There's no smoking in here, right?' Morgan asked, smelling the cigarette smoke.

'Right. I think it must have come in from the street,' Matt said.

'Or you have a resident ghost,' Morgan smiled.

'Ghosts?' Matt said. 'There's a logical explanation for the smoke. I just haven't found it yet.'

He doesn't believe in ghosts. Interesting, thought Morgan. And, if he doesn't believe in ghosts, he won't believe in magic.

That could cause problems.

*

It was raining again, in almost horizontal sheets. The cold and damp were seeping into Matt's body, causing him to shiver briefly, and he zipped up his navy Boss parka jacket. He was rummaging in the shed behind the shop, looking for some more shelving for Justin's display. Thank goodness the shed is waterproof, he thought.

Matt heard a faint *miaow*. He looked around the shed. Nothing. *Miaow*, he heard again. He fetched a stepladder from the shed and climbed up it, leaning over the wall into the alleyway behind the bookshop, peering through the steady rain, wiping it away from his eyes. It was difficult to see, the rain was so heavy. *Miaow* he heard again, fainter this time. He went out of the side gate into the alleyway. What he saw was a tiny ginger tabby kitten, no more than five to six weeks old, huddled against the wall – dripping wet, muddy and frightened. He slowly walked towards it, and it backed away. He stopped and spoke gently to it. 'Hello. Is your mum anywhere around?' he asked, looking over the rest of the alley. He couldn't see any other cats or kittens anywhere.

How on earth had this kitten got here? 'Would you like me to take you inside out of this nasty cold, wet weather and give you some cream?' he asked the little cat. He moved a step closer, and this time it didn't back away. He reached down to touch it. It flinched at first, which tugged at Matt's heart strings. He tried again, speaking gently all the time, and he managed to pick the kitten up, murmuring reassuring, quiet words while walking back to the gate and into the yard. Then he went into the bookshop where he was met by an incredulous Justin.

'What have you got there?' Justin asked.

Matt just smiled, and put his finger to his lips, going to the door leading to the flat with a now visibly shaking kitten.

*

Acacia looked up from her keyboard, and saw that Matt was holding a kitten. 'Oh, what a little darling. He's very frightened isn't he? And very wet.'

'I found him in the alley behind the shop,' Matt said. 'Can you get some cream for him please, Acacia? Do we have any boxes up here? A blanket inside a box next to the radiator would be good, I think.'

Acacia bustled about, getting things for the kitten.

Matt then put the kitten down next to the saucer of cream. The kitten immediately drank the cream, saw the box and climbed in. He looked around him, eyeing the two humans carefully.

'Well, looks like we've got a cat,' Acacia said, smiling. 'No one around anywhere? No mother cat?'

'I'm going down to have another proper look,' Matt said, 'but I couldn't see any other cats or people anywhere nearby. I think he was abandoned, Acacia. He is pretty frightened. When I've had a thorough look round I'll nip over to the pet store and get some supplies. Lucky we're not busy in the shop at the moment. We'll need to put an advert in the paper and stuff asking if anyone's lost him, but I have a feeling he has no one who cares about him.'

Acacia watched her husband. He was dripping wet, but his concern was for the kitten, not himself. He was such a kind person. She loved him so much that sometimes it frightened her with its intensity. She grabbed a towel and started towelling Matt's wet hair.

Matt stared at her, surprised.

'Well, the kitten isn't the only one who's wet,' she said. 'And, the kitten isn't alone anymore. He or she has us now. What shall we call him? Is it a boy?'

Matt nodded. 'I think it's a boy. He's so small though, it's difficult to tell.'

'What about Ginger?' She studied the kitten, who had opened his eyes. A look of horror came over his little face, and his whole body went rigid. 'No, that doesn't suit him,' she said, watching the kitten carefully. 'On second thoughts, what about Tiger?'

The kitten's body relaxed. His name was sorted out to his satisfaction. He assumed a nonchalant expression, starting a careful face wash.

'Yes, I think Tiger suits him,' Matt said.

'Excellent. Tiger it is,' Acacia said, picking the kitten up and giving him a cuddle.

Tiger studied Acacia, and she could have sworn he was wearing a smug expression. She smiled and kissed him on the top of his head. 'You monkey,' she laughed, kissing him again, and she returned him to his box.

*

Matt went back outside, checked the alleyway thoroughly, even asked the nearby shopkeepers. No one knew anything about a lost or stray cat or kitten.

Matt went to look in the road near the church, and sure enough he saw the body of a dead cat, obviously hit by a car. He searched the nearby churchyard in case any other kittens were around. He found nothing, and he hoped Tiger was the only one. He got a box from a nearby shopkeeper and carefully placed the dead cat in the box. He'd take it to the vets and ask them to see if it was tagged so any owners could be notified, but he felt it was probably a stray cat and no one would be looking for it. He put his hand on the cat's head and said, 'I found your kitten, he's fine. He's going to be living with us and will be loved.'

Once he'd been to the vets, he would bury the mother cat in their garden behind the shop. She would see her kitten and know he was okay. He stopped. If he didn't believe in ghosts, why was he thinking the mother cat would see Tiger and know he was okay? He shrugged. Acacia was right – life wasn't always black and white.

*

Tiger was asleep and didn't wake up until Matt and Acacia were preparing their dinner. Acacia put some kitten food on a saucer in front of his box, and Tiger ate some slowly, looking around him all the time. Having eaten about half of it he went on a tour of the flat, checking out all the furniture and each room thoroughly for possible dangers. Finding none, he went back to his food before climbing back into his box and falling asleep again.

'You know, Matt,' Acacia said, 'my Aunt Tabitha always says a house is not a home without a cat, and she's right. I think you were meant to find Tiger. I think he's meant to live with us.'

Matt nodded. He and Acacia had been talking about getting a cat just a few days back, before the cigarette smoke incident had put it out of their minds. Now they had a cat. Strange how things happened like that, he thought.

'I believe Tiger is special,' Acacia said.

And, although Acacia didn't know it at the time, she was right.

*

A light mist covered everything in the square, and people wore scarves and hoods, some had umbrellas, but people seemed to have other things than books on their minds, and the bookshop was quiet this morning. Matt and Justin walked to the centre aisle, deep in conversation regarding a new book display. Suddenly they heard a loud *smack* as a book fell off the bookshelf onto the wooden floor. Matt looked at the book, and was just bending to pick it up when Justin shoved him out of the way. A whole shelf load of books fell where Matt had been standing just seconds before.

Matt went over and checked the shelf, now devoid of books. It seemed sound. No loose screws or anything. He checked the shelf below it and above it. All was well.

Justin started to put the books back on the shelf. 'Has your new kitten found his way into the bookshop, Matt?'

'Good point. I'll have a look round,' Matt said.

No sign of the kitten, so Matt went up to the flat to ask

Acacia. Tiger was playing on his new scratching post with a catnip mouse.

'Problem?' Acacia asked.

'Some books fell off the shelf,' Matt said, 'and Justin and I wondered if maybe Tiger had got downstairs and was playing with the books.'

'Hmm. Well, it's not Tiger, as you can see,' Acacia said.

'Right,' Matt frowned. What had caused it then? 'Glad to see Tiger is safe in the flat.' He liked everything to run normally. First the cigarette smoke, and now this. Should he get the bookshelves altered, maybe put a small lip on each shelf to stop books falling off? That meant some disruption. Matt didn't like disruption. He decided to ignore it.

*

The bookshop was closed, and Matt and Acacia worked unpacking boxes of books and shelving them.

'That was a good Bolognese tonight,' Matt said, sticking the scissors into the top of a box and ripping it open.

'It was soy, you know that, right?' Acacia asked.

Matt laughed. 'Of course. It was very tasty. You can make that again.'

Acacia clutched the scissors and opened another box. 'Ooh, mystery books. Are these for the new display?'

'Yep, a bit of a wider selection as that's what we're pushing at present,' Matt said.

Acacia grabbed the shop's trolley and loaded it, wheeling it over to the mystery display. She was just reaching into the box, when all the books from the top shelf tumbled to the floor.

Matt came rushing over. 'Are you alright?'

'Yes, I'm fine,' Acacia said. 'I was standing a bit to the side with the box, so they missed me. How did it happen?'

Matt and Acacia inspected the bookshelf. It was secured to the floor and didn't shake or move when they pushed it. They checked all around the bookshelf and could see no reason why the books had fallen off.

'Déjà vu,' Matt said. 'Except this time there are more books.'

'Well, Tiger is definitely upstairs,' Acacia said, 'so it wasn't him, and even if he was down here I doubt he'd be able to push off all those books.'

Acacia looked at Matt with her eyebrows raised, but she said nothing more. Matt avoided her gaze and got on with unpacking boxes.

Acacia put the fallen books back on the shelf. She smelt a faint hint of cigarette smoke and smiled.

Matt stoically refused to discuss the books or the cigarette smoke, saying there was a natural explanation for both things, and they just had to find out what it was.

Acacia was becoming frustrated with Matt's closed mind. She found herself banging books and striding about. She needed to calm down. She knew this wasn't something Matt would accept easily. His granddad had brought him up, and they were both prize sceptics.

Matt pushed his fringe out of his eyes, a nervous habit. 'You're obviously tired, Acacia, why don't we call it a day and go upstairs?'

'Sure. In a minute. You go on. I'll just finish this box and I'll join you,' Acacia said.

'I'll make some hot chocolate then,' Matt said, 'it'll be waiting for you, so don't be long.'

Acacia nodded as Matt went upstairs. She sensed a ghost

in the room. She assumed a nonchalant air and walked over to the coffee area. She got the tell-tale sign of smoke – and then a figure materialised.

A man in his fifties, light brown hair, clean shaven, the faint smell of aftershave – what was that? Old Spice! She recognised it from her granddad when she was a child. She loved that smell.

'Hello, I'm Acacia.' She smiled at him.

'Ernie,' he said, putting his hand out. She wondered what would happen if she put her hand out too and so she did. It passed through air where the hand was clearly seen. They both laughed.

'I didn't expect to touch you, but putting my hand out was instinctive with introduction.'

Just then, Matt appeared at the door leading to the flat and called out, 'Acacia, I've made hot chocolate. Are you coming up?'

'I hope to see you again soon, Ernie,' Acacia said quietly. 'Just coming, Matt,' she called out.

'Before I go. The cigarette smoke, that's you letting us know you're there, right?'

'Yes,' Ernie said.

'The books falling?'

'Yes, it was me. I need to talk to you,' Ernie said.

'Right. I have to go now. Can we meet here tomorrow evening about the same time? Matt's going out tomorrow evening.'

'Yes,' Ernie sighed his relief. 'We'll talk tomorrow evening.'

Back in the flat, Matt handed Acacia a mug of hot chocolate. 'I thought I heard you talking to someone downstairs?'

'It was probably me muttering to myself,' Acacia said. 'I do that sometimes.'

'Hmm,' Matt said, sipping his hot chocolate. The right side of his brain told him there was something going on, but the left side of his brain told him to ignore it.

He ignored it.

*

Ernie was relieved. At last he'd made someone take notice of him. He knew Matt didn't believe in ghosts, so it was a relief that Acacia did.

Something was in the air, he could feel it. Nothing concrete, but things were definitely out of kilter. Some unknown danger was heading their way. Did it have to do with Morgan? That was the question he was asking himself.

He didn't know Morgan, he only knew of him. But, he knew that Morgan was Wiladelle's son. And everyone in his sphere knew about Wiladelle. She was bad news with a capital B. So, was Morgan trustworthy? Or was he like his mother?

Ernie felt a responsibility towards Matt. The bookshop was Ernie's home. He knew he should move on, but he wasn't ready. He liked it there. He felt protective towards it and the people who lived and worked there. He'd died in the bookshop during one of his visits there years ago. He didn't know how many years had passed. Years didn't matter once you'd lost your physical life. But he'd known and liked Matt's grandparents, Sam and Tara, and Matt was their grandson.

Morgan visiting the bookshop had made him uneasy. Whether it was because of Morgan, or whether it was because

Wiladelle may be attracted to it because Morgan was visiting, he was unsure.

But, he knew he had to be vigilant. Wiladelle caused trouble wherever she went. He didn't want her coming to his bookshop.

Still, he told himself, I've made contact with Acacia, and I'll put my concerns about Morgan to her. She can then act accordingly.

Would that be the end of it, though? He thought not.

Still, it was a start.

THREE

Justin arrived carrying a bag of doughnuts – and tripped. He tossed the bag of doughnuts in the air, and reached for the nearest bookshelf to steady himself. He slid down the side of the bookshelf onto the wooden floor.

Matt came over and picked up the bag. 'You okay, Justin?'

'Yeah, yeah, fine,' Justin replied. He was confused though. There was nothing he could see that he could have tripped on.

Matt went over to the front door. He inspected the step but could find nothing wrong.

'I think I need a coffee and a sit down,' Justin said. 'I'll get some fresh going.'

'Good idea. I'll take a doughnut up to Acacia,' Matt said.

'Doughnut on the table for you,' Matt called out to Acacia. Tiger came bounding over to see what was going on, and threw his catnip mouse at Matt's feet. Matt smiled, picked the mouse up and threw it across the room. Tiger went hurtling after it.

Acacia took off her headphones and ambled over to Matt. 'Got any fresh coffee downstairs?'

'Sure. Justin's just making some,' Matt said. 'Actually, he tripped as he was coming into the shop. I couldn't see any reason for it. Maybe he's just tired.'

'Oh?' Acacia said. 'Well, I'll come down for some coffee with you guys. I need a bit of a break from those reports.'

Matt looked at his wife. There was coffee up here. She probably wanted to talk to Justin about the incidents.

'No, you can't go down there, Tiger,' Acacia said, as the cat tried to get through the door. 'I'll only be a few minutes. We'll get something sorted out for you soon.' She turned to Matt, 'We need to sort the walled garden out, and we need to get a cat door.'

Matt nodded. 'You're right. I'll look into it.'

Tiger sauntered over to the dining area, and leapt up to the windowsill to watch the birds.

*

Acacia and Matt went down to the bookshop, and Acacia found Justin sitting on the sofa in the customer area, sipping his coffee. There was a lull in sales, and only three regular customers milling around, so Matt and Acacia joined him. Acacia lifted her head and inhaled appreciatively. The smell of freshly brewed coffee – one of her favourite smells in the world.

'You okay, Justin?' Acacia asked.

'Oh sure,' Justin said. 'I didn't hurt myself. I'm just a little shaken, that's all.'

Acacia examined the front door, and looked around. She

couldn't see anything, but she could sense something. She chanted quietly as she moved around, and then went back to the sofa.

'I couldn't see anything there when I looked,' Matt said. 'Did you see anything?'

'I didn't see anything, no,' Acacia said, 'but I sensed something.'

'Sensed something?' Matt asked, panic in his brown eyes. 'What do you mean?'

'Oh, nothing, Matt,' Acacia said. 'It's all fine now.'

Justin looked at Acacia and smiled. Matt took rather a large gulp of coffee and spluttered.

'Can you help?' a customer asked. 'I'm looking for the latest Elly Griffiths and can't find it.'

'I'll show you,' Matt said, and he led the customer to the correct shelf.

'You cleared it, didn't you?' Justin said to Acacia quietly. 'Was it a tripping spell?'

'Yes, I did and it was,' Acacia said. But she felt uncomfortable at being forced to use some magic, even if it was basic. 'You know a bit about this stuff, don't you?'

'Well, my Uncle Peter is a bit of a… I'm not sure what to call him,' Justin laughed.

'Is he a witch?' Acacia asked.

'I suppose he is,' Justin said, 'but his group prefer to be called *charmers*. Please don't tell Matt. Goodness knows what he'd think.'

'Well, I have news too,' Acacia said. 'I met the bookshop ghost last night when Matt went upstairs.'

'You did?' Justin said. 'Wow. What's the ghost like? Is he friendly, or…' He leaned forward, eyes bright.

'He's called Ernie, and he's the one who's been putting the cigarette smoke around. I didn't get a chance to talk to him properly but I intend doing it tonight. I need to get Matt to meet him too. I've no idea how I'm going to do that, though.'

'It's a shame all the books were put away or we could use that as an excuse,' Justin said. 'I'd like to be there if I can?'

'Good idea,' Acacia said. 'Let's come up with something to do after the shop's closed.'

'How about a discussion about a signing event?' Justin suggested.

Matt came back and poured more coffee in his mug. 'Did I miss anything?'

'Well, we were just wondering if maybe we could get together after work tonight and talk about a possible author signing event,' Acacia asked.

'Sounds good,' Matt said. 'I'm out until 8pm though, remember?'

'That's fine. Justin and I can find plenty to do before then. We'll make notes and discuss it with you when you get back here around eight then. Okay?'

'Sure. Sounds like a plan,' Matt said.

*

Matt left before the bookshop closed for the day, and Justin and Acacia enjoyed a takeout meal while waiting for Ernie to appear.

'Vegetable curry and mushroom fried rice,' Acacia told Justin. 'I hope that's okay?'

'Looks great.'

Ernie appeared at 7pm.

'Hello,' he said to Justin.

Justin smiled broadly at Ernie. 'Hello. You're Ernie, I understand. And you already know my name?'

'Well,' Ernie said, looking shy, 'I've known you since you started coming in here as a small boy, Justin. I was very pleased when you started to work here.'

Justin's mouth came open in surprise. 'Are you very often in the bookshop then?'

'Most days, yes,' Ernie said. 'I try not to intrude though.'

'Except when you want to get our attention, right?' Justin asked.

'Right,' Ernie agreed.

Acacia said, 'Matt will be coming back at about eight and I think I'd like him to meet you. Is that okay?'

'It's okay with me, but I doubt it'll be okay with him,' Ernie chortled.

'Do you want to tell Justin and me what it is that's worrying you?' Acacia asked.

'Well, it's Morgan,' Ernie said. 'I'm not sure about him.'

'In what way?'

'How much do you know about Matt's parents?'

'Not much,' Acacia said. 'Only what Matt and his grandparents have told me. Why?'

'Well, Matt's mum, Eliza, had a sister called Wiladelle,' Ernie said. 'She was, is, Morgan's mother.'

'So, Morgan is Matt's cousin?' Acacia frowned. Matt hadn't told her that.

'Yes, but the sisters didn't get on,' Ernie explained. 'Family feuds, you know...'

'Yes,' Acacia said quietly. 'I understand.'

'Well, Wiladelle was, is, a black witch,' Ernie said,

watching Acacia and Justin to see what their reactions would be.

'A black witch?' Acacia said. 'Are you sure?'

'Unfortunately, yes.'

'But what about Morgan?' Justin asked. 'Is he a black witch too?'

'I don't know,' Ernie said. 'I've not heard anything bad about him. But his mother is bad news. And just because she's a ghost now, doesn't mean she can't cause trouble if she wants.'

'I see,' Acacia said. 'So, you think Wiladelle might appear because Morgan's found Matt?'

*

They were so absorbed that they didn't hear Matt open the door. He didn't see Ernie, he just saw Acacia and Justin, and he saw they had notebooks in their hands. Maybe this really was about an author signing event then?

'Hi, you two,' Matt said, sitting down next to Acacia.

Acacia jumped, and Justin looked startled.

Ernie disappeared – and waited behind a bookshelf to listen to the conversation.

Matt frowned at Acacia and Justin. 'What's with you two? Why so jumpy? You look like you've seen a ghost, the pair of you.'

Acacia and Justin smiled at the irony.

'So, which authors do you want to get here?' Matt asked, diving right in. 'This is a small town and I doubt we'd get any big names.'

'Why don't we try local writers?' Justin said, recovering

quickly. 'I'm going to go through our book list and see how many live nearby. What do you think?'

'Sounds good,' Matt said, 'but the books they write will have to be in line with whatever we're pushing that month. Let me know what you come up with.'

'We should get the local paper over here so they can advertise the event,' Acacia said, looking to see where Ernie had gone. 'We should try to involve the library too in some way.' She got up, and said, 'I'll be right back.' She walked around the other side of the nearest bookshelf, and found Ernie.

'Look,' Acacia said to Ernie, 'I don't want Matt to think we've been talking about things behind his back. So don't be surprised if I repeat things we've already discussed, okay? Ready?'

Ernie nodded.

Matt heard his wife talking to someone, and he brushed his fringe out of his eyes. He was sure there was no one else in the bookshop.

'There's just you, me and Acacia here, right?' Matt asked Justin.

'Well…' Justin said.

'There's someone who wants to meet you, Matt,' Acacia said.

Matt looked at her in confusion. He could only see Acacia and Justin. Was Acacia losing it?

Justin smiled and looked in the same direction as Acacia. Matt still couldn't see anyone. Then suddenly, a man materialised in front of him. He was in his fifties, and he was smoking.

'Ernie, this is my husband, Matt,' Acacia said.

Matt just stared at Ernie, and said nothing.

'I'm so pleased to meet you, Matt,' Ernie said, and he went and sat on one of the armchairs near the sofa.

Matt was still silent, unable to believe what he was seeing and hearing.

'What we'd really like to know, Ernie,' Acacia said, 'is, are you trying to get our attention for some specific reason? We now know the cigarette smoke means you're around, but have you been toppling books off shelves too?'

'Sorry about that,' Ernie said. 'Yes, it was me. I need to talk to you. I'm a bit disturbed about something, and I need to discuss it with you.'

'Did you trip Justin up earlier today?' Matt found himself shouting. He was way out of his comfort zone.

'No,' Ernie said. 'That wasn't me. It is related to what I want to talk to you about, though.'

Acacia went and sat next to her husband, and held his hand. 'What did you want to talk to us about, Ernie?'

Ernie stubbed his cigarette out in an ashtray he kept in his pocket, and he took a deep breath. 'Well, it's about Morgan. I don't know why but his presence here disturbs me. I thought you should be warned.'

'Warned? Warned about what? What's my cousin got to do with anything?' Matt was still agitated. He was talking to a ghost? Was this really happening?

'Well, I've been asking around, Matt,' Ernie said. 'It seems Morgan's mother, Wiladelle, walked on the dark side and she hated your mother. So I'm wondering why Morgan is here?'

'Walked on the dark side? Whatever do you mean?' Matt asked, surprised his voice sounded so loud. He didn't seem able to control it.

'He means she practiced the dark arts, Matt,' Acacia said. 'She was a dark witch.'

'She was very vindictive too, apparently,' Ernie said. 'I'm surprised her son, Morgan, has come here, and I think nothing good can come of it.'

'Well, he's my cousin and I think it's up to me if he visits me or not, don't you?' Matt had become dangerously quiet now. He was like a simmering pot, about to reach boiling point.

'I'm sorry if this is upsetting you, Matt,' Ernie said, 'but really in all conscience I had to let you know, didn't I? Just in case.'

'Well, I'll consider myself warned,' Matt said. 'Now if that's all, I'd like you to go please.'

'Matt, it takes effort to materialise like this,' Acacia said, 'I think we should give Ernie a little more time.'

'I'd like you to go now, please,' Matt repeated.

'We'll talk again, Ernie,' Acacia said. 'Thank you for coming tonight, but this is all a bit much for Matt, as you can see. How about I put flowers by the coffee pot any time I need to talk to you? Would that be okay?'

'Sounds a good idea,' Ernie said, and then slowly faded.

'Is that why you two got me here tonight? To talk to a ghost?' Matt asked. 'A ghost who's trying to tell me how to live my life? How dare he. Who does he think he is? Morgan is my cousin, and I like him. I'm going upstairs. You can lock up, Acacia.' Matt went to the door leading to the flat and banged it shut after him.

*

'Oh dear, that didn't go too well,' Acacia said to Justin as Matt stomped up the stairs to their flat.

'Very interesting though,' Justin said. 'I think Ernie will be very helpful. We should have asked him more about the tripping incident. Do you think it could be Morgan's mother? I'll ask Ernie next time I smell the smoke, if there's no one in earshot.'

'Yes, maybe it was Matt's Aunt Wiladelle,' Acacia said. 'I quite liked Morgan, though I only met him for a moment. You've met him, Justin. What do you think?'

'I liked him too,' Justin said. 'I don't think he'd do anything to hurt us. I did sense he had magical abilities, though.'

'Magical abilities, eh?' Acacia said. 'I wonder how advanced he is? Do you think he could've put a spell on the door so you tripped?'

'Well, I think he has the ability to do it,' Justin said, 'but, no, I don't think he did.'

'Hmmm. Well, we have lots to think about,' Acacia said. 'Right now though I have to go up and calm Matt down. He's pretty upset about the whole thing.'

'Yeah, well, he's just had his world turned upside down, hasn't he?' Justin said. 'I can remember that happening to me when I found out my Uncle Peter was... *different*. But, he wants me to learn. He says I have promise.'

'How exciting,' Acacia said. 'Let me know how you get on.'

Justin said goodbye to Acacia, and she locked up. She felt torn. She was interested in magic while at the same time wanting nothing to do with it.

After all, it had caused problems for her parents, and look what that had led to...

*

What the heck?

Acacia sensed someone behind her, but turned and saw no one. And there it was again. That laugh. There was nothing funny about it though. It actually made Acacia's skin crawl. And the atmosphere in the shop seemed supercharged. Like the shop was alive and on steroids, vibrating with energy.

She went over to the counter and spoke to Justin.

'You heard it too, then,' Justin said quietly, noting her flushed face.

'Yes,' Acacia said. 'Eerie sound. Is it someone laughing, do you think?'

'Yes,' Justin said. 'If that's what it can be called. I've never heard another laugh like it.'

Acacia walked around the bookshop, trying to find the source of the laughter, and nearly collided with a customer in the mystery section.

'Great idea that,' the female customer said, and smiled.

'Oh?' Acacia said.

'That laughing,' the customer continued. 'It's real creepy. It's not Halloween though. Are you getting ready to push horror books or something?'

'Just something we want to try out,' Acacia said, thinking fast. 'Glad you like it.'

When the only customer left, Acacia rushed over and hung the *Back in Ten Minutes* sign on the door.

'We have to try to get rid of whatever this is,' Acacia said. 'Any ideas?'

'You think you can get rid of me, do you?' A female voice. Disembodied, but confident. 'How do you think you're going to do that?'

Justin looked panicked.

Acacia was frightened. She could hear her heart pounding, and realised she was taking short, shallow breaths.

A smell of smoke drifted over to them, but it wasn't cigarette smoke. Bright red flames were leaping up the nearest bookshelf. The bottom row was already engulfed.

Acacia grabbed the fire extinguisher and pointed it at the flames, dowsing them with thick foam.

'Ha, ha!' the ghost laughed. 'See you again soon.'

The locked front door was flung open, and wind blew into the shop, scattering newspapers onto the floor.

Justin closed the door, and turned the sign over so customers could come in again.

'What's the damage?' he asked, picking up the newspapers and putting them back on the coffee table.

'Not bad, just singed really,' Acacia said. 'It looked much worse than it was.' She got a paper basket and threw in four ruined books, then fetched a damp cloth and wiped down the shelf. There was a faint smell of burning wood, so she grabbed the polish and sprayed it over the shelf. That helped. The smell was much less now. She took the burnt books outside to the recycling.

When she re-entered the bookshop the atmosphere had changed. Whoever had been there, they'd taken their negative vibes with them.

'Do we tell Matt?' Justin said. 'He's going to be back soon.'

'He's bound to notice the smell,' Acacia said. 'Open all the windows, Justin, that'll help.'

'She'll be back,' Justin said. 'She said she would. What shall we do?'

'I think we might have to have a word with your Uncle Peter,' Acacia said. 'We need help. You say he's experienced in magic. Let's hope he can give us some advice on how to deal with this ghost.'

'Do you think it's Morgan's mother?' Justin asked.

'Who else could it be?'

Cigarette smoke wafted in, and Ernie appeared. 'She found her way here then,' he said. 'I thought she would.'

'It was definitely Wiladelle then?' Acacia asked.

'Probably,' Ernie said. 'If you're going to call Peter, you should do it sooner rather than later. She'll be back, and she might bring company.'

*

Matt was in the office writing out cheques to cover the bills Acacia had okayed for payment. He was finding it hard to concentrate. He was preoccupied. Justin had told him there'd been an accident in the bookshop. Even with bad news, he always preferred to know what he had to deal with, and he felt Justin was hiding something from him. And Acacia had been distinctly guarded when he'd come home earlier. What had really happened? Did it involve that ghost, Ernie?

*

Morgan walked into the bookshop, wiped his feet on the mat, and stopped. Something felt different.

'Hi, Justin,' Morgan said, finding him at the counter. 'Is Matt around?'

'I'll tell him you're here,' Justin said. He paused.

'What is it, Justin?' Morgan asked. 'Something happened here today, didn't it?'

'Yes, it did.'

'What?'

'One of the bookshelves caught fire,' Justin said.

'Does Matt know?'

'He knows there was an incident.'

Morgan nodded, and Justin went to get Matt.

'Morgan,' Matt said, coming over and shaking his hand. 'Great to see you. Got time for a coffee?'

'Always,' Morgan answered. They walked to the coffee area together, and Morgan paused as he passed the damaged bookshelf. He could smell a trace of smoke – and something else. Yes. Darn it. He could smell his mother's perfume. She'd been there.

'So,' Matt said, handing Morgan a mug of coffee. 'How's it going?'

'Great,' Morgan said. 'I am going back to London tomorrow. I don't like leaving my business too long. I was wondering if you and Acacia would like to join me for dinner this evening.'

'I'll check with Acacia,' Matt said, 'but I think we're free. What have you been doing with yourself since you've been in Devon?'

'Site seeing mostly,' Morgan said. 'A couple of old churches, museums, local markets. And beaches are great this time of year – almost empty. I love watching the sea. It's been great fun.'

'Do you think you'll come back?' Matt asked.

'Now that I have a cousin here, yes I do.'

Matt smiled at him. 'So, you're an only child?'

Morgan nodded. 'My parents didn't get on. Dad left when I was quite young. He paid maintenance, but it wasn't easy for a while. My education was funded by friends of my mother. I have a trust fund. They helped me set up in business too.'

'Really?' Matt said. 'Wow, that's great, Morgan.'

Acacia came over and joined them. 'Hello, Morgan,' she said.

'Hi, Acacia,' Morgan responded, looking her over appreciatively.

Acacia was wearing a pair of old jeans and a faded beige top, she had no makeup on, and her fingernails were short for typing. And yet she looked lovely. And she seemed genuinely pleased to see him.

Morgan was mentally comparing her to some of the women in his circle. They were beautiful, well-groomed and wore designer clothes. And yet Acacia was far more attractive in his opinion. He thought it was her personality as much as her beautiful green eyes. She cared about people, he could tell.

'I'll leave you with Acacia for a bit, Morgan,' Matt said, getting up. 'I have to help Justin for a while. Okay?'

'Oh, right,' Morgan said, smiling up at him.

'Justin called me to say you were here,' Acacia said. 'He thinks you're, that is he thinks you might know… We had an *incident* here today,' she finished.

'So I heard,' Morgan said. 'It could have been very nasty.'

'I'm not sure how to say this,' Acacia said, looking very uncomfortable. 'Justin, and I, think you might be…'

Morgan waited, amused at Acacia's difficulty.

'Justin and I aren't sure how to handle this problem, and we think you might be able to help.'

'It was a ghost, right?' Morgan said. 'And you're psychic, I know you are.'

Acacia nodded.

'But you need help handling this particular problem?'

Acacia nodded again. 'Justin is going to speak to his Uncle Peter tonight to see if he has any suggestions.'

'I see,' Morgan said, sipping his coffee. 'Peter Fairbrother, right?'

Acacia nodded, looking surprised.

'I've heard of him,' Morgan said. 'He knows his stuff.'

'Oh,' Acacia said, 'that's good.'

'This ghost, what did it look like?'

'She didn't show herself,' Acacia said. 'But she had an awful laugh, it was quite eerie.'

'Ah,' Morgan said thoughtfully. 'It was definitely a female ghost then?'

Acacia nodded again. 'You know who it was, don't you?'

'I'm afraid it might be my mother,' Morgan said. 'And if so, it's a problem alright.'

'What can we do?'

'Does Matt know?'

'Not yet,' Acacia said. 'We didn't really want to tell him. It's been a difficult few weeks.'

'Out of his comfort zone?'

'Very much so.'

'What stage are your magical abilities?' Morgan asked.

'What?'

'Come on, Acacia,' Morgan said. 'I can sense another *charmer* when I see one. How far along in your magical studies are you?'

'I only know a few basics,' Acacia said. 'My parents. They. It was because of magic that... Look I don't want to talk about it,' Acacia finished, her face flushed. Her eyes were filling up, and she brought out a tissue to blow her nose and wipe her eyes.

'I see,' Morgan said. 'I didn't mean to upset you. Look, how about I extend my vacation in Devon? I could meet up with Peter Fairbrother, and we could try to find a solution to this problem.'

'Thanks, Morgan,' Acacia said, her hand resting on his shoulder.

Morgan sighed. Matt was one lucky guy. 'You're very welcome. I'll pick you and Matt up at six thirty this evening and we'll drive somewhere nice for dinner. Okay? And we won't mention it to Matt, until we think he's ready to hear it.'

Matt came back just as Morgan was pushing himself up off the low sofa. 'Going already?'

'Yep,' Morgan said, 'but I'll pick you both up at six thirty, okay?'

FOUR

February brought hail, high winds and snow, and so for a Saturday the Holsworthy Square shops were unusually quiet. A few brave souls were wading through the six inches of white stuff already on the pavements, their gloved hands gripping their hoods. Some children were laughing and kicking up snow or running and sliding on the slush that was quickly freezing.

Acacia was looking out of the flat's front window. Falling snow always made her think of her time in Canada. She sighed. She knew she had unresolved issues from her time there, but decidedly pushed them back into the box she kept at the back of her mind. Another day, she thought.

*

Morgan pulled up the collar of his city coat, lamenting its unsuitability for a snow storm. He quickened his pace and pushed the door of the bookshop open, snow dripping from his hair, face and coat, his shoes wet and slushy. He looked up and saw Matt coming towards him holding a towel.

'You know what? This towel won't do it,' Matt said. 'I think you should go upstairs to the flat, Morgan. Acacia's up there and she'll give you a pair of my spare jeans – you're soaked through.' Matt ushered Morgan up the stairs to the flat in front of him.

Morgan opened the door to the flat. He was greeted by a scene of happy domesticity. Acacia was just taking a cake out of the oven, and he could smell the freshly brewed coffee. Tiger was sitting in his new faux fur bed, in front of a very warm natural gas flame fireplace, washing his face, an empty saucer in front of him. He stopped mid-wash to give the visitor a penetrating look before continuing his ablutions.

'Acacia, can you show Morgan to the bathroom and give him a pair of my jeans? He's wet through. He might need a dry shirt too under that coat, I'm not sure.' Matt turned to Morgan, 'I'll have to leave you with Acacia, I'm in the middle of something downstairs, sorry.' Matt went back down to the bookshop.

'Oops, I'm dripping on your floor,' Morgan said.

'Don't worry about it. Give me your coat and I'll hang it up somewhere to dry. Take your shoes off – are your socks wet? You really need boots in this weather, don't you?' Acacia bustled about, getting a towel and some of Matt's clothes.

'I think you're about Matt's size, aren't you?' Acacia smiled at him, 'You're a little taller though – try this pair of jeans.'

Morgan headed for the bathroom, and ten minutes later appeared wearing Matt's clothes and looking considerably dryer. The jeans were a bit short in the leg, but Morgan had Matt's high boots over them and the jeans looked fine.

'Here, have some hot coffee. Would you like some cake?' Acacia held out a plate with a piece of Victoria sandwich on it filled with butter cream and jam. 'I always make cake on Saturday mornings, at least when I'm not needed in the shop, and the weather is keeping customers away today.'

Morgan took both the coffee and the cake and sat in an armchair next to the fireplace, facing Tiger. He sipped the coffee, feeling its warmth work its magic. And the cake – wow, it was so good. He looked at Acacia as if she were some kind of domestic goddess.

Morgan admired the flat. It was stylish and comfortable, but otherwise very different to his place. This was a true home, he thought, a place to enjoy spending time. His pad, while also being stylish and comfortable, had an empty feeling to it as though it were a show home and not lived in. Morgan felt a bit envious. Matt was very lucky indeed to be married to Acacia and have the bookshop and flat. The cat was the icing on the cake as far as Morgan was concerned.

'Your cat has green eyes,' Morgan exclaimed, 'that's very unusual. Where did you get him?'

'He found us actually. He was in the alley behind the shop, all muddy and frightened. Matt found him,' Acacia explained, 'just a week ago.' She walked over to Morgan and whispered in his ear, 'We found what we're sure was his mother's body by the church later, and we buried her in our garden. Poor little thing, she was obviously knocked over by a car. Hopefully, she died quickly.' There were tears in Acacia's eyes, and Morgan had to look away as his eyes filled too. He took a deep breath, and turned to Tiger.

'Well, young man, looks like you've landed on your paws, doesn't it? A nice place to live, people who love you and buy you a nice new bed,' he looked around and smiled 'and a scratching post and toys, I see.' Morgan looked up at Acacia and smiled. 'So, Matt likes cats then? We're still getting to know each other.'

'Yes,' Acacia said, 'Matt's very pleased you found him. More coffee?'

'Please, that would be great.' Right then Morgan realised that Matt and Acacia were his family. He wasn't alone anymore. He smiled. Not alone. That was new for him.

Meeting Matt and Acacia was altering his view of life. He never would have believed it a few weeks ago, but he felt his values changing. He had money, sure, lots of it, but his relationships needed some drastic remodelling. He needed what Matt and Acacia had. Loving family, true friends, companionship.

Morgan looked at Tiger, who'd completed his wash and was now playing with a catnip mouse. Morgan had loved animals as a child, but his mother would never let him have a pet. She cared for nothing but herself. Morgan had a sneaking suspicion she had somehow been behind Matt's parents' car crash. He remembered her laughing when she told him they were dead. She had done a little dance in their dirty, untidy living room. He shuddered, thinking his mother had been more than a little unhinged.

'Are you cold, Morgan? Here, put this blanket over your knees,' Acacia said, seeing him shudder.

'Thanks, Acacia,' Morgan said, taking the blanket.

'How about coming to see me?' Morgan asked Tiger, holding out his hand and wriggling his fingers. Tiger gazed at Morgan but stayed firmly in his basket.

'Maybe later?' he asked Tiger. 'Clever cat,' Morgan said. 'Always best to know someone before trusting them.'

Tiger continued to watch him, then approached cautiously, sniffing Morgan's clothing.

'Oh, dear,' Morgan said, 'that's going to confuse you. I'm wearing Matt's clothes.'

Tiger looked up at him, then jumped on the arm of the chair and peered at Morgan's face. He seemed satisfied with what he saw there, went back to his basket, curled up and fell asleep.

'Looks like you've passed muster,' Acacia said.

'Phew,' Morgan said. 'I felt I was being interrogated by the headmaster.'

Acacia laughed, and then changed the subject. 'Have you managed to speak to Peter yet?'

'Yes,' Morgan said. 'I'm meeting him here later this morning to talk about what can be done about our little problem.'

'Let's hope the snow doesn't stop him coming,' Acacia said, frowning. 'It's falling really thickly now.'

*

Snow continued to fall. Not that it mattered to Wiladelle.

She didn't like working in the daylight though, it didn't seem right somehow, but she wanted to scrutinise the bookshop to see what she was up against and how she could disrupt it. The girl she'd passed in the doorway had sensed she was there, but couldn't see her, of course. She smiled. This was going to be easy, she felt it in her bones, or at least she felt that she would if she still had bones. She laughed a cold, brittle laugh that would've brought a chill to anyone who heard it, and a passer-by jumped at the disembodied sound before hurrying past.

'I'll bet he's like his stupid grandfather and doesn't believe in ghosts,' Wiladelle said out loud. 'Well, he's going to get an introduction to one pretty soon.' She smiled again, and shook her long, wavy blonde hair as though clearing her mind. Her blue eyes were bright with fervour and she was on a high, triumphant that her son, Morgan, had located Matt. She'd been able to track Morgan, and he'd led her here unknowingly. She'd send Matt on his way to his maker but not before she'd caused him a lot of grief. That'd make her sister upset. She laughed again. Strangely she hadn't come into contact with her sister since she had passed away. She wondered briefly where her sister was.

She stood observing the bookshop, just a couple of customers browsing, and Matt and an employee at the counter talking over some books. She glided around the shelves taking in what was on offer, went to the coffee area and switched off the hotplate. Silly, she knew, but these little things were disconcerting to the vibrantly alive and she wanted them to feel confused and unsettled. She went round to the little fridge and unplugged it – see how they liked milk that had gone off with their cold coffee.

These simple things had taken her quite a long time to learn once she no longer had a physical body, but she was a good student and had persevered. She went over to the natural gas flame fireplace and switched it off too. It really was too easy. She heard something and turned round.

There was a man, another ghost, glaring at her. He was in his fifties and had that expression of righteous indignation she'd come to hate so much when she'd been alive and well.

'What do you want?' Wiladelle asked.

'No, the question is what do *you* want?' Ernie countered.

'I have business here, and it's none of yours,' she said.

'That's where I'll have to disillusion you. You see, I live here,' Ernie said.

'Live here? In this bookshop?' Wiladelle replied, eager for confrontation, anger building inside her. 'Dear oh dear, maybe it's time you moved on.'

'That won't work with me,' Ernie said. 'Now please leave, or I'll have to make you leave.'

'I'd like to see you try,' Wiladelle laughed. 'I've had a look round. I'll go now, but I'll be back and I don't expect to find you here,' she said.

'Don't come back,' Ernie said. 'I'm not frightened of your kind. I've seen it all before.'

'You've not met me before, and if you're not careful you'll wish you hadn't met me now. I'll give you another warning. Leave this place before I return, or you'll be sorry.'

'Off you go,' Ernie said, 'don't think about coming back again. Really.'

Wiladelle scanned the bookshop one more time, then flew through the front door. The visit had been very illuminating. It was a shame there was a ghost living in the bookshop. He could cause problems if she wasn't careful. He'd have to be dealt with somehow. The important thing was that she had learnt the layout of the shop, and Matt only had one employee so it shouldn't be that difficult to cause him problems. She'd have to plan it out carefully. She had lots of ideas. She'd been waiting a long time for this. She meant to enjoy it.

*

Upstairs in the flat, Tiger was behaving strangely. He was prowling around and growling, staring at the flat's door, marching backwards and forwards, growling, pausing, growling again.

Acacia was alarmed at Tiger's behaviour, and Morgan's mouth was open, his eyes following Tiger's movements.

'Something's obviously wrong downstairs,' Acacia said. 'We'd better go and see what's happening.'

In the bookshop, Acacia saw Matt and Justin talking at the counter. Two customers were browsing, and she saw one of them pull his collar up. Acacia went over to the fireplace and saw it was off, so she switched it on again.

'The fireplace was off, Matt,' Acacia said, walking towards him.

'I switched it on early this morning – you didn't unplug it did you, Justin?' Matt asked.

Justin seemed surprised. 'No. Of course not.'

'Well, I've switched it back on now so no worries,' Acacia said. She then caught a whiff of cigarette smoke and turned round, following the smell to the coffee area.

Morgan was walking around the bookshop. Acacia could see he was checking every aisle for problems.

'Matt, the hotplate's been switched off and so has the fridge,' Acacia was getting concerned now. 'What's going on, Matt?'

Matt and Justin had followed her to the coffee area and watched as she switched the fridge and the hotplate back on, and put more coffee on to brew, removing the jug of cold coffee.

'That's strange,' Matt said. 'I don't know, Acacia, maybe one of the customers is playing a practical joke on us?'

he suggested. He glanced at the two customers currently browsing, both in their forties, neither of them known for their joking personalities.

Morgan joined them in the coffee area, his eyebrows raised.

'Don't look at me,' Matt said. 'I've no idea how this happened.' He went back to the counter and ran some books through the till for a customer.

'What do you think?' Justin asked Acacia.

'Well, I don't think this was an accident, do you?'

'No,' Justin said. 'Something's going on. I'm just not sure what it is.'

'Well, I think I know what's happening,' Morgan said. 'I'm not sure if it'll continue or if that was it, though.'

'What?' Acacia said.

'I think you've had a visit from an unfriendly ghost,' Morgan said.

'Oh dear,' Acacia said. 'We'll have trouble convincing Matt.'

Morgan sighed. 'I think this could be the handiwork of my mother, Wiladelle. She really hated her sister, Matt's mum.'

'Oh?' Acacia said.

Justin said. 'What do we tell Matt?'

'Nothing for now,' Morgan said. 'Let's keep an eye on things but not tell Matt our suspicions at the moment. He's struggling with the ghost thing in any case. I'll tell him soon though, he'll have to know in case other things start happening.'

Morgan's mobile rang. 'Peter! Are you coming over? Oh. Right. Well, we've had some more problems. Right. See you soon then.'

Ernie was pleased his cigarette smoke had brought help to the coffee area to remedy Wiladelle's troublemaking. He'd never taken the time to learn how to manage physical things like that once he'd lost his physical body, but obviously Wiladelle had.

He needed help to stop her coming back. He drifted off to consider his options. He knew this woman would be trouble, and he didn't want anything happening to the bookshop or the people in it.

He had noticed Morgan walking around the bookshop and knew he was trying to work out what had happened. If that was the case, he couldn't be in league with Wiladelle… could he?

*

Wiladelle had been thinking a lot about what she could do to cause problems for Matt. Today was a good start, it would cause discomfort and uncertainty. But what next? Why not burn the bookshop down, she thought, or injure him somehow?

She smiled. This was going to be such fun. A series of little accidents, maybe?

This required some careful thinking.

FIVE

Acacia was upstairs, hoping to catch up on some reports, when she saw Tiger, who sat watching the falling snow from his window seat, stand up and place a paw on the windowpane.

'What's up?' she asked the cat, moving to the window. She saw Peter trudging through the thickly falling snow to the bookshop. 'I'll be right back,' she told Tiger, who blinked, and sat down on his cushion.

Acacia was downstairs in time to see Peter come through the door, shaking snow off his boots.

'You made it,' Morgan said to Peter as he came through the door. 'I'm Morgan, by the way.'

'Hello,' Peter said, 'pleased to meet you. It's not looking good out there. I left my car outside town and walked the rest of the way. They've got the snow ploughs out.'

Acacia looked over at Matt. He and Justin were busy unpacking boxes.

'Hi, Peter,' she said. 'Let's go upstairs.' She knew Matt wasn't ready for the conversation they were about to have. In the flat, she put fresh coffee on. Tiger joined them on the sofa.

'Can you tell me exactly what's been going on, Acacia?' Peter asked.

'Firstly, Justin and I had an experience of a ghost setting fire to one of the bookshelves,' Acacia said. She paused, waiting to see what Peter would say.

'Did you see this ghost?' Peter asked.

'No,' Acacia said. 'We heard her though. She was laughing, but it wasn't funny.'

'Hmm,' Peter said. 'What else?'

'Someone turned things off downstairs,' Morgan said. 'Matt thought it might be a customer having some fun at our expense, but it wasn't.'

'Right,' Peter said. 'Justin tells me you think it might be your mother, Wiladelle?'

'I think so,' Morgan frowned, 'but I'm not sure. She hated her sister, Matt's mum.'

'And why are these things happening now?' Peter asked. 'It's been years since Matt's parents died, and your mum has been gone a long time too. Why now?'

'It could be my fault,' Morgan said. 'I wanted to find my cousin. I think she might have followed me, and now she knows where Matt is.'

'It's not your fault,' Acacia said. 'She could've found Matt without your help.'

Acacia watched Peter. She could tell he was sizing Morgan up. She saw Peter take a deep breath. He'd reached a decision.

'I have a protection spell that would keep Wiladelle out of the bookshop,' Peter said. 'It won't stop her getting at anyone outside of the bookshop though.'

'It's a good start,' Morgan said.

Peter seemed to scrutinise Acacia. 'What are we going to tell Matt?'

'Good question,' Acacia said. 'I don't think we should tell him about spells yet. He's only just getting used to the idea that ghosts exist.'

'Morgan,' Peter said, 'this involves your mum. Would you rather not be associated with this?'

Acacia watched as Morgan sipped his coffee, wriggled in his seat, sat upright.

'Matt and Acacia are family,' Morgan said. 'You said you'd heard of me,' he said to Peter. 'Have you heard anything about my using dark magic?'

Peter shook his head.

'No,' Morgan said, 'because I don't. I'm a *charmer* and a good one. I've made it my business to study magic and I've used it to good effect. But, I believe Wiladelle is,' he struggled to find the right words, 'on a different path to me. If she's trying to hurt Matt and Acacia, she'll have to fight me too.'

'How good are you at this stuff, Morgan?' Acacia asked. 'I mean, how much practice have you had?'

'Quite a bit, thanks to Wiladelle actually,' Morgan said. 'It was like second school each day. And as I've got older, the learning has continued.'

'Do you have a suitable protection spell?' Peter asked.

'Wiladelle knows most of my spells and how I operate. That's why we need you to help us. She needs to be surprised. If I use one of mine, she'll know how to break it.'

Interesting, Acacia thought. Morgan uses his mother's name rather than acknowledging her as his mother, most of the time.

'Sounds logical,' Acacia said to Morgan. She poured more coffee for Morgan, who placed both hands round the mug and sniffed it before drinking.

'Your coffee always smells so great,' Morgan said, smiling at her.

Acacia put on a Canadian accent, 'Gee, thanks.' Then back to her English voice, 'As you'll have noticed, we drink a lot of it in this house. Blame it on my time in Canada.' Morgan smirked, Peter laughed, Acacia smiled.

Acacia poured more coffee for Peter, 'How does your spell work?'

'It works on the principle that everyone is fine except one specific person,' Peter said. 'You have to use a wand for this one. You need wand and words together, spoken with emotion, believing the words. You know what I mean of course, Morgan. I'm saying this for Acacia's benefit really.'

'Right,' Morgan said. 'So this will keep Wiladelle out of the entire building? Not just the bookshop?'

'Ah,' Peter said. 'She's tried to come into the flat then, has she?'

'We're not sure. Tiger alerted us to her presence,' Acacia said, 'he growled and hissed. But whether she was outside the flat door or downstairs isn't clear.'

'Hmm,' Peter said. 'She's rather cheeky, isn't she?'

'Determined, I'd say,' Morgan said. 'Do you know anything about Wiladelle?'

'We in the order know all about her, yes,' Peter said. 'Not a nice piece of work. Not improved by death either, apparently. Sorry, Morgan.'

'I understand. And I agree,' Morgan said. 'It was quite a relief when she died, actually. Sounds awful, doesn't it.'

'Have you seen her since she's passed over?' Peter asked Morgan.

'Yes, once or twice,' Morgan said. 'I asked her not to visit me again. She kept coming, so I had to use a spell to keep her away from me. So far it's worked, but she might find a way round it. She's very accomplished.'

'So I understand,' Peter said. 'Well, she's never met me so she doesn't know the way I work. And I belong to a local group who are willing to help if they're needed, so she's bitten off more than she can chew.'

'What do you suggest we do, then?' Acacia asked. 'Just use this protection spell? Will that be enough?'

'Probably not,' Peter said. 'But it'll stop her getting into the building. You have a garden too, I understand? That'll need a separate spell, and I can come over and do that when the weather gets better in a few days, or Morgan can do it. But for now, the protection spell will stop her getting in and causing problems in the bookshop and your flat. Okay?'

'Brilliant,' Acacia said. 'If you could perform the spell on the flat for us, then Morgan can go down and put the spell on the bookshop when it's closed. We'll have to somehow keep Matt occupied while Morgan's doing that.'

Morgan and Peter talked for about fifteen minutes more, Morgan writing down words and actions.

Tiger jumped on Acacia's lap and looked towards the door. Matt came through a few seconds later.

'Hi Peter, I didn't realise you were here… I think you'd all better stay here tonight,' Matt said. 'Justin's staying over, and he doesn't live far away. Have you looked out the window in the last half hour?'

They all went to the living room window. It was deadly quiet out there. No pedestrians. No moving vehicles. Everything covered in white fluffy snow, which continued to fall. The few cars that were parked wouldn't be moving any time soon and were just visible as shapes under a white blanket.

'Right,' Acacia said, 'I'll make up the spare beds, and the sofa is good for sleeping on too.'

Matt went back downstairs.

Acacia and Morgan watched as Peter got his wand out and cast the protection spell on the flat, starting at the bottom of the stairs and working his way up, moving around the flat chanting.

Later that evening, Acacia and Matt were doing dishes, Acacia washing and Matt drying. Acacia took off her rubber gloves and rummaged in the kitchen drawer for a dry tea cloth for Matt. 'There you go.'

'Do you mind if I show Peter the new metaphysical books you've got in?' Morgan asked Matt from the doorway.

'Help yourself,' Matt said. 'There's no alarm down there. You know where the light switches are?'

Morgan nodded and turned to go, but paused for a second to watch the interaction between Matt and Acacia.

'That must be at least twenty teaspoons I've dried,' Matt laughed.

'Lots of coffee means lots of spoons,' Acacia said, dabbing a blob of washing up bubbles on Matt's nose.

'You're going to have to pay for that,' Matt laughed.

Morgan was smiling at Matt and Acacia's banter as Peter joined him. They headed downstairs.

Once in the bookshop, Peter watched as Morgan brought out his wand and chanted the spell, pausing at each door and window to repeat it, and then covering the door to the flat.

'Here,' Morgan handed Peter a book. 'Take this up with you. It's a good book.'

Back in the flat, Morgan and Peter found everyone sitting on the sofa watching TV, Tiger curled up on Justin's lap.

A sense of peace seemed to pervade the whole building. The walls, the floors, even the ceilings seemed to exude tranquillity.

Tiger lifted his head as Morgan and Peter came in. He gave a knowing cat smile. His people were safe.

SIX

Morgan looked out of the window. It was 6am and snow was still coming down thick and fast.

He was concerned. He didn't usually leave his business this long, but there were problems at the bookshop that he felt were down to him. Well, probably down to his mother following him there. He should be checking out of his hotel and driving back, but this weather…

He put the coffee on and found some bagels for his breakfast.

Acacia appeared, wrapped in her dressing gown. She said a sleepy good morning, cleaned Tiger's litter tray, then went to shower.

Tiger was watching Morgan eat his bagels. He looked affronted.

'Sorry, Tiger,' Morgan said. 'As Acacia is in the shower, shall I top up your kibble dish and put some fresh food down?'

The kitten followed him to the cupboard where his food

was kept, and sat down. Morgan refilled Tiger's dishes, put fresh water in his bowl, and they both ate their breakfast, Morgan listening to the sound of Tiger happily crunching his cat kibble.

'Are you still going home today?' Matt asked, appearing at the kitchen table, already showered and dressed. 'The forecast isn't good.'

'I don't usually leave the business more than a few days, but I don't like the look of the roads,' Morgan said. 'I've been watching the news, and they're advising people to stay at home.'

'I think you should stay put at least today,' Matt said, 'see what the weather's like tomorrow and make a decision then.'

'Well, if you're sure,' Morgan said. 'But I don't even have a toothbrush with me. Everything's at the hotel.'

'We can wade across the road to the pharmacy for a toothbrush,' Matt said. 'You can borrow some of my clothes today.'

Matt joined him at the table. 'Thanks for feeding Tiger.'

'He's such a great little guy,' Morgan said.

'Do you have any pets?'

'Not at the moment,' Morgan said. 'My place doesn't really feel like home. Maybe having a cat around would help.'

Morgan watched Acacia come out of the bathroom and head straight for the coffee. She smiled at Matt and then Morgan. Tiger came and sat on her lap while she sipped her coffee.

'Not a morning person?' Morgan asked her.

'I'm not bad in the morning usually,' she said, 'but I was wide awake last night and had trouble getting to sleep. This helps.' She poured more coffee.

'I was just telling Morgan he shouldn't try to go back to London today,' Matt said to Acacia.

'Too right,' she said, getting up and wandering to the window, holding Tiger in her arms. He jumped onto the windowsill and watched the snow falling, reaching out with his paws to try and catch the snowflakes as they fell outside the window.

Morgan watched Matt and Acacia. They seemed to work in sync. Acacia picked up a clean coffee jug, and Matt ground some fresh coffee. Acacia poured water into the machine while Matt put the fresh coffee in the filter.

Morgan smiled at them. 'How long have you two been married?'

'Oh, years and years,' Matt laughed.

'Two actually,' Acacia said, 'though sometimes it feels longer.'

Matt punched her lightly on the arm, and they all laughed.

Justin went into the bathroom. Peter came over to the table and helped himself to coffee.

'Wonder if I'll get home this morning?' Peter asked.

'Why don't you wait and see if the roads get ploughed first,' Matt suggested.

'What about you?' Peter asked Morgan. 'Will you be staying a few days?'

'Looks like it,' Morgan said. 'Problem is, all my stuff is at the hotel.'

'Ah...'

Morgan watched with interest as Acacia took something wrapped in foil out of the freezer and left it on the counter.

'Devon apple cake,' she said, 'for later.'

'You know, it's almost worth being captive with all the good food on offer,' Morgan said.

Now it was Acacia's turn to hit Morgan on the shoulder, and he feigned a wince.

'Well,' Peter said. 'Neither Justin nor I have far to go to get home, so you should be able to have the spare room tonight.'

'Oh,' Morgan said, 'that's great. Thanks.'

Justin came out of the bathroom and grabbed some coffee. 'Matt, if I can borrow your boots I think I can get to my flat. It's not far after all, and I need some clean clothes.'

'Sure,' Matt said. 'Go slowly though, right? As Acacia says, it's not the snow, it's the ice that's the problem.'

'Right,' Justin said, pulling on a pair of Matt's boots which were a bit too big for him. 'I've got a good pair of winter boots at my flat. I need to get them. It won't take me long, and then I'll be back.' He stopped, looking out of the window.

Morgan joined Justin at the window, looking out at the wintry scene below. 'Matt, you and I'll have to get over the back fence, go round and shovel the snow away from the front door before Justin can get out.'

'I can just climb over the back fence myself,' Justin said.

'It has to be done anyway,' Matt said. 'Let's do it.' The three of them headed downstairs.

'Peter,' Acacia said. 'You should wait for a bit. You live further away, don't you? And your car might be completely covered in snow. In fact, it's almost bound to be.'

'You're right,' Peter said. 'It wouldn't take that long to walk home though, if I'm careful.'

Morgan came back to the flat feeling cold, but thanks to one of Matt's jackets he was still dry. He saw Acacia putting clean sheets on the spare beds.

'Are you sure you'll be able to get home?' Morgan asked Peter, feeling guilty at taking Peter and Justin's room.

'Almost sure,' Peter said. 'I'll stay here for a few hours before I try though.'

Tiger followed Morgan into the spare bedroom and jumped on the bed, looking up at him as he snuggled into the duvet.

'Oh, I see,' Morgan said to the cat, 'I haven't taken your room, have I? I thought your bed was in the living room?'

Tiger settled down for a snooze.

Morgan laughed. 'Go ahead, I don't mind cat hair.' He left the bedroom door open for Tiger and headed for more coffee. Acacia had defrosted the Devon apple cake and the air smelled of cooked apples and cinnamon. After his exertions with the snow shovel he found himself surprisingly hungry.

'OMG, Acacia, this cake is so good,' Morgan said between bites, holding his hands around the coffee mug to warm them up. 'Do you often get this much snow?' he asked, wandering over to the window to look outside. It was still coming down, distorting the shapes of things and creating an eerie scene.

'No, we don't,' Acacia said. 'At least, not since I've lived here. Matt?'

'Not for a long time, actually,' Matt said. 'I guess it was overdue. Will it be okay to leave your business for a few days?'

'Well, it can't be helped, can it?' Morgan said. 'I'll send a text to Sophie, my PA, and tell her I'll be here awhile.'

'Where's Tiger gone?' Matt asked.

'He's sleeping in the spare room.' Morgan said.

'Do you want me to bring him back in here?' Matt asked. 'You'll get cat hair on your clothes.'

'No, it's fine,' Morgan said. 'I feel rather flattered actually that he wants to sleep on my bed.'

'He does seem to like you, doesn't he,' Matt said.

Acacia stood up. 'Matt, I'm going to work for a while in the study. Will you and Morgan excuse me?'

'Working so early?' Morgan said. Acacia raised her eyebrows towards Matt. Right, Morgan thought, I have to speak to Matt.

'It's good to start early, the best reports are there first thing,' Acacia said.

Morgan helped himself to yet more coffee, he was drinking way too much of it, and stood next to the fireplace. He knew he had to talk to Matt about Wiladelle, but he really wasn't looking forward to the conversation.

Morgan looked over at Peter, who nodded briefly and picked up the book from the previous evening, heading into the sitting room with it.

'Matt, while we're alone there is something I wanted to talk to you about,' Morgan said.

'Oh?'

'Yes. My mother really hated your mother. I think I told you that?'

'Yes, you did,' Matt said, clearly confused at the sudden change of topic.

'Well, the thing is,' Morgan took a sip of coffee, 'Wiladelle is a witch, and I think she might have followed me here. I think she's decided she is going to cause some problems for you.'

Matt stared at his cousin, wide eyed. He managed to croak out, 'A witch? She's a ghost *and* a witch?'

'I'm sorry to throw this at you, Matt,' Morgan said, 'but

with what happened yesterday I really think we need to have this conversation. I think my mother may be responsible for turning off those appliances.'

Matt swallowed, but said nothing.

'You see,' Morgan continued, 'my mother is a very accomplished witch. I never liked her, she was, and is, a strange woman.'

Morgan looked at Matt, who was just staring at him. Did Matt believe him? Did he still trust him?

'Matt,' Morgan said, 'I know we've only just met, and normally I wouldn't have discussed this with you. It's not something I usually talk to people about, obviously.' He looked at Matt for any encouragement, but got none. 'I'm worried those appliances being turned off may just be the start of even bigger problems she may cause if we don't do something to stop her.'

Seeing his cousin speechless, Morgan poured some more coffee for Matt and handed it to him. Matt sipped the coffee, and gradually some colour came back into his face, but he still didn't say anything.

'Matt,' Morgan said, 'this is important. She might do something really bad next time. You need to be aware of this.'

'Ghosts can turn off appliances?' Matt asked quietly.

'Ghosts can do all sorts of things,' Morgan said, 'if they take the trouble to learn.'

'You think Wiladelle will do other things? What things?' Matt asked.

'She's taken the trouble to follow me to find you,' Morgan said, 'and knowing my mother like I do, yes, I think she'll keep causing problems.'

Morgan could see his cousin was having issues with this

latest piece of information. A few days ago there was no such thing as the supernatural as far as Matt was concerned. Now there were ghosts *and* witches.

Matt stayed quiet while he digested this information.

Morgan could see Matt was floundering. He could almost hear Matt's mind working. What had happened to Matt's calm, normal world? First there was a ghost, Ernie, in the bookshop, then he had found out Acacia was psychic, and now his dead Aunt Wiladelle was a witch and out to cause problems.

'The thing is,' Morgan said, 'I could help, but I think that might make things worse.'

'Worse? Can it get any worse?' Matt asked.

'Yes, it could get a lot worse,' Morgan said. 'But you're not alone in this, Cuz.'

Morgan saw Matt making an effort to pull himself together. Matt was an action person, but he was out of his depth.

'I have no idea about any of this stuff,' Matt said. 'If I hadn't seen some of these things with my own eyes I'd never believe it. You say you know about this kind of thing though?'

'Yes,' Morgan said. 'I'm an accomplished *charmer.*'

'*Charmer*?' Matt said. 'No, don't explain, I couldn't take it in at the moment. Whether your help makes things worse or not we obviously need it. What should we do?'

Morgan sighed with relief. His cousin seemed to have regained his usual problem solving attitude.

'Acacia is psychic,' Morgan said, watching his cousin for a reaction. But Matt just nodded. 'And there's Justin, he knows a bit about this, not much at the moment, but he's willing to learn. And Justin's Uncle Peter is very knowledgeable. He's willing to help, and he belongs to a group who can also help.'

'Justin is psychic? His uncle is psychic?' Matt said, momentarily floored again.

'More than psychic actually,' Morgan said.

'More? What do you mean more?' Matt sounded edgy.

'You'll see what I mean as we talk this through,' Morgan said. 'I think we need to get Justin, Peter, Acacia and you and I together to talk about things. See what we can come up with. What do you think?'

Morgan watched his cousin Matt as he sipped his coffee. He could almost see the wheels turning in his brain. They still didn't know much about each other though, and he wished fervently that he'd had more time to get to know his cousin before this problem erupted. No point in bemoaning it though. It was what it was, as Acacia would say.

Matt seemed to visibly strengthen. He straightened up. 'Seems a logical course of action,' he said. 'Good job my granddad isn't listening to this. He'd have us all committed.'

Acacia came back into the living room. 'Everyone okay?'

'Oh, we're fine,' Matt said ruefully. 'Ghosts can turn appliances off apparently. Yep, everything's good.'

'Looks like it might be a two pot morning,' Acacia said, making more coffee.

'Maybe three,' Matt said, getting busy with the grinder.

'And another thing,' Matt said, putting the coffee in the filter, 'that cat of ours is different somehow. He seems to know when people are about to turn up, and he alerted you two to the fact there was a problem downstairs, didn't he?'

Acacia smiled at her husband. 'You're right there, Matt.

Tiger has hidden talents. I guess we'll find out about them as he grows up. He could be very handy to have around.'

'Want some more cake?' Matt asked Morgan, looking resigned.

'Yep,' Morgan said, putting his hand on Matt's arm. 'Don't worry, Cuz, we're in this together.'

'Thanks, Morgan,' Matt said. 'I just wish I knew what *this* was though.'

SEVEN

Acacia was in the kitchen making pancakes in the cast iron pan she'd inherited from her grandmother. The smell filled the flat, and down the corridor she could hear Matt singing in the shower.

Matt came into the kitchen, towelling his wet hair. 'Pancakes for breakfast?'

Morgan sat at the kitchen table, watching Acacia cooking pancakes and transferring them to the oven to keep warm.

'Well, it is Shrove Tuesday,' Acacia said. 'A little bird told me that you always had pancakes on Shrove Tuesday, so here they are.' She squeezed some lemons into a jug and put it on the table along with demerara sugar and freshly made coffee. Then she presented them with a pile of pancakes.

Matt and Morgan tucked in. Matt loved pancakes, and Morgan obviously did too.

Tiger looked up at them, his tail curled like a question mark.

'You wouldn't like pancakes, Tiger, not even without the lemon juice,' Acacia said. 'At least, I don't think you would?'

Tiger opened his eyes wider and blinked.

Acacia laughed, and cut up a piece of pancake into small pieces, putting them onto one of Tiger's saucers for him and blowing on them to make sure they weren't hot. To her surprise, Tiger ate the whole lot, and then went back to his basket and gave himself a thorough wash.

'That cat never ceases to amaze me,' Acacia said.

'He's a character, that's for sure,' Matt said.

After they'd polished off the pancakes, Matt went downstairs to work. Acacia started typing reports, while Morgan was engrossed in a new book. Two hours passed quickly.

Acacia paused after sending off another report. She could see Morgan wasn't used to much leisure time. She watched as he put the book down and went over to the window, looking out at the snow. It was much less now, and the roads had been cleared and gritted.

'You're like a caged lion,' Acacia laughed. 'Why don't you go and see if Matt needs any help downstairs?'

Acacia saw Morgan's face light up at the suggestion.

'Good idea. Maybe I could serve some customers or something?'

Morgan was just about to go out of the flat when Tiger rushed passed him and hissed at the door, his fur fluffed up and his eyes wide. He hissed again and paced backwards and forwards in front of the door.

Morgan and Acacia watched, and Morgan put his finger to his lips so Acacia wouldn't say anything. All three of them were listening intently. They each sensed something was there, something unfriendly. The atmosphere felt charged, and they held their breath.

They waited. Nothing happened. Five minutes passed. Acacia put her ear to the door. She couldn't hear anything. Tiger stopped pacing, and Morgan tentatively opened the flat door. No one there.

'That couldn't be Wiladelle,' Morgan said. 'She wouldn't get past Peter's spell that quickly.'

Acacia frowned. She'd thought they'd have some peace, at least for a while.

'Don't worry too much,' Morgan said, seeing Acacia's expression. 'I'll put a spell on the flat that will only allow specific people in. You'll have to give me a list, though.'

'Right,' Acacia said quietly, not liking the feeling of fear that lingered. 'Thanks, Morgan, I appreciate it.' She sighed. 'I've always felt safe here. Now I don't.'

'You will be,' Morgan said, 'the spell I'll use is simple but very effective. Tiger is very intuitive for such a young cat.'

Acacia nodded. 'Clever cat,' she said, picking him up and kissing him, then pouring some cream into a saucer. 'Thanks for alerting us.' She put him down to drink his cream.

Acacia saw Tiger preen as he walked to his saucer. He paused mid-lap and looked up at her. Their eyes connected, and Acacia heard *I love you* in her head. Her mouth dropped open.

'What is it?' Morgan asked.

'I… I'm not sure,' Acacia said. 'I think I just heard Tiger say *I love you*. I heard it in my head, I mean I didn't hear him speaking. Do you think he's communicating with me telepathically?'

'Wow!' Morgan was stunned. He'd heard of this but never experienced it.

They both watched Tiger lap his cream and saunter over to his basket looking distinctly pleased with himself.

'Is there any truth in the old myth about cats protecting against evil?' Acacia asked.

'Well,' Morgan answered, 'I think we've just seen that at work, don't you?'

*

More snow had fallen. Morgan and Justin had shovelled it away from the front and back doors earlier that morning. They'd also sprinkled salt to stop ice forming. The wind was cold and penetrating. Morgan pulled his collar up and went back inside for a coffee to warm up.

Wiladelle saw her son go back into the bookshop, so she tried to follow him in, but found a protection spell blocked her from entering. The pavement was still a bit slippery, and Wiladelle took great delight in tripping up a customer who sprawled half in and half out of the shop.

Matt hurried over. He couldn't see anything, but he could sense someone else was there. He helped the customer into the shop, and poured her a hot coffee.

'Are you sure you're okay?' Matt asked.

'I'm fine,' she replied. 'Just slipped, that's all.'

Morgan watched this exchange, then scanned the front door. He had the feeling an outraged Wiladelle was outside. He beckoned Matt over.

'Sounds like the sort of thing Wiladelle would do,' Morgan said, 'trip up one of your customers. She'd find that funny.'

'Well,' Matt said, 'just be careful if you go out the front again. She might be waiting for you.'

'I hope not,' Morgan said. 'I don't think I'm up to facing her so early in the day.'

'How long do you think you'll stay in Devon for?' Matt asked.

'They're saying the roads will be clear by tomorrow,' Morgan said, 'so I'll probably wait until the day after that and then go back for a week, then come back here again, if that's okay. We need to get this resolved, and it'll probably take a while.'

'Do you miss it?' Matt asked. 'The hustle and bustle of London?'

'A bit,' Morgan said. 'But this place is growing on me.' He smiled. An idea was forming in the back of his mind to buy a second home, in Devon. He didn't need to be in the London office all the time. He felt good about this idea. It made him happy.

'What?' Matt asked, seeing his cousin's happy expression.

Morgan shook his head, 'Oh, nothing.'

'Come on. Something's making you smile. What is it?'

'Well, if you must know,' Morgan said, 'I'm thinking of buying a second home in Devon and splitting my time between London and here.'

'Really?' Matt said, obviously pleased. 'That'd be great.'

'But first,' Morgan said, 'we have to get this little problem of Wiladelle sorted out.'

*

Wiladelle was standing outside the bookshop again, looking in. She noted Morgan and Matt's friendly attitude but couldn't hear what they were saying. Darn it! Well, she had patience. She'd wait and see if Morgan came out again. She'd just missed him the last time, she'd come round the corner as he was going into the bookshop. She waited for hours and had some fun making people slip and slide as they went past. One woman could sense she was there but couldn't see her, and she made sure that woman fell over again when she was trying to get up. It was so easy and oh so funny. She laughed out loud, and the woman obviously heard her because she seemed startled.

The council staff came round sanding the pavements, and Morgan decided he'd nip over to the pet shop to get something for Tiger.

Wiladelle was waiting for him and cornered him as he went down a side street.

'I think you're forgetting where your loyalties lie,' Wiladelle said.

'I told you to leave me alone, Mum,' Morgan said. 'It's time you moved on.'

'I'll *move on* when I'm good and ready,' Wiladelle said. 'I have unfinished business, as you well know.'

'Matt's done nothing to you,' Morgan said. 'Why can't you leave him in peace?'

'So that's the way of it is it? Friendly, are you? Well I want you to help me deal with him. He's my sister's brat, and I want him dead.'

'What for?' Morgan asked. 'What good will that do?'

'It'll make me smile. That's the important thing.'

'Mum, let it be. Please,' Morgan said.

Wiladelle scrutinised her son, and frowned. Her dead sister had tried to appeal to her better nature once. Well, look where that had got her.

'Is that it then?' Wiladelle demanded. 'You won't help me?'

'You'll have to fight me too,' Morgan said. 'I'd rather you moved on, and left us all alone.'

'I'm sorry to hear that, Morgan,' Wiladelle said, 'but if that's the way it is, so be it. I've learnt things you can only dream of since I've been physically dead. Think you have a chance of winning? Think again.'

*

Wiladelle's image faded, and Morgan sighed. He'd expected this would happen. Well, he'd led her here. He'd have to be part of the solution to the problem.

He went into the pet shop and bought some catnip for Tiger, chatting with the owner as if he didn't have a care in the world. But in the back of his mind, his thoughts were churning over possible scenarios and solutions. He stopped off at the bakery and bought doughnuts, talking to the friendly baker. He liked the people here. They were genuine. No pretence.

He walked slowly back to the bookshop, looking at the now familiar square with fresh eyes.

This was a place he could settle. This was a place he could call home.

EIGHT

It being Sunday, the church bells were ringing, reminding people the service would be starting soon. Nate rubbed his hands together in between cleaning his shop's front window. It was frosty outside this morning, but beautiful blue skies met a calm grey sea on Bude's seafront.

Nate finished the cleaning and went inside the shop, drying his cold wet hands on some kitchen roll. He'd earmarked today for reorganising stock and was eager to get on with it. He caught a whiff of Chanel perfume, what was that called? Didn't Wiladelle used to wear that?

Nate turned towards the smell of the perfume, and watched, stunned, as Wiladelle materialised. It was fortunate the store was closed – there could have been complications. She really did have no sense of propriety, he thought.

'I could do with your help, Nate,' Wiladelle said, getting right into it. 'Surely you'd like the opportunity to get back at Eliza? Or at least her son?'

'No,' Nate said. 'I'm not going to cause any problems for Eliza's son, Wiladelle.'

'You must want to get revenge for Eliza dumping you for that Raphael, surely?' Wiladelle said. 'She gave you no warning. She just stopped seeing you, and started seeing him. That's worth at least a couple of little incidents with her son, wouldn't you say?'

'I'm not like you, Wiladelle,' Nate said. 'I don't think there's any point in trying to get back at people. And Eliza's son had nothing to do with it. Why do you want to hurt him?'

'Because he's part of her, of course,' Wiladelle said, surprised. 'Can't you see that?'

Nate sighed. 'It's not in my nature to cause harm to anyone. I can't help you.'

'Why did you study the dark arts then?' Wiladelle said. 'Why take the trouble to study and not use the knowledge?'

'I went along to that class partly because you badgered me into it, as you well know, and partly because I find some of it fascinating,' Nate said. 'I stopped going a long time ago.'

'I know,' Wiladelle said. 'I can't understand why you didn't take it further. You're a very talented witch after all.'

'Well, thanks for that,' Nate said. 'Not like you to give compliments when you're not after anything – but then you are after something, aren't you? You want me to cause problems.'

'Yes, yes,' Wiladelle said. 'Whatever. Just go along to that bookshop in Holsworthy and see if you can find anything out I can use, okay?'

'I might go because I'm curious to see Eliza's son,' Nate said. 'I won't give you any information that could hurt him.'

'Well, if you change your mind let me know,' Wiladelle said. 'Just call my name and I'll pop up, just like magic.' She laughed at her own joke and disappeared.

Nate stood in front of The Devon Bookshop, admiring the façade. He liked Georgian architecture. He wondered why he hadn't been to this town for so long, but then he'd had no reason to. Not since… He pushed the door and went in. It was warm and welcoming. He undid the buttons on his coat.

He looked for a section on the occult but couldn't find one.

Nate saw Matt at the counter. There was no mistaking that he was Eliza's son, but there was something else too, something he couldn't quite put his finger on. He was pleased to see Matt was a smart young man, dark suit, white shirt, deep blue tie. He was about five foot ten, Nate thought, same height as him. He also had chestnut brown hair and brown eyes – this surprised Nate because he knew Eliza had had green eyes. He couldn't remember Raphael's eye colour, but he knew they weren't brown.

'Something wrong?' Matt asked with a frown. He felt himself being scrutinised.

'Sorry,' Nate said. 'Miles away. I was wondering if you have an occult book section. I can't see one.'

'Not at the moment, no,' Matt said, 'but we're thinking of getting one.'

'Oh?' Nate was curious about this possible change in attitude. Matt said nothing else on the subject though, so Nate continued. 'Well, if you need any help with authors and things, please let me know. I don't live far away. In Bude actually.'

'What brought you here today then?' Matt asked, curious.

'I haven't been here for a long time,' Nate said. 'I thought it'd be nice to have a look and see if it's changed.'

'Would you like a coffee?' Matt asked. 'It's good stuff.'

Nate lifted his head up and sniffed. The coffee smelt wonderful. 'Thanks.'

Matt poured them both a coffee, and they went to the seating area in front of the fireplace. 'So, what help could you give me in starting up an occult book section?'

'Well, I could give you the names of some books and authors to get you started if you want. I know a bit about the subject.'

'You're into the occult then?' Matt asked. 'In what way?'

Interesting, Nate thought. Eliza's son doesn't seem to know much about the occult. Why is that? 'I've made a study of it, over the years. It's a very interesting subject.'

'Is it? I wouldn't know.' Matt looked up as more customers came in. 'If you could write your name and phone number down for me, I'll give you a call if I have any questions.'

'I can do better than that. Here's my card. I run an antique shop.'

'Thanks,' Matt said, taking the card and studying it. 'You never know, I might get in touch.'

'Well, I'll just finish my coffee and have a browse around.'

'Bye for now,' Matt said, walking back to the counter.

Nate moved to the thriller section and found a new book by his favourite author. He went to the counter, and was served by Justin. Nate noticed how both Justin and Matt seemed to be watching him, as if they were looking for trouble. Had Wiladelle been here causing problems already then?

'You look a little familiar,' Nate said to Justin. 'Have we met before?'

'I don't think so, no,' Justin said.

'Hmm, I don't usually forget a face,' Nate said. 'Could I ask your name?'

'Justin. Justin Fairbrother.'

'Any relation to Peter Fairbrother?' Nate asked.

'He's my uncle,' Justin said, surprised. 'Do you know him?'

'Yes, we went to school together,' Nate said. 'Say hello to him for me.'

'I will,' Justin said, pleased.

Nate walked away, and Justin turned to Matt. 'Very stylish guy, don't you think? I wonder if one of those long, black coats would suit me.'

'That's an expensive coat, Justin,' Matt said, 'and he didn't buy it round here.'

*

So, Nate thought, Matt has Peter's nephew working in the shop. Does he know Peter's an experienced witch? And what about Justin? Does he know much about the art? Somehow he didn't think so. He would have felt it. But perhaps he had only just started his training? That was a possibility. He took his book and walked to the door. He paused. He could sense something… A protection spell, that was it. That's why Wiladelle had asked for his help. He smiled. Good on you, Peter, he thought. I bet that's one of your spells.

He looked over to the counter and raised his hand in farewell to Matt and Justin, and saw Matt brush his fringe out of his eyes.

*

Morgan came through the bookshop's door just as Nate was leaving, and their eyes met. Morgan's antennae went up. Was this one of Wiladelle's associates? He went over to Matt and Justin and asked them about Nate.

'He's either a *charmer*, or he's a witch,' Morgan said. 'I could sense it.'

'Oh?' Matt said. 'He offered to help me organise an occult section if I'm interested.'

'Hmm ,' Morgan said, worried. 'He could be dangerous.'

'He went to school with Uncle Peter,' Justin said. 'I'll ask him about Nate and let you know what he says.'

'I think we should keep our eyes open for him,' Morgan said. 'There was an incident a while ago. We thought it was an unfriendly ghost, Acacia and I, but it could have been dark magic.'

'Neither of you mentioned this to me?' Matt said, hurt.

'Well, there wasn't any point,' Morgan said, 'whatever it was went away after Tiger growled and paced up and down a bit.'

Matt's eyebrows went up, but he said nothing.

Justin looked at Morgan and nodded.

'Matt,' Morgan said. 'Peter and I have put protection spells on the shop and the flat, so Wiladelle can't get in.'

'You've what?'

'Protection spells,' Morgan said. 'Fairly simple really.'

'Spells. Simple. Right.' Matt brushed his fringe out of his eyes, retreated to his office and firmly closed the door.

*

Nate drove slowly back to Bude. The roads were clear now

and hopefully there wouldn't be any more snow. He looked at the sky. It was grey. No. Not more snow surely? Then it started to fall again, softly at first, then with increasing urgency as though it was trying to fill up the roads as quickly as possible. He put the windscreen demister on and turned the heater up.

He drove home carefully, thinking about meeting Matt and Justin. He liked them. But, what would he tell Wiladelle if she came back?

NINE

Ernie had mastered the art of moving objects now, and could get a book onto the coffee table and turn the pages. He was thrilled about this and wondered why it had taken him so long to learn. When he first tried, of course, objects just fell through his hands, but he'd taken lessons from the teachers *upstairs* and now he could read earthly books again.

Jett, an attractive teenager even as a ghost, watched Ernie. He'd seen Wiladelle confront Ernie, and he'd seen her switching off appliances. He materialised for Ernie.

'Who are you and what do you want?' Ernie asked, rather rudely.

'I could ask you the same question,' Jett asked. 'What gives you the right to be here?'

'I live here. I've been here for years. This is my place.'

'Well, I'm just visiting, that's all. I used to know Matt a long time ago.'

'Oh? And what's your name?'

The newcomer smiled at him, then drifted out of the building.

Ernie was a bit unsettled by this. Why hadn't the visitor wanted to give his name?

*

Snow had fallen most of the night, and trees and hedgerows resembled lumpy unfinished pottery pieces. Morgan was in Matt and Acacias' flat, which was a warm and happy place to be. He smiled as he watched Acacia typing her reports, but the sound of her tip tapping on the keyboard was distracting him from his conversation.

'So, I'll be about a week, I think,' he told his PA. 'Any problems, email or call me. Okay?' He hung up.

Downstairs in the bookshop, Matt looked disconsolately through the window at the council workers clearing snow from the roads. And then Justin appeared with a shovel on the pavement in front of him, and started clearing the snow away from the bookshop entrance. After about ten minutes Matt was able to open the front door.

'Wow, thanks Justin,' Matt said. 'I couldn't get the door open to do that.'

'That's what I thought,' Justin said. 'Are you going to open the bookshop today? People might be bored of TV and want some books.'

Matt smiled. 'I suppose so. It's worth a try.' He flipped the sign on the door and set the coffee maker going. The fireplace was already on, and the shop was cosy.

Morgan came down the stairs, carrying Tiger, and then saw that Matt intended opening the shop.

'What shall I do with Tiger?' Morgan asked. 'Shall I take him back upstairs?'

'Seems a shame,' Matt said. 'He's starting to get bored up there all the time. We really should get working on the walled garden for him, then he can have a cat door out there and his world will be bigger and more exciting.'

'Maybe in March?' Morgan laughed. 'For now, we're stuck with this weather. I hope you don't mind, but I called the office and said I'd be here for another few days yet. Acacia said it was okay.'

'Of course, Cuz, no worries,' Matt said. He stroked Tiger. 'I don't want him getting out of that front door, though. We need to be careful.'

Morgan nodded.

The morning went slowly with two customers in four hours, but there were still things to be done. Tiger helped Matt in the office by sitting on the desk next to his computer and patting at the mouse every time Matt reached for it. Tiger then got bored and ran around the bookshop chasing imaginary – Matt hoped – beings. Then he jumped on the windowsill and watched people and cars outside.

Morgan fetched a pet blanket from upstairs and put it on the windowsill, and Tiger promptly fell asleep on it.

*

By lunch time the square was safer. Snow had been cleared, then dumped in heaps, leaving a good width for vehicles to pass, and the roads were gritted. Traffic was starting to move. Matt watched a Range Rover drive into the square and park opposite the bookshop. Nate jumped out of the car, and came in. He went straight to the fireplace and rubbed his hands together, then over to the coffee area and poured a coffee. Matt went over and said hello, and then Morgan came and stood next to Matt, waiting to be introduced, watchful.

'This is my cousin, Morgan,' Matt said. 'Morgan, this is Nate. He lives in Bude, runs an antique shop there.'

'Hello,' Morgan said. 'I'm surprised you called in today. The roads are pretty bad, aren't they?'

'Well, I have four wheel drive, and I was bored,' Nate said. 'I closed my shop today. No customers. So I thought I'd come here for something to do. I didn't know if you'd be open or not.'

'What was the drive like?' Matt asked, sitting down.

Nate joined him on the sofa. 'Pretty hairy, actually. I shouldn't have done it I suppose. I don't know what possessed me.' Nate laughed.

Morgan sat in the chair opposite Nate and Matt. 'If the temperature doesn't go up it'll freeze later.' Morgan was watching Nate intently.

'Hey, Morgan, weren't you looking for an old chest for your house?' Matt asked. The tension between Morgan and Nate was obvious. 'Nate might have just the thing in his shop.'

'We have two or three, actually,' Nate said. He scrutinised Morgan and then Matt. 'You know, you two don't resemble each other.'

'Our mothers were sisters,' Matt said.

'Your mothers were sisters?' Nate repeated, startled.

'Yes,' Morgan said. What was going on? Why did Nate seem alarmed?

Nate went pale. This was Wiladelle's son, and he was in Matt's shop.

'Did you know my mother?' Matt asked, leaning forward, always keen to talk to anyone who knew his parents.

'I did,' Nate said. 'I knew Eliza, and Wiladelle, actually.' The smile was gone from Nate's face.

'Tell me something about Mum,' Matt said. 'She died when I was young and I don't know much about her.'

'Yes, tell us something,' Morgan said. He didn't believe this man had known his mother or his aunt. Let's see what he comes up with, he thought.

'Your mum, Matt,' Nate said, 'was one of the best people I ever knew.'

Matt smiled broadly. 'In what way?'

'She was kind and considerate,' Nate said, 'and she was very gifted.'

'Gifted how?' Matt asked.

'Well, I don't know if I should say,' Nate said. Changing the subject, he saw Tiger on the windowsill. 'Hey, is that your cat?'

'Answer the question,' Morgan said, 'tell us how my Aunt Eliza was gifted.'

'Morgan!' Matt said. He turned to Nate. 'Yes, the cat is ours, mine and Acacia's. His name is Tiger.'

Nate got up and walked over to Tiger and stroked him. The cat seemed to like Nate.

'Morgan,' Matt said quietly. 'Nate must be okay if Tiger lets him stroke him.'

'We'll see,' Morgan said. 'I don't trust him. Anyone who knew Wiladelle might be trouble.'

'Justin's Uncle Peter knew Wiladelle, and Peter's not trouble,' Matt said. 'He's been a big help.'

Justin came over to join Matt and Morgan. 'I called Uncle Peter,' he said quietly. 'He says Nate is not a dark witch.

Although, apparently he did study the dark arts when he was younger.'

'That's interesting. I need to find out more about him,' Morgan said to Matt, getting up and going over to Nate.

'I think I should take Tiger upstairs now,' Morgan said, picking Tiger up. 'I'll see you later, Matt.' And with that, Morgan marched back to the flat, with Tiger in his arms.

*

'Sorry about that, Nate,' Matt said. 'My cousin isn't usually rude. We've had a few incidents, and he's on alert I'm afraid.'

'Ah,' Nate said. 'That explains it.'

'Please, have another coffee before you drive back,' Matt said, 'although you shouldn't leave it too long. Morgan's right about the temperature dropping and the ice on the roads.'

Matt smelt smoke. He hoped it wasn't that ghost Ernie again. No, the smell was different. It wasn't cigarette smoke. He stood up and ran his eyes over the room. He saw smoke coming from the coffee maker. He switched it off and unplugged it and, despite the weather, he opened the nearest window to clear the air.

'Is that a new coffee maker?' Nate asked, joining him.

'No, but it's not very old,' Matt said. 'We've had it for a year, and it's never caused any problems before.'

'Seems like you need a new one, now,' Nate said. 'I think I should probably get going. But Matt, I want you to know I'm on your side, okay?'

'On my side? What do you mean?' Matt asked.

'You said there'd been a *few incidents*,' Nate said. 'I'm wondering if this coffee maker is another?'

Matt looked at Nate. He didn't know him at all. This was only the second time they'd met. Was he responsible for the coffee maker nearly causing a fire? Morgan didn't seem to trust Nate. Matt was upset. He didn't like conflict.

'I didn't do it, Matt,' Nate said, seeing Matt's suspicious expression. 'I promise you that. I mean you no harm. But Morgan's mother, Wiladelle, is another matter. Do you trust Morgan?'

'Yes, I trust him,' Matt said, frowning. Who was this man to be questioning Matt about his cousin?

'I'll see what I can find out about him,' Nate said. 'I'll let you know if I find any problems.'

Matt chose to ignore this offer. 'Well, maybe the coffee machine is just an accident, a coincidence.'

'I don't believe in coincidence,' Nate said.

Justin joined Matt and Nate in the coffee area. 'Maybe there's another explanation. Something we haven't thought of yet.'

'Maybe,' Nate said. 'But I'd like to help if I can.'

Matt stayed silent. He was uncomfortable with the tension, and he was confused that another *incident* had taken place. What was going on?

Justin took charge of the situation. 'Thanks, Nate. We appreciate you offering to help us. You'd better be on your way now before it gets dark, though. We'll call you if we need you – is that okay?'

'Right,' Nate said. 'Well, you have my number still, Matt?' Matt didn't respond, so Nate turned to Justin and handed him a card. 'Here's a card for you too, in case Matt's misplaced the one I gave him before. I hope to see you both again soon.'

Matt watched Nate brush his fringe out of his eyes. He

noticed that Nate's eyes were the same shade of brown as his. Matt frowned. What was the matter with him? What did Nate's eye colour matter for goodness sake?

Matt pulled himself together and got up to see Nate off. 'Drive safely,' he called.

*

Upstairs in the flat, Morgan was talking to Acacia, telling her his fears that Nate might be trying to cause problems.

'But, Tiger was okay with him, you say?' she asked.

'Yes, that's the confusing thing,' Morgan said.

'Well, I think if Tiger was okay with him he must be alright.'

'I hope that's true,' Morgan said. He couldn't shake the feeling something was wrong. The problem was, if Nate hadn't caused that electrical problem with the coffee maker, what or who had?

*

Jett had watched earlier as someone had fiddled with the coffee maker. He had wondered what they were doing. Then later, from his hiding place at the back, he'd seen the smoke. So, whoever it was had vandalised the machine deliberately. He knew it couldn't be Wiladelle this time. She'd been blocked from coming in.

Who could it be? Why had they done this?

TEN

The air was crisp, and people were bundled up as they went about their business in the square. Wiladelle paced outside the bookshop, oblivious to the cold.

She would rather not hurt her son, but he'd betrayed her. He'd taken his cousin's side over her. She couldn't forgive treachery. She'd have to end their relationship. And the best way to do that was to kill him. Yes, she'd have to kill him. The question was, how?

She paced some more. She moved to the churchyard at the back, where it was quietest. She liked it there. It was peaceful. She couldn't remember having much peace when she was alive. There'd always been something. And her sister, Eliza, had been most of the problem. Her parents always took her sister's side. Why? And Matt was her sister's son. She had to deal with him. But first she had to deal with her own son, Morgan.

Wiladelle paused, listening to the roofing work going on near the pet shop. Morgan had a habit of visiting the pet shop to get things for that stupid cat. She considered the building site. The workers had stopped for a tea break and left the scaffolding unattended while they visited a local coffee shop. She smiled. She was sure she could use this somehow. She flew over to the scaffolding and inspected it. It was sturdy and safe. Hmm. She flew up to the roof and saw what they were doing. They were replacing all the slates. Now, what if some of those slates happened to fall off the roof just as Morgan was walking past? Maybe that would work. But would it be enough to kill him? She might have to use a whole box.

She found an unopened box of slates on the scaffolding and put a *Hide* spell on it, moving it to the other side of the roof where the builders wouldn't accidently trip on it. Not that she cared about injuring the builders, but she needed a full box for maximum effect.

The builders came back, and she watched them working for what seemed like an hour but really was twenty minutes. She moved some of their tools around so they had difficulty finding them. It was funny seeing the bemused expressions on their faces. So predictable.

She was growing tired of this and was about to go back to the churchyard when she heard the foreman say, 'Come on lads, it's POETS day. One more hour, and then we're finished till Monday.'

POETS day? What the heck was that? Oh, right. A memory came back of her husband telling her Friday was POETS day and he'd be home early. She laughed. Push off early, tomorrow's Saturday. But what time would they leave? And could she get Morgan to come over to the pet shop this afternoon? Not that it mattered. She could do it tomorrow if necessary. They wouldn't be back till Monday, after all. But it would be so much better to get this dealt with today. She laughed again. She couldn't help it. Sometimes things just seemed too funny.

One of the builders stopped and listened. Nothing. He resumed work.

So, one of them could hear her, eh? But he couldn't see her, she was sure. Let's have some fun then, she thought. She manoeuvred herself in front of him and pushed the upside down wooden crate he'd been using to put things on. She watched his face as he saw the crate move seemingly on its own. He scanned the area and couldn't see any reason for the crate to have moved. Then he seemed to look right at her. So, he was a little psychic, eh? Well, what could he do to hurt her? Nothing.

Wiladelle went back to the churchyard where she'd pitched a concealed tent and fell fast asleep. She didn't often rest these days, but the peaceful atmosphere in the churchyard made her sleepy.

She awoke a few hours later refreshed and calm. She sat up and saw the fabric of the tent around her. It was wishy-washy blue. Why did she have that colour tent? A nice mint colour would have been good. She yawned and stretched. How long had she been asleep? It was starting to get dark now. She climbed out of the tent and walked through the churchyard and back into the market square. She had an idea.

She flew up to one of the windows in the bookshop flat and peered in. There was that stupid cat sleeping in his basket. She tapped on the window, and he was immediately on alert. He raced over to the windowsill and fluffed himself up and hissed at her. She laughed at him. As long as the window was between them she was safe. She wondered if he knew? He was still very young. Feisty though.

Acacia came over to see what the problem was, and sensed Wiladelle on the other side of the glass. She picked Tiger up protectively and moved him away from the window.

'Go away,' Acacia said. 'You're not welcome here.'

Morgan joined Acacia at the window. 'What's the matter with Tiger?'

'Something he saw through the window upset him,' Acacia said.

'Oh dear,' Morgan frowned. 'Would a new toy help? I could go and get him one if I hurry, before the pet shop closes.'

'Good idea,' Acacia said. 'That should take Tiger's mind off whatever it was.'

Morgan smiled at her. 'I'll go now.'

'Thanks, Morgan,' Acacia said. She felt as though she'd known Morgan for years. He was part of the family now. She understood how happy Matt was that Morgan had found him. She was pleased too. She didn't have much family of her own, but Matt's family was her family.

*

Wiladelle grinned. It had worked very well. Excellent timing! She flew over to the scaffolding, now quiet as the roofers had gone home. She moved the box of tiles she'd hidden to the front of the roof, and waited for her son to appear on the street below. There he was, on his way to the pet shop. She opened the box and tipped the whole thing over, watching as the tiles fell in a steady stream towards Morgan below.

Just as the slates were about to land on and around Morgan, Nate appeared and pushed him out of the way. At least a quarter of the slates still managed to hit Morgan, and he was sprawled on the pavement unconscious, his expensive shoes muddy and scratched, the sleeve of his coat torn. He lay there absolutely motionless, his blond hair sticky with blood.

Wiladelle watched anxiously. Was he dead? She really would like to get it over and done with. And if he was dead, it would take him a long time before he was ready to do anything to stop her. And where had Nate come from? Drat the man! Why did he have to interfere?

*

Nate pulled out his mobile and called for an ambulance. People came out of the pet shop with a pile of pet blankets and put them underneath Morgan's head. A woman from another shop came out with a blanket to cover him and keep him warm.

Nate then called Matt, who rushed over and found his cousin on the ground surrounded by people, Morgan's blood on the pavement.

'How on earth did that happen?' Matt asked, looking up at the scaffolding, and then down at the smashed slates on the pavement. He couldn't see any roofers. Had they left an open box of slates up there? Surely not.

Nate saw Matt lean down and speak to Morgan, but Morgan was still unconscious.

An ambulance pulled up in a flurry of sirens and whirring lights.

'Will he be alright?' Matt asked the paramedic, as

Morgan was carefully transferred, still unconscious, to a stretcher.

'We'll know more when the doctor's examined him,' said the paramedic, closing the ambulance door.

'Which hospital?' Matt asked.

'Barnstaple,' they called as the ambulance drove off.

'I'll drive,' Nate said, handing him his mobile. 'You call Justin and Acacia and tell them what's going on.'

Matt called the shop and told Justin what had happened. 'Please can you call your Uncle Peter and ask him to come and sit with Acacia?'

'Sure,' Justin said. 'Do you think this is Wiladelle's handiwork then?'

'I'm not sure,' Matt said, 'but I don't want to leave Acacia alone. Wiladelle might try something else.'

'Hang on, I'll call him on the shop phone,' Justin said. Barely a minute later, he said, 'Okay, I've spoken to him. He's on his way. I'll lock up. You get to the hospital. I'll tell Acacia, and I'll wait here till Uncle Peter comes.'

Nate took the road to Barnstaple. He saw Matt watching him, eyes narrowed. He knew Matt was wondering how he just happened to be there when the tiles fell.

'I know what you're thinking, Matt,' Nate said. 'I had a strong feeling something was about to happen and drove here as quickly as I could. I found myself at the pet shop, then saw the tiles falling from the roof with Morgan below. I pushed him out of the way, but I wasn't quite quick enough, and some of the slates hit him. I'm sorry.'

Nate sensed Matt's conflict. How could he reassure Matt and still concentrate on his driving? The road had been gritted, but there were still patches of ice. He turned the car's heater up.

'You spoke to the pet shop staff, right?' Nate continued. 'They told you they'd seen me try to save Morgan? They saw me push him out of the way?'

'Yes,' Matt said. He was very quiet. Nate had seen the way Matt dealt with conflict. He knew Matt retreated into himself, giving time to process whatever was happening.

Nate's mind was working overtime. If someone, probably Wiladelle, had tried to kill Morgan then obviously Morgan was on their side. That was a relief. He knew Matt was fond of Morgan. He also knew Morgan was knowledgeable in the art and would be very helpful to have around. If only he'd been there five minutes earlier he could have stopped it happening. But then, Wiladelle would have found another way to get at Morgan.

'Keep positive, Matt,' Nate said, changing gears as they took a bend. 'Morgan is a healthy guy, and he wants to live. I'm sure he'll make a good recovery.'

Nate stole a glance at Matt's face. He could see something of Eliza there. He'd started by wanting to help Matt because he was Eliza's son, but now he knew Matt a little he liked him and wanted to help him for his own sake.

Matt nodded, silent, studying the scenery as they drove the quiet country lanes.

Nate, despite his words to Matt, was worried. Morgan's face had been covered in blood, and his legs had been at an odd angle. Was his spine injured? Did he have a brain injury? Would the physician's work be enough? Or was it something that would require magical intervention? What spells did he know that could help? He'd have to think about that when they got there.

'Matt,' Nate said. 'I know Morgan is your cousin, and you don't want to lose him. You won't. Trust me.'

ELEVEN

Matt kissed his grandmother, Tara, and took her coat, hanging it on the coat stand near the fireplace so it was warm when she put it on again. It was cold out, and his grandmother was, well, she was older than he was… he never thought of her as old.

Acacia poured some tea, and Tiger padded over and sat on Tara's lap.

'Well, Matt,' Tara said, 'you've had a bit of a time of it, haven't you?'

'You could say that, Nana,' Matt said.

'How is Morgan doing?' Tara asked.

'He's stable. Peter, Justin, Nate, Acacia and I take it in turns to sit with him.'

'I'm glad we're having this conversation,' Tara said. 'I think you should know your mother was very gifted. I'm hoping you've inherited some of your mother's talent.'

Acacia looked excited. Tara smiled at her.

'Talent?' Matt asked. 'What talent?'

Tara sighed. 'Come on, Matt, you must know your mother was a very talented witch.'

Matt went pale, but said nothing.

'Your grandad and I think differently about these things.'

'More tea?' Acacia asked. Tara nodded, and Acacia topped up their cups.

'Now,' Tara said, 'I understand some things have happened here that are not quite understood yet. Is that right?'

Matt looked at Acacia, and she nodded at him to go on. 'Yes, we're working on it,' he said.

Tara looked at him closely. 'Matt, please don't do this. It's like trying to prise the lid off a tight jar. I'd like to be brought up to speed on these *things* please, before we discuss what happened yesterday.'

Acacia looked at her husband. She saw him swallow, then reach for his tea and drink some of it, but he said nothing.

'Shall I explain?' Acacia asked Matt. He nodded.

Acacia gave Tara a quick overview of what had been happening and what precautions had been taken so far.

'Sounds like Morgan is a big help,' Tara said. 'I'm glad you've met up with him, Matt.'

'Why didn't you tell me I had an aunt and a cousin?' Matt asked.

'We always felt your aunt was a little, well, strange, Matt,' Tara said. 'So we just felt it best not to mention her or her son. We're still not sure how your parents' car accident happened. We thought it best if you were kept away from Wiladelle, and her son. It seems we were wrong about your cousin, but we were right about Wiladelle.'

Matt was becoming more and more agitated. Was his grandma hinting Wiladelle might be responsible for his parents' deaths?

'Nana,' Matt said. 'Do you think my aunt caused my parents' deaths?'

'She hated your mum,' Tara said. 'She really was unhinged.'

Matt's eyes were big as saucers.

'But, Matt, you must know that your mother was perfectly sane. And so are you. There's no cause for alarm on that score.'

Acacia poured three small tots of brandy and passed them around.

Matt tossed his back in one go, and Acacia put a bit more in his glass. He stared at his grandmother. He'd lived with his grandparents most of his life, ever since his parents had been killed. He'd never heard her talk about this kind of thing before. He was annoyed. Why hadn't he been told any of this?

Tara watched her grandson as his mood changed from confused to downright miffed.

'Look, Matt, you must understand that your grandpa doesn't believe in this stuff and neither did you. How could I broach this subject with you before? You just weren't ready.'

'I might have been,' Matt said, 'if you'd only given me a chance. You just assumed I wouldn't believe you, is that it?'

'Your grandpa felt it was best not to discuss your aunt or your cousin.'

Matt put his remaining brandy in his tea and took a gulp. So, all this time he'd lived in ignorance of the fact that his aunt may have killed his parents, and he had a cousin.

'Now,' Tara said, 'I've not met Morgan, but Acacia tells me he's a good man, right?'

Matt said nothing, not yet trusting himself to be civil to the grandmother he loved.

Acacia sat next to Matt and held his hand. 'We both

like Morgan and so does Tiger. Tiger is pretty savvy when it comes to people. Morgan came looking for Matt after his mother died because he has no other family, and he wanted to know if maybe his cousin and he could be friends.'

'Has Peter met him?' Tara asked.

'You know Peter?' Matt asked, surprised.

'Of course,' Tara said. 'He was a regular customer in the bookshop when we ran it. He never discussed his occult tendencies in Sam's presence, of course.'

'Yes,' Acacia said. 'He's met Morgan, and he likes him.'

'Well,' Tara said, 'then Morgan is definitely okay. That's a relief. I've been a bit worried about that, with him being Wiladelle's son. And Nate? You've met Nate I understand?'

'What?' Matt said. 'Do you know Nate?'

'I've known Nate for years,' Tara said. 'I've always liked him.'

Matt nodded. That was a good thing. That was something he could accept with no problem. He liked Nate.

Tara stroked Tiger, who was still on her lap, purring contentedly.

Matt's mind was racing. Of all the things that had happened in the last few weeks, this was the most surprising, that his grandmother believed in the supernatural. He thought back to when he was a child and still open to lots of things, and he heard his grandfather's voice, *If you can see it and touch it, it's real. If you can't see it and touch it, it's not real. Always remember that.* His grandmother had never said anything like that to him, she never reinforced what her husband said about the supernatural, she had just looked at him and looked away. Now he knew why.

'What about Mum?' Matt asked.

'She was very talented, Matt,' Tara said. 'Don't listen to Sam saying she was crazy. I saw some of the things she could do.'

'What kind of things?' Matt asked.

'I saw your mum fly once,' Tara said.

Matt's eyes widened. He laughed uncertainly. She had to be joking, right?

Matt looked at his grandmother. She didn't look as if she was joking. It occurred to him now that she was not just his grandmother, not just his Grandpa Sam's wife. She had different beliefs to his grandfather. She was her own person. His world had shifted on its axis again, but he was getting used to that.

'Okay, Nana,' Matt said. 'What happened?'

'She didn't need a broomstick,' Tara said. 'She just launched herself above and across the lawn when you fell in the fish pond. You were about two years old.'

'How far away was she?' Matt asked.

'You know where the fish pond is?' Tara asked. 'We were sitting at the garden table drinking tea. That's a long way from the fish pond, isn't it?'

Matt nodded. No way could it have been just a leap. It was too far. He straightened up in his seat. His mother had been a witch. His cousin was a witch. Justin's Uncle Peter was a witch. There was a ghost in the bookshop. His dead aunt was causing him problems. Okay, then.

Matt's mind went into overdrive. If his cousin and his mum were witches, or *charmers*, maybe he really did have some of this talent. Once he got the bit between his teeth he didn't let go till he'd achieved whatever it was he set out to do.

'Well, if Mum could do these things,' Matt said, 'maybe I

can too. We have Morgan, Peter, Justin and Nate to help us. Aunt Wiladelle may have bitten off more than she can chew.'

Tara smiled at her grandson. 'That's more like the Matt I know and love.'

Acacia held up her teacup and clinked it against first Matt's and then Tara's teacups.

'To unknown possibilities and talents,' she said. 'And to Morgan's full recovery, and our successfully overthrowing anything Wiladelle comes up with to hurt us.'

'Here, here,' Tara said.

'Too right,' Matt said.

TWELVE

Morgan was sitting upright in the hospital bed, his usually attractive face a mess of bruises and cuts. Matt felt his eyes fill with tears.

'Sorry about this, Cuz,' Morgan said. 'Guess I was in the wrong place at the wrong time.' He groaned, and shifted around the bed, trying to get comfortable, then said, 'I didn't get Tiger the toy I promised him. Can you tell him I'm sorry? I'll get it when I get out of here.'

Matt and Nate exchanged a look. 'Morgan, don't worry about Tiger,' Matt said, 'he's safe and healthy, which is more than you are at the moment.' Matt scrutinised Morgan's face, and then his eyes travelled over Morgan's normally robust body. Morgan was in obvious pain, dishevelled, face and forearms grazed and sore. Matt was worried. He'd been told there was a problem with his cousin's leg. He didn't even know which leg it was. He didn't want to ask.

'That's it now, leave him in our hands,' a nurse said. 'You can see him tomorrow, but call first, okay?'

Matt and Nate waved at Morgan and tried to look cheerful for him, but neither of them felt upbeat about Morgan's situation. How badly was Morgan's leg injured? Would he be able to walk on it after an operation? Were there internal injuries? They could get no answers now, and so they headed back to the bookshop.

Nate drove while Matt brooded.

'It could've been a lot worse,' Nate said. 'If those tiles had fallen on Morgan's head instead of his leg he'd be dead now.'

Matt nodded, but stayed silent, and after three quarters of an hour Nate parked near the bookshop. The square was busy with shoppers, and the smell of a lit cigarette wafted over them as a man hurried past.

Acacia greeted Matt with, 'I called the builder about the roof tiles. He couldn't understand how a box of tiles could've fallen. They don't leave stock there when they leave the site. He is completely mystified.'

'You don't think the builder is just trying to cover his butt, do you?' Matt asked.

'He sounded genuinely surprised. Outraged actually,' Acacia said. 'He's on his way over there to check things out, and will call me later.'

'Well, if this is Wiladelle again we have to step up the game plan,' Nate said. 'We have to somehow make sure nothing else happens to any of us.'

Matt looked alarmed, and Acacia came over, and put her hand in his.

'Will Morgan's leg be okay?' Justin asked.

'We won't know anything else until tomorrow morning,' Matt said.

Peter walked into the shop. 'I've called my local group.

We'll make sure a couple of guys are outside the hospital and looking at anyone who goes through the doors, just to make sure nothing happens to Morgan while he's in there.'

Matt felt his stomach clench. Did this mean Morgan was still in danger?

'That's great, thanks, Peter,' Nate said. He turned to Matt. 'Best to be on the safe side.'

Peter left soon after, to take a turn at the Hospital Protection Rota as he called it. None of them got much sleep that night. They were all worried about Morgan.

*

'The operation went well,' Matt told Acacia, putting the phone down. 'He'll be allowed to leave hospital soon. His leg was broken, but no internal injuries, lots of bruising and slight concussion, but nothing else serious. He can come here, right?'

'Of course,' Acacia said. 'It'll be great to have him here.'

Matt looked at Acacia. His wife liked her privacy, but she always seemed happy to see Morgan. That was a good thing, right?

Matt shivered and went over to the fireplace to turn it up a notch. He watched Acacia topping up Tiger's kibble dish. Tiger came over to inspect what was on offer and put his paw into the dish to pull out some food. Matt could hear Tiger munching his kibble, and realised he was hungry himself. He poured a coffee and pulled out the cake tin, holding it up to Acacia, a question in his eyes.

'No cake for me, thanks, Matt,' Acacia said, pouring herself some coffee.

'New recipe?'

'I don't think I've made it for you before, but it's an old favourite of mine. It was one of Mum's recipes. Do you like it?'

'It's very good. Maybe you should be running a tea shop rather than typing medical reports.'

Acacia laughed.

*

A few days' later, regular visits to Morgan were allowed. The weather had warmed up a bit, and the roads were clear of ice. Matt and Acacia visited Morgan more frequently. Peter and his group still had their lookouts, but nothing untoward had been seen.

'How're you doing?' Matt asked Morgan, sitting next to the bed and handing him some grapes.

'Good,' Morgan said, looking at Matt and Acacia through dark rimmed eyes. He took a grape and ate it slowly.

Acacia sat the other side of the bed and took one of Morgan's hands in hers. 'You'll be able to leave tomorrow,' she said, 'so Matt and Nate will pick you up, and you're going to recuperate with us. Your bedroom is all prepared, and Tiger is looking forward to sleeping with you.'

Morgan's eyes misted over. 'Thanks, Acacia.'

Matt saw his cousin swallow, and knew Morgan felt a bit emotional about having family support. Matt realised his cousin must have been quite lonely before he found him and Acacia. Matt noticed his own throat constricting. He felt very protective towards Morgan, even though Morgan was capable of looking after himself. They were kindred spirits, even though they were different in so many ways.

'It'll be good to have you with us for a bit,' Matt said, looking at Morgan and Acacia smiling at each other.

*

The following day, Nate and Matt went to collect Morgan, leaving with a wheelchair, medication, and numerous instruction sheets.

Morgan and Matt were laughing and joking. The journey seemed much shorter this time around, and Nate pulled into a parking space in the square after what seemed like minutes.

'There you go, Morgan,' Nate said as he and Matt took an arm each and helped Morgan up the stairs to the flat.

As soon as Morgan was in bed, Tiger jumped on the bottom and then gently made his way up Morgan's side until he reached his arms, snuggling in and purring.

'You see?' Matt said. 'We're all pleased you're here.'

Morgan smiled. He felt his eyelids drooping, and he nodded off.

*

Later, Tiger jumped on the windowsill and looked out. Nothing menacing out there today. He looked at Morgan. I think maybe I keep it at bay, he said, by way of a meow, getting back on the bed and batting Morgan's hand. Morgan stroked Tiger and then went back to sleep. Tiger's instincts were spot on.

*

Wiladelle had seen them arrive and watched as they got Morgan into the bookshop. She'd kept her distance as the cat jumped onto the windowsill. She didn't want him to alert anyone that she was there.

Would you reconsider? she asked Morgan telepathically. *This accident was a warning. Think about it. Let me know if you change your mind.*

Morgan dreamt about Wiladelle, and the question appeared in his dream. He tossed and turned, and called out 'No!' in his sleep.

Wiladelle frowned. She'd heard the *No* from Morgan. She had also seen Peter's group at the hospital and realised there were a lot of them. Darn it. And what about Nate? She was confused about Nate. Was he really on Matt's side? She'd have to have another word with him. She needed to be sure.

Unknown to Wiladelle, Peter called the bookshop and spoke to Justin. 'Stay vigilant, okay?' Peter said.

'Will do, Uncle Peter,' Justin agreed. 'Nate's been in a few times to see how Morgan's doing.'

'I thought he would,' Peter said. 'I'll be in tomorrow. See you then.'

*

The weather had improved considerably, if rain could be considered an improvement. Better than snow and ice, Acacia thought.

Matt had allowed himself to believe things were getting back to normal, but Acacia was still watchful. Her instincts told her this was just the beginning, and she didn't allow herself to relax.

After a week, Morgan hobbled into the living room and fell onto the sofa. He could see Tiger sleeping in his basket next to the fireplace. The room was warm and, as always, Morgan felt at ease in Matt and Acacia's home.

'Well, hello,' Acacia said. 'Coffee?'

'Nice to get back some normality,' Morgan said. 'I'm so bored of being in bed. Just coming into the living room is a great change of scenery. Coffee would be wonderful.'

Tiger woke up, saw Morgan, and joined him on the sofa, snuggling at his side.

'Plaster comes off next week, I think?' Acacia asked.

'I hope so,' Morgan said. 'I can hardly wait. I'm so tired of all this.'

THIRTEEN

Matt came upstairs for some lunch, and he found Morgan and Acacia laughing and chatting in the dining room. Acacia was serving Morgan his favourite toasted cheese sandwich.

Matt caught a look in his cousin's eye that he recognised only too well.

'You seem a bit better each day, Cuz,' Matt said, taking a seat at the table.

'Would you like a toasted cheese sandwich?' Acacia asked Matt.

'That'd be great,' Matt said, watching as Morgan's eyes followed Acacia around. 'Have you spoken to your office lately?' Matt asked him.

Matt watched as Morgan mentally shook himself.

Morgan studied Matt, whose eyes clearly told him he suspected his cousin was in love with his wife.

Matt saw his cousin's face show confusion, dismay and regret.

Morgan smiled ruefully. 'I spoke to them this morning. I told them I'd be back in a couple of weeks' time. I even managed to send some emails today.'

*

Acacia frowned. What was going on here? Something felt off. Matt and Morgan were awkward with each other. Why was that? She put her hand on Matt's shoulder, and lent down and kissed him lightly.

Matt smiled up at his wife. He glanced over at Morgan, and Morgan shook his head at him.

'I'll be out of your hair in a couple of weeks' time,' Morgan said. 'You've both been great, supporting me, but I really need to pay more attention to my business.'

Acacia was confused. She frowned. What on earth was going on here? Did Morgan really want to leave so soon?

'Are you sure you're ready?' Acacia asked.

'I will be,' Morgan said. 'Not much longer and I'll be up and running around again.'

'What about Wiladelle?' Acacia asked.

Morgan shrugged.

Matt took a deep breath. 'Maybe Morgan being out of the area for a while is a good idea. Nate and Peter will keep an eye on things. It's me she's after, not Morgan.'

'I think she's after both of you,' Acacia said. 'You be careful, Morgan.'

'I will be. Don't worry about me, I'll be fine.'

'Don't stay away too long, okay?' Acacia said.

Morgan studied the table, and Matt coughed. Acacia frowned again. What was going on here?

'Okay?' she repeated.

Morgan seemed uncomfortable, and still didn't answer. His usual self-assurance was gone.

Matt decided to rescue him. 'Morgan knows we're here for him, don't you Morgan?'

'Yes,' Morgan said haltingly.

'Are you feeling okay?' Acacia asked Morgan, concerned. 'Do you need anything?'

'He probably needs more coffee, Acacia,' Matt said. 'Right?'

Morgan nodded, and Acacia went through to the kitchen to get some.

'Listen, Matt,' Morgan said. 'You know I'd never... I wouldn't do anything...' He couldn't go on.

'I know, Cuz,' Matt said. 'We're good. No worries.'

But, much as he wanted to believe that, Matt couldn't shake the feeling that was not the end of the matter.

*

The street lights were struggling to shine through the grey mist hanging over Bude, like a single candle trying to light up a concert hall. Wiladelle was in Nate's antique shop. She'd been gliding around inspecting the stock. She'd never liked antiques. Why did people buy this stuff? Although, that desk in the corner was interesting, she thought. She opened the flap and was investigating the compartments in the top when Nate appeared, ready to open up for the day.

Wiladelle launched straight into it – no preamble. 'So, you managed to cause some disruption in the shop then?'

'What?' Nate asked.

'The other day in the bookshop,' she said. 'The smoke with the coffee maker.'

'That wasn't me,' Nate said.

'Oh?' Wiladelle was puzzled. 'Just a coincidence then?'

'No idea,' Nate said. 'Look, Wiladelle, you've caused a lot of problems. I'd like to ask you to stop.'

'Stop?' She was astonished. 'Stop? I've only just begun.'

'Well, I've no intention of helping you,' Nate said. 'I'm on Matt's side, and Morgan's.'

'Oh?' she said. 'Matt is Eliza's son. You do remember what she did to you, don't you?'

'That was a long time ago,' Nate said, 'and had nothing to do with Matt.'

'Matt's her son,' Wiladelle repeated. 'If you hurt him, you hurt her. Stands to reason.'

'I don't want to hurt anyone. I would ask you again to reconsider your actions. Stop this, Wiladelle, before we have to make you.'

'You're threatening me?' Wiladelle said, outraged. 'Eliza was unfaithful to you and laughed at you behind your back. Yet you take her side over me?'

'She must have had her reasons. I'm not perfect, you know.'

Wiladelle stared at him. He still believed Eliza had been unfaithful to him. Good.

'Do you really want me for an enemy?' she asked.

'I don't want anyone as an enemy,' Nate said, 'but if you're determined to wage war on Eliza's son, and your own son, then so be it.'

Wiladelle shook her head. 'You'll be sorry.'

'I think you're the one who'll be sorry,' Nate countered.

116

Wiladelle was watching Nate carefully. He seemed confident that he could beat her in a fight. She knew they were evenly matched. Did she want to take him on?

'Wiladelle, think about this,' Nate said. 'Matt's not on his own, you know. And he doesn't just have me and Morgan to help him either.'

'I know that,' Wiladelle said. 'I saw Peter and his little band of helpers at the hospital. No problem to me. I've got friends too, you know. You'll be meeting some of them soon.'

She flew out the door, and Nate cast a protection spell on his shop.

*

Morgan opened his bag on the bed. The bag really wasn't big enough, but he'd had no idea when he'd packed it that he'd be in Devon this long. Who could've foreseen it? His blue eyes filled up, and he grabbed a tissue from the box Acacia had thoughtfully placed in his room. Acacia. He sighed. Well, he'd only be away for a few weeks, and then he'd be back.

Where were his brown shoes? He found them in the wardrobe, where no doubt Acacia had tidied them away. Why did he even have brown shoes? All his suits were grey, black or blue, for heaven's sake. He put them back in the wardrobe and instead put two pairs of black shoes in his bag. He folded his shirts up neatly and put them on top of his shoes, then remembered his bathroom stuff and got that together in his toilet bag, putting it next to his shoes under his shirts.

Morgan sat on the bed. His heart wasn't in this at all. Did he have to go? Stupid question – of course he had to go. He needed to put some distance between himself and Acacia before she realised how he felt. Matt had already sussed it. He really hoped Matt knew he wouldn't act on his feelings for Acacia.

He'd been away from his business way too long anyway, and there was only so much he could do by phone, video conference and email. Ah – he'd need his laptop. He put that into its carrying case and put it next to the bag. Where was his suit? He'd only brought one. Well, he didn't need suits here, did he?

Ties? Did he bring any ties? Right, there they were, one red and one silver-grey. He folded them in the bag along with his underwear. He never wore pyjamas, and he'd been using Matt's spare dressing gown.

He picked his bag and laptop up, and as he left his room the smell of freshly brewed coffee wafted towards him. Matt and Acacia were sitting on the sofa, drinking coffee and obviously waiting for him.

'Coffee, Morgan?' Acacia asked.

Morgan swallowed, and shook his blond hair. This had become home to him, and Matt and Acacia were family.

'I'll only be a few weeks,' Morgan said. 'When I get back we'll see how things are, and I'll make some decisions. Don't forget you can reach me on the phone any time, day or night, if you need to talk to me about stuff, okay?' He went over and kissed Acacia lightly on the cheek, then shook Matt's hand before Matt went one step further and hugged him.

'We'll miss you, Cuz,' said Matt. 'Here, let me take that bag.' Matt and Morgan walked to Morgan's car.

Morgan said, 'Matt, you do know…' But he couldn't finish the sentence.

'I know, Morgan.'

'Yes, but you do know I wouldn't…' Morgan said, again unable to finish the sentence.

'I know,' Matt said. 'See you when you get back, okay?'

'I'm thinking of buying my own place here,' Morgan said. 'That way— '

'Close, but not too close?' Matt nodded. 'Good idea. I'll keep my eyes open for something suitable.'

'We're good, right?' Morgan asked.

Matt hugged him again. 'We're good, Cuz, no worries.'

Matt watched his cousin's car drive off. Morgan waved out of the car window and drove away, looking in his rear-view mirror until he couldn't see Matt anymore. Then he turned on the radio needing to hear voices in the car.

Suddenly he felt very lonely indeed.

FOURTEEN

Being so near Cornwall, spring came a little earlier in Holsworthy. Snowdrops were everywhere and, now the snow had gone, daffodils were starting to come up.

Acacia hugged Tiger close as they looked out of the window at the walled garden.

'I promise we'll get working on that walled garden soon,' she told Tiger. 'Then you can have a cat door from here down the stairs and another cat door into the garden, okay? But we don't want you going into the shop when it's open.'

Tiger looked at Acacia seriously. So, he was going out into the garden soon. Thank goodness for that. He was bored. He longed to be outside.

He used telepathy to tell her *thank you.* She hugged him again, and sat him on his cushion on the windowsill.

There was a knock at the flat door. Acacia was surprised to see Nate standing there. She invited him in, and handed him a coffee.

Nate laughed. 'It's guaranteed I'll get coffee when I visit you, and it's always good. I wanted to sound you out about my offering to mentor Matt in the magic arts,' Nate said.

'Oh, I see,' Acacia said. 'Before you go into the lion's den, you want to talk to his mate?'

'I get the impression he's got rather mixed views on the subject.'

'Yes,' Acacia said. 'Until recently he didn't believe magic was real. Or ghosts. It's all been a bit of a shock.'

'That's what I thought, but the thing is, I think we need to be ready for problems, and Matt really needs to start learning stuff. Right now.'

'Yes, you're right,' Acacia said. 'Actually, around now would be good timing for that conversation as it doesn't get really busy in the shop till about noon.'

'Do you think he'll go for it?'

'I hope he will,' Acacia said, 'but only one way to find out. Sorry I can't be more help.'

'That's fine,' Nate said, finishing his coffee and putting his mug on the coffee table. 'I'll go talk to him downstairs.'

However, just then, Matt appeared in the flat. 'I thought I saw you coming up,' he said to Nate.

'Nate has something he wants to ask you,' Acacia said. 'I'm going to put my headphones on and get back to work.' She left them to it. She knew it was best she took a backseat, knew Matt needed to do this, needed to be intrinsic to solving the *Wiladelle problem*.

*

'I wondered how you felt about my mentoring you,' Nate asked.

Matt looked puzzled. 'In what?'

'The magic arts,' Nate said.

Matt was silent. He hadn't expected this. He poured himself a coffee, topped up Nate's cup and gestured him over to the sofa.

'How would the whole mentoring thing work?' Matt asked. 'Where would we practice? How often would we meet for training?'

'I think twice a week for lessons, around 6.30pm. I'm not sure where the lessons should take place yet. I have to think about that. I just wanted to know if you're up for it.'

Matt sipped his coffee and looked over at Acacia. She was busy typing reports, so he couldn't ask her what she thought. They made all big decisions jointly. He would've liked to talk to her about this.

Nate saw Matt looking over at his wife and said, 'I asked Acacia what she thought about it, and she said she thought it was a good idea.'

Matt nodded, then drank some coffee. In the back of his mind, he'd known it would come to this. No point in hiding his head in the sand.

'Okay,' Matt said. 'Let's give it a go then. No idea if I'll be any good at it though.'

'Any magical experiences you've had that you'd like to share?' Nate asked.

Matt looked at him. 'Not really. Have you been talking to my grandma about this?'

'No. Should I?'

'Grandma told me some of the things my mum could do,' Matt said.

Nate leaned forward and waited, the expression in his brown eyes carefully neutral.

'Grandma says Mum flew to my rescue once. When I was very young.'

'Ah,' Nate said. 'Well, your mother was very talented, Matt.'

'Is that usual? The flying thing I mean?'

'Not very usual, no,' Nate said. 'In the past witches and *charmer*s have used brooms, of course. That much of conventional belief is true.'

Matt nodded. He was starting to feel excited about the possibilities. Peter popped into his head. 'Peter has a big basement in his house,' Matt said, 'and Peter has been talking about training Justin apparently.'

'Brilliant!' Nate said. 'We could do the lessons together, the four of us. I'll call Peter and ask him. Don't say anything to Justin yet, we'll leave it to Peter to talk to Justin. But it would be more powerful with four of us.'

'More powerful?' Matt asked. 'How's that?'

'The power increases with numbers,' Nate said. He smiled. He'd never mentored anyone before. 'Okay,' Nate said. 'I'll have a word with Peter and give you a call.'

'Good,' Matt said. Now the decision had been made, he found himself feeling quite enthusiastic.

*

Acacia took her headphones off and looked at Matt and Nate. 'Well?'

'Nate's going to be my mentor,' Matt said. 'He's going to teach me magic.'

'That's great news,' Acacia said. She was relieved. Maybe once Matt knew some of the art she should learn some too.

No. She couldn't do that. Best to leave it to Matt.

Tiger jumped on Nate's lap, looking up at him with a question in his eyes.

'What do you want to know, Tiger?' Nate asked.

Acacia was watching closely. Would Tiger communicate telepathically with Nate? So far, it had only been with her.

Tiger licked Nate's hand, and looked up at him again.

Nate laughed. 'You're still a bit young, Tiger,' he said. 'But we'll see if you and I can do some magic together. How's that?'

Tiger seemed to smile at him, and then went over to his food bowl.

'Did Tiger ask you to teach him?' Acacia asked. 'Did he use telepathy?'

Nate's eyes widened. 'I didn't know he could use telepathy! No, it just seemed obvious from the way he was acting, and I just felt that's what he was asking.'

'So far he's only used telepathy with me,' Acacia said smugly. She knew she and Tiger had a special relationship.

'Can you teach Tiger magic?' Matt asked, incredulous.

'I think Tiger knows more than we realise,' Nate said. 'But he could probably do with some lessons too. I'll have to see what I can do about that. There's this very talented young *charmer* I know. She's called Samantha, and she's very good with animals. Maybe she could teach Tiger?'

Matt's eyes were as wide as Acacia's.

'Why so surprised?' Nate asked. 'You said yourself Tiger is a very special cat.'

FIFTEEN

'It's all set,' Matt told Acacia. 'The first lesson is tonight, in Peter's basement.'

Acacia squeezed Matt's hand in response, then kissed him lightly on the lips before going back to her desk and her transcription work. Matt smiled as he closed the door to the flat and headed back downstairs.

Nate and Peter called at the shop just before it closed. Justin was cashing up the till as the door closed behind them. 'What's this?' he asked. 'An armed escort?'

'In a way, yes,' Peter said. 'Wiladelle may have got wind of this, and we don't want any little surprises before we're ready for it.'

Matt and Justin looked at each other. They'd been excited all day about the training, but the reality check was a dampener on their enthusiasm.

'Don't look like that,' Nate said. 'Don't let her stop you having fun.'

They drove to Peter's house, an Edwardian detached home

at the end of a country lane with a large, well-kept garden. Out of the car, it was dark and cold, but at least it wasn't raining.

'There's only me here, since my wife died,' Peter said. 'It's about time it had more people in it.'

'Well, it will have us a few times every week,' Justin said, giving his uncle's arm a squeeze as they went into the house.

'Let's get the niceties out of the way first then,' Peter said, showing them to a table weighed down with sandwiches, cakes and a trifle.

'Peter, you needn't have gone to all this trouble,' Nate said.

'Nonsense,' Peter said. 'This first lesson is a cause for celebration. We won't usually have all this food first, but I felt in honour of the fact that training is beginning we should have something nice to eat. We've got about thirty minutes, then we have to start,' Peter said. 'So dig in.'

A little later, Matt started to wander around the house, taking in the tall windows with the window seats, the shrubs and flowers he could just see through the windows in the dark garden. The understated elegance everywhere surprised him. Very unusual, Matt had thought bungalows a fairly modern innovation, but this one had character, and a basement... Peter was a practical man, and this house didn't seem to sit with the Peter he thought he'd come to know.

'What do you think of the house?' Peter asked Matt. 'My wife chose it,' he said. 'She loved the Edwardian era. The house is full of things she bought, and it's decorated to her taste. I love it too, but it's a bit too big just for me.'

'Ah,' Matt said. 'That explains it. I didn't think it was your style. I love it, though. It has a good atmosphere. I can almost see Edwardians at the dining room table. Your wife had a good eye.'

Justin joined Matt and Peter. 'Have you ever thought about how stylish Nate is? I mean, that long, black coat, those Oxford shoes (he gets them from London), his dark brown hair is so, I don't know what the word is, 'him'. Who does his hair? He always looks immaculate.'

'Nate's legendary, you know,' Peter said. 'He's not just cool to look at, he's original with his spells. He's beyond knowledgeable in the art. He achieves everything he sets out to do. We're so lucky to have him helping us.'

Nate was reading one of Peter's books, and he brushed his fringe out of his eyes. Justin frowned. Matt raised his eyebrows at Justin – *what*?

Justin said, 'Some of Nate's mannerisms remind me of someone…'

'Who?'

'Can't put my finger on it, but I wish I was as good looking as Nate,' Justin said, 'then I'd have no problem getting women.'

Peter laughed. 'You're right there. Women throw themselves at him, I understand, but he doesn't seem interested. And before you ask, no, he's not gay. Rumour has it he lost the love of his life, and he's never looked at a woman in that way since.' Peter paused. 'Rumour also has it that he rescues animals from abusive situations and puts spells on people who mistreat them.'

Matt looked over at Nate. No doubt about it, he was certainly attractive and stylish. He'd have to tell Acacia about the animal rescue thing, she'd be pleased about that.

'Time to go down to the basement,' Peter said. 'By the way, no need to worry, the whole house is protected so there's no way Wiladelle or any of her associates can get in here.'

Nate and Peter both pulled out wands.

'Wands?' Matt said. 'I didn't think you guys really used wands.'

'Bit old school, I know,' Nate said, 'but they make the spells that bit more powerful. Watch.' He turned to Peter. 'Do the *Disappear spell* without the wand, Peter.'

Peter placed an empty glass jar on the table at the other end of the room, walked back to where the others were and chanted a spell:

You're no longer needed, you're not needed here
So go away, vanish, yes, please disappear

They watched as the glass jar seemed to melt and vanish in front of them.

'Now, with the wand please, Peter,' Nate said.

Peter placed another empty glass jar on the table, took out his wand and repeated the spell, this time flourishing his wand as he chanted. The jar was gone instantly.

'Did you see the difference?' Nate asked Matt and Justin.

'It was much quicker,' Matt said, and Justin nodded.

'Right, now you try, Matt,' Nate said.

'I don't have a wand,' Matt said.

'Try this one,' Nate said. 'It belonged to your mother.'

'How did you get it?' Matt asked.

'I'll tell you the story sometime, but not today,' Nate said. 'Here's the spell written down. Try it without the wand first. Let's see what happens. Now, focus just on the jar, we don't want to make anything else disappear.'

Matt took the spell from Nate. He read the spell in his mind and then focused on the jar and chanted aloud. Nothing happened.

'Now you try, Justin,' Peter said.

Justin did the same, and nothing happened again.

'What do you think you were doing wrong?' Nate asked.

'No idea,' Matt and Justin said in unison.

'It's what you were *not* doing,' Nate said. 'Now, watch Peter closely as he does it again.' He nodded at Peter.

Peter looked at the glass jar and repeated the spell, and Matt and Justin began to watch him more closely than they had before. They now realised that he didn't even blink when he was chanting the spell. He was completely focused on the jar, and his body was turned facing the jar full on.

Matt tried again. This time the jar slowly melted away, but much slower than when Peter had done it.

'Well done,' Nate said. 'You try now, Justin.'

Justin succeeded too this time.

'Now, with the wand,' Nate said to Matt.

Matt picked up his mother's wand. He felt a tingling sensation in his fingers and he tightened his grip. He could almost feel his mother's influence coming through the wood. He felt as if his mother was encouraging him, and he grasped it firmer. Yes, he could sense the connection between the wand, himself, and his mother. He chanted the spell again, flourishing the wand, and the jar disappeared instantly.

Peter stared at Matt. Matt had a particular flourish with the wand that looked very much like someone else's.

'Well done!' Nate and Peter exclaimed. 'Your turn, Justin.'

Justin succeeded, too. 'Well done, Justin,' they all said.

'Now, let's try rocks,' Nate said. 'This is more fun. Watch this.' Nate focused on the rock and chanted a different spell, the *Reduce to Basics spell*, aloud:

We don't need you here, and we'd like you to go
So back to your fragments and please don't be slow

The rock turned into a pile of rubble. Matt and Justin's mouths were open.

'Now watch this,' Nate said. 'With the wand, please, Peter.'

Peter took out his wand and chanted the spell at the next rock on the table, flourishing with his wand as he spoke. The result this time was dust.

'Impressive,' Justin said.

'Bloody brilliant,' Matt said.

*

Acacia poured coffee for Nate, and handed him the mug.

'Mmm… tastes as good as it smells, as always.'

She looked at him closely. His big brown eyes and long dark eyelashes were just like Matt's. Come to think of it, Matt and Nate did look somewhat alike. Maybe they were long lost relatives?

'Thanks, Acacia,' Nate said. 'This is just what I need this morning.'

'Is business slow?' Acacia asked. 'I'm a bit surprised to see you here in the morning.'

'No, business is very good actually. I have an assistant now as I have other interests at the moment.' He smiled.

'How's Matt coming along then?'

'He's doing very well, and so is Justin. Of course magic runs in their veins, but I've been surprised at just how quick they are to grasp the concepts. They're both quite old to be just starting out.'

'Is it true you rescue abused animals?' Acacia asked.

'I see the rumour mill is alive and well.'

Acacia put her head on one side.

'I will admit to interceding sometimes when the need arises,' Nate said.

'Good. I wish I could do something to help, but I get so upset.'

'Send out good thoughts,' Nate said. 'That always helps. Really.'

She smiled. Once you got to know Nate, he was very likeable indeed. At first he'd appeared a bit remote.

Matt came into the flat. 'Hi, Nate. To what do we owe this pleasure?'

'I had to come into town and took the opportunity to pay a visit,' Nate said. 'I hope that's alright?'

'Of course,' Matt said. 'We're always pleased to see you, aren't we Acacia?'

Acacia laughed. 'We sure are.' She noticed Nate looking at Tiger. 'Do you have any cats?'

'Unfortunately, no,' Nate said. 'Maybe I should get one though. I've been thinking about that lately. I expect the right cat will appear in my life pretty soon.'

Acacia looked at him. Nate had a strange way of talking sometimes, but Acacia thought she knew what he meant. When you expected something, it usually appeared.

'Do you have time to talk?' Nate asked Matt.

Acacia disappeared into the kitchen, and Matt said, 'Of course. Any problems?'

*

'I've heard a disturbing rumour,' Nate said. 'Wiladelle has been recruiting allies. Goodness knows what she's told them, but she has around twenty, I hear.'

'Do we know what she's going to do?' Matt asked.

'No,' Nate said. 'But Peter and I are going to teach you and Justin some attack spells now, rather than concentrating on the protection spells. We want you to be prepared. Peter's going to give Justin a call this morning to let him know.'

'Okay,' Matt said quietly. 'You think she's coming again then?'

'Well, we always knew she would, didn't we?' Nate said. 'When's Morgan due back here? We could do with his help.'

'I haven't heard from him for a while,' Matt said.

Nate looked surprised. 'Oh? Any problems?'

'Nothing we can't work through,' Matt said, looking uncomfortable.

'Ah,' Nate said, glancing up as Acacia came back into the room, and put her headphones on to type reports. He looked at Acacia, then looked at Matt.

'Does Acacia know?' Nate asked quietly.

Matt was startled. Nate seemed to know things without being told the full story. 'No, she doesn't realise Morgan's in love with her if that's what you mean. I don't want her to, okay?'

'Of course. Morgan will get over it. He has to.'

'That's a bit harsh,' Matt said. 'Morgan can't help his feelings.'

'Well, he'll have to learn then,' Nate said. 'We all have to.'

It sounded like Nate had been thwarted in love.

Maybe Peter is right, thought Matt.

*

Another cold and damp evening, Matt thought as he and Justin arrived at Peter's home. Matt pulled his collar up as he got out of his car. Inside Peter's house it was warm and welcoming, and Matt took his coat and scarf off and hung them in the hall.

Nate and Peter had two specific spells they wanted Matt and Justin to learn quickly.

'These are not spells to be used lightly,' Nate said. 'But they're very necessary in times of crisis.'

Peter nodded. 'Unlike some factions, we never practice on animals. So we have to practice on objects and each other. The effect is the same, and you get the idea of how the spells work.'

'But what you must remember,' Nate said, 'is that when a dark witch is coming at you, you won't have time to think or reason. You have to act instinctively and instantly. Remember that. Don't question yourself. It'll be you or them. That's it.'

Matt and Justin exchanged looks. Neither was comfortable at the thought they might hurt someone. They both turned to Nate.

'Listen to me,' Nate said. 'These people mean business. Wiladelle has told them whatever lies she's come up with, and they think you're the enemy. You and anyone you care about. That includes family, friends, anyone you care about.'

Matt looked startled. 'They might hurt Acacia and Tiger?'

'Yes,' Nate said. 'Now you're getting the picture. So you need to attack these people before they can hurt the ones you love. Okay?'

'So,' Peter said, 'imagine the coat we've hung over there is a person, Wiladelle, or one of her associates. He or she may not look threatening at first, but when they act they'll be fast. Lightning fast.'

133

'You need to be on guard at all times,' Nate said, 'no matter where you are or what you're doing. At the moment, you need to have half your brain looking for possible problems and situations that need to be dealt with. Got it?'

Matt and Justin nodded.

'Look at the coat,' Peter said. 'What do you see?'

'Just a coat,' Justin said, frowning.

Matt peered at it. There was something else there. A bulge in the fabric? 'There's something in the pocket,' he said.

Nate smiled. 'Yes, there is. It's a weapon. What would you do?'

'I suppose it depends where it happens,' Matt said. 'I mean, if this person was in the shop I'd watch him or her very closely to see what they'd do. If it was in the street, I might not notice them.'

'And therein lies the problem,' Nate said. 'When you're walking down the street, from today onwards, you have to be vigilant. When you're anywhere at all, you have to be vigilant. Think about when you're driving your car. You're driving along watching the road in front of you, right? But if you're a good driver, you regularly check your rear-view mirror, and you look to the right and the left watching for possible animals or anything else that might dash in front of you. Half of you is automatically doing the driving while the other half is looking for possible problems. That's how you have to live at the moment. All the time. You have to be looking for possible problems, and you have to react instantly.'

'Now, say you see something that you think is questionable,' Peter said, 'but you don't think the threat is imminent. When that happens, you call me or Nate at once. Tell us the situation and we'll come to you.'

'It doesn't matter what time it is,' Nate said.

Peter nodded. 'But if something is about to happen, you need to respond yourself, immediately.'

'So, this is the first spell,' Nate said. 'Remember to carry your wand with you wherever you go. If you're in a public place, obviously you can't use the wand in full view of the general public, so you'll just chant the spell. Make sure you don't panic. Stay calm, and chant the spell as you've been taught. Here it is: *Immobilise*.'

'That's it? *Immobilise*?' Justin asked.

'Try it on me,' Peter said. 'It won't hurt me, but it'll stop me doing whatever I'm doing.'

Peter picked up his wand and aimed it at Justin, pretending to be threatening him, and Justin used the *Immobilise* spell. Peter seemed to freeze.

Nate went over to Peter and reversed the spell. 'Good job, Justin,' he said. 'You try it on me Matt.' Nate aimed his wand at Matt, and Matt flourished his wand at Nate, using the spell. Nate immediately froze.

Peter and Justin looked at Matt and Nate, then at each other. Peter mentally shook himself, then said, 'Good job, Matt.'

'What's the reversing spell?' Matt asked. 'We might need that. They might use the spell on us.'

'Good point,' Peter said. 'To reverse the *Immobilise* spell you say *clearimmobilise,* all one word and focus, of course. Always focus.'

'Really?' Matt and Justin said together.

Peter and Nate laughed. 'It sounds improbable, but it's true.'

'Now, this next one is a bit more complicated,' Nate said.

'Let's have a cup of tea before we do anything else,' Peter said. 'I think we need a quick break.'

*

Peter and Justin went upstairs to make the tea, and while the kettle was boiling they remained quiet. Then Justin spoke. 'So, are we going to pretend we didn't notice anything?'

'I don't know what to say,' Peter said.

'Are they related, do you think?' Justin asked.

'I think they must be,' Peter said. 'But I don't know how. And they obviously don't know how alike they are.'

'That was weird, that spell,' Justin said. 'It was like looking in a mirror. Nate one side of the mirror, and Matt the other side. They both stand the same way, they both flourish their wands the same way. And they both have that habit of brushing the fringe out of their eyes. They both have those big brown eyes and long dark eyelashes. Other people are bound to notice. We need to tell them before someone else does, or before someone tries to use the similarities against them.'

'You're right,' Peter said. 'I wonder…'

'What are you wondering?' Nate walked into the kitchen, and took the tea tray from Peter.

'Let's have it up here,' Peter said, heading for the living room.

'Matt!' Nate called. 'We're having tea up here.'

Peter poured the tea, and Matt helped himself to a biscuit. Peter and Justin were unusually quiet.

'What's up?' Matt asked.

Peter took a deep breath. 'Haven't you two noticed the similarities between you?'

'Similarities?' Nate asked. 'What similarities?'

Matt looked puzzled.

'You have the same colour hair and eyes,' Justin said.

Nate said, 'Lots of people have similar features.'

'You flourish your wands the same way,' Peter said.

'You stand the same way when you're casting spells,' Justin said.

'We do?' Nate said, looking at Matt.

'And you both have that habit of brushing your fringe out of your eyes,' Justin said.

'You must be related,' Peter said. 'You need to check your family trees.'

'What does it matter?' Matt asked. 'What's the problem?'

'The problem is,' Peter said, 'that Wiladelle and her cronies will suss you're related in a heartbeat and will find some way to use it against you. You need to be aware of that, and you need to have the answers, before they do. If there's something in your history they can use against you, they will.'

SIXTEEN

Matt arrived home feeling a bit bewildered. If Nate was related to him somehow, how could Wiladelle use it against him? He was unsure. Nate had promised to check his family tree and see if there were any links. Matt had never noticed similarities. He needed to ask Acacia. He opened a bottle of wine and poured two glasses, handing one to Acacia.

'Thanks, Matt,' Acacia said. 'You look a little shaken. What's up?'

'Have you ever noticed any similarities between Nate and me?'

Acacia took a sip of wine, and then looked at her husband. 'Now you come to mention it, yes I have.'

'In what way are we similar?'

'Well, you look quite alike, you know.' She smiled up at him. 'You're both very attractive men.'

'Seriously, Acacia,' Matt said, 'okay, we look a bit alike, but are there other things you've noticed?'

'You look very similar when you frown at something,

and you both have that habit of pushing your fringe out of your eyes when something disconcerts you.'

'Anything else?'

'You walk the same way. You both stride about the place and you're both quite graceful when you move.'

Matt raised his eyebrows. 'Graceful?'

'Yep,' Acacia said. 'And the eyebrow thing when you're sceptical about something. He does that too.'

'He does?' Matt asked.

'Are you related?'

'Well,' Matt said, 'that's what we're trying to find out. Peter and Justin think it's important we know all the details just in case Wiladelle and her cronies try to use it against us in some way. Although how they could use that information I really don't know.'

'You should talk to your grandparents about it, see if they know anything,' Acacia said. 'On another note, my Aunt Tabitha called while you were out. She's wondering if she can pay us a visit soon.'

'Not a good idea at the moment, is it? With all we've got going on here, we don't want to have to worry about protecting your aunt too.'

'Well, the thing is,' Acacia said, 'Aunt Tabitha has magical abilities, Matt. She's more than good with herbs as you know, but is also very talented in other, so far undiscussed, areas. Anyway, she sensed there was something wrong, and that's why she's coming over. She's going to help us. I don't know how yet, but I'm very grateful to her, AND, it turns out she knew your mum, Matt. She and Eliza met when your mum had that trip to New England when she was young.'

'Really? She knew Mum? How strange is that?'

Acacia laughed. 'A few weeks ago the first words out of your mouth would have been, "Magical abilities? Whatever do you mean?" Now the big thing is the fact she knew your mum.'

Matt laughed. 'You're right there. Focus has changed somewhat.'

*

Aunt Tabitha arrived in a taxi from Exeter airport. Matt saw an older version of Acacia emerging through the bookshop doorway. He rushed over to greet her, and they exchanged hugs. Tabitha wore a long multi-coloured scarf, blues and greens mostly, and a long black woollen coat and stylish boots. Her long, wavy blonde hair was clipped back with pretty combs, and she wore green eyeshadow to highlight her green eyes. She certainly looked the part, he thought.

'Aunt Tabitha I presume?' Matt smiled.

'Well, I certainly hope you don't greet your regular customers with a hug,' Tabitha laughed. 'Where's my girl?'

'Acacia's upstairs in the flat. Let's go up,' Matt said. 'Justin!' he called over to the till. 'I'm going upstairs with Tabitha, okay? Oh, sorry,' Matt guided Tabitha towards the till, 'this is Justin, valued assistant. Justin, this is Acacia's Aunt Tabitha from New England. She's come for a visit,' Matt said.

Justin looked at Tabitha and smiled broadly. 'I can see where Acacia gets her good looks from, Tabitha.'

'Why, thank you young man!' Tabitha laughed. 'I see English gentlemen do still exist.'

Matt and Tabitha climbed the stairs just as Acacia opened the flat door and practically threw herself into her aunt's arms.

'Aunt Tabitha, I'm so pleased to see you,' Acacia smiled, hugging her aunt.

'Okay, Acacia,' Matt laughed, 'let the dog see the rabbit. We need to get into the flat.'

*

Matt put the coffee on and watched as Acacia and Tabitha chatted and laughed on the sofa. Tiger was right there, sniffing Tabitha's legs and then jumping on the sofa and sitting next to her.

'What a little darling!' Tabitha exclaimed, stroking the top of his head. 'You must be Tiger.'

Tiger gave a double blink to acknowledge her, and rubbed his face against her arm, claiming her as one of the family.

'What beautiful green eyes you have, Tiger,' she continued, 'green is one of my favourite colours, as you can see.'

Tiger gazed up at her and gave another double blink, and then he promptly sat on her lap.

'Well, I see you've met our Tiger,' Matt said proudly, putting the coffee tray on the table in front of them. 'We have freshly made cake too. Acacia made it this morning knowing you'd be here today,' Matt said, slicing the cake and handing her a piece on a plate.

'Mmm,' Tabitha said, 'this is good cake, sweetie. Thank you so much.'

Matt hadn't heard the term *sweetie* before, and he smiled quizzically at Acacia.

'One of Aunt Tabitha's endearments,' Acacia explained. Tabitha looked confused. 'Matt isn't used to the term *sweetie*, Tabitha, that's all.'

'Oh I see. Well, you'll get used to all my little Americanisms in due course. On another note, I had thought I'd be exhausted by the time I got here, but I find I'm not at all tired. At least, not at the moment. I'll just have a wander around your lovely apartment if that's okay with you? I want to get familiarised as quickly as possible for lots of reasons.' She smiled at her niece, got off the sofa and had a thorough reconnoitre of the flat. Tiger accompanied her, walking by her side with a proprietorial air. She laughed and bent down to pick him up.

'Here you go, Tiger,' Tabitha said, 'you get a better view from up here, plus I get the benefit of holding you close to me, as you're so very handsome. Oh, I see you have a walled garden out there. Needs some work by the look of it?' She turned to Acacia. 'I'd like a look in the garden if that's okay?'

'What do you think, Matt?' Acacia asked. 'Can we take Tiger into the walled garden? It's quite safe out there, it's just overgrown.'

'Okay, maybe he should have his first visit outside. He's been inside the flat for weeks now, and he probably wants to explore.' Matt took him from Tabitha and carried him down the stairs and into the garden.

Tabitha paused as Matt opened the door into the walled garden.

'This has such possibilities,' Tabitha said, 'I love it. It has a wonderful atmosphere, this garden. I think maybe...'she left the sentence unfinished as she explored.

Matt put Tiger down, and the cat tentatively investigated his new territory, sniffing and prodding things, working his way around the walls until he reached the garden shed.

'Ah, you want to go in there I expect?' Matt asked, opening the door.

Tiger promptly went into the shed for a sniff around, jumping on the shelves and moving things. He seemed to get very excited about a small box that had been hidden behind a plant pot, and he pushed it around the shelf with his paws.

'You want to see what's under the box?' asked Matt. He lifted the box up to show the cat there was nothing underneath and then put it down again. Tiger batted the top of the box with his paws and looked up at Matt, who laughed and opened the lid. Tiger peered inside and put his paw in the box, hooking something with his claw and pulling it out. To everyone's surprise it was a cat collar, and not just any old cat collar either. It had inlaid green and black stones. The collar itself was blue, and with the green and black stones it was beautiful.

Tabitha lifted the collar up and looked at it, rubbing at the stones with her dress, and she looked at Matt and Acacia.

'I'm pretty sure these are not glass, you guys,' Tabitha said. 'I think you should get this collar to a jeweller and ask for an opinion, but I think these are either emeralds or green diamonds, and I'm sure the others are black diamonds.'

'Green and black diamonds?' Matt asked. 'I didn't know there were such things as green and black diamonds.'

'Oh yes, there are,' Tabitha said. 'I have some of my own. The diamond is a protective stone you know, and green diamonds are very special in a lot of ways. If these are green diamonds, or emeralds, then whoever had this made must've loved their cat very much. Not only are they expensive, but they provide protection. Plus black diamonds help develop your potential.'

'Clever cat!' Acacia said to Tiger. 'We'll clean this up and get it to a jeweller for an opinion. It's too big for you at the moment, Tiger, but you'll grow into it, and as soon as you do you can wear it, okay? We'll just need to maybe replace the safety elastic, I'll have a look at it.' Acacia placed the collar in her pocket and stroked Tiger, who, job done, left the shed and sat on the bench surveying the garden.

Snowdrops were in flower to the side of the shed, and daffodils yawned open by the bench.

Spring had arrived.

*

Matt was tossing and turning. He couldn't get the nagging thought out of his mind that Wiladelle may have been responsible for his parents' deaths. Tara had hinted that this might be the case when she visited recently.

He got up and quietly moved into the living room, where he considered sleeping on the sofa. He didn't want to disturb Acacia.

He'd accepted the fact that his grandmother, Tara, knew about and believed in magic. That was surprising enough. But he was still struggling with the fact that Morgan's mother was Wiladelle, and that Wiladelle was his mother's sister. Because Wiladelle was obviously a dark witch, and his parents had not practiced the dark arts. That much he was sure about.

Surely even Wiladelle wouldn't kill her own sister? He couldn't relate to anyone who would do such a thing. To protect yourself, or loved ones, that was one thing. But to kill out of jealousy, or hatred, or whatever, that was another thing altogether. But then Wiladelle was insane, wasn't she? Or was she?

And what about Morgan?

He liked Morgan. How could Morgan be so very different from his mother? Had he been duped by Morgan? No, he didn't think so. And anyway, Peter and Nate both got on with Morgan, and they'd know if he was a dark witch.

And what about the fact that Morgan was in love with Acacia? How did that fit in? Was it some kind of plan, to infiltrate Matt's home and lure Acacia away to hurt Matt? That sounded like Wiladelle, but it didn't sound like Morgan. Morgan had told him he'd never act on his feelings for Acacia. He had to believe that. He had to.

But the question of how his parents died was different. Matt was a person who liked order and information. For Matt, it was as necessary as breathing. He had a genealogy chart on his study wall for goodness sake. Although obviously that would have to be altered now he knew he had an aunt and a cousin… He had a physical need to know whether Wiladelle was responsible for their deaths. He knew there were different scenarios. Which one was true? Did his parents die trying to save him and his sister? Did they swerve to avoid an animal, and crash because of that? Or was it just a mechanical problem with their car?

Matt got up and went to look out of the window at the town square. The street lamps were on, and the pavements appeared damp. He listened. Yes, rain was falling.

He went back to the sofa and plumped a cushion to place under his head. Then he sat up again. Darn it. If Wiladelle really was responsible for his parents' deaths, could he and Morgan stay friends? One side of his brain told him that wasn't fair. Morgan wasn't responsible for the actions of his mother. But the other side of his brain couldn't let it go.

He got up again and paced around the living room. He'd

only just found Morgan. He felt close to Morgan, more like a brother than a cousin. He didn't want to lose that friendship. His sister now lived up north, and he hardly ever saw her. Morgan seemed to have filled the gap somehow. Was that coincidence? Or was it contrived?

What could he do? He knew he should drop it. Yes, that would be the best thing. That's what his head told him to do. Drop the question. Forget about it. Keep Morgan's friendship. But his heart, the wounded orphan, needed to know the truth of his parents' deaths.

Tiger came over and looked up at him. He put a paw on Matt's leg.

'Okay, you're right,' Matt said. 'Let's snuggle on the sofa and see if we can get some sleep.'

He grabbed a blanket from the storage chest, then picked Tiger up. They settled on the sofa, Tiger lying next to Matt's chest.

But Matt didn't fall asleep for a long time. The problem was going round and round in his mind.

SEVENTEEN

Tabitha and Acacia were wrapped up warmly. Tabitha closed the front door and they stepped into the frosty street. They were taking the cat collar to the local jeweller's shop.

The manager inspected the stones in the collar carefully, using a magnifying glass. 'No doubt about it,' he said. 'Those are green and black diamonds alright. Did you want to sell it?'

'Oh no, thanks,' Acacia said. 'We just wanted to know if the stones were real or not.'

'Are you going to put this collar on a cat?' he asked, disapprovingly.

'When he's old enough, yes,' Acacia said.

'Lucky cat!' he said. 'If you change your mind, I can give you a good price.'

'We won't change our minds,' Acacia said, 'but thanks anyway.'

They left the jeweller's and walked to the coffee shop, where they sat watching the people going by.

'I like this town,' Tabitha said. 'I know I haven't seen much of it yet, but it has a good feeling to it.'

Acacia smiled at her aunt. 'I still can't quite believe you're here.'

Tabitha sipped her coffee, and bit into a piece of chocolate cake. 'This is good.'

Acacia smiled at her aunt. 'The last time we had coffee and cake together in a coffee shop we were in Boston.'

'I've always wanted to visit Devon. You know our family is from Devon originally, right?'

'Yes, of course,' Acacia said. 'I've always felt Devon was my home, and now it really is. I'm very happy here.'

Tabitha watched her niece's face closely. 'Even with the current problems?'

Acacia sighed. 'If only Wiladelle would just go away. But that's not going to happen without a struggle. I know that.'

'What's with Wiladelle?' Tabitha asked. 'Why does she hate Matt so much? I think there's more to this than just the fact she hated her sister. I think something else is going on, but I don't know what. We should try to find out. It might help us.'

'Hmm,' Acacia sat thinking. 'I don't know, Tabitha. How would we find out? We do have help, that's the good news. We have Morgan, Matt's cousin, who's in London at the moment but will come back soon I hope. Then we have Nate, he used to know Matt's mum apparently. And we have Peter, who belongs to a local group of like-minded people, and his nephew, Justin, is just starting to learn. He and Matt are taking lessons from Nate and Peter. And now we have you too.'

'I'd like to meet Peter and Nate as soon as possible,

Acacia,' Tabitha said. 'I need to get up to speed on what's been happening and what steps you've already taken.'

Acacia picked up her mobile. 'Nate? It's Acacia. Yes. My aunt is here, from New England. She's come over to help and would like to meet you and Peter as soon as possible. Tomorrow? Okay, that's good – 7pm? Sure. See you then.'

Acacia laid her phone down. 'All done. Nate's coming over at 7pm tomorrow and will bring Peter with him.'

'Oh good,' Tabitha said, holding up her coffee cup. 'Could I get some more coffee?'

An hour later they were back in the flat, and Acacia noticed a brown paper parcel on the coffee table. It was addressed *To Matt and Acacia*. She turned it over. No return address. It must've been hand delivered. She opened it and scanned inside, but there was no note. It contained a book on archaeology in Egypt, written in the 1920s.

'Look at this, Tabitha,' Acacia held it out to her aunt, who took the book and opened it.

There was an inscription inside the book which Tabitha read out. *To my darling Elizabeth with love, in memory of our happy years digging in Egypt, love Rupert.*

'How intriguing,' Acacia said. 'I've always been interested in archaeology but never done anything about it. I'll just pop down and ask Matt who delivered it.' She rushed downstairs to find Matt.

'Parcel on the coffee table?' Matt asked. 'Justin! Did someone drop off a parcel for Acacia and me?'

Justin came over. 'Not that I know of. Are you expecting something?'

'No, but it's on our coffee table upstairs,' Matt frowned. 'How did it get there then?'

'Strange,' Acacia said. 'Well, Tabitha's going through it now. It's on archaeology in Egypt, very interesting stuff.'

'I'll come up,' Matt said, and together they went up to the flat.

They found Tiger sitting on the coffee table with his paws touching the book, Tabitha turning the pages.

'Can I have a look?' Matt asked, gently removing Tiger's paws and taking the book from Tabitha. He turned it over, opened it, read a few paragraphs and put it down again. Tiger promptly sat on the book and started a thorough wash.

'Tiger likes it,' Tabitha laughed. 'It's very interesting actually. From what I can see, this couple, who came from Devon, went out to Egypt in the 1920s and made some interesting discoveries there. They brought back quite a lot of stuff for our museums apparently.'

'Can you sense anything from the book, Aunt Tabitha?'

Tabitha paused, placed her hand on the book and was quiet, eyes closed. Then she smiled at them both. 'It's a gift,' she laughed. 'It's a present from one or both of these people, Elizabeth or Rupert, for you.'

'Curiouser and curiouser,' Acacia said.

'I think we should do some digging,' Tabitha said, 'pardon the pun, and see what we can find out about these people. I've a feeling they may have lived here before your grandparents owned this bookshop, Matt.'

'Really?' Acacia's face was lit up with excitement. 'Ooh. I wonder if these are the people who owned the cat collar?'

'By the way, Matt, Nate and Peter are coming over tomorrow around 7pm,' Acacia said, 'to meet Tabitha and discuss Wiladelle.'

'Good,' Matt said. 'We can tell them about this book and see what they think.'

'It's nothing sinister, Matt,' Tabitha said. 'I think you have a well-wisher and they want you to know they're here, that's all.'

'Another ghost in the bookshop?' Matt asked. 'Why hasn't Ernie mentioned him or her?'

'He may not have felt it was relevant to the problem at hand,' Tabitha said. 'Or maybe he doesn't know.' She sat upright and smiled. 'I've got it. I think this ghost spends most of his or her time in the walled garden. Didn't you feel a harmonious presence out there?'

'Oh, yes, you're right,' Acacia said. 'I did feel something, but it was a happy presence. It's female, I'm sure.'

'It's Elizabeth!' they said together, then laughed.

'I'm going to call Tara,' Acacia said. Then she turned to her aunt, 'Tara is Matt's grandmother. I'll see if she can remember the names of the people they bought the bookshop from. I bet it's Elizabeth and Rupert!' Excitedly she called Matt's grandparents.

'Oh, hi Sam,' Acacia said. 'Do you remember the name of the people you bought the bookshop from?' She waited while he called his wife.

'They were called Rupert and Elizabeth,' Sam said. 'I was very interested to talk to them as they were archaeologists and had spent a lot of time in Egypt.'

'Why did they sell the bookshop?' Acacia asked.

'I can't remember, dear,' Sam said. 'Hold on a minute. Tara!' He had a conversation with his wife, and she came on the phone.

'Hi Acacia,' Tara said. 'Yes, definitely Elizabeth and Rupert. I can't remember their last name though. If it's important, maybe I can find it somewhere. They told me they were sorry to sell the bookshop – well, it was a house then, but they wanted something smaller and more rural. They bought a bungalow. Very modern at the time. Rupert couldn't manage the stairs anymore. He'd had an accident in Egypt and had broken his leg. His wife sensibly chose a bungalow to prevent any possible accidents with stairs, although she told me there was a basement, very unusual for a bungalow… it gave extra space, and they didn't have to go into the basement regularly for anything.'

'Were they nice people?' Acacia asked. 'Did you like them?'

'Oh, yes,' Tara said. 'Sam and I liked them immediately. But I couldn't say we knew them. It was only a business transaction.'

Acacia sighed into the phone.

'Why are you asking about them, dear?' Tara asked.

'Oh, just some research, that's all. Thanks, Tara, and please thank Sam for me. Will you be coming to visit us for coffee soon? My Aunt Tabitha is here at the moment. From New England.'

'Oh?' Tara said, surprised. 'I didn't know she was coming? Yes it would be good to meet her. I'll call you soon to arrange a visit.'

They signed off.

Acacia was pleased. Tara was quite prescient and, if Tara had liked them, they were good people.

*

Jett had been watching the bookshop all morning and had

seen Elizabeth lay the parcel in the flat. He didn't know what was in the parcel. Why should she be giving them gifts? Who was she? He sometimes found it difficult to focus, but on this occasion his curiosity overcame his mental fog, and he followed Elizabeth.

Jett watched as Elizabeth entered the walled garden and sat on the bench, her black Edwardian ruffled skirt almost touching the wet earth. It had rained again, but she was completely dry. The earth had that sweet, fresh smell it gets after rain. He watched her breathe deeply, taking in the smell, and saw a squirrel climb a nearby tree.

'Who are you and why are you in Matt's garden?' Jett asked, his black hair and black clothes in stark contrast to his pale face.

'And you are?' Elizabeth asked, calmly.

'Never mind who I am,' Jett said. 'Who are you, and why are you here?'

'My name's Elizabeth,' she said. 'I used to own this place and lived here for a long time.'

He sat next to her, and peered into her face. She had kind eyes. He liked her eyes, they were deep blue, and she had blonde hair like his mum had.

She tried again. 'What's your name?'

'My name's Jett,' he said. 'I went to school with Matt. He's my friend.'

'Ah,' she said. 'How long ago did you pass over? You seem quite young.'

'I can't remember,' he said. 'That's not important. Are you a friend of Matt's?'

'In a way, yes,' she answered. 'He hasn't seen me yet. Acacia senses I'm here though. They're a nice young couple.'

'What was in the parcel you took up to their flat?' he demanded. He needed to know Elizabeth was not a threat.

'A book on archaeology. I thought he and Acacia might like it.'

He lost interest. This was a boring conversation. Why was he here again? He stood up and walked around. 'They need to do some work in this garden. It could be nice.'

'Yes,' Elizabeth said. 'They'll be starting work on it soon. They've done a little bit of tidying up, but they've been having some problems in the bookshop, and it's taken their attention away from this work.'

'Yeah. What's with that woman? Why does she hate Matt so much?'

'No idea,' Elizabeth said. 'If you're a friend, though, you could maybe help keep an eye out and warn Matt and Acacia, or me, if you see anything suspicious?'

Jett's head ached. He got a lot of headaches. He needed to go and lie down. Without responding to Elizabeth, he disappeared.

*

Jett returned to the church for a nap in the vestry. It was quiet and peaceful there, and he always felt safe there. He believed nothing bad would happen when he was in the church.

When he woke up, he went back to the bookshop and searched for books on life after death. It always interested him, seeing what people thought happened to them when they died. It was funny really. Some of it was quite fanciful, and some of it was spot on. He moved a book out, placed it on the table near the fireplace, and turned the pages.

A woman nearby saw the book on the table, and saw the pages turning seemingly by themselves.

She went over to Justin, placing her purchases on the counter. 'How clever, to have that book set up near the supernatural section. The pages turning by themselves gives a super creepy atmosphere to that section.'

Justin smiled at the customer but said nothing. When she'd gone, he went over to the table and found the book she had mentioned. No pages were turning though. He picked it up, and inserted it into the right place on the shelf, slightly bemused.

Jett had become bored and gone back for another nap in the church. He was finding it harder to stay awake. Still, it didn't matter how much he slept did it?

*

Justin shivered and went to Matt's office to check the radiator. 'Matt, the radiators are off.'

'Oh?' Matt touched the radiator. It was ice cold. He frowned and turned the knob so it was on. 'That's strange. Check the others, will you? Make sure they're on. We're going to have another cold spell tonight according to the weather forecast.'

Justin was switching the radiators back on, when Peter came into the shop looking thoroughly dishevelled, his jeans damp with mud on the hems. He headed for the coffee machine, and poured himself a hot drink.

'What's up, Uncle Peter?' Justin asked.

'Bit of car trouble,' Peter said. 'Nothing serious, but annoying, and I got thoroughly chilled waiting for it to be fixed.' He went and stood next to the fireplace. 'Bit nippy in here?'

'We just discovered some of the radiators were turned off,' Justin said. 'No idea how that happened. It'll warm up again in a minute. As you can see, the fireplace is still working.'

'Can't be Wiladelle,' Peter said, rubbing his hands together in front of the fire. 'She can't get in here now. Maybe your cleaner inadvertently turned off the radiators this morning?'

'I'll leave a note for her tonight,' Justin said.

*

Tabitha felt the need for a new book. Acacia was busy, Tiger was napping, so she walked down the stairs into the bookshop. Today she was wearing a long, floating blue skirt and light green blouse. Her hair was pinned up, and she'd applied her usual green eyeshadow.

Justin looked up as she approached. He found himself smiling at her. She was very *alternative lifestyle*. He liked it though. It suited her.

'Can you point me to the metaphysical section, Justin?'

'Sure thing,' Justin said, then turned to his uncle. 'Will you excuse me a minute, Uncle Peter?'

But Peter's eyes were fixed on Tabitha. 'You must be Tabitha. I recognise the accent.'

Tabitha laughed and held out her hand. Peter grasped it. They stood there, gazing at each other, holding hands.

Justin felt that time was standing still. He coughed, and Tabitha and Peter moved apart. Justin studied his uncle and Tabitha. There was definite chemistry there. Well, well, this was a surprise. His Uncle Peter hadn't looked at a woman, not like this, since his aunt had passed away. It was time he got involved with someone. Jumping the gun a bit, he reprimanded himself.

'This way, Tabitha,' Justin said. He led Tabitha over to the supernatural section, and Peter followed. Justin left them talking avidly about books and beliefs, and went back to the counter.

An hour later, Peter and Tabitha were still talking. By now they'd moved to the coffee area in front of the fireplace and were discussing the pros and cons of various authors.

Matt saw Justin watching Peter and Tabitha. 'Looks like they're getting along well.'

'It sure does,' Justin mimicked an American accent, and Matt laughed.

'Er, Matt,' Justin said, looking at his computer, 'there's no power.'

'It's been unplugged,' Matt said, frowning and plugging it back in. 'Maybe one of us knocked the cable.'

'Hmm,' Justin said.

'I'm off now, Justin. See you later,' Peter said, waving to Justin and Matt. There was a pause, then Peter waved at Tabitha.

Tabitha came over to Matt. 'Peter confirmed he and Nate will be over at 7pm to meet up. And, I'd like to buy these books.'

'Oh, right,' Matt said. 'Yes, that's fine, Tabitha. Justin will ring them up for you.'

A minute later, Peter rushed back into the shop, clutching his mobile. 'There's been an accident. A tractor collided with Nate's car, and he's been taken to hospital. I'm going there now. Do you want to come with me, Matt? Justin can look after the shop?'

'Tell Acacia, please, Tabitha,' Matt said, pulling on his coat and following Peter outside. 'They say things come in threes,' he said to Peter. 'We'll use my car as yours has been giving problems.'

EIGHTEEN

Matt and Peter sat in the hospital waiting room, drinking coffee from the machine.

Matt pulled a face. This wasn't what he expected coffee to taste like. It was hot though. He was grateful for that.

'Was it an accident, do you think?' Matt asked Peter.

'That's the question, isn't it?'

They watched nurses and staff in white coats going about their business, and people coming and going.

Matt's mobile rang. 'No, nothing yet, Acacia. We're waiting to talk to a doctor. I'll call you when I know what's happening. Bye, love.'

Matt got up and went over to reception. 'Any news on our friend, Nate Parish?'

The receptionist checked her notes and the computer. 'They're finishing up with the initial assessment. He's being taken into surgery.'

'Surgery?' Matt gasped.

The receptionist said, 'Someone will talk to you after the

operation. It'll be a long wait. You might want to go home and come back.'

'We'll stay,' Matt said. He went back to Peter. 'Nate's gone into surgery. The receptionist doesn't know anything else yet. She says it'll be a long wait. I said we'd stay, but if you want to go home that's fine, Peter.'

'I'm not going anywhere until I know how Nate's doing,' Peter said. 'You know, this could be a way of getting us away from the bookshop, to distract us.'

'Hmm,' Matt said. 'What can we do about that?'

Peter picked up his mobile. 'I'm going to talk to Tabitha. I'll tell her what we suspect.'

Tabitha picked up the phone in the flat. 'You think this accident is Wiladelle getting you out of the way so she can do something to the bookshop and us?'

'Maybe,' Peter said. 'We're not sure. But I thought I should mention it.'

'Just as well you did, actually,' Tabitha said. 'We were thinking of coming to the hospital to sit with you, bring you some food and give you some company. Now I see that's maybe what Wiladelle wants. We'll stay where we are.'

'Good. We'll call you when we know anything,' Peter said. 'Can you have a word with Justin? Wiladelle might send one of her associates into the bookshop.'

'Will do,' Tabitha said. 'Call us regularly, even if you don't have any news, eh? We're on pins and needles here. Oh, before I forget, Justin is staying with us in the flat for a few days.'

Peter sighed with relief. 'That's good. Talk later.' He dropped his mobile into his pocket.

Matt and Peter walked to the café and grabbed some sandwiches, then bought some magazines and a couple of books to try to take their minds off what might be happening in the operating theatre.

Matt was starting to doze off when Peter nudged him. 'See that guy over there?' Matt nodded. 'He belongs to a dark sect in Somerset. What's he doing here?'

'Should we follow him?' Matt asked.

'You follow him,' Peter said. 'He might recognise me. Watch yourself!'

Matt got up and followed at a distance. Matt thought the man looked like a businessman, with his smart grey suit, blue shirt, silver-grey tie. The man sensed he was being followed and stopped abruptly. Matt kept walking and went past him to the next reception desk, pausing to ask a question. The man continued past Matt and into a hospital coffee shop. Matt waited a bit, and then went to see what the man was doing. He was sitting at a table talking to someone. Matt hurried back to Peter.

'What does the other man look like?' Peter asked.

Matt described the other man, and Peter looked alarmed. 'He belongs to the same sect. Two of them in this hospital? They're here for Nate.'

'What can we do?' Matt asked. 'What can *they* do?'

'I need to find out where the surgery is taking place so I can put a protection spell on it,' Peter said, heading for reception. He came right back. 'Come with me, Matt.'

They walked down a corridor, turned left, right, and finally came to the surgical theatre. The timing was good, no one was around. Peter pulled out his wand and chanted a protection spell on the area and on Nate. He'd just finished when a nurse came round the corner. They sat down and opened their books, and the nurse continued on her way.

'I'll call my group and get a protection rota going,' Peter said. 'This is déjà vu. We haven't had so much action for a long time.'

'Well, Morgan recovered. Let's hope Nate does.'

An hour later six of Peter's group were in the hospital, stationed around the operating theatre.

Matt and Peter were talking to one of the Devon Crew, Alan, when the two guys from the dark sect walked by. They were about to produce their wands when they saw the Devon *charmers*. They turned and stalked off, faces taut with anger.

'Wow,' Matt said, 'they weren't expecting to see all of us here!'

Matt and Peter looked up as a doctor approached. 'You're friends of Nate Parish?' he asked. They nodded. 'Surgery went well, but we won't know how he's doing for a while yet. He could be in a coma for a while.'

'What surgery did you perform?' Matt asked. 'I mean, what parts of Nate's body are injured?'

'His right leg was broken,' the doctor said, 'but that's been set and will heal well. His chest was crushed and the ribs took a bashing. We removed some bone splinters, and the ribs will heal fine. The concern is his brain. He took a nasty hit on his head...'He paused. 'I have every reason to believe he will make a full recovery.'

Matt was too shocked to speak.

'Thank you, doctor,' Peter said. The doctor nodded and went on his way.

'Do you believe him?' Matt asked Peter. 'I mean, he might've just said that to make us feel better. It didn't ring true somehow.'

'We'll have to wait and see, Matt,' Peter said. 'Let's see

which ward they put him in. Then we'll cast some healing spells over him when we get the opportunity.'

*

There was a chill in the air, but no rain, so Holsworthy was busy, and so was the bookshop.

Acacia was heading to the office to pay some invoices, when she saw an attractive young woman, with long, wavy blonde hair and blue eyes, nudging the door open. She went straight over to Justin.

'Hello,' she said. 'My name's Samantha. Nate asked me to call in. Could I see Matt or Acacia, please?'

'Oh?' Justin asked. 'When did you talk to Nate, then?'

'Last week,' she said. 'He knows I love cats, and he wanted me to meet Matt and Acacia's cat, Tiger.'

Acacia realised Justin wasn't sure if this girl was on the level or not.

He asked Samantha to call Nate for him. It was obvious she didn't know he was in the hospital. Samantha pulled her mobile out of her handbag and called Nate's number. It rang and rang, and went to the answer machine. Justin could hear Nate's voice asking her to leave a message.

'Not to worry, Samantha,' Justin said. 'Acacia!'

Acacia came over to meet Samantha and held out her hand. 'Good to meet you, Samantha. Let's go up to the flat.'

Samantha followed Acacia. 'I've been trying to get hold of Nate for a few days but can't get any reply. I just get his answer machine. So I thought I'd come over and introduce myself. I understand we need to get Tiger's training underway.'

Acacia chewed her lip. Is this girl the one Nate talked about? She said, 'Oh, you know the problem then?'

'Nate touched on it briefly, yes. He said he and Peter are teaching Matt and Justin, but that Tiger really needed to have some tools in his arsenal too.'

Acacia and Tabitha smiled at each other, reassured she was the Samantha that Nate had mentioned.

Tiger had been watching this conversation and listening with interest. He jumped off the windowsill and sauntered over to Samantha, sat at her feet and looked up at her.

'My goodness,' Samantha said, 'you're a very handsome cat indeed, aren't you.'

Samantha turned to Acacia. 'Today I'd like to get to know Tiger a little bit. Then maybe we can work out a routine that suits us all?'

'Sure,' Acacia said. 'I'll put some coffee on, and you and Tiger can get to know each other.'

Tabitha followed Acacia into the kitchen. 'She's the real Samantha, I'm sure of it,' Tabitha said.

'Let's see how Tiger is with her,' Acacia said, 'before we arrange any lessons.'

Acacia and Tabitha came back into the living room with coffee and cake, and saw Samantha pulling a piece of string along the floor for Tiger to stalk and pounce. They were both absorbed in their game. Acacia placed the coffee and cake on the table.

'He has great natural instincts,' Samantha said, 'and I can tell he's reading me well.'

'Reading you?' Acacia asked.

'He's reading my character. He studied me carefully before letting me touch him. He's very prescient. He'll be a good student.'

'Would one evening a week be enough, do you think?' Acacia asked. 'Or would Saturday afternoon be better?'

'I think at the moment I'd prefer to come here in the daylight. Saturday afternoon, say 2pm, for about an hour?'

'That'd be great,' Acacia said.

'How do you take your coffee?' Tabitha asked, handing her a piece of cake.

*

Saturday arrived with blue skies and hardly any clouds, and Samantha arrived promptly at 2pm.

Upstairs in the flat, Tiger was watching Samantha get out of her car and walk towards the bookshop.

Justin smiled at Samantha when she came in, and introduced her to Matt who was serving a customer.

Acacia went down to fetch Samantha, and back upstairs Tiger was waiting eagerly at the door. He was hopping about in front of her with excitement.

'Acacia,' Samantha said, 'I heard about Nate. Do you know how he's doing?'

'He still hasn't woken up,' Acacia said, 'but the doctors are hopeful. Would you like some coffee?'

'Not at the moment, thanks,' Samantha knelt down on the soft, cream carpet in front of Tiger.

Acacia and Tabitha retreated to the dining room.

'Right, Tiger,' Samantha said. 'I'm going to be teaching you one spell today, and then each time I come we'll do two spells, okay?'

Tiger gave the double blinkie with his eyes to show he understood.

'This first one is a protection spell,' Samantha said. 'If you need to protect yourself, or Matt or Acacia or anyone else, you can use this one. It's quick and easy. Okay?'

Tiger put his paw on her leg to acknowledge he understood.

'Say a bad person appears in front of you, and you know that person means you harm, the first thing you must do is protect yourself. When you're safe, you can help others. Right?'

Tiger again put his paw on her leg.

'So, you visualise yourself enclosed in a halo of golden light. Think about a big bubble of soap, only this is a bubble of protection. It's important to see in your mind the colour of gold, do you know what that is?'

Tiger put his paw halfway up to her leg and down again to indicate *no.*

'Okay, I'll show you,' Samantha said. 'See this ring?' Samantha showed him a gold ring she was wearing. 'It was my nana's ring. This ring is made of something called gold. It's a deep yellow colour. You're a ginger tabby so that's close to the colour gold but not quite. Think a mixture between ginger and yellow. Got it?'

Tiger again put his paw on her leg.

'Good! Now, having thought about the golden bubble and pictured yourself in it, you say in your mind, *Protective Halo,* and that's it. The bad person will no longer be able to see you. Now before you try it, you have to know how to get out of it afterwards, otherwise we won't find you!'

'I'll do it first, okay?' Samantha visualised the golden bubble and said the spell. She disappeared. Tiger jumped and ran round. He could feel her, but he couldn't see her.

She reversed the spell and appeared again, and Tiger leapt up into her arms.

'Oh, Tiger,' Samantha said, 'you're such a darling.' She cuddled him and kissed the top of his head. 'Back to business, though.' She put him back on the floor, and he sat looking up at her.

'To reverse the spell when you want to be seen again, you say the spell, *Dispel Protective Halo.*' You try it now, Tiger. First hide yourself. Close your eyes, think of the golden bubble, say the spell in your mind, *Protective Halo.*'

Tiger closed his eyes and disappeared in front of her.

Samantha clapped her hands in glee, and Acacia looked up, startled. Samantha shook her head at Acacia and mouthed *okay.*

'Now, Tiger,' Samantha said. 'Say the reverse spell, *Dispel Protective Halo* in your mind.'

Tiger appeared in front of her.

'You are such a clever boy! Now, I'd like you to imagine someone is trying to hurt your toy mouse. Visualise your toy surrounded by the golden bubble and say the protective spell.'

Tiger went over to his toy mouse and closed his eyes, thinking the spell. The toy disappeared in front of him. He used the reverse spell and the toy reappeared.

'That is *so* clever, Tiger. You know what? As this is our first lesson, I think that's enough for one day. We'll do more next Saturday, okay?'

Samantha sighed, and walked over to Acacia. 'I think I'd like that coffee now please, Acacia.'

'How did he do?' Acacia asked, walking to the kitchen.

Samantha followed Acacia into the kitchen. 'Tiger did

really well. He learnt the first spell quickly. His communication skills are good too.'

Tiger seemed to preen himself a little, and jumped on the kitchen counter looking up at Acacia.

'Yes,' Acacia said, 'you did very well and do deserve a treat.' Tiger followed Acacia as she put treats on his bed, and rolled on them before eating them.

'Tabitha, do you want to join us for coffee?' Acacia called at Tabitha's door.

Tabitha came out of her room, and they settled down to coffee and cake while Tiger threw his toy mouse around the room before settling down for a well-earned nap.

'How did you come to have Tiger?'

Acacia relayed the story of Tiger and his mum.

Samantha's eyes filled with tears. 'I'm so glad Tiger found you and Matt, but it's such a shame about his mum. How sad.'

'Yes,' Acacia said. 'It is. We could have taken them both in, if we'd only known.'

'His mum's buried in the walled garden, though,' Tabitha said. 'There are snowdrops and daffodils all around her. She knows her kitten is safe and loved, so she's happy.'

NINETEEN

Acacia was in the bookshop, going through invoices, when Peter called in, a bunch of flowers clutched tightly at his side.

Justin gave what sounded to Acacia like a snigger. She pretended she hadn't heard it.

'You've come to see Tabitha, I expect?' Acacia asked.

'Oh, um, yes,' Peter said, 'I saw these in the Co-op. We've all had a rough few weeks. They might brighten up your living room.'

'That's a lovely thought, Peter,' Acacia said, leading him upstairs to the flat. 'I like to have fresh flowers in the house when I can. I'll get a vase, and then make some coffee. You'll stay for some?'

Peter relaxed and smiled. 'That'd be great. Thanks, Acacia.' He gazed round the warm, comfortable room, but no Tabitha.

Acacia knocked on Tabitha's bedroom door. 'Tabitha, Peter's here. I'm making coffee. Want to join us?'

Tabitha came out of her room wearing a long black skirt and a blue silk top, her wavy blonde hair loose, shoulder length. She was holding her spell notebook and her glasses, and her eyes were reddened from too much reading. 'Oh, that's just what I need. And a visit from Peter, how lovely.' She smiled at him, her face radiant.

They sat at the kitchen table. Acacia poured coffee. Tabitha went to the kitchen, and came back with a plate of biscuits. Tiger came over and sat next to Peter, not wanting to be left out.

'Can you give Tiger a treat, please, Tabitha?' Acacia asked, pushing his treat tin towards her.

'You're such a sweetie,' Tabitha told the cat as she dropped some treats on the floor in front of him.

Tiger munched the treats, smiled back at her, went to his basket, picked up his toy mouse and dropped it at Tabitha's feet.

Tabitha had a quick game with Tiger while Peter and Acacia chatted about Nate's progress. After a few minutes, Tiger went back to his basket and settled down to listen to their conversation.

'Any more problems at the hospital?' Acacia asked Peter.

'They tried again, yes,' Peter said. 'But we were ready for them, they knew they were outnumbered, and after some threatening banter they left. Good job we were there, though.'

'What do the doctors say about Nate's recovery?' Tabitha asked.

'He's still in a coma,' Peter said. 'They're being a bit tight lipped actually. They won't commit themselves regarding the outcome. We cast healing spells on Nate okay, when the nurses changed shifts. Now it's a waiting game.'

'What do your instincts tell you, Peter?' Tabitha asked.

'I think he's fighting for his life,' Peter said. 'He might be being attacked in the spiritual realm. Wiladelle is very knowledgeable and very cunning. She's on the other side, so she can do things we can't do on the Earth plane. It's frustrating. His physical body is protected, but we can't protect his spirit. We don't know what else to do.'

Tabitha furrowed her brows, and gave a deep sigh. 'We had a similar case in New England.'

'What did you do?' Peter asked.

'Well, we had to enlist the help of someone we knew had passed over,' Tabitha said. 'It wasn't easy finding someone available to help, actually. Either they were available and willing to help and they knew nothing of the art, or they weren't available. It was touch and go, but eventually we found someone to help who knew what they were doing. The woman we were helping came out of the coma and had a frightening tale to tell. We all learnt a lot from it though.'

'So, we need someone who's passed over, who knows the art?' Acacia asked.

'I think so, yes,' Tabitha said. 'Know anyone suitable?'

'Not that I can think of,' Acacia topped up Tabitha's and Peter's coffee cups.

'Tabitha,' Peter said, 'why does it have to be someone *we* know? Could it be the same person you used in New England? I mean, distance isn't the same in the spirit world, is it?'

'Hmm,' Tabitha said. 'Maybe we could.' She drank some coffee and ate a biscuit while she thought about it. 'It's worth a try. But I'll need help. Would you like to see an old fashioned séance, Acacia? The person I'm thinking of asking likes a séance.'

'Would I ever!' Acacia exclaimed. 'When would we do it?'

'Tonight,' Tabitha said. 'Peter, could you bring your group over here this evening at 7pm please? As many as can come. I know you have to leave some at the hospital to protect Nate.'

'Sure,' Peter said. 'We'll be there.'

*

It being best not to have animals around during a séance, Tiger had been lured into Tabitha's bedroom with his favourite blanket, toy mouse and some treats, and was now fast asleep. In the living room, the curtains were drawn, lights were off and candles were lit.

'Okay everyone?' Tabitha asked as Peter's group were seated.

The group nodded, quiet, waiting.

A car horn sounded outside. Matt peered out of the window and saw Morgan there, waving his arms about. He rushed downstairs and let him in.

'Cuz!' Matt exclaimed, giving him a hug. 'Why didn't you let us know you were coming?'

'My phone's dead,' Morgan said. 'It was working fine in London, and I thought I'd call you on the way here, but the bloody thing wouldn't work.'

Matt bustled him in. 'We're having a séance. Nate's still in a coma, and Tabitha has an idea of getting help from someone who's passed over.'

'I know,' Morgan said. 'Peter called me at work. I thought I should be here with you all. I know you have Tabitha staying with you, so Peter suggested I stay with him while I'm here this time.'

'Oh, right,' Matt nodded. 'I wonder why Peter didn't mention it.'

'I wasn't sure I could get here,' Morgan said. 'Peter didn't want to say anything unless I was definitely coming.'

They'd reached the top of the stairs by now. Matt opened the door. 'Look who's here, everyone. Morgan's come to lend some support.'

Acacia took his coat and hugged him. Morgan smiled at her.

Peter brought another chair to the table, and patted Morgan's shoulder. 'Glad you could make it.'

'We're doing an old fashioned séance, hence the candle light,' Tabitha told Morgan. 'Ever been to one?'

'Oh yes, but not for a while,' Morgan said, settling into his chair and opening his hands on the table in receptive mode.

Peter sat next to Tabitha and placed a pad and pencil in front of her. Tabitha laid her hand over Peter's, and gave it a squeeze. 'Thank you.' Their eyes met. They smiled at each other.

Peter's group were watching this interaction with interest, and Justin couldn't resist grinning.

Tabitha took a sip of water. 'Right, let's begin.' Tabitha used her favourite protection prayer. The group waited expectantly. 'Sylvia, are you there? We need to talk to you. This is very important. We need your help, like last time. Someone is in a coma, and we believe they're being attacked spiritually.' Silence, so Tabitha repeated, 'Are you there, Sylvia?'

They waited.

Nothing.

Then, all the lights went on and off again. The room temperature dropped a bit. Justin's eyes grew wide as the notepad on the table moved seemingly on its own.

To everyone's surprise, Tabitha laughed. 'Oh Sylvia, no need for all those theatrics.'

'Shame,' said Sylvia, who materialised in front of the table. 'I enjoy that bit.'

'Thank you for coming,' Tabitha said. 'This is about our friend, Nate.'

'I thought it might be,' Sylvia said. 'I'm glad you called me. I've been doing some research into this Wiladelle person. She's a piece of work, isn't she?'

'Yes,' Tabitha said. 'Very clever though.'

'So I've heard,' Sylvia said. 'Would you allow me to ask others to assist?'

'Of course. Who do you need?'

'You have two resident ghosts here, I understand?' Sylvia said. 'Do I have your permission to enlist their help, if needed?'

Tabitha turned to Peter, her eyebrows raised in question.

'Of course,' Peter said.

'Also, I have a friend here who will help if I ask. You might remember him. His name is Raphael.'

Matt blanched. Raphael was his dad's name.

Acacia looked at Matt, then Tabitha, then back at Sylvia. 'Do you mean Matt's father?'

'Yes, I do,' Sylvia said. 'He's been attending my group sessions up here and learning all he can. He feels somewhat responsible for the current predicament, as Wiladelle was his wife's sister. He really wants to help, if you'll let him.'

'I never actually met Raphael,' Tabitha said, 'although I

174

did meet Eliza, his wife. What do you think, Matt? Are you okay with this?'

'Yes,' Matt stuttered. 'If he wants to help, that'll be great.'

'Peter?' Tabitha asked. 'Are you okay with this?'

'Of course,' Peter said.

The rest of the group nodded their agreement.

'Right, Sylvia,' Tabitha said. 'What do you need us to do?'

*

It was midnight, and all was quiet.

Now for some fun, Wiladelle thought. It hadn't taken her long to overcome the protection spell and get into the bookshop.

She made a pile of books by the fireplace. She cast a *Jumble* spell at each book section, and pretty soon all the books were in the wrong order and the wrong sections. Wiladelle paused. What else?

She headed to Matt's office. His computer – oh yes, she could have some fun with that. She sat on his chair and studied the computer. Damn it, she thought, it's password protected. I'll come back another time and destroy it.

Wiladelle went back to the pile of books and took out her wand. She was just about to cast the *Incendiary* spell when Ernie appeared.

'Having fun, are you?' he asked.

'Get out of here,' Wiladelle shouted. 'I've warned you before to stay out of this.'

'Last time I checked I wasn't answerable to you.'

Wiladelle took her wand out to attack Ernie. Tabitha, Matt and Acacia rushed into the bookshop, prepared for a fight.

'I wouldn't do that if I were you,' Tabitha said.

Wiladelle's face lit up. At last, some real competition. This would be interesting.

'Come on then,' Wiladelle said. 'Let's see what you've got.'

*

Wiladelle was wearing a long black dress, tight at the waist, flared, reaching to the floor. She wore dangling silver earrings with green gemstones in them, and her blonde hair was pinned on top of her head with little curls tumbling around her neck. If it wasn't for the madness in her eyes, Tabitha thought, she'd look very attractive.

In contrast to Wiladelle, Tabitha, Matt and Acacia were clearly dishevelled, having tumbled from their beds and grabbed dressing gowns on their way out of the flat. Acacia only had one slipper on.

Wiladelle kicked off with a *Disable* spell, but Tabitha countered it.

Tabitha used the *Confuse* spell, but Wiladelle blocked it.

They hurled spells at each other through their wands, using their free hands to block spells coming at them. Wiladelle pushed her wand up and brought it down again, and part of the ceiling fell towards Tabitha. Tabitha managed to sidestep most of it but was caught on the shoulder with some masonry. She ignored the pain and carried on.

Wiladelle was enjoying herself immensely. Tabitha was cool and professional, but they were each gauging the other's talents and knowledge. Spells went back and forth, light flew through their wands.

Acacia watched, holding her breath, as the two seasoned witches warred. Spells from their wands lit up the shop.

Suddenly, Tabitha said, 'Okay, I'm tired of this. *Banish.*' She flourished her wand, and in an instant Wiladelle was gone.

Ernie checked the bookshop. No sign of Wiladelle.

'I don't think she'll be able to get through the *Banish* spell,' Tabitha said. 'It should keep her out of here forever.'

Acacia felt exhausted, but she had to be sure Tiger would be safe. 'Is the flat secure?'

'I'll see to it,' Tabitha said.

'How's your shoulder?' Acacia asked.

'I'll live, but I could do with some pain relief and a healing spell.'

Acacia left Matt and Tabitha discussing healing spells, and went over to Ernie. 'Thank you so much, Ernie. If you hadn't found Wiladelle here, we could've lost everything.'

'My pleasure,' Ernie said.

'We met someone last night who's agreed to help Nate. He's protected physically, but we believe he's being attacked in the spirit realm.'

'Oh?'

'The person's name is Sylvia,' Acacia said. 'She's helped Tabitha once before with a spiritual realm fight for survival, and succeeded.'

Ernie opened and closed his mouth, but nothing came out. He said, 'That's really advanced stuff.'

Acacia nodded. 'She said she might need your help and Elizabeth's too, so she'll probably contact you soon. Are you alright with that?'

'Of course,' Ernie said. 'I'll tell Elizabeth.'

'One other thing you should know,' Acacia said. 'Raphael, Matt's dad, has also agreed to help.'

Ernie smiled, and his blue eyes twinkled. 'I wondered where he was. It'll be good to catch up.'

'I think we deserve a stiff drink,' Acacia said to Tabitha and Matt. 'What a mess!'

Aside from the books in a pile by the fireplace, books were scattered on the floor in every section, tables and chairs were overturned, and now there was a hole in the ceiling and plaster over the floor.

'We'll deal with it in the morning,' Matt said. The bookshop clock said 2am.

'Stiff drink, then bed,' Tabitha said.

'Goodnight, Ernie!' they called as they went upstairs.

Tiger was pacing anxiously in front of the door.

'We got rid of her, Tiger. It's okay,' Acacia said, stroking him.

Acacia poured three brandies, and they sipped their drinks. 'I'm wide awake,' she said. 'I don't think I'll get any sleep.'

'Me neither,' Tabitha said, walking to the nearest window and chanting a spell, using her wand in a cross-wise fashion on each window as she chanted.

'Well, if we do manage any sleep, we'll be safe,' Tabitha said. 'It'll take her a while to break that one. It's one of my own spells.'

'Goodnight,' Matt mumbled, exhausted, on his way to the bedroom.

'How can he sleep after what we've been through?' Acacia asked Tabitha.

'Sometimes after the adrenaline, the body and brain shut down,' Tabitha said.

Acacia yawned. 'Mmm, see what you mean,' she murmured. 'Maybe I'll get some sleep after all. Goodnight, Tabitha.'

'I'm going to bed too,' Tabitha said, hugging her niece.

Tiger followed Tabitha into her bedroom and curled into a ball by her pillow. She fell asleep with her arms wrapped round him.

*

Outside, Wiladelle had watched while Tabitha worked at renewed protection for the flat. Wiladelle was angry now. This was all taking far longer than she wanted it to. Well, if she couldn't get in she might as well go to her den. Her den was well hidden in the woods, away from prying eyes. She'd equipped it with a comfortable bed and a warm quilt. She liked it there. She fell asleep, dreaming of revenge.

TWENTY

Acacia drove Matt and Tabitha to Peter's home that evening. The sky was a clear, deep blue, and stars were twinkling down at them.

Peter's group were gathering to discuss *the Wiladelle problem,* but Acacia wasn't really happy about all the magic going on. She still felt conflicted about it all. They parked, and went into Peter's house.

Peter gave Tabitha a hug, and greeted Acacia and Matt warmly.

'You look good,' Peter said to Tabitha. She was wearing a light green, flowing skirt and silky top with a gold necklace and earrings. Her hair was piled up on her head.

Peter realised the group were watching him, expectantly. 'Right,' he said, removing his attention from Tabitha, 'we all know why we're here. Who wants to kick off first with suggestions on how to get rid of Wiladelle?'

Alan spoke first. 'What are our intentions here? Are we talking hurting her, or stopping her coming back to Devon, or stopping her coming back to Earth?'

'Good question,' Peter said. 'Anyone want to share thoughts on that?'

Some muttering, people frowning in concentration. Then silence.

'I think we have to see the bigger picture,' Peter said. 'If we stop her coming into Devon that helps us, but what if she causes problems for other people elsewhere? And what happens when we travel out of Devon? I think we have to stop her coming back to Earth.'

Tabitha spoke next. 'You're right. This is bigger than just us and our problems. She's dangerous. She mustn't be allowed to continue to hurt people, wherever they are.'

Everyone nodded agreement.

'What exactly would that mean, though?' Matt asked. 'I mean, I know she's mad and dangerous, vicious even. But, I don't think I could be responsible for affecting her spirit forever. Can you explain?'

'There are different levels, Matt,' Peter said. 'We could come up with a version of the *Banish* spell to keep her from coming to Earth. That way she's not obliterated. Her spirit still lives,' Peter explained, 'but she can't visit this planet again.'

'She can go to other planets though,' Alan said. 'Who knows what havoc she could wreak?'

'Other planets?' Matt asked, eyes wide.

'You don't really think this is the only planet with life on it, surely?'

'I'd not really thought about it.'

'Well, you should think about it,' Peter said, 'but not today. Today we have to figure out what we're going to do about Wiladelle, and how we're going to do it.'

Acacia saw Matt's mouth open and shut. She knew he was having trouble digesting this latest piece of information.

Acacia got up and made coffee while the discussion continued, then brought it in. People poured coffee and kept talking, drinking in between speaking. Most of what was said was beyond Acacia, so she just listened.

'Does anyone know a spell that would force Wiladelle to go into the Higher Realms?' Morgan asked. 'If she was up there, it could save her soul.'

'I've heard of such a thing,' Tabitha said, 'but I've no idea how to do it.'

'Anyone?' Peter asked. The group shook their heads, no.

'What about Sylvia?' Acacia asked. 'The woman who's helping Nate to fight spiritually. Would she know?'

'Maybe,' Peter said. 'It's a thought.'

'If I can use your laptop, Peter,' Tabitha said, 'I could make a call to a friend in New England and ask if anyone there knows how to do this.'

'I'll set it up,' Peter said. 'Take a break, everyone.' He and Tabitha went into the study.

'Wow,' Justin said to Matt and Acacia, 'I had no idea these kinds of things were possible.'

Alan joined Acacia, Matt and Justin, clutching his coffee mug. 'How are your lessons going?'

'Not bad,' Justin said, 'we've only just started though. So much to learn.'

'I know,' Alan said, 'shame you didn't start earlier. But from what I hear from Peter, you're both quick learners. Just keep at it.'

'How many people are in Peter's group?' Acacia asked. 'We only ever see part of the group, and I see some different people here to the ones who've been doing the hospital rota.'

'There are twenty-five of us in total,' Alan said. 'We'd love new recruits, but it's hard these days. People don't believe this stuff. They think it's fiction. We're all thrilled to have new blood in the group.'

'Thanks,' Matt and Justin both said.

Acacia watched Peter and Tabitha walking back, very close together. Tabitha appeared a little flushed, but happy. So, Acacia thought, their relationship is progressing.

'Good news,' Peter said. 'Tabitha's group are confident they can find out how it's done. So, in the meantime, we need to discuss other things. We can't just wait for the New England group to get back to us. We need to take some action now.'

Simon coughed and stood up. 'It would really annoy Wiladelle if she couldn't hurt any of us individually. Can we work out a *Protection from Wiladelle* spell? I know that won't protect us from her associates, but they're not quite as dangerous as she is.'

'Good idea, Simon,' Peter said. 'We'll add that to the list. Anyone else got any ideas?'

Morgan went rigid, then slowly turned to the living room window. A black blur shot past. Acacia followed Morgan's eyes, and she lifted her eyebrows to Peter.

'No one but us can get into this house,' Peter said. 'But I should really protect the garden too. They can't hear what we're saying, but this underlines the point doesn't it? It's not just Wiladelle we have to deal with, it's her associates. Do we use the same process on all of them? Getting rid of Wiladelle may not finish the matter. They may continue even when she's gone.'

A man at the back of the room spoke up, a quiet man in his sixties. 'I've been working on something you might be interested in,' he said to Peter.

'What's that, Milton?' Peter asked. 'Tell us, please.'

Milton wasn't happy about speaking in public. He was okay with Peter's group, but Morgan, Tabitha, Matt, Acacia and Justin were all fairly new to him, and he was shy around them.

Acacia got up and poured some coffee into Milton's cup, smiling at him encouragingly.

Milton smiled back, took a sip, and spoke. 'Well, I've been working on this, I don't know what to call it, it's a bit controversial I suppose.' He stopped and sipped some coffee.

Peter smiled at him, and raised his hands in a 'tell me more' gesture. 'Sounds very interesting, Milton, please go on.'

'It repels the person who's attacking you.'

'What do you mean, *repels?*' Peter asked.

'It literally throws them backwards,' Milton said, 'they land on their backside, they'll have scorch marks on their hands and,' he paused here and swallowed, 'it'll burn and destroy their wands.'

Acacia saw that the group was stunned. This was obviously innovative.

No one spoke for a few seconds. Then everyone spoke at once.

Acacia beckoned Morgan over, and he joined her, Matt and Justin. 'We never usually attack people's wands,' Morgan explained. 'Wands are personal, almost like an extension of the person. But this all-in-one spell is perfect for this situation. If they haven't got their wands it'll set them back months!'

Everyone gathered around, shaking Milton's hand and congratulating him. He blushed with pleasure, and stuttered his thanks.

'We'll have to come up with a name for it,' Peter said.

Milton said, 'I was thinking maybe *Repulse*?'

'Perfect,' Peter said. '*Repulse* it is.'

Tabitha had gone into the kitchen and came back with three bottles of wine that had been chilling in the fridge, and glasses. Peter poured the wine, and Acacia handed out the full glasses.

'To Milton,' Peter said. 'Our clever researcher.'

'To Milton,' they all said, clinking glasses.

*

Matt studied Nate, saw his pale skin and the dark circles around his eyes. 'So, they've released you from hospital, so you must be making good progress?'

'Yes, I'm almost recovered,' Nate said quietly. But he had a haunted look.

'Like to join us for lunch?' Matt asked.

Morgan answered for him. 'Thanks, Cuz, but we can't stay long. I'm going to go home with him for a while, help him recover.'

'Want to talk about it?' Matt asked Nate.

'Yes and no,' Nate answered. 'I get tired so easily. Later, though?'

'I understand,' Matt said. 'Would you like a coffee? We can have it here?'

'That'd be good,' Nate said.

'You stay here and talk to Nate and Morgan, Matt,' Acacia said. 'I'll get the coffee.'

'How long are you down for then, Cuz?' Matt asked Morgan.

'A couple of weeks probably, but I'll stay as long as it takes.'

Matt nodded.

Acacia came back with coffee and biscuits.

Nate nibbled absently on a biscuit and drank a little coffee, but the effort seemed too much for him, and he looked as if he was going to keel over.

'Okay, I think we'd better go,' Morgan said. 'Nate needs to be in bed really.' He turned to Nate. 'I'll bring the car to the front of the shop. I'll just be a few minutes.'

'Sorry,' Nate said to Matt and Acacia. 'The spirit's willing but the flesh is not up to it.' He tried a weak laugh.

'It's lovely to see you,' Acacia said, kissing him on the cheek. 'Thanks so much for dropping by on your way home. When you're ready, we'll come and visit you and Morgan in Bude, okay?'

Nate smiled at her sleepily.

Morgan pulled up outside the bookshop, and between Justin and Matt they got Nate out to the car.

Matt made a *call me* sign to Morgan, who nodded and waved.

*

They made the drive to Bude in silence. Nate had fallen into a deep sleep. Morgan parked the car right outside Nate's shop. His flat was at the back of the shop with just two steps down. It's chilly, Morgan thought, but thank goodness it's not raining.

Samantha opened the shop door as they drove up.

'Hello, Samantha!' Morgan said, surprised to see her there.

Samantha nodded to Morgan, then turned to Nate. 'The guy who's been helping out has the flu, so he called me.'

Nate nodded.

They got Nate to his flat between the two of them, and then Morgan parked the car round the corner in the garage. Nate sat on the sofa, clearly completely exhausted, and Samantha helped him take his coat and shoes off.

'I feel like an old man,' Nate said to Morgan when he came in.

'You'll feel better in a few days' time,' Morgan said.

'I'm just in the shop if you need me, okay?' Samantha said to Morgan and Nate. Morgan nodded and closed the flat door. He checked Nate's bedroom. It was spick and span. Samantha had even put clean sheets on the bed, and some flowers on his chest of drawers. Daffodils. Nate's favourites.

'Do you want me to make up a bed on the sofa for you?' Morgan asked. 'Or do you want to sleep in your bedroom?'

'I think I'd like to stay in here with you till bedtime,' Nate said.

Morgan knew Nate didn't want to be alone. He got some bedding from the blanket box and settled Nate on the sofa. 'Do you want anything?' Morgan asked, but Nate was already asleep.

Right, Morgan thought. He took out his wand and went to every window and door in the flat, chanting one of Tabitha's protection spells. Then he went into the shop. 'I was thinking of putting a protection spell on the shop, unless you've done it?'

'I did a protection spell as soon as I got in here,' Samantha said. 'In fact, I'm afraid I gave Nate's assistant the flu, so I could be here. He's not one of us you see.'

'Ah,' Morgan said. 'I've just done protection for the flat – had you already done that?'

'Yes,' Samantha said, 'but another charm will be good. You're way more experienced than I am. You should do one for the shop too. It'll be higher grade than mine.'

Morgan nodded and went round the shop, pausing at each window and door. He stood quietly, breathed deeply. Had anyone from Wiladelle's group been in?

'There was someone in here this morning,' Samantha said, 'who appeared suspect. I didn't trust him. I played innocent though, and I don't think he realised I was a *charmer*. I've done that with success before,' she smiled. 'Anyway, he was asking about the shop's owner, and I said he was in hospital, like he didn't already know that. He asked when Nate was coming back and I said I thought it'd be in a week or so. He seemed content and went away. That's another reason I wanted to be here. If it had been Roger, Nate's regular assistant, he'd have told him honestly that Nate was due back today, and I didn't want an unwelcome party waiting for Nate when he came through the door. He's fit to drop, I'd say. How's he actually doing?'

'Well, he's better than he was,' Morgan said, 'but obviously not up to much at all and won't be for a while, I don't think. I'm staying here with him for as long as it takes. Peter and other people will be visiting, but I'll tell you who they are, okay?'

'Good,' Samantha said. 'I suppose I should work in the shop for a while?'

'That would be a great comfort, Samantha, if you don't mind,' Morgan said. 'To have one of us in the shop would give me peace of mind, and Nate too. Thanks.'

'You think they'll try again, then?' she asked.

'Yes, I do,' Morgan said. 'But they won't be expecting to find me here. Keep playing the regular girl, Samantha, and they'll not touch you. Have you used a masking spell?'

'Yes,' she said. 'I suppose Nate and Matt told you about my teaching Tiger?'

'Yes,' Morgan smiled. 'I love that cat… We'll shut the shop this Saturday. I don't want to be distracted by customers when I'm watching out for trouble, and it's important you keep teaching Tiger. The more prepared he is, the better.'

'I love him too,' Samantha said. 'We've only had a couple of lessons, but he's one of my favourite cats ever.'

Morgan smiled at her. She was very attractive. He wondered how experienced she was in the art. He mentally shook himself. He had to concentrate on protecting Nate while he recovered. He'd get to know Samantha better over the next few days. The most important thing was that she was trustworthy.

'Right, well, I'm going to sit with Nate,' Morgan said. 'If you need me, you know where I am.'

Samantha nodded a greeting at a customer coming in. Morgan paused, checking it was a regular person. It was, and he bought a Georgian chair. Morgan went back to Nate, whose eyes flickered, then closed again when he saw it was Morgan.

I think I'll sleep next to Nate's bed for a few nights, Morgan thought. Pity Nate doesn't have a dog. They're so good at giving warning when someone comes near. Maybe we should get one?

TWENTY-ONE

Morgan was in the living room, checking his emails. Nate was in his bedroom, sitting up in bed, a laptop on his knee.

'Can you confirm your mother's maiden name was Evans?'

Morgan wandered in from the living room. 'Sure. It was.'

'Good. So Wiladelle and Eliza were both Evans.'

'And?' Morgan said.

'I promised Matt I'd see if we're related somehow.'

'You think you may be related to Matt?'

Nate took a deep breath. 'Peter and Justin told Matt and me, at our last training session, that we looked alike, we stand the same when we're doing magic, we have some of the same characteristics.'

'Now that you come to mention it,' Morgan said. 'Yes, you are alike in a lot of ways. I've thought that myself. Do you think you might be related to me too?' Morgan would have loved to have thought that Nate was related to him. He had no relatives that he knew about, other than Matt, and Sarah, who he'd never met.

'Maybe,' Nate said. 'I don't know yet. I've just started searching.'

'Don't overtire yourself, Nate. I can help if you want?'

'Okay, thanks. Can you see what you can find out about these two people? They're my grandparents on my dad's side. I'm doing my mum's side at the moment.'

Morgan and Nate worked on their laptops for an hour before Nate had to stop and sleep, but Morgan kept going. He was bored anyway, and this was something to focus on. He was used to being busy at work, and he missed it. By the time Nate woke up, Morgan had found a whole load of information about Nate's family, but nothing to suggest a link to Matt's parents, or his.

Morgan called his cousin. 'Matt? Yes, everything's fine. Nate's doing well. In fact he's been working on his family tree. He says you talked about that. Oh? Sure, he's right here.' Morgan handed his phone to Nate. 'Matt wants to talk to you.'

Nate took the phone and brought it to his ear. He frowned. 'Tara thinks I may be your father? Wow! Yes, it is a lot to take in. DNA test? Sounds like a good idea. When I'm a bit better, though. Doctor says about another week in bed should do the trick. Yes, Morgan's still here.' Nate handed the phone to Morgan.

'Yes, I heard,' Morgan said. 'Your grandma thinks Nate might be your biological father? Bombshell! Yes, a DNA paternity test is a good idea. I'll arrange that for next week and take Nate for it. Are you okay? Yes, big shock for you, and for Nate! It would explain a lot though. Okay. Talk later.' He slipped the phone back in his pocket.

'So,' Morgan said to Nate. 'You might have a son. How do you feel about that?'

'Well, if it's true, it'd be great,' Nate said. 'But if so, why didn't Eliza tell me? Why did she leave me, and then shortly after marry Raphael? It makes no sense.'

Morgan nodded. 'It is strange… I'll get on the phone and arrange the test, then. You and Matt both need to know one way or the other, don't you?'

'Thanks, Morgan,' Nate said. 'It's a bit of a shock. I'm going back to sleep for a bit, okay?'

Morgan left Nate and went into the living room to arrange the test. He saw that Samantha had placed fresh flowers in two vases in the living room, one held daffodils and one red tulips. He noticed a new cushion on the sofa too. It was blue and green and uplifted the muted cream and white of the living room walls. The thought crossed his mind that maybe Samantha had a bit of a crush on Nate. Did it matter, though? Probably not.

*

Acacia and Matt parked near Nate's shop. They were armed with shortbread, cream and organic coffee. Acacia pushed the door, and the bell gave its welcoming ding-a-ling.

'What a nice surprise,' Nate said. 'I've done the DNA thing. It'll be a few weeks before we know anything though.'

'They told me the same thing,' Matt said. 'Still, the tests are done. That's one hurdle over.'

'Shall I make coffee?' Acacia asked.

'I can help,' Morgan said, 'if that's okay?'

'Good idea, Cuz,' Matt said. 'We'll be with you in a minute.'

Acacia frowned. Why was Morgan asking Matt's permission to help her?

Samantha was out, and Nate was minding the shop for a few minutes. He flipped the sign to closed.

'Shall we?' Matt asked, offering Nate his arm to lean on. Nate took Matt's elbow and they went into Nate's flat. A wonderful smell greeted them from a pot of blue hyacinths.

Acacia and Morgan were chatting in the kitchen. Soon they went through to the living room with the coffee and shortbread. Acacia gave Nate a hug. 'How are you doing? You look better than last time we saw you.'

'That wouldn't be difficult,' Nate laughed. He sat down in an armchair and took the coffee Acacia offered him. He sipped the coffee and sighed. 'You know, Acacia, you make the best coffee of anyone I know. You should be running a coffee shop.'

Acacia laughed. 'I did for a time. When I lived in Canada, before I came home to England.'

'That explains it,' Nate smiled. The coffee was good, but he couldn't disguise his tiredness.

Morgan noticed, and asked if he needed to rest.

'It's so annoying,' Nate said. 'I've been so bored. Then I get visitors I love, and my brain tells me I have to sleep.'

'You must listen to it, Nate,' Matt said. 'These things take time.'

'Well, don't hurry off on my account,' Nate said. 'Stay and talk to Morgan. He's been stuck with me for ages.' He drifted into his bedroom, and fell sound asleep.

'He is doing better,' Morgan said, 'it's just that we had a trip to the hospital, and it was a bit emotionally draining as well as physically tiring.'

'Our timing wasn't the best, was it?' Matt said. 'We should've called first, but we wanted to surprise you both.'

'When did you get your DNA test done then?' Morgan asked Matt.

'Last week,' Matt said. 'I won't know anything for a while yet though. We have a friend who works in the lab, luckily.'

'Nate's never married,' Acacia said. 'He must've loved your mum a lot, Matt.'

'I guess so,' Matt said. 'I don't know how much grandma knows, but she did know her son wasn't my biological father. And, she knew about Nate.'

'Your dad, Raphael, helped Sylvia with the spiritual battle for Nate, didn't he?' Acacia said. 'Would it be possible to ask your dad?'

Matt brushed his fringe out of his eyes. 'No way.'

'That might be too painful for Raphael,' Morgan said, 'two men in love with the same woman. It's an old story.' He smiled ruefully at Matt.

Matt patted Morgan on the shoulder.

Acacia was puzzled. She was obviously missing something. She poured more coffee.

Matt's phone pinged. 'A text from our friend at the hospital.'

'What is it?' Acacia asked, coming over to read the text. 'Oh… our friend in the lab was working today. She saw Nate's sample and ran it straight away.'

'And?' Morgan asked.

Matt sat down, gripping the arm of the chair. He felt his world tilt on its axis. 'She says it's a match. Nate is definitely my biological father.'

Acacia reached for Matt's hands, holding them tight.

'Are you okay with that? Knowing that Raphael was not your biological father?'

'I was very young when my parents died, but of course I've always thought my dad was, well, my dad. I guess he still was, though. Just, not biologically.'

Morgan came over and sat next to Matt. 'This does explain why Nate and you have been targeted.'

'What do you mean?' Acacia asked.

'Well, Wiladelle hated her sister. Nate was in love with her sister. Matt's her sister's son. Looks like Wiladelle is out to get anyone who had anything to do with her sister.'

'And you? Why did she target you?'

'I wouldn't play ball. It made her very angry.'

*

The weather matched Wiladelle's mood. The Atlantic winds were wild today. People were clutching their headgear and struggling to stay on their feet. She was unable to get into Nate's antique shop. She was pacing, desperate to know what Matt was discussing with Nate. She crept up to the window and peered in. She still couldn't hear what they were saying. Were they discussing plans to defeat her and her group?

Eventually Matt and Acacia came out of Nate's shop, and headed towards the car park. She followed them. They were talking excitedly. She listened to every word they said. She gasped – Nate had fathered a child with her stupid sister. Nate was Matt's father.

'You idiot,' Wiladelle said, hoping Nate could hear her, but knowing he couldn't. 'I loved you. I still love you. Why did you have to fall in love with my sister?'

She paced again. She could feel her blood pressure rising. Blood pressure? She didn't have any blood. She couldn't die of a heart attack no matter how angry she became. She was already dead. She laughed, and felt the anger subside a bit.

'Okay, Nate. I'll leave you till later. Right now I'm going to concentrate on killing Matt. But I'll make him suffer first. How would he feel if his beloved Acacia, or someone else he loves, was hurt or killed? You should have chosen me!'

*

Peter was looking out of the window at the clear evening sky. His wife had always said that shade of deep blue reminded her of velvet. She'd passed over a long time ago, but even now something she'd said would come to him now and then and make him catch his breath.

Outside all was calm, but the atmosphere inside Peter's house was charged.

Peter clapped his hands and called the meeting to order. 'Right everyone. I have some important news. Alan has found out that his old friend, Ezra, has been signed up by Wiladelle.'

There was a shocked silence. Then, Simon, a quiet man in his forties, spoke up. 'Are you sure about this?'

Alan sighed heavily. 'I'm afraid so. I spoke to him yesterday.'

'You're on speaking terms with one of Wiladelle's group?' Matt asked shakily.

'Ezra and I go way back. We were best friends as kids. We went to school together. He… chose a different path to me. But in my heart, he's still my friend. I don't want to fight Ezra.

For lots of reasons. But the most important reason is that in the past we were close.'

'Why did he tell you he'd been recruited by Wiladelle?' Morgan asked.

'He wanted to warn me,' Alan said. 'He doesn't want to fight with me, either.' He shook his head sadly. 'Ezra is one of the greats. He's truly gifted. It's such a waste, him being involved with Wiladelle and her cronies.'

Even though it was May, tonight it was chilly, and Peter increased the temperature of the natural-flame fire.

'The good thing is that we've been warned,' Peter said. He realised he was pacing about, and slowly sat back in his armchair.

Milton spoke up. 'Ezra is extremely knowledgeable. If he's joined Wiladelle, this is bad news. This isn't just Matt and his family now, or even our group. If they beat us, they'll go on and challenge the rest of the UK *charmer*s and then, who knows how far they'll go?'

'I've heard of Ezra,' Morgan said. 'He's brilliant, innovative. Don't we have any information at all that would turn him away from Wiladelle?'

Peter could see Alan's mind working.

'What?' Peter asked. 'Alan, what is it?'

'Well, I did hear a rumour,' Alan said.

'Well?'

'You won't like it.'

'Who cares if we like it or not?' Peter said. 'Will it help us?'

'I'm not sure.'

'For goodness sake, Alan, what have you heard?'

Alan turned to Morgan. 'What do you know about your father?'

'My father left us when I was small,' Morgan said, 'I don't remember him.'

'The man who married your mother was not your biological father,' Alan said. 'Well, this is just rumour, I don't have any proof.'

'What?' Morgan gripped the chair arm. 'First Matt, now me?'

'Who was Morgan's biological father, Alan?' Matt asked quietly.

'Well, it's just a rumour,' Alan said.

'Who?' Morgan demanded, angry now. 'Who was my biological father?'

'Ezra.'

Morgan was stunned. 'What?'

Matt asked, 'Does Ezra know?'

'I don't know!'

TWENTY-TWO

Peter was walking up and down, clutching the phone. 'Are you sure you're up to it?' he asked Nate. 'Teaching can be tiring.'

'Yes,' Nate said. 'I'm fine now. And besides, I'm getting bored. Honestly, Peter, I really am okay. Matt and Justin need to progress their training.'

Peter sat on the sofa. 'You're right there. Alright then, see you this evening at 7pm.' He lay down the phone on the coffee table. It would be good to be doing something positive again. He'd been itching to get on with something, anything, for days. Truth be told, he missed Morgan being in the house. It seemed oddly quiet without him.

Thoughts of Tabitha flitted through his mind. He picked up the phone again.

*

Acacia was stroking Tiger, who was sitting on the windowsill.

'Really, Matt, I don't mind you going to training,' Acacia said. 'I'll be fine. Tabitha is here, and so is Tiger. This is important to you. I understand.'

'Thanks, Acacia,' Matt said, kissing her lightly on the cheek.

Acacia could see how excited he was.

Tabitha came in and placed a box of chocolates on the table. 'Coffee?'

*

Peter heard the sound of Morgan's BMW, and opened the door to Justin, Nate, Matt and Morgan.

They hung their coats in the hallway, while Peter poured coffee into mugs for everyone.

'Is it okay if I watch the lesson?' Morgan asked Peter. 'I had to bring Nate over, and I'm very interested.'

'Of course,' Peter said.

In the practice room, Peter could see from Matt and Nate's body language that a shift had taken place. They were more comfortable with each other. Now that he knew they were father and son, the likeness was unmistakeable.

'Right then,' Peter said. 'We're going to practice Milton's *Repulse* spell.'

Matt and Justin grinned and stood, holding out their wands.

'Now obviously, we won't be using our own wands for this. We've got generic wands. They don't handle like ours, of course, but are ideal for this lesson.'

Matt nodded. Then he backtracked. 'Milton said it throws people backwards and scorches their hands, as well as destroying their wands...'

Nate produced heavy-duty gloves. 'Ta-da... fire resistant!'

'Ready?' Peter asked Justin, who nodded.

Justin chanted the spell, flourishing with his wand. Peter was thrown backwards, his wand in flames. He threw the gloves off, and grinned widely.

'That was brilliant!' Peter said to Justin. 'Well done.'

'Awesome,' Matt said.

Nate and Matt went next with the same impressive result.

'Can I try?' Morgan asked Peter.

'Sure,' Peter said, picking up a new pair of gloves and a fresh wand. 'Ready?'

Morgan cast the spell, and Peter was thrown across the room – another wand destroyed.

'This is brilliant,' Morgan said. 'It'll stop them in their tracks.'

Justin helped Peter to his feet. 'Okay?' Peter nodded, brushing ash from his jeans.

'Uncle Peter,' Justin said, 'what happens if they don't stop coming? Are there spells that will, that will...'

'Yes, Justin,' Peter said. 'There are spells that will kill. But we only use them when we absolutely have to. We won't be teaching you and Matt killing spells, not until you're well and truly along in your training. You have to be ready for it, on so many levels.'

'Have you both memorised that spell?' Nate asked. 'We don't really want to lose any more gloves and wands.'

Matt and Justin nodded.

'Good,' Peter said. 'Nate has a spell he wants you to learn. It'll be very useful.'

'It's a spell Samantha has taught Tiger, actually,' Nate said. 'It reminded me that you guys don't have a lot of the basics. This is a Hide spell and it's predictably called *Hide*.'

There was some laughter as Justin made the table, and not Peter, disappear.

Peter saw Morgan watching Matt and Nate, wearing a wistful expression.

'If you find someone you want to mentor, Morgan,' Peter said, 'join our training sessions. In fact, you can join us whenever you want anyway. You may find spells you think Matt and Justin should learn.'

'Thanks, Peter.'

*

Nate picked up the phone.

'Yesteryear, can I help you? Oh, hi, Peter. Tonight? Yes, that'll be good. We need to move forward with this. I'm fine, really. See you later.'

Samantha came over. 'Are you okay? Do you need to rest for a bit?'

Nate sighed. He was getting frustrated with all the well-intentioned concern. 'I'm good, but actually there is something I wanted to do. I'm going out. I'll be about an hour or so.'

Samantha nodded, then got on with her dusting. Samantha had a natural flair for design. Nate had told her to present things as she wanted, so she moved around stock as she went, standing back and checking it was eye-catching.

Nate walked out of the shop and down the street. He needed to have coffee in his favourite place without anyone asking him how he felt. He found a table by the window, and sat there people watching. Outside, the rustic wooden tubs were brimming with multi-coloured pansies and iris.

He watched the butterflies on the flowers, and felt his spirits lift.

Nate ordered chocolate cake, and a cappuccino. He nodded to a young couple he recognised as customers. Thankfully they just smiled and didn't stop to talk. He needed a few hours, just a few hours, without thinking about spells, or Wiladelle, or danger, or his health.

After two hours, Nate went back to his shop feeling revived. He gave Samantha the rest of the day off, and closed the shop early. He smiled at Samantha's latest display. She'd somehow moved some solid Georgian furniture to the front of the shop and created a little Georgian enclave. There was a blue cotton Georgian dress (where had that come from?) next to a dressing table, a tea table with a rosewood tea caddy on top, a linen press and a mahogany commode. There was a box of second-hand books next to the display with a couple of Jane Austen books on top. He nodded. She had a good eye alright. He'd have to persuade her to work for him permanently.

Nate knew he had to get his mind around what was going to be discussed at the meeting that evening. They'd want to know about the spiritual fight. Was he up to reliving it?

Morgan had moved back to Peter's place the day before. He was surprised how much he missed him. He shook his head at his conflicting thoughts. Do you want to be alone, he asked himself, or have company?

*

Nate shook Peter's hand and went inside.

Peter's house was always welcoming. The fireplace

was on, and people were sitting around drinking coffee or beer. The atmosphere felt charged though, at odds with the comfortable expressions on peoples' faces.

'Right, everyone,' Peter said. 'First item on the agenda.'

Nate read the agenda in front of him. The first item was, 'Nate's spiritual fight. What can we learn?' Well, Peter had warned him. He had to deal with it. He stood up.

'Firstly, I want to thank Tabitha for bringing Sylvia and Raphael in to help. For Wiladelle to take the fight into the spirit realm like that, when she realised I was in a coma, was very clever. My brain was in a fog. My spiritual self should've been unaffected by my physical problems, but it wasn't. I'm still not sure why. Anyway, Wiladelle repeatedly threw the *Headache* spell at me, and the pain in my head was so bad I wasn't able to fight back when she threw other spells at me too, including one that made every muscle hurt. Sylvia and Raphael appeared just in time.'

'What did they do?' Peter asked.

Nate saw the group were completely absorbed in his story. It gave him the strength to go on. 'Sylvia and Raphael joined hands and chanted something. I've no idea what. I was out of it. Before they came, Wiladelle had been coming daily, piling on the pain.'

'How long did it take,' Alan asked, 'after the chanting?'

'A couple of minutes, and Wiladelle was gone,' Nate said. 'Next thing I knew I was back in my body, and opening my eyes. Whatever they did, it protected my spirit. If they hadn't come, I wouldn't be here now.' He sat down, surprised at how tired he felt.

Acacia came over and topped up his coffee. She whispered something to him. He nodded, and smiled at her.

'Well,' Peter said, 'hopefully that won't be repeated. If it is, we'll have to call on Sylvia and Raphael again. Once the current situation is overcome, I suggest we all take some time to learn some of this spiritual realm protection stuff.'

There was a murmur of agreement.

'Milton,' Peter said, 'would you please tell us about the *Repulse* spell? Not everyone here knows about it, and it's going to be very handy in the coming fights.'

The members who'd not heard of this before were very excited and had questions, which Milton, in his calm, ordered way, answered.

'The *Repulse* spell will be a huge help,' Peter said. 'But, what's our plan of action?'

'We have to do something,' Alan said. 'At the moment, we're just reacting. We have to take control.'

Peter nodded. 'The problem is that once one of us has used *Repulse*, they'll know about it and be ready for it.'

'Not if we take them out,' Nate said. 'Individually, I mean. Okay, say one of them attacks. We use the spell, they get thrown back and their wand is in flames. We have to take that opportunity to get rid of them. We can't afford to muck about. They have to be removed from the field permanently.'

The room was hushed. They knew what this meant, but most of them had never done it before.

'What do you mean, *remove* them?' Matt asked, eyes wide.

'What he means, Matt,' Peter said, 'is that after the *Repulse* spell we use the *Disintegrate* spell or something similar. There's no coming back from that.'

'There is a third option.' Tabitha got up and stood in the middle of the group. 'My New England associates have now discovered how to remove people from the physical realm to one of the astral planes. There's nothing dark about it. They get rehabilitated. They're different when they're released. All darkness is stripped from them. It works absolutely.'

People surrounding Nate were slowly taking in what Tabitha had said. Gradually the group became animated, excitedly asking questions.

Again, Tabitha stood up. 'I promise I'll give more information as soon as I get it.'

*

'Usual place?' Tabitha asked. 'Fifteen minutes?'

She put the phone down and made a quick trip to the bathroom. She brushed her hair, pinned it up with clips made from New England seashells, and applied fresh, pink lipstick. 'Back later,' she called to Acacia as she went out the door.

When she arrived, Peter was waiting in the coffee shop, at a table by the window, and no sooner had she sat down than a latte appeared in front of her. She smiled up at the waitress, who smiled back.

'So,' Peter said, 'we need to keep our wands with us at all times. Where's yours?'

'In my purse,' Tabitha said. 'Where's yours?'

'Your purse? Is that big enough?'

Tabitha frowned in confusion. Then, realisation hit. 'I keep forgetting. You call it a handbag over here.'

'Ah.' Peter smiled at her. He reached over and took her hand, giving it a squeeze.

'Two countries, divided by a common language,' she said, 'or something along those lines.'

'What will you do when this is over?' Peter asked.

'When what's over?' Tabitha pursed her lips. 'Oh, you mean our current problem?'

'Yes.' He gazed into her eyes, waiting for her answer.

'I suppose I'll go home,' she said, 'although this is feeling more and more like home.'

'Could this be your permanent home, do you think?'

'Well, I do have family and friends here.'

'Would you ever think about living here permanently?'

'That depends.'

'On what?'

'You see, I'm not as young as I once was and decisions of this magnitude need to be made with great care. Mistakes can't be remedied so easily as we get older. We don't have the time left for us to put things right.'

'What if you had a home to come to? A home with someone who loved you very much already living in it? A home where mutual beliefs were shared. A home where mutual friends were shared. What then?'

'Well, then I think I'd give it some serious consideration,' Tabitha said.

'It could be made legal too, if both parties were agreeable.'

Tabitha laughed. 'Why are you talking in the third person?'

'It's easier. It distances me from a possible negative response.'

'Ah. I've heard that somewhere before.' Tabitha sipped her coffee. As she looked at her hands, she realised she hadn't been wearing her wedding ring the past few weeks. Her first husband had been dead more than twenty years, and yet she'd worn his ring always. Until recently.

Tabitha could see Peter was struggling with the situation. 'Was that a proposal?' she asked him.

'Maybe,' he answered.

'Well, it does sound very tempting. How about we deal with the current problem, and then revisit this conversation when everything has died down? How does that sound?'

'It sounds good,' Peter said.

They drank their coffee, mulling over what had been said.

Tabitha was watching people pass by the window. She did a double take. 'Peter, who's that peering into your car window?'

Peter glanced out of the window, then got up. 'That's the opposition. Stay here. Please. I'll deal with this.'

Tabitha was eager to follow, but she sat back down. She didn't really want Peter going out there alone. She watched as he went over to his car and had a conversation with a young man in his twenties, tattoos on his arms and gel in his short, spiked hair. She saw Peter motion to him, and they moved across the road to a side street. She got up and peered through the window. She saw Peter's arm move out of his pocket, and then he was out of her line of vision.

Twenty minutes later, Peter came back into the coffee shop and sat down.

'What happened?'

'I used the *Repulse* spell and it worked great. But I couldn't let him go and warn his colleagues. He didn't leave me any choice. I had to use the *Disintegrate* spell.'

Tabitha put her hand over Peter's and gave it a squeeze, then went to the counter and ordered more coffee.

Peter was staring out of the window. He was pale and shaking.

'If you used that spell, he must have forced your hand. It can't be helped. But we do need to know how to remove people without violence. I'll chase up my New England group again.'

Peter nodded. 'He said they're going to kill us all, one by one. I couldn't let him tell them about the *Repulse* spell.'

Tabitha wanted to give Peter something else to think about. 'What about Ezra possibly being Morgan's biological father? Do you think if he found out, he would come over to our side?'

'Let's hope so. But as none of us talk to him, how are we going to find out?'

'Hmm. Unsure. Maybe Alan can talk to him?'

TWENTY-THREE

The bookshop was closed, and Jett was sitting in an armchair next to the coffee table. It was quiet, just as he liked it. He didn't like too much going on around him. He'd started a new book, but he often forgot what was going on and had to reread bits of the previous chapter.

'Hello there,' Ernie said. 'You're back, I see.'

'Yes,' Jett said, frowning. 'Do I know you?'

'We've met a few times now,' Ernie said, bewildered. 'I'm Ernie. I live here.'

'Oh, right,' Jett said. 'What do you want?'

'I don't want anything. I spend a few hours with books every evening.'

'Oh?' Jett was confused. What did the man want?

'Mind if I join you?'

'If you must,' Jett said, picking up the book and starting to read. Ignoring Ernie.

'Have you been reading that book long?'

Jett sighed, and placed the book on the coffee table. 'I started it a few days ago.'

Ernie suddenly changed the subject. 'Do you know Wiladelle?'

'What does she look like?'

'She's blonde, blue eyed, attractive, passed over years ago. Very dangerous.'

'Oh,' Jett said. 'I've seen her. What's with her?'

'She doesn't like Matt.'

'Why not?'

'Long story,' Ernie said.

Jett got up and walked around the bookshop, picking up books, putting them down, staring at the pictures on the wall, peering through the window into the square in front of the shop. Not much cloud tonight. It was dark out there now, and the stars were clearly visible.

'You know Matt, I think?' Ernie asked.

'We were at school together. We both loved cricket. We were on the same team. That's how it happened. The accident. He really should pay for that.'

'What happened?'

'What?'

'You said that's how it happened. But what happened?'

'No idea,' Jett said. 'Look, I want to read some of that book, okay?'

'I won't disturb you,' Ernie said. 'I'll go to another section.'

After a few minutes, Jett replaced the book, bored. His black hair fell over his eyes and he pushed his hand through it. He gazed absently around, then down at the floor. He saw he was wearing odd coloured shoes. How had that happened? His blue jeans were clean though, so was his shirt. His denim jacket had a rip in it by the pocket. Had he caught it on something? He stamped his foot. Why couldn't he remember things?

Jett went over to the window again. There was someone out there, watching the building. He'd seen him before, but he didn't know who he was. It didn't seem as though the person had seen him, though.

He wandered over to a bookshelf and swept his right hand along a shelf holding mystery books. They fell in a heap on the carpet. He frowned. What were those books doing on the floor?

He drifted out of the bookshop, and went back to the church. He felt safe there. Once in the vestry, he curled up on the floor with three hymn books replacing a pillow.

*

Tiger was sprawled out on the windowsill. Acacia had told him Samantha was coming today. He scrutinised every car that went by.

Acacia went over and kissed him on the top of his head. It being Saturday, Acacia had made pancakes for breakfast, and Tiger always had a little pancake with his food. 'You know it's Saturday, don't you?' she asked him. He gave one of his cat smiles, and laid his paw on her arm. She kissed him again. 'You know, I do believe I love you more than anyone. Apart from Matt, of course. You and he are equal on that score. But don't tell him I love you as much as I love him, okay? He'll be jealous.'

*

Justin was opening the bookshop when Samantha arrived. He liked her. About his age, he thought – early twenties. She had beautiful blue eyes with long, dark eyelashes and long, wavy blonde hair. Bright blue nail varnish today, and a bright blue necklace. He laughed. 'Blue day today, eh?'

Samantha smiled at him, blinked a couple of times, then dropped her gaze. 'I guess so. I like the colour blue. Do you?'

Is she flirting with me? Justin asked himself. 'I've never really thought about it. Matt says Tiger has been waiting for you.'

'See you later, then,' Samantha said, going up the stairs to the flat.

*

'Come in,' Acacia called when Samantha knocked on the door.

Tiger rushed over to Samantha and wound himself around her ankles.

'He's been waiting for you,' Acacia said.

Samantha leaned down and picked Tiger up, giving him a cuddle and kissing him. He purred. 'I see he has a new collar?'

'Yes,' Acacia said. 'He's grown enough that he can wear it now. The stones are black and green diamonds.'

'Oh, wow!' Samantha said. 'Those are protective! And did you know they'll also help enhance his magic?'

Acacia picked up her latest novel. 'Yes, someone did tell me that. Thanks for confirming it. I'll leave you to it, but I'll be just over there in the dining area if you need me.'

Samantha stood in front of Tiger. 'This spell will enable you to get out of locked boxes or locked rooms. It's very handy. It's called *Dematerialise*.'

Samantha placed Tiger in his cat basket and locked it. 'Okay, try the spell. Let's see if you can get out.'

Tiger was out in an instant. Samantha excitedly called, 'Look at this!' to Acacia.

Acacia had mixed feelings about it. 'I can see that's a very handy spell, but what about when I want to take him to the vets? I can't have him getting out of the basket and getting lost.'

'Good point,' Samantha said. 'Let's think about that.'

Tabitha, coming back from her morning coffee with Peter, overheard this. 'Have you asked Tiger?'

'What do you mean?' Acacia asked.

'Tiger,' Tabitha addressed the cat, 'will you promise that if Acacia or Matt use your basket to take you to the vets or take you anywhere, that you'll stay in the basket, unless there's danger and you have to escape?'

Tiger seemed to consider the question. He didn't like trips to the vets. He saw Acacia's worried face though and made his decision. He said *I promise* telepathically.

Acacia picked Tiger up and cuddled him. 'Thank you,' she said to him.

'Am I missing something?' Samantha asked.

'Tiger talks to me sometimes, telepathically,' Acacia said, a little smugly.

'Wow!' Samantha said. 'That's a first for me. I've not heard of that before.'

'Tiger and Acacia have a very close relationship,' Tabitha said.

Acacia set Tiger down, and he went over to his bed, where he performed a nonchalant face wash. Acacia placed some treats in front of him and he daintily ate them.

'Lesson over for the day,' Samantha said. 'Um, on another note, do you know if Justin has a girlfriend?'

Acacia smiled broadly. 'No, he doesn't have one that I know about. Interested?'

'I am rather. Yes.'

'You wanted to see the walled garden, didn't you?' Acacia said. 'Why don't you and Tabitha take Tiger, and I'll bring some coffee down? I'll ask Justin if he wants to join us, and Tabitha and I will make sure you two sit together. Okay?'

*

Tabitha took a deep breath as they entered the walled garden. Sweet peas and chrysanthemums were in full bloom. Birds were singing. Tiger started chasing butterflies.

Tabitha was leaning over some sweet peas, smelling them, when a dark presence appeared, casting the garden into shade. She heard the diamonds in Tiger's collar hum, and she took a step towards him. Tiger paused mid-swipe at a bee, just as the dark witch aimed his wand at the cat. Tiger immediately used the *Dematerialise* spell and hid behind the garden shed.

'Think you can outsmart me, cat?' the dark wizard asked.

'No, but I can,' Tabitha said, using the *Repulse* spell. The dark wizard flew across the grass, clutching his burnt hand, as his wand went up in flames. Tabitha took a deep breath. Nothing for it. It had to be done. *Disintegrate.*

Samantha, frozen in shock, stumbled over to a garden seat and sat down.

Acacia and Justin came into the garden carrying coffee and cake on trays. They saw Tabitha standing there holding

215

her wand, and watched as the dark wizard seemed to melt in front of their eyes. Tiger came out from behind the shed, lifted his tail and peed where the wizard had died.

Tabitha reached for a mug of coffee. 'Just what I need.' She sat down on the bench, decidedly wobbly.

Acacia hugged Tabitha. Justin handed coffee to Samantha. They all sat on the bench in silence.

Acacia took a mouthful of coffee, then another. It revived her. 'Thank goodness you taught Tiger that spell, Samantha!'

'Yes, thank you, Samantha,' Tabitha said. 'Tiger would be dead if he hadn't known that spell.'

'We mustn't let this ever happen again,' Acacia said. 'This is our home. We need to be safe here.'

Tabitha stood up, and again brought out her wand. 'Yes. I'll make sure of that.' She walked around the perimeter of the garden, chanting and waving the wand as she placed her own protection spell on the entire area.

Justin walked over to where the dark witch had fallen. The grass was a shade darker there. He pulled his wand out and walked around the area, criss-crossing the ground with the wand. '*Ego te absolvo a peccatis tuis in nomine Patris et Filii et Spiritus Sancti.* Go in peace.'

He realised the others were watching him. 'Something Uncle Peter taught me. He's Catholic. Didn't you know?'

TWENTY-FOUR

Six o'clock was early for one of their Devon group meetings, but they had a lot to talk about, and Matt was pleased the meeting was taking place at his and Acacia's flat. Acacia had been fussing around cleaning, fluffing up cushions. To Matt's eyes, the flat was always clean and tidy.

Peter arrived and hugged Tabitha. She squeezed his hand.

'Thanks, Peter,' she said. 'It's good to have you here. Knowing you've already been through the same thing really helps.'

Matt topped up Tabitha's brandy as they sat waiting for the rest of the Devon group. Tabitha was still a bit shaken. Matt could see guilt warring with the knowledge that she had done what was needed.

Tiger sat on Tabitha's lap, purring.

'Thanks for saving Tiger, Tabitha,' Matt said. 'I really don't know what we'd do without him.'

'You're very welcome, Matt,' Tabitha said. 'But it was Samantha's training that saved him. And I'm pretty sure the stones in his collar had a positive effect. I heard them humming. They were warning him. I just finished the job. I wish I'd had the information I have now, though. Then I wouldn't have needed to…'

'You did what you had to do, Tabitha,' Peter interjected. 'We both did. Now we have options. At the time, neither of us had those options.'

'You did the right thing,' Raphael appeared in their midst – his expression serious. 'I'll be interested to hear about your new spell, though, Tabitha.'

'Dad?' Matt gasped.

'Hello, Son,' Raphael said, moving nearer to Matt. 'I've wanted to visit lots of times. In fact, I've been keeping an eye on you for years, but I thought it best not to let you see me. You didn't believe in ghosts until recently, after all.'

'Sorry about that,' Matt said. 'I had no idea ghosts and magic were real.'

'Yes, well, my parents did a great job raising you. I just wish my dad hadn't foisted his beliefs onto you. Anyway, I wanted to let you know your mum and I are pleased you and Nate know the truth about your parentage, Matt,' Raphael said.

'Really?'

Raphael nodded.

'Thanks, Dad. I'm a bit confused though… I mean why did Mum leave Nate?'

'Things were murky at the time, Matt. I don't feel it's my place to explain. But I wanted you to know I'm pleased you and Nate are working together. You're like him in so many ways. He's a brilliant *charmer*.'

'Thanks, Dad.' Matt felt as though a burden had been lifted off his shoulders. He no longer felt guilty about loving both Nate and Raphael as his fathers.

A knock at the door was followed by Nate and Justin coming in. Nate saw Raphael, and joined him.

'It's good to see you after all this time,' Nate said. 'Will you be staying for the meeting?'

'If no one has any objections, I would like to stay, yes,' Raphael said. 'Although, as Wiladelle is my wife's sister, I don't think I can be involved in any confrontation.'

'Nate, could I have a quiet word?' Raphael gestured Nate over to the window. 'Don't blame Eliza for what happened. She loved you very much, you know. But when she found out, well, she couldn't cope with it, and she needed a father for her child. I hope you understand?'

'Found out what?'

Raphael just shook his head. 'I can't say any more. Eliza needs to explain.'

'She was happy with you, wasn't she?' Nate asked.

'Yes, we were happy together. But there was always a part of her that belonged to you. I wanted you to know that.'

'That's very generous,' Nate said. 'Thank you. Her leaving always confused me, though. Will I ever find out why?'

'You really don't know, do you?' Raphael asked.

Nate shook his head.

'Hopefully you'll find out soon. I don't feel it's my place though…'

'I understand.' Nate went over to Tabitha, gave her a hug and sat on the sofa.

The remainder of the group arrived in dribs and drabs. Another fifteen minutes saw the whole group assembled.

*

'Right, everyone,' Tabitha said. 'I'm sure you've all heard what happened to Peter a few days ago, and then to me today. It wasn't pleasant for either of us, as I'm sure you realise, and we certainly didn't use that spell lightly. The good news is that my New England group has come up with the steps for a third option. We can use this in good conscience. It takes whoever you're dealing with to a good place where they'll be turned back to the light before continuing on their evolutionary journey. We've come up with a name for it. We've called it *Metamorphosis* – which we thought was appropriate.'

Tabitha laid out the steps for the new spell, questions were answered, and eventually the talking stopped.

Acacia poured wine all round. They raised their glasses. 'To *Metamorphosis*.'

'And happy endings,' Acacia said, sipping wine, then added in a whisper, 'hopefully.'

*

Tabitha watched Tiger running down the stairs to his cat flap to the walled garden. As she opened the door, she saw him cross over to the bench and launch himself at a butterfly, which sailed over his head. She felt at home surrounded by plants. And today, the sun was shining, flowers were blooming, bees were buzzing. She gave a sigh of contentment.

Elizabeth the ghost was watching Tiger's antics. She turned to Tabitha. 'I love watching Tiger. He has such joy in him.'

Elizabeth glided elegantly over to the herbs, where Tiger was watching an insect carrying a blade of grass. She moved her attention back to Tabitha. 'Thank you for including me and Ernie in the garden's protection spell.'

'You're welcome,' Tabitha said.

Elizabeth sat on the bench. 'There's been a rather dubious visitor, both here and in the bookshop. I don't *think* he means any harm. He seems rather confused. Still, he won't be able to get into the garden now.'

'What visitor?' Tabitha asked.

'He says his name is Jett. Ernie has had a couple of conversations with him, although Jett forgets what was said, afterwards. He says he went to school with Matt.'

'Really? I'll talk to Matt and see what I can find out.'

Tabitha wandered around the garden, pulling up the occasional weed. The earth was still damp from the morning dew and had a wonderful smell to it, a mixture of wet earth and ozone.

'You lived in Egypt for a while, I understand?' Tabitha said.

'Yes. Egypt gets into your blood, you know, and archaeology is an absorbing subject. My husband was on lots of digs out there, and sometimes I accompanied him. We sailed down the Nile on a number of occasions. The pyramids. Such splendour. And the markets! The crowds, the smell of the spices, the handmade carpets, the jewellery, the chaos!' Elizabeth laughed. 'Did you read the book I left in Matt's flat?'

'I had a quick look, but I haven't read it all yet.'

Tiger was sitting under the oak tree, watching a spider. He lost interest, and walked over to the newly created herb garden. He lay down, relaxing in the warm sunshine. Nearby, a bee landed on some lavender.

Tabitha joined Elizabeth on the bench. She sipped some coffee, admiring the overflowing wooden flower tubs. 'How long did you live here?'

'About three years, while we were having a bungalow purpose built for us. All mod cons. Very modern, back then. We loved that bungalow. And the garden. I filled it with herbs and flowers. There were already big ancient trees there. They seemed to stand guard.'

'Was the bungalow in this town?'

'Yes,' Elizabeth said. 'Peter bought it, after we passed away. It was for sale for a long time. People said it was haunted and wouldn't touch it. We were pleased Peter bought it.'

'Peter? Not Peter Fairbrother?'

'Yes,' Elizabeth smiled. 'He was a lot younger then, of course. But his character has remained the same. He's a very good man.'

'Yes, he is,' Tabitha agreed.

'Actually,' Elizabeth said, 'I've been meaning to tell you for a while now. There's a wooden trunk in the attic of that bungalow. In the trunk is a necklace of black and green diamonds that came from Egypt. I'd like you to have it. It will give you added protection when you need it.'

'That's very kind of you. Why me?'

'I've got a feeling you'll need it. It protected me once when I was vulnerable.'

'Oh?'

Elizabeth sidestepped the question. She nodded, 'Will you accept it?'

'Thank you, yes. Why black and green diamonds? Tiger has the same stones on his collar.'

Elizabeth nodded. 'I had a conversation with a wise

woman in Egypt. She recommended those stones for both me and my cat. So I got the necklace and the collar made at the same time. My cat lived a good, long life. He's with me still. We have a cottage in heaven with a nearby stream. Wild flowers grow all around us. It's lovely there.'

Tabitha noticed how content Elizabeth seemed when talking about her cottage in heaven. 'I hope you don't mind me asking, but I'm wondering why you visit this garden so often.'

Elizabeth got up from the bench, bending down to smell the rosemary. 'I've been wondering the same thing. I was always fond of this walled garden, but I think once this Wiladelle problem is sorted out, I'll not visit so much. I feel as though I'm keeping guard somehow. Not that I can do much. I'm not very knowledgeable in that area. But I can alert people to danger.'

'We're glad you're here. Thank you so much for the necklace. I'll give Peter a call and tell him about it. I wonder if he knows about the trunk in the attic.'

Tabitha stood up and called Tiger's name. She waved goodbye to Elizabeth, and she and Tiger went back to the flat. 'How exciting,' she said to the cat, 'now I'll have a necklace with precious stones like the ones in your collar.'

Tiger gave his cat smile as they opened the door. He wandered over to his bed, where he promptly fell asleep.

'I expect you're dreaming of butterflies and bees,' Tabitha said to the cat. 'Good idea. I think I'll do the same.' She'd meant to call Peter right away, but instead settled on the sofa for a nap.

TWENTY-FIVE

Acacia took her headphones off and went into the kitchen. She measured coffee into the cafetiere and added boiling water, leaving it to steep. The flat was rather quiet. Where was Tiger? And where was her aunt?

She found Tiger on his bed, smiling in his sleep. She peeked in Tabitha's bedroom. No sign of her aunt.

'Is that fresh coffee I smell?' Tabitha said, stretching on the sofa and then sitting upright. 'What time is it?'

'Oh, there you are,' Acacia said. 'I wasn't expecting to see you lying on the sofa. Why so tired?'

'No idea. Tiger and I had a nice time in the walled garden earlier, then we felt drowsy, so we both had a nap.'

'It's not even noon,' Acacia said. 'Aren't you having coffee with Peter this morning?'

'Not till this afternoon. He had something he wanted to do this morning. But, I have something interesting to tell you.'

'Go on,' Acacia said. She poured two mugs of coffee, and handed one to Tabitha.

'Elizabeth says the bungalow Peter lives in used to belong to her and her husband!'

'Really? How's that for coincidence?'

'And, she says there's a necklace with green and black diamonds, like in Tiger's collar, that she wants me to have. The cat collar and her necklace were both bought by Tabitha in Egypt. She had a much loved cat, she told me. Well, still does, but the cat's not on the Earth plane anymore obviously… Anyway, the necklace is in a trunk in the attic at Peter's place, she says.'

'Curiouser and curiouser, cried Alice,' Acacia said.

'I can't wait to tell Peter. Oh,' she paused, mid-sip. 'What if the trunk isn't in the attic anymore?'

'Only one way to find out,' Acacia said, handing the phone to her aunt. 'Call Peter.'

*

Wiladelle's eyes were wide, but her mouth was pinched. 'Are you questioning my authority?'

Romany squirmed. He was usually self-possessed, arrogant even, but not when Wiladelle was around. She frightened him.

'Not at all,' he said. His voice cracked. He was finding it difficult to swallow. 'It's just that I think we should kill Matt and get it over with. The others will be weakened by that, distraught. It'll make it easier.'

'Oh?' Wiladelle asked coldly. 'How come you know so much about it? Done this kind of thing before, have you?'

He shrugged, uncomfortable. No point in lying. She'd know it straight away.

Wiladelle turned her attention to the rest of her group. 'Right, as I was saying. I want to focus on hurting or killing Acacia and Tabitha. Get those two out of the way first. It'll bring pain to Matt, and that's what I want. It's time he suffered.'

A man in his forties spoke up. 'We can't get into the garden now either. That's the flat and garden off limits to us. How do we get at them?'

Wiladelle sighed. 'Do I have to do everything?' Outwardly she appeared annoyed, but really she was delighted. Planning to hurt Matt and his family and friends was such fun. She scrutinised the people in front of her. 'We've already lost two witches to them. I don't know what happened. I can't be everywhere at once. We have to lure them out, or wait till they leave the bookshop and pick them off, one at a time. But it's Acacia and Tabitha I want first. Stewart,' she turned to a man in his fifties with tattoos on his cheek. 'I want you to keep watching that bookshop. The first one of that group who comes out, I want you to follow them, see where they go. See what they're up to. Don't do anything to stop them. Your job is surveillance. Alright?'

Stewart nodded.

Wiladelle watched him. She could almost hear his brain turning. He didn't need to work. He had more money than he knew what to do with. What he craved was action. He smiled, and Wiladelle sighed. She knew he was thinking of making something happen, just so he'd have to act. 'Surveillance only, right?'

'Right,' he said.

'So, you'll watch and report back to me. Got it?'

'Yep.'

Wiladelle turned to a smart, attractive man in his thirties. 'Warwick, you're back-up to Stewart. If either of you see anything you tell me. Anything unusual at all. Right?'

'Will do,' Warwick said.

'How are we going to single out Acacia and Tabitha?' asked Savannah, a dark haired woman in her forties. She looked as though she'd been squeezed into her dress, like too much filling in a pie.

Ezra was obviously smitten. He didn't say a word but stood so close to Savannah he was almost touching her. His eyes followed her lipstick red lips as she talked.

Wiladelle shook her head, and smirked. 'Samson and Delilah. That's what you two should be called.'

Everyone laughed, including Savannah, but Ezra just stared at Wiladelle, unsmiling. He wasn't happy about any of this.

'Savannah,' Wiladelle said, 'Stewart and Warwick will follow anyone *but* Acacia and Tabitha. If Acacia or Tabitha appear, I need to be told. I want to be the one to kill them. Got it? I'm going to be outside the bookshop at regular intervals throughout the day. If I need assistance, I'll press the autoalert button, so you need those devices turned on at all times. If the autoalert button goes off, you all meet up at the market square. Someone will be there to tell you what's happening.'

Wiladelle could see Savannah was getting excited about the possibility of causing pain. She sidled over to her and whispered in her ear, 'Keep your masochistic needs under control. This is business.'

Savannah flushed.

'We need to be cold about this, people,' Wiladelle said.

'Keep your emotions in check. Once we've defeated this ramshackle group, the whole of Devon will be ours for the taking. Then we can move onto Cornwall. I hear they do a great cream tea down there.'

The room erupted in laughter. Ezra nearly choked on his beer.

*

Alan took the next turning, to see if the car behind took it too. It did. 'Don't look now, but we're being followed.'

'And I thought we were going to have a nice pub lunch,' Milton said, getting his wand out of his pocket, and peering through the car windows at the rain.

Alan drove on until he saw the entrance to his favourite pub's car park. He reversed into a space overlooking a grassed area with picnic benches. They got out of the car, and calmly started talking about darts matches. They held their wands in their hands, hidden in their coat sleeves, and nonchalantly walked past the other car.

Savannah and Ezra got out of their car and went on the attack, but Alan and Milton were ready.

'*Repulse.*' Milton aimed his wand at Savannah. She flew across the wet tarmac of the car park, wand in flames.

'I warned you,' Ezra shouted at Alan, aiming his wand and firing off a spell.

Alan aimed at Ezra and got the *Repulse* spell out just before being hit by Ezra's spell. Alan fell to the floor clutching his arm.

Ezra's eyes grew large, and the *Repulse* spell scorched his hands, wand in flames on the floor next to him.

Distraught by Alan being hit, Milton didn't follow up with the *Metamorphosis* spell quick enough, and both Savannah and Ezra vanished.

Milton helped Alan up, both of them dripping wet. 'Come on. Let's get to the bookshop so Tabitha can attend to your arm.'

*

Acacia saw Alan and Milton arrive at the bookshop, holes in their jeans, dirt on their coats, Alan holding his arm, pale and shaken. 'This way. Tabitha's in Matt's office.'

Acacia moved her head to the right, indicating to Justin that he should distract his customers, who were obviously startled at Alan and Milton's dishevelled appearance. Justin launched into a spiel about the free coffee, and offered to make some fresh for them, distracting them and blocking their view of Alan and Milton.

Tabitha removed Alan's coat and shirt carefully. His arm appeared badly burnt, a jagged gash on his elbow. She applied antiseptic cream and a dressing, followed by a healing spell.

'It'll be okay in a few days, but you'll need to rest it.'

Acacia produced a bottle of brandy and a couple of glasses from one of Matt's filing cabinets, pouring good tots of brandy in each before handing them to Alan and Milton.

Alan's hands were shaking.

'We thought we were ready, but we weren't quick enough,' Milton said. 'Their wands were burnt alright, but we didn't get a chance to use *Metamorphosis*. Now they'll go back and tell the others about *Repulse*. We've lost the element of surprise.'

Acacia chewed her lip. What could she say? 'They don't

know about *Metamorphosis*, though. So we still have that up our sleeves.'

'I can't do this anymore,' Alan said, his hand gripping the brandy glass.

'What do you mean?' Matt asked, startled.

'Just that,' Alan said. 'I can't do this anymore. I'm taking the family away for a while.' He drank the brandy in two swallows, his face flushed. 'Sorry.' He got up to leave.

Milton helped Alan with his jacket. 'Let me drive you home.'

'Alright. But don't try to talk me out of it. My family come first.'

Acacia frowned.

What did he mean? His family? They weren't in the group, why should they be in danger?

*

The clear sky and warm summer air did nothing to ease the tension in Matt and Acacia's flat that evening. The Devon group were subdued.

Milton stood up. 'Just before Alan took the hit, I heard Ezra shout, *I warned you*, at him.'

'Why would Ezra warn Alan? And what about?' Matt asked.

'Ah,' Peter said. He seemed distracted, far away. Justin nudged him, bringing him back to the present.

Peter stood up, walked over to the cafetiere and poured himself more coffee. 'I'm starting to drink way more of this than I should.' He took a deep breath, staring into his coffee as though the right words were hidden in its dark depths. 'Ezra used to be close with Alan, but they chose different paths. Alan didn't want to fight his friend. I know that much.'

Milton stood up. 'Alan said, "My family comes first."'

'So, he thinks his family is in danger?' Peter said. 'That's certainly possible. I suppose all of our families are in danger.'

Acacia heard someone say, 'Oh my God,' and she turned, but couldn't see who had spoken. She certainly sympathised.

*

Two days later, Tabitha received a phone call from Toby, one of her New England group.

'I remember you telling me about the Devon group members, but I didn't know one intended to pay us a visit. Alan is here. Did you know he was coming?'

'No,' Tabitha said. 'He got injured a couple of days ago in a fight. I should've realised though. He did say he wanted to see New England. And he had asked me where we usually meet. He didn't actually say he'd visit you though.'

'Hmm. Things have moved rather quickly. Linus wants to fly over and join you guys. He says he's willing to take Alan's place until this problem is sorted out.'

'Oh? That's generous of him.'

'Well, he always wanted to visit Devon. His grandparents were from Devon, you know.'

Was that serendipity, Tabitha asked herself? Something didn't feel right, but Linus was brilliant and would be a serious help to the group.

'Oh, I see. We'll meet him at Heathrow. When's he coming?'

'That's the thing. He didn't want to wait. He's on the evening flight. He'll be at Heathrow tomorrow morning.'

TWENTY-SIX

Acacia sat in the window seat, stroking Tiger. As the group assembled, the mood in the flat grew tense. The weather showed sympathy, rain lashing against the window panes.

'Are you sure Alan and his family have left?' a frowning man in his forties asked Milton.

'Yes,' Milton replied quietly. 'I drove them to the airport.'

'Is he coming back?'

'I hope so.'

'Did she threaten his family then?'

'I'm not sure. I think so.'

Acacia walked around, offering tea and coffee, and chatting. People were talking quietly in little groups. Acacia could almost see the worry as a colour... a very muddy brown.

Tabitha stood up. 'Okay, everyone, I want you to meet Linus. He's from my New England group, and he's come to take Alan's place until we have this problem resolved. He's very experienced and has helped with quite a few similar problems in our home state.' She smiled at a man in his fifties, dark brown hair, large brown eyes and a mouth used to smiling. He wore blue jeans, and had a silky black waistcoat over his checked shirt.

Samantha had recently joined Peter's group, and her eyes widened at the vision of American manhood who stood before her. Older than her, of course, but very handsome. She smiled at him.

Justin, seeing Samantha's rapt expression, frowned.

'Hi, everyone,' Linus said. 'Before I say anything else, I want you to know that we can win this battle. I know all about you from Tabitha, and I'm impressed with your collective credentials. I've been checking out this problem, otherwise known as *Wiladelle*,' the group laughed, 'and I've found that, already a very talented witch before her death, she's continued to hone her skills since then.' The group murmured agreement. 'Something else I've found out is what I think is one of the reasons for this campaign of hers. She's a vengeful person, of course, doesn't like to be brushed aside, and it would appear that she's been in love with Nate for a very long time.'

Heads turned towards Nate, now sitting with his mouth open in surprise.

Linus continued. 'She's jealous, of course, and we all know she's unhinged and dangerous. There's nothing we can do about these facts. But I believe we need to know as much as we can if we're to defeat her and her cronies.'

Nate sat quietly, stunned. People were gazing at him, trying to monitor the effect of this revelation on him. 'Are you sure about this?'

'Yep,' Linus said. 'No doubt. Reliable source.'

Acacia came and stood next to Nate, her hand resting lightly on his shoulder. 'If she loves Nate, why would she try and kill him? It makes no sense.'

'He's not interested in her,' Linus said. 'Right?'

Nate nodded. 'Of course.'

'Hell hath no fury and all that,' Linus said, sitting down.

Nate swallowed, clearly trying to absorb this information.

No doubt about it, Acacia thought, this information has thrown our usually composed Nate.

Nate stood up. 'Did she… I mean did she…' He couldn't finish the sentence and sat back down.

Acacia saw Matt had gone pale, gripping his mug of tea tightly. She went and sat next to him, placed her hand on his arm, then put her arm round his shoulders.

'Nate, we'll discuss this more in private, okay?' Linus said. He steered Nate into Acacia's work area.

Morgan came over to Matt and Acacia. 'You okay, Cuz?'

Matt nodded dumbly. 'You?'

'Not really, no. I feel such guilt, knowing Wiladelle is my mother and what she's done and is doing,' Morgan said.

'Not your fault, Cuz,' Matt said.

Acacia gave Morgan's hand a squeeze, then went to brew more coffee and tea. She saw Nate and Linus talking intently and couldn't help overhearing some of their conversation.

Nate's eyes blazed. 'Did she definitely kill Eliza and Raphael?'

Linus nodded, calm and business-like. 'Pretty sure she did, yep.'

'Did she feed Eliza and me false information so we'd split up?'

Again, Linus nodded. 'Well, ninety-nine per cent sure on that.'

'She altered the course of my life,' Nate said. 'She lied and manipulated Eliza and me. And she murdered Eliza and Raphael. She's going to have to pay for this.'

*

Jefferson lounged on a bench in the square, watching the bookshop, trying to get a feel for the place.

'Seems a pretty mixed age group,' Garrick said to Jefferson, smiling at a woman who batted her eyelashes at him. His blond hair, blue eyes and open, friendly face were highly deceiving. He was not what he appeared to be.

Jefferson nodded. 'Although a lot of them seem to be twenties to thirties.'

'Hmm,' Garrick said. 'Maybe we can pick up a couple of women while we're at it.'

Jefferson sighed. He had known Garrick would be a problem. 'We're here on business. Keep your eyes on the bookshop.'

Jefferson, tall, dark and extremely attractive to the opposite sex, ignored his seemingly magnetic pull on women. This, of course, only made the attraction stronger. But he concentrated mainly on his work and his witchcraft. Wiladelle had recruited him and Garrick recently, and he found the project intriguing.

They walked into the shop and began browsing the shelves, stopping at the metaphysical section. Jefferson found an interesting book. He held it up to show Garrick, who just shrugged.

Matt rang up the book Jefferson put on the counter, and chatted to him. 'There's free coffee for customers if you want?'

'Great,' Jefferson said. 'Thanks.'

Matt joined Jefferson in the coffee area. Both businessmen, both readers, they had a good discussion.

Justin's eyes were following Garrick. And Jefferson noticed. 'Can I help you find anything?' Justin asked.

'Probably not,' Garrick said. 'How long have you worked here?'

'Years,' Justin said. 'I wouldn't work anywhere else.'

Garrick frowned. 'Really?' Then he saw two attractive young women in the health section. 'Oh, right. I guess you get a lot of interesting women in here.'

Although Jefferson couldn't hear their conversation, he saw Garrick's eyes on a trim, smart young woman, and he could imagine the conversation. He'd have to distract Garrick before Justin smelled a rat.

Jefferson waved Garrick over. 'Find anything interesting?'

'Yeah, right.'

'Join us for coffee?' Jefferson asked. He poured coffee for Garrick, who sat next to Matt.

Justin went back to the counter.

Jefferson's mind went into overdrive. He should've used the *Conceal* spell on him and Garrick before they entered the shop. Darn it. He didn't want anyone to know they were witches. A good chance to try the *Befuddle* spell on Matt and Justin, too. He'd wanted to use that for a long time. It would be interesting to see what effect it had.

'Excuse me, Matt,' Jefferson said. 'Garrick? Can I have a quick word?' He turned back to Matt. 'Just remembered an important phone call I have to make. I'll be right back.'

Garrick's mouth opened, ready to deliver a sarcastic diatribe. Jefferson caught his eye, and Garrick followed him outside. Jefferson surreptitiously chanted the *Conceal* spell over himself and Garrick.

'We should have done that before we went in.'

Jefferson swallowed a smart reply, and they rejoined Matt in the coffee area. Jefferson leaned over and whispered the *Befuddle* spell to Matt, gripping his wand in his pocket. Momentarily surprised, Matt started laughing. Soon Matt and Garrick were laughing at silly things. Jefferson smiled. It had worked well. He could see Justin watching and frowning, though. Justin would have to be dealt with too.

Jefferson waited until Justin finished serving a customer, and then he headed in his direction. Choosing his moment carefully, he repeated the *Befuddle* spell, and within a few minutes Justin chatted easily with him.

*

Upstairs, an agitated Tiger paced up and down. Acacia also sensed something wrong. She went down into the bookshop to talk to Matt and saw him chatting with two attractive men. She felt as if someone had thrown cold water in her face. She staggered slightly, and caught hold of a bookshelf. Ah, she thought. Dark wizards. Matt saw her and waved her over.

'Hey, Acacia,' Matt said. 'This is Jefferson and Garrick. They're new customers. We're going out for a drink later. Want to come?'

'Hello,' Acacia said, coldly polite. 'No thank you, Matt. I have lots of things to do this evening. You go and enjoy yourself. We'll talk later.'

'Okay,' Matt shrugged his shoulders. 'Women. Can't live with them, can't live without them.' The three men laughed, and Acacia went back upstairs.

Acacia found Tabitha in her room. 'There's a problem. Two dark wizards are downstairs talking to Matt. They've hoodwinked him. I think they used the *Conceal* spell on themselves. I got the usual warning our family gets. And that spell never works on us, does it? But there's something else. I think some sort of confusion spell has been used on both Matt and Justin. They're acting strangely.'

'Oh dear,' Tabitha said. 'We need to find out what the spell is. This could be tricky.'

TWENTY-SEVEN

Jett watched Matt leave his desk, get coffee, and then settle back to his computer work.

A slow anger built inside him. Jett had had ambitions, but his life had been cut short. His eyes narrowed. Matt was twenty-six, happily married, ran a successful bookshop, had friends and family. Jett was stuck at the age of sixteen, drifting from one place to another, lost.

Matt was absorbed in his work, so Jett moved to the door and knocked. Matt got up to see if anyone was there. No one. Matt went over to see Justin. Jett saw Justin shake his head, no.

Jett took out the piece of paper he'd scribbled the spell on. Would it work? He'd never used magic before. But then until recently he'd not been able to manoeuvre physical objects either. He stood over Matt's coffee mug and chanted the spell.

Matt came back, and sat down, reading his notes and checking the computer screen. Jett moved away and waited, holding his breath.

Matt picked up his mug and sipped his coffee. Silently, he clutched his throat and slumped forward.

Jett smiled. Maybe Matt wouldn't wake up? He could but hope. His thoughts drifted, and he left.

*

Justin was serving customers and working on a new book display in between sales. He glanced at the clock. Matt usually came out of the office by 10am. It was now ten thirty, and no sign of him. He went and knocked on the office door. Silence. He knocked again. No sound. He tentatively pushed the door open, and saw Matt lying with his head on the keyboard. He went over and felt Matt's pulse. It was very faint. He stood there frozen for a second before adrenaline kicked in, and he picked up the phone and called the flat upstairs.

'Acacia? Is Tabitha up there with you? Can you both come down? Something's wrong with Matt. I don't know if I should call an ambulance.'

*

Acacia and Tabitha rushed into the office. Acacia went over to Matt and spoke to him, but got no answer. She sat next to him, holding his hand, her eyes begging her aunt to make it alright.

Tabitha saw the coffee mug on the desk and picked it up, sniffing at the contents. 'I think I know what this is.' She gently lifted Matt's face up with one hand and moved the other hand over his head and neck murmuring what sounded like Latin.

Matt stirred slightly.

'Can you bring me a mug of water, please?' she asked Justin.

Acacia was still holding Matt's hand, tears falling, making her mascara run.

Justin handed the mug to Tabitha, and she waved her hand over it, chanting more Latin.

'Matt, sip some of this water for me.'

Matt didn't answer. Tabitha dipped her fingers in the water and wiped some on his lips. She motioned to Acacia, and Acacia dipped her fingers in the water and gently pushed Matt's mouth open so some went in.

Matt swallowed, and brought his head up a little. 'What happened?'

'Please can you drink a little water, Matt?' Tabitha said.

Matt frowned, feeling woozy. He took the mug of water Tabitha held out to him and took a sip. The wooziness eased a little. He took another sip, and then sat up straighter.

Tabitha sighed, relieved. 'That's working. Good. But you'll need to rest up for a few days, Matt.'

Matt saw Acacia's tearstained face, then, to Acacia's dismay, he edged away from her and frowned.

'What's going on?' Matt asked.

'Someone poisoned your coffee, Matt,' Tabitha said, 'with a spell. I've reversed it, but it will take time to recover.'

Justin helped Matt upstairs, while Acacia minded the bookshop.

'Wiladelle can't get in,' Matt said to Justin, 'so who poisoned my coffee?'

'I really don't know,' Justin said, 'but you need to rest. I'll call Uncle Peter, let him know.'

'Hmm,' Matt said, as his head touched his pillow and he fell asleep. He had nightmares that Peter and Acacia were trying to kill him. He tossed and turned, and slept fitfully for hours.

Acacia made fresh coffee for Tabitha, and then waited as her aunt called Peter.

'Who could have done this?' Peter asked Tabitha on the phone. 'It must've been one of Wiladelle's associates, but we can't keep everyone out of the bookshop or Matt'll have no business.'

'I don't know,' Tabitha said. 'It was a very basic, but nasty spell. I'd say it must've been Jefferson or Garrick, but Justin says they haven't been in this morning.'

Matt woke up and used the bathroom.

Acacia asked him if he wanted anything. Matt eyed her suspiciously, edged away from her, and said no.

Acacia frowned. Surely Matt couldn't think she had anything to do with this?

*

Peter nodded, phone to his ear. 'I know what you mean, Milton, and I agree. I'll have a word with Nate. There's no point him leaving the South West. Wiladelle will only follow him.'

'And she'll still come after us, because that's who she is,' Milton said.

'Yes, you're right. I'll send an email and get everyone round here this evening. We need to start making headway.' Peter sighed. Just as he opened the cupboard where the vacuum cleaner lived, the phone rang again. 'Hello?' He grinned broadly. 'Hi, there. What are you doing today? Well, would you like to come over? I'm emailing the group for a get together this evening. It'd be great if you'd help me get some food ready. Right now? That would be great, Tabitha. See you in about fifteen minutes.'

*

Tabitha placed the phone down on the kitchen worktop. 'I'm going over to Peter's place, dear,' Tabitha said. 'Is it okay to use your car?' Acacia nodded. 'We don't seem to be progressing with this *Wiladelle* problem. There's going to be a meeting at Peter's tonight.'

Acacia frowned.

'You don't want to tell Matt?' Tabitha nodded her understanding.

Acacia shook her head.

'I expect Peter's already sent the email by now.'

Acacia gazed at the floor. 'Talking to him about anything is difficult these days. Matt and Justin don't seem to trust me now, and I'm afraid I don't trust them either.' A ping on Acacia's laptop, an email to the group. Too late. Matt and Justin were included.

Tabitha studied Acacia. She knew her niece hadn't slept much since the introduction of Jefferson and Garrick.

'I'll talk to Peter about getting that spell off Matt and Justin, and I'll call my group and see if they've found anything to help.'

*

That evening, rain fell from the sky as if someone above was emptying the bath. Acacia sat in Matt's car with him and

243

Justin, the atmosphere strained. She pulled a tissue out of her pocket to wipe the steam off the car window, and watched the scenery as they drove by.

Acacia knocked on Peter's door, and he opened it to find them dripping. Tabitha handed them a towel each, and took their damp coats.

Linus came in carrying a flip chart. Acacia followed him, interested to know his plans. Each sheet contained details of individual adversaries. Good idea, she thought.

Linus started his presentation, but Matt and Justin were laughing and joking in the corner of the room, only listening sporadically to what Linus had to say. She felt her face grow hot with embarrassment. Linus had spent a lot of time on this.

'So you see,' Linus continued, 'Ezra's weakness is the fact that he's besotted with Savannah. I don't know how we can use that at present, but it's worth remembering. If Savannah is in danger, Ezra will be right there. Maybe we could lure Savannah into a trap and Ezra would follow, that way we could deal with two of them at once.'

Matt frowned. 'I don't see why we have to do this. Why don't we just leave it alone and see what happens?'

Justin spoke up. 'Yes, I agree with Matt. Let's give this up.'

Peter's face registered disbelief at what he was hearing.

'We've taken serious injuries to Morgan, then Nate, and now you, Matt,' Samantha said. 'Why should we forget about that? Do you think it's going to stop?'

'I don't think my *accident* had anything to do with Wiladelle or her friends,' Matt said, narrowing his eyes at Acacia.

Acacia's mouth opened, and stayed that way until she pulled herself together and closed it.

Linus gave Peter a look, and turned the flip chart to the wall. 'Maybe you're right, Matt. Let's forget about it for now.'

The rest of the group were clearly confused, and sat in groups talking quietly. Matt and Justin though were tucking into some quiche, laughing and joking again.

Acacia walked over to Tabitha and Peter.

'You're right, Acacia,' Peter said quietly. 'We'll have to exclude Matt and Justin from any meetings until that spell is removed from them. Think of something to get Matt and Justin out of here so I can talk to the group.'

Acacia's mind went blank. She turned to her aunt.

'The silent alarm?' Tabitha suggested.

Acacia nodded and went over to Matt, holding up her mobile phone. 'The silent alarm has gone off at the bookshop. Could you two go and check it out? I don't really want to leave just yet.'

'Sure,' Matt and Justin said together, eager to go. They grabbed their coats and waved goodbye to the group in general, studiously ignoring Acacia.

Once they'd seen Matt's car drive away, Peter clapped his hands. 'You obviously noticed something wrong with Matt and Justin. We're going to have to exclude them from meetings for a while.'

Acacia stood up. 'Two dark wizards came into the shop the other day. I'm pretty sure they cast a spell on Matt and Justin. The four of them have been out every night since then. Tabitha and I no longer trust Matt and Justin. So far, we haven't come up with a way to remove the spell, mainly because we don't know the spell used.'

'Matt barely acknowledged me this evening,' Nate said.

'I've only just found out I've got a son. Now it seems I'm in danger of losing him to the other side.'

'Nate,' Peter said. 'Don't think about leaving the South West. It won't work. Wiladelle would only follow you. And she'd still come after us. You may be the catalyst, but she thrives on conflict. It's exciting for her to think about destroying us. We have to get rid of them all.'

Acacia felt extremely uncomfortable hearing this. Why did magic have to play such a role in their lives? Why couldn't things go back to the way they were? And she felt she'd lost Matt. She wanted her husband back.

'I know it's disappointing and worrying,' Linus said, 'but we have to face the fact we've lost Matt and Justin for the time being. Don't pass any information to them until we find a way of removing that spell.'

'So, now we have two main problems,' Peter said. 'We have to find out how to remove that spell from Matt and Justin, and we have to start luring Wiladelle's people into situations where we can use *Repulse* and *Metamorphosis*.'

Acacia poured herself a stiff drink. Tabitha would drive them home.

'Why not assign us to named adversaries?' Tabitha asked. 'That way we're focused on one or two people each.'

'Great idea,' Peter said. 'Who wants to concentrate on Ezra?'

TWENTY-EIGHT

'You only have four weeks before you have to go back to America?' Acacia said, stunned.

'You know how it works, Acacia,' Tabitha said. 'You lived in Canada for years, but you got citizenship. I could apply for an extension, but my focus is on solving this problem, not on paperwork.'

Acacia smiled at her aunt, but her eyes filled with tears. Acacia and her aunt had been apart so long, and she felt reluctant to let her go again. 'It's just gone so quickly. It doesn't seem like you've been here that long.'

Tabitha sighed. 'A whole lot of stuff has happened since I've been here. To me it seems longer than five months.'

Acacia changed the subject. 'Have you noticed that Tiger is avoiding Matt?'

'Of course.'

'Matt doesn't seem to have noticed. He's just not himself anymore.'

Tabitha squeezed Acacia's hand, and said, 'No. He isn't.'

'I don't know how much longer I can stay here, Tabitha. It's not home now.'

'I know what you mean. I don't know what to say. None of us have come up with the anti-spell.'

Acacia's words came out slowly. Her throat felt tight. 'I'm thinking of getting myself a flat, for Tiger and me. You could stay with us till you go back, of course. We'd love to have you.'

'Hang on for a bit longer, Acacia,' Tabitha said. 'Let's see what we come up with, okay?'

Acacia nodded. 'Going back to your six months being nearly up, why don't you at least try phoning the embassy and talking to someone about it?'

Tabitha smiled ruefully. 'And say what? That my niece is having a problem with dark wizards and I need to stay here to sort it out?'

'I see what you mean. We'll just have to bring this to a head within the next two to three weeks then, won't we?'

'We sure will.'

'What does Peter say about it?'

'Pretty much the same thing. He wants us to wrap this up, and then he wants to come to New England with me and stay there for six months.'

Acacia saw the wistful expression on her aunt's face. 'He does? That's wonderful.' She thought about them living in New England, in Tabitha's period home ten minutes' walk from the harbour. Tourists would be starting to arrive now. The town always got busy in the tourist season. And Christmas, with snow in the garden and a roaring wood fire, Peter meeting her friends.

'Yes,' Tabitha said, 'it will be so good to show Peter my New England home.'

Acacia wandered over to the window seat and gazed down at the town square. 'Who have you and Peter decided to deal with?'

'Garrick, first of all,' Tabitha said. 'Jefferson is the brains behind that duo. He's a cool customer, focused, clever, instinctive. But Garrick is hot headed, acts before he thinks. He should be easier to deal with than Jefferson. Peter and I are working on a strategy, which we hope to test out tomorrow.'

'Exciting stuff.' Acacia's could feel her stomach clench with anxiety, but she couldn't let her aunt know.

'You'll hear, one way or the other.'

'Are you worried about this?' Acacia asked. 'Surely you and Peter are more than a match for Garrick?'

'Yes, we are. But where Garrick is, Jefferson isn't usually far behind, and to deal with Jefferson will take more planning. We need to get Garrick on his own.'

'There's something else, isn't there?'

Tabitha sighed, brows together in concentration. 'There's something in the back of my mind telling me to go cautiously. I never ignore those feelings.'

'I think you should wear that green and black diamond necklace Elizabeth gave you. The one you found in Peter's attic. It's for protection, right? Wear it always until this is sorted out. I feel strongly about this, Tabitha.'

'You're right. Something unexpected is going to happen, I can sense it. Yes, I'll wear the necklace. Thanks, Acacia.' Tabitha hugged her niece and went to her room to get the necklace.

*

Tabitha unbuttoned her jacket. The day was getting warmer. She watched a delivery van unloading goods at the Co-op. She and Peter were waiting for Garrick and Jefferson to arrive. They didn't have long to wait.

Garrick walked over to one of the seats in the square, and Jefferson headed to the bookshop to talk to Matt.

Tabitha sat down next to Garrick. He glanced up. They'd all had strict instructions to leave Tabitha to Wiladelle. She saw confusion on his face. He watched the bookshop, as though willing Jefferson to come out, but there was no sign of him.

'All on your own, this morning?' Tabitha asked.

Peter came around the war memorial and sat the other side of Garrick, hemming him in. 'How about we go and have a chat?'

'No, thanks,' Garrick said. 'I'm quite happy here.' Garrick was watching a couple of sixteen-year-old girls over the road. One of them gave him a dazzling smile, and he smiled back.

'Much as we like it here,' Peter said, 'it really would be best if we had this conversation somewhere quiet – see that alleyway? We won't be disturbed there.'

Tabitha watched as Garrick considered the odds. He must've decided they were in his favour.

'Alright,' Garrick said. 'If you insist. Can you make it that far? It's a five-minute walk and you might get tired. I can see you're both OAPs.'

Tabitha laughed, delighted that Garrick thought she and Peter were too old to be a threat. He obviously didn't rate their experience and expertise.

The three of them walked to the alleyway. At the end was a treed area, and Tabitha sent up a prayer that it would be deserted.

At the end of the alley, Garrick turned his wand on Peter, but Peter was ready. Spells flew through the air. Tabitha's analytical mind was trying to read each attack. The green light from Garrick's wand smelt faintly of water lily. Yes, that was the *Break Bones* spell. Then a red light accompanied by a smell of fireworks – what was that? She pulled herself back from her scientific musings, and watched for an opening to use the *Repulse* spell. It came soon, and Tabitha was pleased to see Garrick lying on the ground, clutching his hand, his wand burning beside him.

Peter waved his wand and cast the spell – '*Metamorphosis!*'

Garrick's expression changed from anger and fright to one of surprise as he saw two luminous beings coming towards him. They were more than eight feet tall, both blond and blue eyed. An overwhelming sense of peace and goodness was emanating from them.

'Angels?' Garrick stammered.

They took hold of his arms firmly, saluted Peter and Tabitha, and carried Garrick upwards.

Peter and Tabitha had been so caught up in this, their first experience of the *Metamorphosis* spell, that they hadn't heard Jefferson running towards them.

'What have you done with Garrick?' he asked, wand held out towards them.

'He'll be fine,' Peter said. 'He's not dead.'

'What?'

'Your friend isn't dead,' Tabitha said. 'He's gone to another realm, that's all.'

Jefferson's expression underwent rapid change, first surprise, then curiosity, disbelief and finally anger in the space of a few seconds. He flourished his wand and hurled a spell at Tabitha, and she was thrown across the grass towards the woods, where she collided with a tree. She folded over onto the damp earth.

Peter ran across to Tabitha, and placed his hands underneath her head. She was breathing shallowly and trying to say something, but she was having trouble speaking.

Tabitha was trying to sit upright, but stopped when in her mind she heard the word *danger*. Frantically she grabbed Peter's arm, and opened her eyes wide, her face turned towards Jefferson.

Peter looked up in time to counter a *Disintegrate* spell from Jefferson, before Jefferson disappeared back into the alleyway, running towards his car.

'I'm fine,' Tabitha said, recovering, sitting up. 'Just a little bruised and dazed, that's all.'

'Your necklace looks red hot,' Peter said, leaning over to touch it. He pulled his hand away quickly as the heat hit his fingers.

'It doesn't feel hot to me. I think it saved my life.'

Peter pulled his mobile out of his jacket and called Acacia. 'Tabitha's fine. I'm taking her back to my place. In fact, I'll come over later and get her things. She can stay with me till she gets back to America.' He paused and listened to Acacia. 'Are you sure? Okay, if you want to bring her things over to my place that'd be great. Can you get away without Matt wondering where you're going? Good. See you later.'

'Acacia needs me with her at the moment, Peter,' Tabitha said. 'I really should stay with her until we've removed that spell from Matt and Justin.'

'And I need you with me. No arguments. Okay?'

Peter got Tabitha to her feet, and they walked slowly to

his car. 'This evening, I'm telling the group we're engaged. It's time we made it formal.'

Tabitha smiled, and kissed him. He squeezed her hand as they drove to his home. 'Where will we live?'

'How about six months in New England, and six months in Devon?'

'Sounds good to me.'

*

The sky was a dark, midnight blue, reminding Acacia of a velvet dress she'd had when she was younger. She bundled the last of Tabitha's things into her car. She felt desolate at the idea of being left alone with Matt. She knew Tiger wasn't happy anymore either. What could she do? She knew the answer, of course, but couldn't quite bring herself to leave. Not yet.

She drew up outside Peter's house, and immediately Peter and Tabitha came out to greet her. She and Peter belonged together. It felt right.

Unfortunately, seeing Peter and Tabitha made her think about her relationship with Matt. They'd always been close, but now they were just living in the same home. She reminded herself yet again that it wasn't Matt's fault. If only they could break that spell.

'Peter's cooking dinner and there's more than enough for three,' Tabitha said. 'Will you join us?'

'That's kind, but I'm not hungry.'

Tabitha gave her niece the once over, shepherding her inside. 'You've lost weight. You're not eating properly.'

Acacia studied the floor. 'I know. Okay, it'd be nice to have some company for dinner. Thank you.'

Peter grated cheese in the kitchen, and Tabitha poured herself and Acacia a glass of wine.

'One won't hurt,' Tabitha said, handing a glass to Acacia.

Acacia sipped the wine. 'The quiche smells good. I didn't realise Peter did real cooking.'

'He's quite the talent in the kitchen,' Tabitha said. 'And he cooks a lot of vegetarian stuff. The quiche today is vegetarian, of course.' Tabitha steered Acacia into the living room. 'Talking of talent, I think it's time you and I had a discussion about yours.'

'What do you mean?' Acacia frowned. 'Okay, I know I've not been cooking much lately and I used to love it, but, well, with Matt not being himself I've not felt like it.'

'Oh, honey, that's not what I mean,' Tabitha said, taking her hand as they sat on the sofa. 'You have other talents too, and you know it.'

'Do I?'

'Don't be coy. It doesn't suit you.' Tabitha laughed. 'Magic, of course.'

'Magic? Well, I'm psychic, but that's different, isn't it?'

Peter poured himself a glass of wine. He wanted to join them, but then he saw Tabitha's expression. He took his wine back into the kitchen.

'I know we don't usually discuss your parents,' Tabitha said, 'but you know how talented they were in that area.'

Acacia's eyes filled up, and she gulped some wine.

'Acacia, do you remember when you were about ten? You came to stay with me in New England.'

'Yes, of course I remember,' Acacia said. 'I should've stayed there. Or at least, when I emigrated I should've gone to America, not Canada. I love your home town. It's perfect.'

'I wouldn't say that,' Tabitha said – but her eyes said something else. She loved her place in New England. 'But I wanted to remind you of the time you flew. Do you remember that?'

'Flew?' Acacia frowned. 'What do you mean?'

'My cat got stuck in the tree. Darkness had fallen, and I never leave my cats out at night. You were trying to get him in. Snow and darkness, and then a coyote started to howl.'

'Timmy? That lovely black and white cat?'

'That's the one. You reached up as high as you could, but you couldn't get to him. I said I'd go and get a stepladder.'

'Yes, I remember.'

'Do you remember what happened next?'

'I remember reaching out and touching his foot. Then I stretched some more and I grabbed him. I brought him back into the house.'

'That branch Timmy had reached was six feet from the ground, Acacia.'

'What?'

'You were about four feet at that age, I think.'

'How?'

'You stretched up until your legs left the floor, and then you hovered there until you reached Timmy. Then you gently floated back to the ground and came inside. I watched you do it. You didn't realise what you'd done.'

'You mean my feet left the ground so I could get Timmy?'

'That's when a lot of us realise we're magical, Acacia. When we're trying to help people or animals and our natural instincts take over. We find we're doing things regular folk can't do.'

'You said flew, though?'

'Well, kind of flying, or hovering,' Tabitha said.

'Dinner's ready,' Peter called.

Acacia and Tabitha joined him in the dining room, and the three of them were laughing and chatting, enjoying each other's company and the food. She sighed. She thought she'd found a home with Matt and Tiger. She knew Tara and Sam still loved her, and so did Tiger, but had she lost Matt for good?

Tabitha saw Acacia's expression change from one of joy to one of sadness. 'We will figure this thing out with Matt and Justin.'

'Oh, Tabitha, I'm so glad you're here.'

'Me too, sweetie,' Tabitha said. 'Now, what about your magical talents? Just because something bad happened to your parents through magic, doesn't mean you should throw it all out.'

Peter studied Tabitha. She'd never told him what had happened to Acacia's parents.

'I know you're right, especially with what's going on at the moment,' Acacia said. 'It just makes me feel uncomfortable. I'm not ready.'

Tabitha nodded, but Acacia could tell she was sad.

'And, I'm afraid to see what I can do. Mum was prolific, always making new spells and doing things no one had done before.'

'Your dad had as much talent as your mum,' Tabitha said. 'You get your reticence from him, Acacia. He quietly went about saving people and animals without even acknowledging it. Your mum got in the spotlight more, and that's what attracted attention from unwanted sources. Dark sources.'

256

Peter cleared the dishes off the table, and stayed in the kitchen clearing up.

'You know, Acacia, Peter and I are your family too. Just because your parents aren't around, and Matt is playing up, doesn't mean you're not wanted and loved. You're loved by Peter and me, and you'll always have a home with us, wherever we are. Remember that. If we can't bring Matt back from the brink, you can come here. And bring Tiger with you. We both love him too.'

Peter placed some fresh fruit salad and clotted cream on the table. 'We'll break that spell, Acacia. Don't worry. Nate's coming over tomorrow to work with me and Tabitha. And he's bringing Morgan with him. Between us, we'll do it. You'll see.'

'And another thing,' Tabitha said. She went to fetch her purse. Inside she located a small box. She opened its lid and there, nestled in a bed of black velvet, sat a beautiful ring, with a big emerald in the centre, diamonds surrounding it. She slid it on the third finger of her left hand. 'It's official.'

Acacia hugged her aunt and then Peter. At last. Something to be happy about.

TWENTY-NINE

Acacia felt threatened by Matt's behaviour and language. She backed away.

'What's happened to Garrick then?' Matt asked angrily. 'Peter used some kind of spell on him, and he disappeared. He'd done nothing to Peter. Why did Peter do that?'

'Matt, Peter was defending himself. He used a spell to send Garrick somewhere in heaven where he'll be changed for the better. He's not dead. Peter didn't kill him.'

'What do you mean, *changed for the better*?' Matt paced up and down, then stopped and moved to within a couple of inches of Acacia's face. 'He didn't need changing. I don't want Peter coming in this shop or our flat ever again, and Justin agrees. Right, Justin?'

Justin nodded, and Acacia noticed how depressed and withdrawn Justin looked. He now showed no interest in the books they sold or the authors.

'And that aunt of yours,' Matt continued, 'I never want to see her again. Got it?'

Acacia nodded, and went upstairs to their flat.

She gazed around at their belongings, all much loved, and all chosen with care. The pink, grey and white Persian rug in the living room, and the coffee table they'd bought on a trip to London. They'd had such fun on that trip. The blue and white Wedgewood ornaments, each piece a gift from Matt on birthdays and Christmas. The copper bottomed saucepans hanging from a beam in the kitchen ceiling, well used pans. She'd always loved cooking. Now she had no interest in cooking or eating.

She switched her computer on and considered the list of reports waiting to be typed. She just couldn't face it. She switched the computer off again.

Tiger came over and jumped on her desk, watching her intently.

'I know, Tiger, I know. I just can't bring myself to leave though. You think we should go, don't you?'

'Miaow,' Tiger responded, placing his paw on her hand.

'I'll go down and see if I can get any sense out of Justin. I just want to be sure I'm doing the right thing. If so, I'll call Peter and Tabitha, okay?'

Tiger nuzzled his face against Acacia's and sat on her open diary, awaiting her decision.

Acacia took a deep breath, blew her nose, and walked back downstairs. Just as she reached the bookshop door she heard Jefferson talking to Matt and Justin.

'Do you really think you can trust Acacia? She's Tabitha's niece, after all. And she's hiding something, I know she is. You can't trust her, Matt. Don't tell her anything. Look, tonight Wiladelle is holding a meeting of our group. I'd like you both to come with me. You trust me, don't you?'

Acacia peered through the crack in the door. Matt and Justin both nodded.

'I'll pick you up at 7pm then, okay?'

Again Matt and Justin nodded. Jefferson left the shop. Matt and Justin went back to the shop counter to serve a customer.

Acacia sighed. Decision made, she crept back upstairs, and dialled Peter's number on her mobile. 'Peter? Jefferson has invited Matt and Justin to a meeting with Wiladelle and her group, and they've agreed to go. It's no longer safe for me and Tiger here. Can we stay with you for a while? Tabitha said she thought it would be okay if we needed to.'

'Oh, Acacia, I'm so sorry,' Peter said, 'but, Nate's here with Morgan. We're working on an anti-spell. They'll come over and get you in Nate's Range Rover. You can get a lot of stuff in the back of that, and Matt and Justin won't try and stop you if Nate and Morgan are there. Okay? They'll be with you in fifteen minutes. Pack a quick suitcase, and Nate and Morgan will come up to the flat and get you and Tiger. Alright?'

Acacia placed the phone on the kitchen worktop, and started crying. 'No time for that, idiot,' she chided herself, wiping her eyes with a tissue. 'Get a suitcase packed, quick.'

She moved Tiger's scratching post and bed to the door, which she locked in case Matt tried to get in. Then she shoved toiletries into a bag, and underwear and clothes into a suitcase. She packed up her laptop and work files in a large carrier bag, and tucked her purse and mobile into her handbag. About fifteen minutes passed before a knock at the door.

'Acacia, it's me, Nate. I've got Morgan with me.'

Acacia opened the door, and fell into Nate's arms. He

hugged her. Morgan patted her shoulder, then picked up Tiger, hugged him and gently placed him into his carrying box, then picked up his scratching post.

Between the three of them they carried Acacia and Tiger's basic belongings downstairs and out the door of the shop.

Matt and Justin watched this open-mouthed. 'Not even going to say goodbye?' Matt called.

Acacia turned a tearstained face to Matt but said nothing. She just stared at him for a few seconds. Then she left the bookshop, and the Range Rover drove away, taking Acacia and Tiger out of Matt's life.

*

Matt watched Wiladelle. She was attractive, he could see that, but something about her expression wasn't quite right. As if her eyes and her brain were not in agreement with each other. Maybe a touch mentally unstable?

'Nice to meet you at last, Matt and Justin,' Wiladelle said.

Matt nodded. 'You're my aunt, right?'

'I am indeed,' Wiladelle said. 'So we should be allies, not enemies.'

A small part of Matt's logical mind was now assessing Wiladelle. She reminded him of a cat watching a mouse. A small voice in his head asked if he was the mouse. He ignored it.

Wiladelle turned to Justin. 'And you're the nephew of the famous Peter Fairbrother?'

'Yes,' Justin said quietly.

'Well, we'll have to see if we can turn you into our kind of wizard, then, won't we?' She laughed, and the group chuckled agreement.

Wiladelle held up her hand, and the laughing stopped. 'You've been hoodwinked by Acacia and Tabitha. We need to let you know what we're all about. Nothing concealed here, nothing hidden. What do you want to ask us?'

'What's the purpose of this group?' Justin asked.

'Good question,' Wiladelle said. 'Maybe Jefferson can answer that.'

Matt could see Wiladelle trying not to laugh. Was she finding this funny? The voice inside his head gave clear warning, but he stifled it. He felt a headache coming on.

'Our purpose is the advancement of knowledge,' Jefferson said. 'We're all on a learning curve. We seek information about new spells, all things magical.'

'Anyone want to add anything?' Wiladelle asked.

'We need to stop anyone who gets in our way,' Warwick said.

Matt admired Warwick's black shirt and blue silk tie. He looked the part, Matt thought, sophisticated, slightly dangerous. He emanated self-confidence. People listened when Warwick spoke.

'What do you mean by "stop anyone who gets in our way"?' Justin asked.

'We persuade them to leave us to get on with our business,' Warwick replied calmly.

'What tactics do you use?'

'We just talk to them usually,' Warwick lied. 'Most people know what we're about. We only want to increase our knowledge and where possible add to the numbers of our group.'

Justin was about to ask another question, but Wiladelle spoke. 'Savannah, what did you find out about Acacia that you wanted to share?'

Matt felt his heart skip a beat. Then he remembered that Acacia had left him, and taken Tiger with her. He thought maybe Morgan and Acacia were an item now. He'd been betrayed by his cousin *and* his wife.

'Yes, you're right about Acacia, Wiladelle,' Savannah said. 'She knows the dark arts alright. She just doesn't let anyone know.'

Matt frowned. His wife knew the dark arts? He tried to remember if he'd ever witnessed anything out of the ordinary. No – he couldn't remember one instance. He must be wrong though. Wiladelle and Savannah were saying Acacia knew the dark arts. They must be right. His head started to throb.

'And what about Nate Parish?' Wiladelle asked. 'He's not really Matt's biological father, is he?' Wiladelle smiled at the lie.

'No, he isn't,' Savannah turned to Matt. 'Those DNA tests were fixed, Matt. Nate's not your father.'

Matt felt tears in danger of falling, so he pushed his fringe out of his eyes, surreptitiously wiping his face at the same time.

'Now, as the people in Peter's group have shown active hostility towards us,' Wiladelle said, 'and they've killed two of us, we have no alternative. Much as we don't want to do it, we have to take action. I think it's retribution time.'

The group shouted a loud *yes*.

'Who wants to kill Acacia?' Wiladelle turned to Matt. 'It could be your privilege, Matt. She's your wife. You could make it as quick or as slow as you want.'

Matt opened his mouth to answer, but no words came out. His brain seemed to be holding a war with itself. The throbbing became more insistent.

Wiladelle continued. 'And who's going to kill Peter? It has to be someone experienced.' She turned to Stewart. 'What do you think, Stewart? Are you interested?'

He made a little bow. 'It would be my privilege.' He turned to Matt and Justin. 'It's a shame, but it has to be done.'

Matt noticed a smirk on Stewart's face before he turned away. The fight inside Matt's brain ramped up a notch.

'Right,' Wiladelle said. 'As you know, Tabitha is mine. No one touches her but me.'

Matt could tell people were excited and trying to hide it. A treacherous thought crept through his mind. Were they setting him and Justin up? The thought angered him. Why would he think that? Wiladelle was his aunt. These people had welcomed him and Justin.

'Well, Matt?' Wiladelle said. 'I take it you're with us? Will you kill Acacia? Or should I assign Jefferson that honour?'

'I'll do it,' Matt said. 'She's betrayed me. She has to pay for that.'

*

Jett watched as Matt and Justin left Wiladelle's group meeting. He felt confused. Didn't Wiladelle want to kill Matt and his friends?

Jett felt increasingly conflicted. Matt had been his friend, and the friendship had only stopped when Jett died in an accident at a cricket match. He should warn Matt about Wiladelle. But surely Matt knew already?

Matt and Justin were driving back to the bookshop. The two of them seemed close, they laughed and chatted all the way home, oblivious to the fact that Jett sat in the backseat listening to their conversation.

'You're not really going to kill Acacia, are you?' Justin asked.

'I'm not sure,' Matt said, brushing his fringe out of his eyes. 'Wiladelle wants me to. She told me after the meeting that I was right to think Morgan and Acacia have been seeing each other. She says they've been having an affair for months. I've been a fool.'

*

Justin's head felt strange. It felt as though cotton wool was being pulled out of his brain. A light went on in his head.

'Matt, I think Wiladelle and her group are trying to trick us.'

'Don't you start,' Matt said, furious. 'I've had enough of that from Acacia and your uncle.'

'Sorry,' Justin said, realising Matt wouldn't believe him. 'It's been a difficult day. A lot to take in.'

Matt nodded, then geared up.

*

Back at the bookshop, Justin waited till Matt started a stock check, then pulled out his mobile and called Peter.

'Uncle Peter,' Justin said, 'I'm so sorry. It's like I've just woken up. We've had a spell on us, haven't we? Matt and I?'

'Justin!' Peter exclaimed. 'You're back. What a relief. How did you get free of it? We're still working on the anti-spell.'

'I've no idea. Maybe the spell only half hit me or something? Matt's still under its influence.'

'Try to keep Matt out of trouble while we work on this anti-spell. It's proving difficult. I wish I knew how you'd shaken it off.'

'You don't think…' Justin frowned, chewing his lip. 'No, that couldn't work, could it?'

'What? What are you thinking?'

'Grandma. Did she know I wasn't quite right?'

'Yes. She went into the bookshop last week and said you were being an ass. She said you acted strangely.'

'I see,' Justin said. 'Do you think grandma used the power of prayer?'

'Hmm. Maybe we've been going about this the wrong way. Maybe this spell needs a higher power to remove it. If so, we should get Tara involved for Matt. I'll talk to Tabitha, Nate and Morgan and see what they have to say. I'll ring your grandma first though and ask if she's been praying for you, and if so tell her the prayers were answered.'

'Matt's calling for me,' Justin said. 'I'd better go. I'll call you again. Call me on my mobile if you have any news.'

'Justin, there you are,' Matt said. 'Did I ever tell you about my friend, Jett?'

'No,' Justin said, a little thrown by the topic. 'Does he live in Holsworthy?'

'He used to. He's dead now.'

'What?'

'Never mind. I haven't heard anything since he died, but then I wouldn't, would I? I mean, it was my fault he died. Well, the coroner said a freak accident. Anyway, he suddenly appeared and said he wanted us to go to the quay at Bideford. He has something important to show us.'

'Are you sure?'

'Yes. Get your coat.'

THIRTY

Jett watched Matt and Justin lock up and head into Bideford just as the sun slid behind the horizon. The sky exhibited a blend of pinks, reds and dark blues. All quiet, no one else on the quay. Usually there were dog walkers and joggers at that time of the evening. Not tonight, though.

Matt and Justin sat on one of the benches, gazing out at the water and the boats bobbing up and down. They'd been waiting for an hour and still no sign of Jett, because Jett had climbed under the car and was doing something to the brake cable. He smiled. This stuff seemed easier than he remembered. As a teenager, he'd worked on his dad's car with him. Another wave of resentment hit him. If Matt hadn't bowled so fast, he'd still be alive and enjoying time with his parents and friends. Matt's fault, all of it. He finished his work and stood near them, watching.

'Doesn't look like he's coming,' Justin said. 'Let's go.'

Matt frowned. 'I don't understand it. He definitely said to meet him here.'

Jett sat in the backseat, unobserved again. They drove home in silence, each with their own thoughts.

Matt tried to slow down as he approached a tight bend, but the brakes wouldn't work. He pumped them. Nothing. The car veered to the left.

Jett smiled and flew away, job done.

*

'Jump out!' Justin shouted at Matt, fighting with his seatbelt.

Justin and Matt got their seatbelts off and rolled out of their respective car doors before the car plunged down the hill, into the muddy, fast flowing water below.

Justin sat up, dazed. He put his hand on his head, and it felt wet. He held out his hand – it was covered in blood. He tried to stand up and couldn't. What about Matt? He couldn't see him. Then he heard a groan.

Matt was hanging over the edge of the hill. Luckily his foot had caught under a tree, keeping him from falling down the bank into the water.

Justin tried to move towards Matt, but he went dizzy and had to stop.

'This is a pickle,' Justin said, trying to reach for his mobile phone and instead falling into unconsciousness.

*

'Something's wrong,' Acacia said to Peter and Tabitha. 'Matt's in trouble. I feel it. And look at Tiger!'

Tiger paced up and down, alternately jumping on Acacia's lap and running to the door.

'You're right,' Tabitha said. 'We should go to the bookshop.'

Peter reached for his coat.

'I think you should stay here, Peter. Tiger shouldn't be left alone,' Tabitha said. 'Acacia and I will go. Don't worry, we'll be vigilant.'

*

Acacia gazed up into a clear, dark blue sky. All the stars were visible, a beautiful evening – but she felt a sense of dread. She and Tabitha got into the car, and she pulled out of the driveway. Then she stopped.

'He's not at the bookshop,' Acacia said. 'I'm just going to follow my instincts, okay?'

Tabitha nodded.

Acacia seemed to be picking up some kind of telepathic signal.

They found themselves on the road to Bideford, and as they turned a tight corner Acacia instinctively slowed down and pulled into a layby. They couldn't see Matt's car, but Acacia felt it was the right place, so she and Tabitha got out. They saw tyre tracks but nothing else. Then Acacia heard a noise. She went towards it and found Justin in some bushes trying to pull himself into a sitting position.

'Justin, are you alright?' Acacia asked.

Justin gazed blankly at her.

Tabitha felt his pulse. 'Pulse is steady, but that's a nasty gash on your head. We need to get you to the hospital. It should be cleaned and stitched.'

'Where's Matt?' Acacia asked.

Justin's eyes widened as he remembered. 'He's hanging over the edge of the cliff!'

Acacia and Tabitha rushed over to where Justin pointed. As they got nearer they saw a leg under a heavy tree branch, and they could see the rest of Matt's body resting on a rock overlooking the river.

Acacia dialled 999 while Tabitha spoke to Matt, trying to get a response.

'Is he okay?'

'He's unconscious,' Tabitha said. She wanted to gauge his injuries, but the cliff didn't seem safe, and she was worried if she added her weight to the edge, it might give way and send them both down the rock face.

'Is he stable there? Is that tree strong enough to stop him falling?'

'For the moment, yes. Did they say how long they'd be?'

'Fifteen minutes.'

Tabitha kept talking to Matt, telling him help was on the way, and Acacia went and sat with Justin, her arm round his shoulders.

Flashing lights and sirens heralded the arrival of the emergency services. Paramedics got Justin into an ambulance, while firefighters secured themselves to rocks and trees and managed to reach Matt, hooking a harness around him and slowly bringing him back to safety. They checked out Matt, lifted him onto a stretcher, and he joined Justin in the ambulance.

Acacia and Tabitha followed the ambulance to the hospital and waited while Matt and Justin were assessed. Justin was released after being stitched up, and the three of them stood around Matt's bed as his eyes slowly opened.

Matt saw Acacia, Tabitha and Justin. He frowned. Why were Acacia and Tabitha there?

'What's going on?' he asked Justin, ignoring Acacia and Tabitha.

'We were in a car accident,' Justin said. 'Acacia and Tabitha found us and called the emergency services. If they hadn't come, we might not have made it.'

Matt realised Acacia was holding his hand. He pulled his hand away. An enemy wouldn't have saved them, so why had she? He watched Tabitha on the phone to Peter. She appeared upset. Nothing seemed as concrete as it had before. The car accident had somehow shaken some of the spell off him.

'Matt,' Justin repeated, 'Acacia and Tabitha found us and called the emergency services.'

'How did they know where we were?' Matt asked, narrowing his eyes suspiciously.

'I love you,' Acacia said. 'I followed my instincts. I sensed the route you'd taken. I tracked you.'

'That was no accident,' Tabitha said. 'It's time to ask who your friends are, Matt.'

*

'They're still alive?' Wiladelle asked. 'You're sure?'

'I'm sure,' Warwick answered.

'Darn it. I thought we'd got rid of them. How did the accident happen, does anyone know?'

'No one knows,' Warwick said. 'It wasn't one of our group, that's for sure.'

'Shame. Well, we still have enemies to dispose of. Let's review our strategy. Maybe we should up the game plan.'

THIRTY-ONE

Acacia sat on a bench overlooking the sea. Wild grasses and flowers surrounded the bench, and bees hummed as they hopped from flower to flower. She gazed at the water, watching it rise and fall. She loved the sea. She'd always been a little claustrophobic, and so living near the sea gave her a feeling of escape if she needed it. She smiled. Self-knowledge is a wonderful thing, she thought as she contemplated the scene around her.

Seagulls cawed overhead. She could see a small fishing boat hauling in a net. More gulls were bobbing up and down on the sea next to the boat, some called to friends, 'Breakfast!'

The ocean breeze caressed her face, and she smelt cigarette smoke. 'Hi, granddad,' she said, shifting her gaze from the sea to the space on the bench beside her. No answer, but she smelt his aftershave, Old Spice. 'Thanks for being there for me,' she said. Still no response, but she felt better knowing her granddad had come, because she knew absolutely that he was there. 'I can't seem to pull myself out of this fug I'm in,' she said. 'Matt and Justin nearly died, you know. I shouldn't have left Matt. But I just couldn't take his negativity anymore. He's not the same person since that spell changed everything. All magic should be banned.'

Another whiff of cigarette smoke, and she knew it meant she wasn't alone. He provided moral support, just as he had when she'd been a child. She smiled, but her words contradicted the smile. 'Nothing seems to matter anymore.'

Acacia got up and meandered down the cliff path to the car park. No other cars yet, it was only 6am after all. She unlocked her car and got in, automatically fitting her seatbelt, adjusting the mirror to check behind.

She frowned at herself in the mirror. She saw a thin tired face, no lipstick, dark shadows under her eyes because she wasn't sleeping well. Her hair appeared lank and scruffy. When had she last washed it? She used to wash it every morning in the shower. Now she often forgot to take showers, having a quick wash. And food. She hardly ate now, taking a couple of bites out of her toast before discarding it. She smelt her granddad's aftershave again and gave a weak laugh. 'Yes, granddad, I know. I should take better care of myself. But I seem to be so tired all the time, you know?'

She put the car in gear and drove slowly along the cliff road back to Peter's bungalow. Soon it would be Peter and Tabitha's bungalow. That thought did make her smile. She loved her aunt so much, and Peter had become an intrinsic part of her family. She'd lost Matt, but she had Peter and Tabitha, and Morgan and Nate.

And she had Tiger. Dear Tiger. What would she do without him?

As she pulled into the driveway, Tabitha came out of

the front door to greet her. 'We were a bit worried when we realised you'd gone out in the car so early.'

'Sorry, Tabitha. I just wanted to sit by the sea for a bit. Clear my head.'

'I understand,' Tabitha placed her arm around Acacia's shoulders. 'I'm making pancakes. Will you have some with us?'

Acacia saw the worry in Tabitha's eyes, and she felt guilty. She must make an effort to pull herself together. Acacia's eyes filled up, and she blotted her lashes with a tissue. 'I think I've got some dust in my eye.'

Acacia sat at the dining table while Tabitha bustled about making fresh coffee, and Peter placed two pancakes on a plate in front of her, moving the maple syrup within easy reach. She smiled. A reminder of her time in Canada.

Tiger jumped on the chair next to Acacia and sat studying her. She could feel his loving vibes, smiled at him and stroked his head.

'I love you lots, Tiger,' she told him. 'Thank you for coming to live with us. I'm so glad you're with me.'

Tabitha poured coffee into Acacia's mug. 'Your favourite blend, dear. I haven't been able to get it for a while, but they had some when I went shopping yesterday. Try it.'

Acacia dutifully took a sip. Good coffee, no doubt about that. She smiled up at her aunt. 'Thanks, Tabitha.' She realised Peter was waiting for her to eat some breakfast, so she took a piece of pancake in her mouth and chewed. It seemed such hard work.

Peter and Tabitha resumed their morning conversation. She realised they were studiously avoiding discussion about Matt, Wiladelle or magic.

Tiger had decided to lie down on the chair, but one of his paws touched her leg, letting her know he was there for her.

Acacia managed one whole pancake before placing her fork on the table. She drained her coffee mug though and, seeing Tabitha and Peter's concerned faces, she announced, 'I'm going to take a shower. I feel a bit grubby.'

*

Matt and Justin were at a meeting in the lounge of Ezra's smart, detached Victorian house. In a secluded, rural area, it suggested power and success. The kitchen where the meeting was held had lots of shiny, stainless steel equipment on display, spotlessly clean.

'What are you saying?' Wiladelle asked Matt. 'Are you suggesting one of my people had something to do with your car accident?'

'Not at all,' Matt said. 'But you know people who are capable of doing this kind of thing, and I wondered if you had any idea who could have done it?'

Wiladelle glared at him. 'I have no idea who did it. Some people are just crazy and will do anything. What I want to know is, when are you going to get rid of Acacia?'

Justin had to stop himself laughing out loud at Wiladelle's reference to crazy people. She had no idea how deranged she was herself.

Matt studied the floor in silence.

'Well?' Wiladelle demanded. 'I'm waiting. What's your plan for finishing Acacia?'

'I can't do it,' Matt admitted. 'She's my wife. I just can't do it.'

'That's what my group said you'd say. Right then. I think we're finished. Don't you?'

'What do you mean?' Matt asked.

Justin got up to leave, and took Matt's arm. 'Matt, let's get out of here.'

'No, wait,' Matt said. 'Give me another task. Something not so hard.'

'Leave,' Wiladelle said. 'Before I change my mind and do something you wouldn't like. You're no use to me. Just go.'

Savannah got up and pulled out her wand, aiming it at Matt, her whole body oozing excitement.

Justin stopped breathing, expecting the worst. Surprisingly, Wiladelle stopped Savannah.

'Let them go,' Wiladelle said.

'But, they know stuff,' Savannah said, outraged.

'They don't know much,' Wiladelle countered. 'Nothing we can't change. Let them go. We have important things to discuss and I want to get on with it.'

Justin grabbed Matt and pulled him out of the room, down the hall and out of the house. He kept looking behind them as they headed for the car. He couldn't believe they'd got out of there in one piece, but no one followed them.

'What just happened?' Matt asked as Justin shoved him into the passenger seat and closed the door.

'We're of no further use to them,' Justin said. 'She only wanted you because she thought there was a chance you might kill Acacia, and because she wanted to know what we could tell them about Peter's group. Seems she's learnt all she can from us, so she's cut us loose.'

Matt had one of his headaches. He placed his hand on his head and closed his eyes.

'I'm glad you couldn't kill Acacia, Matt. You made the right choice.'

*

Matt felt confused. His head still hurt. The spell Jefferson had used on him, although losing its hold, was still there, just not as strong. He felt as though there were two people in his head fighting, wanting different things.

Once back at the bookshop, Justin waved goodbye and Matt headed up the stairs to his flat. But he couldn't face it. It was cold and lonely. No Acacia. No Tiger. He turned back, and, curling himself up on the comfortable bookshop sofa, he fell asleep.

Ernie wanted to help but had no idea what to do. He sat on one of the chairs opposite the sofa and watched Matt sleep, keeping him company even though Matt was unaware of his presence.

*

The following morning, Justin felt as though his heart would break as he watched Matt, lonely and confused, stumble into the bookshop.

Justin called Peter to tell him they were no longer in Wiladelle's group, so he'd have no further inside information to pass on.

'At least you and Matt won't be subjected to Wiladelle's poisonous diatribe anymore,' Peter said. 'Good job, Justin. You can get a good night's sleep tonight.'

'I don't want to be alone tonight, Uncle Peter. Can I come and sleep on your sofa?'

'You don't even have to ask. Tabitha and I will get some hot chocolate ready for you.'

*

Wiladelle leaned against the cream wall in Ezra's living room and addressed her group. 'That went better than expected, last night. Matt and Justin still think Peter and his group are the dark wizards, and we're the good guys.' She laughed.

'I don't understand why you didn't finish Matt off,' Ezra said. 'Why did you let Matt and Justin go?'

'I want Matt to suffer more before I kill him. He's confused, he's living alone, and he's alienated from the people who could help him. I want him to suffer real emotional pain before I put him out of his misery.'

THIRTY-TWO

'What do you think?' Morgan asked Acacia, standing back and studying the attractive Victorian cottage that was for sale.

'I think it's perfect.'

'If this were in London, it'd be four times as much, at least.'

'Well, it's in Devon. So you have countryside all around you and most of the facilities you need right here in Holsworthy. Will you make an offer on it?'

Morgan laughed. 'Make an offer? I'm going to buy it, Acacia.'

They walked out of the kitchen door and around the walled back garden, and Acacia bent down to smell some lavender in a tub. 'All the plants are healthy, even though the owner died a while ago. This lavender smells divine! I wonder if a gardener comes regularly.'

Acacia wiped a garden bench off with some tissues from her pocket. The dew had been heavy that morning. 'I was wondering. Does it bother you? Her dying in the house?'

'Not at all,' Morgan said. 'I've had a chat with Tara who tells me the lady, Virginia, was quite a character, involved in the local Cats Protection League and also volunteering at one of the charity shops in town. I think she'll be pleased I'm living here, even if it's only at the weekends.'

'Do you think you'd ever move down here for good? Sell your home in London?'

Morgan studied Acacia. She'd made a little effort today. She wore pale pink lipstick, her hair pinned up, but she still wasn't eating enough, she was thin, and instead of the old smile there were lines around her mouth. The campaign was taking its toll on her, and she missed Matt.

'Maybe I will, Acacia. But for the moment it's somewhere for me to stay at the weekends and whenever I'm needed. My flat in London is too sterile. This cottage will be a real home, I know it. The first priority though is to get Matt back to his former self. We need to get rid of that spell. I'd love to see you two back together.'

Acacia's eyes filled with tears. 'Yes, that would be good.'

'Right, I'm going to tell the estate agent to offer £5,000 above the asking price. I need to ensure this cottage is mine. Coming?'

'You know, Morgan, I can see you having your own cat here. It would be safe in this garden. You just have to install a pet door and you're good to go. That would be an incentive to live down here all the time, wouldn't it?'

'Did Virginia have a cat?'

'That's a good question,' Acacia said. 'We should check. Would you take it on, if so?'

'I'd give it serious thought,' Morgan said, 'but what would Tiger say? I guess we'd have to keep the subject of my cat from Tiger. I wouldn't want him getting jealous.' Morgan laughed.

'Your own cat. It would make everything perfect. Would you consider living here twenty-four-seven? I know things are strained at the moment, but once the spell is lifted Matt should be back to normal, and he'll need your support. It would be great if you were here permanently.'

'I'm thinking about it. I could maybe open an office in Exeter and commute, but work mostly from home. It's something to aim for. For now, though, let's buy this cottage. It'll be for weekends to start with.'

Morgan considered Acacia's hopeful face. 'And yes, if Virginia left a cat when she died, I'll take it. It'll have to live in London with me until I get an Exeter office sorted out. And yes, I'll bring it with me whenever I come down.'

The estate agent smiled at Morgan's offer and made a phone call. The offer accepted, Morgan signed the paperwork.

'Did the previous owner leave a cat, do you know?' Morgan asked.

'She did,' the estate agent replied. 'It's staying with her niece at the moment, but the niece can't keep it unfortunately.'

'Would you be able to give me the niece's telephone number?'

*

Acacia had a good feeling about the cottage. Although a bit dated, it had a lovely atmosphere and a pretty façade. It even had clematis growing up the front wall. All it needed was some new kitchen equipment and a spruce-up of the bathroom. The garden would feed Morgan's soul with its herbs, apple trees and shrubs. It seemed to exude peace and wellbeing.

'Let's go and tell Peter and Tabitha about this,' Morgan said.

Acacia tucked her arm through Morgan's, and they walked back to his new blue BMW. 'Things will start to get better now,' Acacia said. 'You'll see. We're giving a sign to the universe.'

*

Justin shook Nate's hand.

'It's great to have you back on board, Justin,' Nate said.

'Glad to be here,' Justin said. 'My head seemed full of jelly, a super strange feeling. Nothing seemed to matter much. Not the bookshop or the books, not my personal life. All Matt and I wanted to do was hang out with Jefferson and Garrick.' He paused. 'While Garrick remained alive, that is.'

'Garrick is in the best place,' Peter said. 'At least we managed to use the *Metamorphosis* spell on him. We didn't have to kill him.'

'You need to learn as much as possible as quickly as possible,' Nate said.

Peter nodded. 'We need you to be able to protect yourself and anyone else who needs it. We'll do the attacking, Justin, but I need to know you're safe, okay?'

Justin nodded and picked up his wand from the desk.

'Now, remember the words to the spell we've just gone through,' Peter said. 'I'll try to disarm you, you'll counter with the *Repulse* spell. Ready?'

Peter used the regular *Disarm* spell, but Justin wasn't quick enough. His wand flew across the room.

'Let's try that again, shall we?' Peter said.

Justin retrieved the wand again and readied himself. Peter again disarmed him. This went on for half an hour, and then Nate said they should have a coffee break.

'What do you think the problem is?' Justin asked Peter, as they drank their coffee in the lounge.

'I'm not sure,' Peter said. 'It could just be that you're out of practice. We lost you there for a few weeks. Maybe your brain has to get back in tune or something.'

'Let me try to disarm him next time, Peter,' Nate said. 'It could be a subconscious reaction to the fact you're his uncle and he doesn't want to hurt you. And Justin, remember we're using old wands, not our own personal ones, so don't worry about burning these wands, okay?'

Justin nodded.

'Ah,' Peter said, 'I didn't think of that.'

'Let's try again,' Nate said. This time Justin countered the *Disarm* spell and used *Repulse*. Nate's wand flew out of his hand and erupted in flames. Nate was thrown across the room and his protective gloves were singed.

Peter and Nate clapped Justin on the back, both saying, 'Well done!'

*

Acacia came down the stairs into the basement after hearing what sounded like a small explosion. 'Is everyone alright? I thought I heard a bang.'

The three men nodded and smiled.

'Nate, your hand is burnt!' Acacia exclaimed. 'Here, let me apply ointment to that. Follow me.' She led him to the bathroom, held his hand under the cold tap and then found some ointment and a bandage. 'Better?'

'Much better,' Nate said. 'Thanks, Acacia.'

'I wish everything didn't have to be about magic,' Acacia said. 'Someone's always getting hurt.'

'If we could stop Wiladelle without magic we would, but we won't be able to. You do know that, don't you?'

'No, I don't,' Acacia said. 'There must be another way. All these accidents and injuries we've had in the last few months. I can't stand it.' Her eyes filled up, and she hurried out of the bathroom.

Nate went back to Peter and Justin. 'Acacia's upset about the physical trauma.'

'I wish she'd learn some magic herself,' Peter said. 'It'd be such a help.'

'We'll have to keep our eye on her, and protect her when necessary,' Nate said.

'Oh good, here's Morgan,' Peter said. 'We can get back to trying to break that spell.'

Justin got up to leave, but Peter stopped him. 'No, don't go, Justin. I'd like you to describe to Morgan how your brain felt with the spell on you. It might help him come up with something. We're going to do some brainstorming. You can take part if you want? Tabitha will be joining us too.'

However, after two hours of talk, checking references, checking spell books, and diagrams on the whiteboard, they were no further forward.

Acacia brought them hot chocolate, looked at the whiteboard and their frustrated faces. If they couldn't break this spell on Matt, what chance did they have of defeating Wiladelle? She'd always be one step ahead of them.

THIRTY-THREE

Acacia waited in her blue Vauxhall Astra until she saw Matt come out of the bookshop and drive off. She scrutinised her car, dusty from her trips to the beach. Matt was a stickler for clean cars, at least he had been before that spell… Didn't matter, though, did it? She didn't care what he thought, plus Wednesday was darts night. Justin had told her Matt had started to play again. They were both pleased about that. It restored some order to Matt's changed life.

Eight o'clock, a little early for Ernie to show himself, but Acacia felt hopeful he'd appear when he heard her in the shop. Sure enough, as Acacia stood making some fresh coffee, Ernie appeared.

'Acacia,' Ernie exclaimed. 'I'm so pleased to see you. Does this mean you're living here again with Matt?'

Acacia studied the reclaimed wooden floorboards. 'No, I'm still living at Peter's place. I'm here for another reason, and I can't let Matt know.'

'Ah,' Ernie said, waiting as Acacia poured coffee into a

cup, then switched the coffee maker off and settled herself on the plush bookshop sofa. She patted the seat next to her, and Ernie sat down.

'You know Justin is back to normal, right?'

'Yes, I noticed that. What a relief,' Ernie said.

'They're still working on getting the spell off of Matt. Anyway, I wanted to talk to you and Elizabeth about a solution to the Wiladelle problem without using magic. Any ideas?'

'Hmm,' Ernie sat thinking. He frowned, got up and moved around the bookshelves, picking up books and putting them down. He sat again, started to say something, stopped, and again got up.

Ernie lit a cigarette, and Acacia sniffed the air as the smoke wafted towards her. Acacia felt a bit rebellious. Part of her hoped the smell was still there when Matt got back. He wouldn't like that.

Acacia sighed, got up, poured herself more coffee. It was lukewarm. 'No ideas? It's just that, as she's a ghost, and you and Elizabeth are ghosts, I thought she might be willing to listen to you, and leave us alone.'

'I'll talk to Elizabeth, and we'll come to Peter's house to consult with you,' Ernie said.

'Can you do that? I thought you might be stuck here?'

'No. We can go wherever we want. We'll have a chat and visit you at Peter's house tomorrow evening, how would that be?'

'Sounds good.' Acacia brightened a little. She stared at her cup, surprised to see it empty. 'Can you find Sylvia and ask her to help too? Then you can run your ideas by me and hopefully between us we'll have a solution. What do you think?'

'It's worth a try,' Ernie said. 'Sorry I don't have any ideas off the bat, but I wasn't expecting this. I'd like the opportunity to help with the Wiladelle issue. We'll see if we can come up with something suitable for tomorrow. Will Tabitha be there?'

Acacia smiled. She knew Ernie had a soft spot for Tabitha. 'Actually, tomorrow is Peter's birthday, and they're going out to dinner. They may not be keen on this approach. They'll prefer to use magic. We'll keep this to ourselves for the moment, okay?'

Ernie leaned over to hug Acacia and realised he couldn't. He laughed. 'I don't think I'll ever get used to not having a physical body. A hug says so much, doesn't it? Consider yourself hugged.'

Acacia smiled, said goodbye and locked up the shop. Halfway back to Peter's house, she realised she'd left her cup and saucer on the coffee table.

Would Matt realise she'd been there? Would he change the locks?

*

Tara watched heavy winds pushing clouds around dark skies. She was drinking coffee with Acacia, Peter, and Tabitha in Peter's living room.

'What happened to the rain?' Tabitha asked.

'Gone with the wind.' Tara laughed at her own joke, and they all tittered.

Acacia went around topping up the coffee cups.

'What are we going to do about Matt?' Tara asked, nodding thanks to Acacia. 'We can't let this go on any longer.'

'We've tried a whole lot of things, but none of them worked,' Peter said. 'We're stuck.'

'Well, I have an idea,' Tara said. 'Now, you may not agree with this. Brace yourselves.'

Peter and Tabitha seemed alarmed. Acacia sat down in her favourite armchair, relishing the soft velvet and the supportive padding. She leaned forward.

'You're not church goers, Peter and Tabitha, I know that,' Tara said, 'but I am. And Matt's my grandson. The bible tells us *whatsoever you ask in my name it shall be given unto you*. I believe that. I'm a Christian, and I have the right to stand on the Lord's word.'

Tabitha's eyebrows were as high as they could get. Peter choked mid-swallow. Acacia sat quietly, listening.

'You do know that the spell on Justin was broken by his grandmother's prayers, don't you?' Tara continued.

'It seemed like coincidence,' Tabitha said.

Acacia smiled, but said nothing.

'Now who's being judgemental?' Tara laughed. 'You're not the only ones who can work a little magic, you know. The Lord himself worked a whole lot of magic during his time here. We call them miracles, but they're magic just the same.'

'You're right, Tara,' Acacia said. 'Go on.'

'I'm going to get Matt into the church somehow. I don't know how yet, but he won't let me down if he thinks I need help. I'm going to ask the Lord and his angels to intercede on my behalf and remove this spell from my grandson. They'll come through for me.'

Peter looked sceptical. 'You think this will work?'

'You *charmers* have had your opportunity and not come up with anything. It's my turn.'

'When are you going to do this?' Acacia asked.

'Tomorrow. Tonight I'm going to pray and meditate. Tomorrow morning I'll call Matt early and ask him to meet me at the church for some reason. Once he's in the church and angels get their hands on him, that spell will be removed. I'd stake my life on it.'

*

Saturday morning arrived with blue skies and a warm breeze. Tara called into the bookshop for Matt, and he grabbed his jacket. He caught Justin smiling at Tara knowingly, and he frowned. He opened his mouth to ask Justin what was going on, but customers were waiting, so he let it go.

Matt and Tara walked to the church in companionable silence, but as they got to the door, Matt stopped, unwilling to go in.

'Standing outside won't help me, Matt,' Tara said. 'Now you promised me you'd help me stack those benches. Come on.' She tucked her hand through his arm and pulled him inside the church, and as they closed the door a bright light filled the interior.

Matt shielded his eyes. 'What's that?'

Tara smiled but said nothing.

Vibrant music – was that harps? And singing like Matt hadn't heard before filled the church. Its harmonies seemed to fill his head, his body tingled, and he felt happy. 'Is the choir here? They're early, aren't they?'

'They don't limit their singing to specific times of the day, Matt,' Tara said. 'These angels sing all the time. They're so happy to be in the presence of God.'

'Angels?' Matt's eyes widened as he saw two luminous beings approaching. They had to be at least eight feet tall. Their long blond hair was shining like polished gold. He sensed overwhelming kindness and compassion coming from them, while at the same time they had immense strength and power. He didn't know how he knew that, he just did. He tried to back away, but Tara held him firm.

'We're here to help you, Matt,' one of them said. Matt shielded his eyes from the light, but the angel waved his hand over Matt's head, and Matt found he could see without being dazzled.

'Your mind has been invaded, Matt,' the second angel said. 'Tara belongs to the Lord, and you belong to Tara. She has called on us to remove this spell from your mind.'

'Spell? What spell?' Matt turned to Tara. 'What does he mean, Grandma?'

'Your pals, Jefferson and Garrick, planted a spell on you, Matt,' Tara said. 'It's time it came off.'

'In the name of the Lord Jesus Christ, I banish all spells of any kind that have been used against this man,' the first angel said, making the sign of the cross over Matt's head.

The other angel ran his hands over Matt's aura while chanting a prayer.

Matt's mind cleared. He saw a black mist floating away from him. He opened his mouth to speak but didn't know what to say.

One of the angels came over and wafted the black mist into a jar, clicking on the lid. He turned to Matt. 'This will be cleansed. It will hurt no one else. Go in peace.'

The angels left, and Matt saw his grandmother, Tara, on her knees thanking God for His help. He went over to her and hugged her. Tara got up, wiped tears away, and smiled at Matt.

'How do you feel?' she asked.

'I feel like I've been away somewhere, and I've just come home.'

'Good. Time to go back to your bookshop. Justin will be so relieved to have you back to your normal self, Matt. We all will.'

THIRTY-FOUR

Matt couldn't help smiling as he studied Peter's living room. Tabitha and Acacia had outdone themselves. There were fragrant multi-coloured sweet peas in vases on the windowsill and on the dining room table. Flames of the white candles in the brass candlesticks flickered and danced. The table was laid with a brightly flowered cloth and it was covered in plates of cakes, sandwiches, pies and quiche. A *Welcome Back Matt and Justin* poster sat over the fireplace, and the drinks trolley held a dizzying array.

'So, Matt, you're back in the land of the living!' Peter draped his arm around him, and the Devon group clapped. 'Sorry for the old chestnut. I just couldn't resist an opportunity to use it.'

Matt contemplated the company. These people cared about him, and he'd been estranged from them for weeks. Wiladelle had made him feel completely isolated. But he was not alone. Not at all. 'I'm sorry for the way I behaved. That spell completely altered my perception. To think I attended a couple of Wiladelle's meetings! I can hardly believe I did that.'

Justin clapped Matt on the shoulder. 'Me too. It's scary to think about what we were like.'

'The good thing is,' Peter said, 'we've had information from you and Justin about Wiladelle and her group that's been extremely helpful, so it wasn't wasted. Nothing ever is.'

Acacia came over, and Matt stiffened as she hugged him. He couldn't allow himself to love her like before. He was sure she and Morgan were in a relationship now. She could never be his wife again. He gently removed her arms from his shoulders.

Acacia's eyes filled up. 'I still love you, Matt. Always remember that.' She moved away and went to talk to Tabitha, who handed her a glass of wine.

Morgan watched this exchange, and went over to Matt. 'Cuz, it's so good to have you back with us. Acacia and I have been so worried about you. We all have.'

'Right,' Matt said, looking over his shoulder at Justin who was chatting with Samantha.

'Matt,' Morgan said, trying to get his attention, 'Acacia and I are just good friends. Neither of us would do anything to hurt you. You do know that, don't you?'

Matt saw genuine concern on his cousin's face. He glanced over at Acacia, realised how much weight she'd lost, how the spark seemed to have gone out of her. He returned his attention to Morgan. 'I hope that's true. But so much has happened. I need some time to process things.'

'Acacia will get back to her old self now that spell's been removed from you, Matt,' Morgan said. 'She's been through the wringer in the last few weeks. She's been so worried about you.'

'It's not been a picnic for me either,' Matt said, placing his glass on the coffee table and moving across the room.

Morgan sighed, and swallowed some wine.

Matt moved to the centre of the room and held his hand up. 'Can I just say something, please?'

Everyone stopped talking and turned to Matt.

'Wiladelle has put us all through a whole load of stuff and we need to make her pay for that. I want you to consider letting me be involved in her downfall. What she did to me and Justin, via Jefferson and Garrick, has caused a lot of problems.' He turned towards Acacia. 'Problems that won't be sorted out quickly.' He turned back to the centre again. 'Will you think about letting me participate?'

Nate held up his hand as people started to talk. 'We hear what you're saying, Matt, and we understand. But it needs to be someone way more experienced than you are to deal with Wiladelle.'

'I just want you to consider it,' Matt said. 'I'll resume my training and maybe there'll be a way I can be involved in her comeuppance.'

'We don't want to destroy Wiladelle, Matt,' Tabitha said. 'We want to change her for the better.'

'That's all well and good,' Matt said, 'but I've seen what she can do. She's cunning. If you give her the opportunity she'll have you fighting among yourselves. You won't even realise the problem has been caused by her. She has to be dealt with, and soon.'

Peter said, 'We all agree with that, Matt. But let's talk about this at our next meeting. This evening we're here to welcome you back. We just want to have a pleasant get together.'

Matt smiled and nodded his agreement. He picked up his glass of wine and headed over to Justin and Samantha. 'So, I take it you two are an item?'

*

The next evening, in Peter's living room, Matt sat back in the blue padded couch, hands behind his head, as Milton showed his new invention to the group.

'You see the hands of the dial are blue? That means no dark wizards around,' Milton said. 'No worries at all. Now, watch this.'

He produced an object from his chocolate leather briefcase, wrapped in thermoplastic insulator. It was a thick, black wand with the words ROMANY'S – HANDS OFF stencilled in silver across its length. He put gloves on and removed a little of the thermoplastic from its tip. He walked away from the wand, left the watch next to it, and asked the group to check out what happened. The hands of the dial became red.

'So you see, whenever a dark wizard, even his wand, is nearby, the dials of the watch will turn red.'

'This is brilliant,' Matt said. 'How near to the watch does the wizard have to be before the dial turns red?'

'About four metres,' Milton said. 'I know that's not far, but if someone's following you and getting close it's a warning, and if someone is up ahead and hiding you'll know.'

'What are you going to do with Romany's wand?' Acacia asked. 'How did you get it?'

'How I got it is a long story. It's proving difficult to destroy. It has a protection spell on it. Anyway, it's proved useful in this instance.'

Acacia shivered. 'I don't like it being here. It feels like it's spying on us.'

Milton wrapped it up again and put it back in his briefcase. 'I'll keep working on a way to get rid of it.'

'Couldn't you just bury it?' Matt asked.

'Yes, I could,' Milton said, 'but it may have a beacon on it so it can be found. I don't really want to give the dark community one of their tools back. Maybe I could use *Repulse* on it though…'

'How many of these watches have you made?' Peter asked.

'Just two at the moment. I'll make more when I get time. I feel the ones I've made should be given to Nate and Peter. Don't ask me why, but I've learnt to trust my instincts.' He handed the watches over, and Nate and Peter put them on.

'Brilliant,' Matt said to Milton.

Matt picked up his wine glass, took a sip, and watched as Tiger circled the room. He could feel Tiger watching him in return, unsure whether he could trust Matt or not. Matt picked up one of Tiger's toys, and dangled it in front of him, but Tiger didn't want to play. Instead, he jumped on Acacia's lap, and Matt watched as Acacia kissed the cat and cuddled him. Matt felt totally dejected.

Nate came over to talk to Matt. 'It'll take Tiger a while to accept you again, Matt. You ignored him for weeks when that spell was on you. You didn't speak to him or feed him or play with him. Give him time, though. You used to be very close. I'm sure you will be again.'

'Wiladelle took my happy home life away from me,' Matt said. 'I just took it for granted until I didn't have it anymore. I'd give anything to have my life back the way it was before Jefferson and Garrick came into the bookshop.'

'We were all surprised at Tara getting you into the church for that intervention,' Nate said. 'Some people would say that was *old magic*. Maybe it is. I suppose we just approach things from a different angle.'

'Tara always came through for me when I was growing up. She and Sam were so good to me and Sarah.'

'Is Sarah still happy living in Lancashire?' Nate asked.

Matt nodded. 'She loves it up there. The countryside is beautiful, and the people are friendly. It's cheaper to live up there too, you know. I'm glad she's out of the way of Wiladelle. I don't believe she even thinks about Sarah, although Sam and Tara tell me that Sarah looks a lot like our mum. It's just as well Sarah isn't in Devon, or Wiladelle wouldn't leave her alone.'

Nate glanced at the bright stainless steel watch on his wrist, the dial happily blue. 'This will be very handy to have. I wonder why I got one of the prototypes.'

'Let's hope it never turns red,' Matt said.

'Here, have another glass of wine. I'll drive you home.'

'Would you stay over tonight?' Matt asked, feeling rather embarrassed. 'It's so lonely in the flat without Acacia and Tiger there, and it's hard going from this happy home to my empty flat.'

'Of course. I'll be very pleased to. I didn't get to do that when you were little. If I'd known you were my son, I'd have had you stay with me often. I missed out on a lot.'

'Wiladelle said you weren't my dad,' Matt said. 'She said it was a lie.'

'We know the truth, though, don't we?' He raised his glass. 'To family,' he said, clinking glasses with Matt.

'Family,' Matt said, feeling somewhat better.

*

It was a warm sunny day, a day for picnics. Tiger wanted to be outside, running around, chasing leaves. However, Samantha had come to teach him cat magic. He knew it was important. Reluctantly, he left his soft window seat in Peter's living room, where he'd been watching bees and butterflies.

'Let's try this new spell,' Samantha said. 'It's called *Leap Away*. Normally you would reach the sofa in a leap from here, right? Well, this spell will let you leap a long way, much further than the sofa. Want to try?'

Tiger nodded in agreement.

'So, think where you'd like to go, hold the spell *Leap Away* in your mind, and then leap. Trust yourself to end up where you want to be.'

Tiger closed his eyes, thought of somewhere else and leapt into the air. He vanished.

Samantha searched the room, and then the kitchen. She saw Tiger sitting on top of the kitchen cabinet. He'd leapt there directly from the lounge.

'Clever boy, well done!'

Tiger allowed Samantha to pick him up and settled him on his pet bed.

Next, Samantha opened her sturdy backpack and took out a brown paper bag. She crinkled it. Tiger loved the sound. Samantha opened it so he could see the brown velvet toy mouse Milton had made for him.

'Okay, Tiger,' Samantha said. 'This toy mouse is special. Milton has made it for you. It's called the *Remove from Danger* mouse. If you're in any danger at all, just pick the mouse up and it'll transport you to somewhere safe. The toy mouse will know if where you're thinking of is safe or not, Tiger. Let's say you're thinking of Acacia, but she's in a magic battle and it's not safe there. It won't take you there, it'll take you to somewhere peaceful. It knows.'

Tiger studied the toy mouse Samantha had set on the floor in front of him. He reached his paw out, and patted it tentatively.

'It won't do anything until it's in your mouth.'

Tiger stared at the toy, considering it. He looked up at Samantha, unsure.

'The first time you use it, even though you're already in a safe place, it will take you somewhere else also safe. It's been programmed to do this. It needs to get to know you, and it does that by you picking it up in your mouth. Ready?'

Tiger batted it with his paw again, but wouldn't pick it up.

'Acacia!' Samantha called.

'What's up?'

'I need Tiger to pick up the magic toy mouse, and he's a bit reluctant. It'll transport him somewhere out of danger. Remember what Milton said? This first time, even though Tiger's not in danger, the toy mouse will still transport him. It's a trial to make sure it works and so the mouse recognises Tiger. We need to know it's functioning properly.'

'Hmm,' Acacia said, 'what happens if *I* pick it up?'

'Nothing will happen. You're not a cat.'

'Will it work for any cat at all, then?'

'That's the thing. It needs to recognise Tiger. Once Tiger has picked this up, it'll know Tiger as its owner.'

Acacia nodded. 'It's safe, Tiger,' Acacia told him. 'Milton is a friend, right? This mouse is to help you in times of trouble. We just need the mouse to recognise you as its owner, so you need to pick it up. It'll take you somewhere else, though hopefully not far.'

Tiger considered the situation, and again patted the mouse with his paw. Finally, after one more look at Acacia and then at Samantha, he picked it up and instantly disappeared.

Acacia and Samantha both gasped, then set about searching the house. Tiger was nowhere to be found. They went out into the garden, and found him sitting in a lilac shrub behind the garden shed, washing his face.

Acacia rushed over and stroked him, telling him he was a clever boy. He smiled up at her, allowed himself to be picked up and kissed, then struggled to get down. He decided he liked the mouse, and trotted back into the house with it.

'He hasn't disappeared again,' Acacia said. 'It knows it's in a safe place.'

'It worked great,' Samantha said. 'Milton is brilliant!'

THIRTY-FIVE

Rain poured down the windscreen. Linus's wipers could barely keep up with it. 'Darn British weather.'

He pulled into the drive of a detached Victorian house. Wiladelle materialised outside his car door. He nodded in greeting, pulling up the hood on his green cotton-twill parka. He ran from the car to the house as quickly as possible, but his trainers were damp, and his trousers were sodden.

Wiladelle stood at the front door with Ezra, seeming impatient to get him inside.

'This your house?' Linus asked Ezra.

Ezra nodded, and indicated Linus should go into the living room. Linus stood in front of the warm gas fire, his clothes steaming as they dried. He threw his Parker on the pristine cream sofa as no one offered to take it from him.

A charismatic woman appeared in the doorway to the living room. Linus watched as she glided into the room, sitting opposite him. He raised his eyebrows in an 'aren't you going to introduce us?' question, but Ezra ignored him.

'Linus,' Wiladelle said, 'this is Savannah.'

'Pleased to meet you,' Linus said, smiling at Savannah knowingly. The woman exuded sexual invitation. And she was extremely good to look at. The ruby red lipstick was a bit OTT though.

'Now,' Wiladelle said. 'What do you want to know?'

Linus asked Wiladelle questions about her early life, about when she had started using magic, about her family. He wrote notes on a student pad.

Wiladelle was surprised at the questions, but she gave him the answers and watched him carefully. 'Why are you so interested in me?' she asked after about fifteen minutes.

'Well,' Linus said, 'your life story is unusual. You've learnt so much and, even though your physical body has gone, you're still learning and using magic. I'm a historian, and I would like to write your biography, if you agree?'

Wiladelle frowned. Could he be for real?

'Oh?' she said. 'How many biographies have you written before?'

'You would be my first,' Linus smiled at her eagerly.

Ezra came and stood over Linus. 'Why are you really here? Did Peter send you?'

Linus frowned and said, 'Of course he didn't. He doesn't know I'm here. I wouldn't admit that to Peter or any of his group.'

'You're friendly with Tabitha, aren't you?'

'I belong to Tabitha's group in New England, yes.'

'Then why are you here?' Ezra kept up the interrogation. 'Are you spying on us?'

Linus laughed, but Ezra remained silent.

'No,' Linus said. 'I'm not spying on you. I wanted to interview Wiladelle and write her biography.'

'Let me see your notepad,' Ezra demanded, holding his hand out.

Linus passed his notebook over to Ezra, and he read the first paragraph. '*Wiladelle is an unusual witch, highly intelligent, self-motivated, creative, lightning quick. When she was living in Devon she had a string of new spells to her name. After her tragic death, she continued her studies and is the leader of a well-known Witch's Coven, passing on her knowledge to younger and less experienced witches.*'

'So what else do you want?' Wiladelle asked.

'I'd like to join your group,' Linus said.

Wiladelle laughed. Ezra coughed. Savannah seemed intrigued.

'Really? Why should I let you join us?'

'I could tell you what Peter's group are doing, keep you informed on their latest intentions.'

'You're in,' Wiladelle said, silencing Ezra's protests with a wave of her hand. 'But know this. If you betray us, you'll wish you were never born. Got it?'

Linus nodded and got up to leave.

Ezra passed Linus his damp Parker, and held open the front door. 'And keep your eyes off Savannah. She's mine, alright?'

*

Gale force winds were buffeting the trees in Peter's front garden. The sky was dark and threatening rain. Inside, the gas fireplace gave out a welcoming warmth, and Peter's group were munching homemade chocolate cake and drinking coffee from Acacia's French press while finalising the plan to remove Wiladelle.

'I don't use magic,' Acacia said, clearly confused at this unreasonable request, 'you know that. Why do you want me to be the one to do this?'

'Because Wiladelle won't be expecting it,' Tabitha said. 'Wiladelle knows you don't use magic, Acacia. You'll have the element of surprise.'

'I can't do it,' Acacia said. 'Please don't ask me.' Acacia shifted from side to side in her chair, trying to get comfortable. She moved the cushion to a spot just above her backside. It felt better. More support.

'Look, Acacia,' Matt said, 'we know you're uneasy using magic. If there was another way, we'd go for it, but we've been trying to figure out how to fool her and this seems like a good idea.'

'Right,' Acacia sighed. She turned to Peter. 'What's the plan again?'

'You learn how to use the *Persuasion* spell,' Peter said, 'you arrange to meet Wiladelle somewhere, we're not sure where yet, and tell her that you want to talk to her about things. Tell her that you want to find out why she's carrying out this campaign against Matt and the rest of us. Tell her you want to act as an intermediary and resolve any issues. She won't be willing to do that, of course, but she'll probably go along with you just so she can get you alone and finish you off. We'll be hiding nearby. We'll get there way ahead of any meeting time arranged. Then you use the spell, it works, and you can persuade her to come along with us, because once the spell is on her, she'll agree to whatever you want. Then we can use the *Metamorphosis* spell on her, and she'll be rehabilitated.'

'Why can't I just use the *Metamorphosis* spell on her myself?'

'It takes a really strong *charmer* to use that spell, Acacia,'

Peter said, 'and you're a novice. Or you will be, once you recommence learning. Whereas the *Persuasion* spell is simple to use, and you'll be able to master it quickly.'

'I don't know...'

'Sweetie,' Tabitha said, getting up and putting her hand on Acacia's shoulder, 'we'd love to give you lots of time to think about this, but we can't. We need to get this done. Wiladelle is getting stronger by the minute. We've just found out she's recruited two more witches to her group. They already outnumber us. We must act. Now we have the *Metamorphosis* spell, we ought to use it.'

Acacia pursed her lips, considering options. She came to a decision. She'd learn the words and actions of the spell, she'd go along with what they wanted. But she wouldn't use it. She would take Sylvia with her. She'd already had discussions with her about this. Acacia was sure that because Sylvia was a ghost, Wiladelle would listen to her when she wouldn't listen to one of their group.

'Okay, I'll do it,' Acacia said with her fingers crossed behind her back.

Milton came over to Acacia. 'I'm going to teach you the spell, Acacia. I usually just invent them, but now I'm branching out.' He laughed.

'Okay, when do you want to meet up for training?' Acacia asked.

'Now is as good a time as any,' Milton said, handing her a spare wand.

*

Linus drove to Ezra's house. He knocked. The house was

quiet, if the hall light hadn't been on he'd probably have driven away.

A dishevelled Ezra answered the door. 'Do you know what time it is?'

Linus ignored him and went straight in. Ezra pointed to his muddy boots, and Linus wiped them on the doormat.

'Let's get this right,' Wiladelle said, walking backwards and forwards, frowning. 'Acacia is going to ask me to meet with her to discuss things, but really she's going to use a spell to persuade me to do what she wants?'

'Yep,' Linus said.

'But Acacia doesn't use magic. She hasn't used magic since her parents disappeared all those years ago.'

'She agreed to do it after some coaxing from the group.'

Linus could feel Wiladelle's eyes boring into him. He knew she was trying to figure out if he was telling the truth.

'I find this difficult to believe.'

'Well, you'll be hearing from her soon,' Linus said. 'And if you do meet her, Peter's group will be hiding and, if Acacia fails, they'll attack.'

'Are you sure about this?'

'Absolutely.'

'Good. We can get there before them. My group will be well hidden. I'll talk to Acacia first and see what she says, though. I'm intrigued to find out.'

Linus shook his head, sighed, then decided to speak up. 'That could be dangerous. You shouldn't listen to her at all. Just attack.'

Wiladelle's eyes blazed. 'Are you questioning my judgement?'

Linus backed off. 'I guess you know what you're doing.'

'You've got that right. I'll listen to Acacia first and see what she says.'

'Do you know what happened to her parents?'

'Why should I know?'

'I just wondered.'

THIRTY-SIX

'We'll be in hiding before you get there,' Peter told Acacia. 'You'll be perfectly safe. Don't worry. Just do your best, okay?'

They were standing on Peter's doorstep. Tabitha had her arms around Acacia's shoulders. The weather had been lovely all day, blue skies and a warm breeze. That didn't stop Acacia shivering though. She pulled her padded green coat around her, nodded to Peter and Tabitha, then got into the Vauxhall Astra and drove off.

She didn't go to the meeting place yet, however. It was too early, and anyway she'd arranged to meet Sylvia at a quiet place overlooking the sea.

She pulled off the road, and got out of the car, sitting on a bench and watching the waves lapping gently on the beach below. There weren't many trees here, and the trees that were, were stalwart, determined to survive the winds that flattened their tops and stunted their growth. The gorse was thick and covered in yellow flowers. Yellow always made Acacia smile.

'You're here early,' Sylvia said, materialising in front of Acacia.

Acacia smiled, reassured by Sylvia's calming presence. 'Yes, I wanted to gather some strength from this view before we face Wiladelle.'

'Peter's group still don't know I'll be there, eh?' Sylvia asked.

'No. I thought it best. They want me to use magic, but I really don't want to,' Acacia turned away and admired the sea again, breathing in the ozone and trying to centre herself.

Sylvia followed Acacia's lead. She contemplated the view and steadied herself. Although a naturally calm being, she knew she had to be ready for Wiladelle, a superior adversary.

'Overcome evil with good,' Sylvia said to Acacia.

'Sorry?'

'Overcome evil with good,' Sylvia repeated. 'It's a well-known phrase. That's what we're intending to do, isn't it?'

'Yes. Let's hope we succeed.'

'We'll give it our best shot,' Sylvia said, 'and if we don't succeed then you'll have to use the *Persuasion* spell. You're not going to harm Wiladelle. You have nothing to feel bad about, Acacia. Come on.' Sylvia floated through the car door and sat in the passenger seat.

Twenty minutes later, Acacia pulled up at the prearranged meeting place in the local ancient woods. She checked out the area, no picnickers or dog walkers around. It was quiet. She looked up at a sky dotted with white fluffy clouds and wished she could fly up and touch them.

Then she had a moment of panic. Were Peter's group here?

'They're here, Acacia,' Sylvia said, sensing Acacia's

concern. 'I can feel them. You're not alone. And I'm here too, remember.'

Acacia nodded. Getting out of the car, she was surprised to see Wiladelle already there. She came over to Acacia right away.

'Who's this?' Wiladelle asked, surprised.

'This is Sylvia,' Acacia said. 'She's a friend, and I wanted her to talk to you as well. I hope you don't mind?'

Behind a large oak tree, Peter and Tabitha's eyes were wide with surprise. They looked at each other, mouthing *what?* before turning back to Acacia and Sylvia.

'What could you possibly have to say to me?' Wiladelle asked Sylvia.

'Well, despite what you may think, I know exactly how your mind works,' Sylvia said, 'because, believe it or not, I was a dark witch for a long time. I found the light only a short time before I died.'

Wiladelle laughed. 'Finding the light didn't stop you dying, did it.'

'No, but it helped me enormously after.' Sylvia kept her serene expression.

'What do you mean,' Wiladelle asked, 'helped you after?'

'Because I'd found the light, when I died I was surrounded by angels. They welcomed me, and they taught me whatever I asked about. It's so fascinating in the Halls of Learning, Wiladelle. You'd love it.'

Wiladelle's expression changed from one of scorn to one of interest. She loved learning. 'What sort of things?'

'Well, everyone should be healthy. We learn how to heal the body.'

Wiladelle seemed riveted. 'What else?'

'Some lucky people can fly. It's rare, of course. They teach us to do that, no props needed.'

'I fly now,' Wiladelle said, poking her chin out.

'Yes, most of us do when we're released from the physical, for short distances, but wouldn't it have been fun to be able to fly when we had physical bodies? And fly a long way without using aids like broomsticks?'

'What else?'

'Even muddy water can be made clean with the right incantation.'

Wiladelle sat by a wild, red rhododendron bush and placed her wand on the grass. 'Tell me more.'

Sylvia and Wiladelle sat next to each other and talked while Acacia stood a little apart, listening to them. Sylvia had caught Wiladelle's attention.

'I understand all too well why you turned to the dark side,' Sylvia said. 'I did it too. We saw other people who had things we didn't have, and it made us angry. We used dark magic to obtain stuff we wanted. But if someone had told us there was another way, we would've listened, wouldn't we?'

Wiladelle nodded and studied the ground. They talked quietly.

It was the best scenario possible. Acacia realised she'd been breathing shallowly up till now, and started breathing normally again.

*

Unknown to Acacia or any of Peter's group, Wiladelle's team, The Assembly, was approaching from their hiding place on the opposite side of the wood. Composting leaves rustled under their feet. A light breeze moved small branches around, but no one noticed.

Peter's group, Devon Crew, engrossed in the conversation between Wiladelle and Sylvia, missed the tell-tale signs of danger. However, Nate noticed a red flash and glanced at his watch. The numbers had changed from blue to red, which meant dark wizards approaching. He looked over at Peter and saw him stare at his watch, his mouth open in surprise.

*

Ezra had seen Wiladelle place her wand on the ground, and this alarmed him. He kept watching, waiting for the signal she'd promised, but it didn't come. Then he saw Acacia get up and approach Wiladelle. He saw her hand go into her coat pocket and take hold of something. Acacia was reaching for a photograph of her mother. She wanted to ask Wiladelle if she'd met her, but Ezra didn't know that. He thought she was reaching for a wand. He went into action, giving the attack signal himself.

*

Wiladelle, Acacia and Sylvia were all startled to hear sounds of fighting. Acacia's eyes widened. Sylvia looked as though she'd lost a race. Wiladelle, her interesting conversation with Sylvia interrupted, was clearly incensed. She went running towards the sound of fighting.

The Assembly and Devon Crew were hurling spells at each other in the woods. The two groups were fighting hard, and flashes of spells could be seen from where Acacia and Sylvia stood.

'You'd better leave, Sylvia,' Acacia said. 'We've failed. I'll be in touch. Go.'

Sylvia dematerialised and Acacia stood in the clearing, watching the mesmerising spells. She knew that Devon Crew's wands emitted a silver-blue light while The Assembly's wands gave off a black mist. She moved forward to get a better view. Who was winning?

Completely absorbed in the scene, Acacia didn't see Savannah approach, but she did hear a malevolent laugh.

'All on your ownsome, are you?' Savannah asked. 'Dear, oh dear. What a shame. What can we do about that?' Savannah pointed her wand at Acacia, and Acacia, too stunned to move, just stood there. A red hot pain shot up her right arm – and she realised her coat was on fire. She hastily undid it and threw it on the grass. She gripped her arm, and slid down to the ground.

Savannah stood over her. 'Thought you were so clever, didn't you? Well, we're quite clever ourselves.' She aimed her wand at Acacia again just as Milton threw himself in the space between Acacia and Savannah. He took the full force of Savannah's death spell, and he crumpled onto the grass. Acacia, tears running down her face, leaned down to check Milton's pulse. No pulse. Milton was dead.

Tabitha came rushing into the clearing and hurled the *Repulse* spell at Savannah. Savannah's wand flew out of her hand and went up in flames, while she was thrown across the clearing, clutching her burnt wand hand.

Chaos surrounded Devon Crew. They'd hesitated, shocked, when The Assembly arrived, and it had taken too long to get their brains around the facts. Their plan had not worked. Wiladelle's crew had been ready, and they had the upper hand. They had superior numbers, and they'd attacked first with the element of surprise. The battle was lost.

'Into the car with Acacia, quick,' Peter shouted at Tabitha, jumping in the driver's seat and starting the engine.

'What about the others?' Tabitha asked, unceremoniously pushing Acacia into the back of the car.

'The van is right behind them,' Peter said, 'I shouted at them to leave. They'll be okay.'

'Are you sure?' Tabitha asked. 'Will we all get away?'

Peter frowned but didn't answer.

'What about Milton?' Acacia asked. 'We can't leave him there!'

Peter studied Acacia's stricken face, swallowed a retort, and saw Nate running over to Milton with Matt close behind him. The white Vauxhall Vivaro, driven by Morgan, screeched to a halt beside Nate and Matt. They carried Milton's body to the van and drove off.

Acacia breathed a sigh of relief. Most of them were safe, except Milton. Milton was dead, and it was all her fault. She should've used magic like she had promised.

Tabitha and Peter were silent all the way home. Acacia could see how angry they were with her. Rightly so, she thought. Milton – a brilliant scientist and a great friend. He'd be sorely missed.

THIRTY-SEVEN

Sunlight filtered through the curtains. Time to get up yet? Tiger seemed to think so. He yawned and did a ballet stretch on the bed next to Acacia. She forced an eye open and saw Tiger watching her. She laughed. 'Okay, I know it's daylight. You want to go out, don't you? And you want your breakfast? What do you want first? Out or breakfast?'

Tiger stretched again and jumped onto the windowsill studying the garden. He turned to Acacia.

'Okay, got it,' Acacia said. 'Out first, then breakfast.' She leaned over and opened the window leaving enough space to allow him access. She glanced at the clock on the bedside table – 6am. She got up and pulled on her mint-green dressing gown, then went into the kitchen to make coffee.

Tabitha was ahead of her. She filled a mug with hot black coffee for Acacia, and they sat gazing out at the garden, windows slightly open. Bees hummed as they gathered nectar. The birds were pecking at the wet earth to bring up worms.

They could see Tiger out there, checking his territory, inspecting the healthy raspberry shrubs and peeing wherever he needed his ownership reinforced. Tiger peered through the French doors at them, and patted the glass with his paws.

Acacia got up and let him in, then filled his dish with fresh food.

Peter joined them. They were all still in their nightclothes, drinking coffee and mentally gearing themselves up for the day, still dazed from the events of the night before.

Tiger sat on his plump blue cushion on the windowsill next to the dining table, joining the group, watching the interactions, listening to the conversation, seeming to provide moral support.

'The time for talking is over,' Peter said. 'We have to make some decisions.'

Acacia studied Peter. Even though he and Tabitha weren't married yet, Acacia now thought of him as an uncle. 'You're right, and before we say anything else I want to let you know that I realise it was my fault Milton died. I need to learn magic. I've been selfish and pig-headed. Can I join the lessons you give Matt and Justin?'

Peter and Tabitha exchanged glances. 'We were hoping you would, yes,' Peter said. 'We have a meeting this evening, and I know people will want to know how we'll proceed. Apart from your learning magic, I'm not sure what our next steps should be.'

'Why don't you get Morgan and Nate over here to talk about it?' Acacia suggested. 'That way you'll have some ideas to share with the group later.'

Peter looked at the clock. 'Bit early, but I'm sure they'll be up.' He picked up his phone.

Nate answered on the first ring, and agreed to come over within the hour.

Morgan was in the shower when Peter rang, but he called back and said he'd be there in an hour too.

'I guess I'd better get ready then,' Acacia said. She felt worried. She knew they must be upset with her. It was all her fault. That had become her mantra over the last few hours. All her fault.

'Nate and Morgan won't berate you over this, Acacia,' Tabitha said. 'We all know how sorry you are. It's too late to change the outcome.'

'I feel so stupid,' Acacia said. 'I should've listened to you.'

'Yes, well,' Peter said, coughing to clear his throat, 'we all wish you had, but as Tabitha says what's done is done.'

When Acacia was in the bathroom, Tabitha picked up Acacia's breakfast plate and placed it on the draining board. 'I suppose half a slice of toast is better than no toast,' she said to Peter.

'At least she's starting to care about her appearance again,' Peter said. 'Small steps.'

Morgan and Nate arrived within five minutes of each other and were welcomed with fresh coffee and homemade shortbread biscuits.

Morgan went over to Acacia and hugged her, noticing how thin she'd become. 'Milton knew what he was doing, Acacia. He wanted to save you, and that's what he did.'

Acacia's eyes filled up, and she turned away, topping up her tepid coffee with hot.

'Any suggestions what our next move should be?' Peter asked.

'I'm attending magic class with Matt and Justin,' Acacia said. 'I know that doesn't help, it's a bit late to be starting out, but I just wanted you to know.'

'Everyone will be relieved to hear that, Acacia,' Nate said, 'including Matt.'

'What I want to know,' Peter said, 'is how did they know we'd be there?'

'Have they planted a listening device somewhere?' Nate asked.

'Or have they been following us, unseen, and overhead some conversations?' Morgan asked.

'We'll have to be extra vigilant,' Peter said.

'Do we know Wiladelle's weaknesses?' Acacia asked. 'Maybe we could work on those.'

'She's crazy,' Tabitha said. 'That's a weakness.'

They all laughed.

'I don't know so much,' Acacia said. 'It's like she has a split personality, and you don't know which Wiladelle you're going to get. There's the deranged Wiladelle, and then there's the intelligent Wiladelle.'

'You're right,' Tabitha said. 'There's a part of Wiladelle that's extremely clever. We mustn't underestimate her.'

They spent the rest of the morning talking through possible plans, discounting them, finding new plans, discounting those too. By the end of the morning everyone felt frustrated. No progress.

'I've got a headache,' Nate said. 'I think we should stop for now. What time is the meeting tonight?'

'Six thirty if you can make it?' Peter said.

'We'll have food,' Tabitha said, 'so don't worry about eating before you get here.'

*

Matt arrived at Peter's home a few minutes late, and the group were talking about the disaster of the night before. When the group were told Acacia was joining the magical training group, someone muttered, 'Better late than never.' Acacia heard and looked downcast.

Matt went over to her, and gave her a hug. 'We all make mistakes,' he said quietly.

Sylvia held her hand up as though stopping traffic. 'In defence of Acacia, we nearly had Wiladelle where we wanted her. She was extremely interested, excited even, about the possibility of the Halls of Learning. She should've been an academic. She loves studying. Anyway, if Ezra hadn't shouted that attack alarm we'd have had a different outcome.'

'The fact is though,' Peter said, avoiding Acacia's gaze, 'that we didn't. We're still faced with the same problem, and now we have to come up with a different plan.'

'Any ideas, anyone?' Tabitha asked.

'Why don't we split into groups and see what we come up with?' Justin suggested.

Peter nodded, and organised them into four groups. Soon they were brainstorming possible plans.

Matt, though, wasn't paying much attention to his group. Something was wrong with Linus. He just didn't seem his usual self. Matt felt it, but no one else seemed to pick up on it.

At the end of the evening, no definite plan had been determined, but a lot of ideas had been proposed for further consideration.

Matt decided to follow Linus. He had to trust his instincts.

*

The evening sky was overcast, with that ever-present mist that seemed to have been lingering for days. Matt parked in a lane close to where Linus had stopped, and got as near as possible without being seen. He used the *Conceal* spell and moved closer. To his astonishment he saw Linus in another vehicle with Savannah. They were way past foreplay, and Matt's eyes narrowed. He realised there was no point in him being there. He'd learn nothing from waiting about, and anyway he felt like a voyeur. He left.

He walked back to his car and started the engine. His mind whirled. If Linus and Savannah were an item, then Linus might be feeding Savannah information about Peter's group. But, surely not? Tabitha had known Linus for a long time. If she didn't think he was reliable, she wouldn't have introduced him to Peter and the group.

He needed a drink. He headed to The Dog and Duck and ordered a pint. The barman was in a chatty mood and tried to engage Matt in conversation, but Matt just nodded sullenly and found a table. He downed the pint in record time. He'd known a problem existed, but it hadn't occurred to him it was this bad. Linus involved with Savannah? Romantically involved? Well, he wasn't sure romance came into it, but they were sexually involved. And he felt pretty sure Savannah wouldn't be interested unless there were little snippets to be had either before or after sex. He went to the bar and ordered another pint. He'd left his silver-grey Jeep in the car park. He would walk home. He picked up his mobile and dialled Justin's number.

Ten minutes later, Justin came through the pub door and

joined Matt at his table. He saw the expression on Matt's face and headed to the bar, coming back with two pints. This was Matt's third pint now, and it didn't look as if he would stop drinking any time soon.

'Tell me what you saw,' Justin said, glancing about to make sure they wouldn't be overhead. Although there were people sitting at the bar, the tables nearby were empty with no one within earshot.

Matt smiled sadly at his friend, then studied the bar, and then his pint. He was finding it difficult to voice the concerns he had about Linus. He liked Linus. He appreciated the way he dressed, always smart but casual. He liked his sense of humour. He admired his skill with magic.

'Matt,' Justin said, 'out with it.'

'It's Linus,' Matt said.

'What's the matter with Linus? Is he ill?'

'I think he's spying on us for Wiladelle.'

'What?'

Matt could barely meet Justin's eyes. He felt such a traitor voicing concerns like these about Linus. Linus who'd shone as a rising star in the magic world. Linus who had them laughing frequently at meetings. Linus, the man Matt had wanted to emulate.

'Matt,' Justin said, 'answer me. What's wrong with Linus?'

'Something seemed wrong. I trusted my instincts, and I followed him. After the meeting.'

'And?'

Matt took a gulp of beer, then another. He finally faced Justin and said, 'He met up with Savannah, down a country lane. They were making out in the car.'

'Are you sure?'

Matt gave him a look.

'Okay, so you're sure,' Justin conceded. 'What does it mean?'

'It means that Linus is spying for Wiladelle, and that's probably how The Assembly knew we'd be there and were waiting for us.' Matt sighed. He felt exhausted. So much had happened already, and now this.

'If he's having sex with Savannah, yes, he's probably telling her stuff to pass onto Wiladelle. I'll call Uncle Peter.'

Matt was startled. 'Do we have to speak to Peter about it now?'

Justin raised his eyebrows at Matt, then punched in the numbers. 'Uncle Peter? Matt's uncovered something serious. Yes, I'm here with him now. We're in The Dog and Duck in town. Can you come over? Ten minutes? Right.'

'He's on his way,' Justin said. He saw Matt's empty glass and headed over to the bar for refills. He knew his uncle would need one when he heard the news.

Justin handed Matt his next pint. 'I'm sorry, Matt. I know you admired Linus.'

THIRTY-EIGHT

Acacia finished her wholemeal toast and took her plate to the kitchen. She paused at the draining board. So many cupboards and drawers – she wished her own kitchen, at the flat, had this many drawers. She loved the granite topped kitchen island, too. They rarely used the stools, preferring the dining room. However, it wasn't Acacia's kitchen, but Peter's. She missed her own kitchen. She mustn't think about that, though. No point. To replace any morbid thoughts, she looked out of the window into the garden. Tiger was patrolling his territory. She smiled. Tiger still loved her. She gave herself a mental shake. 'Get over it, you have to move on.'

Pleasingly, a good distraction was on the way. Tabitha and Acacia's morning schedule now included two hours in the basement, training – spells, wand actions, magic lore.

They went downstairs together, and Tabitha opened a window. The weather was warm and the air in the basement smelt stale.

'Have a look at this book,' Tabitha said, handing over a thick black book, titled *Magic Potions*. 'What do you think?'

Acacia opened the front page. It had her parents' names written in blue ink at the top of the fly leaf.

Memories of her parents flooded Acacia's mind. She missed them. She wanted them back.

'I found that book in a box at home. I brought it for you, but until now I'd forgotten I had it,' Tabitha continued. 'Your mum loved that book, and I loved your mum, you know that.'

'Thanks for the book. I'll treasure it. I've been really silly, haven't I? I shouldn't have waited this long. But after Mum and Dad, you know, I just didn't want anything to do with magic.'

'I understand, sweetie, don't worry about it. But now we have a lot of ground to cover.'

*

The following day brought drizzle, and Tiger was inside curled up on his blue cushion, surveying the garden. Matt and Justin arrived at Peter's place for their lesson, and were surprised to see Acacia waiting in the basement with Tabitha.

Tabitha turned up the temperature on the wall heater. 'Bit nippy down here,' she said to Peter.

Peter nodded, then turned to Matt and Justin. 'Tabitha tells me Acacia has come on really well, so she'll be joining us today. Now, Nate has a new spell he wants to try out with you.'

'It's one of Milton's of course,' Nate said, 'and I thought it'd be lovely to use it in his honour. It's the *Hovering* spell and allows you to hover above the ground for as much as ten minutes if you want. Ready?'

Matt, Justin and Acacia listened to Nate's instructions, and then took out their wands.

Acacia cast the *Hovering* spell first and immediately found herself a foot above the ground. She laughed in delight and moved around the room, using a sliding motion, a foot above the floor for a few minutes, before becoming aware of the fact that everyone was staring at her. She stopped.

Matt had watched Acacia with his mouth open. Acacia had performed a brand new spell perfectly, like it was second nature to her.

'What's the matter?' Acacia asked, standing on firm ground again. 'Did I get it wrong?'

Nate walked over to her. 'Acacia, that was brilliant. I'd never have thought a novice would realise she could move around like that on the first attempt. Well done.'

Acacia blushed, and studied the floor. 'Is there a spell for going higher?'

Justin laughed at her. 'Wow, hang on a minute! Let Matt and me catch up. We haven't even done the *Hovering* spell yet.'

Acacia stuttered, 'Sorry,' and waited while Matt and Justin mastered the new spell. It didn't seem to take long, but they both had a few tries.

'Right,' Peter said, once they'd mastered it, 'you were asking about flying?' He turned to Tabitha.

'Flying was a speciality of your parents,' Tabitha said to Acacia. 'I mean, without aids, no broomsticks. Let's see if you can do it, shall we?' She turned to Matt and Justin. 'Please join us and try this too.'

Tabitha gave them the words and actions for the *Flying High* spell, and Matt went first. He spent ten minutes trying but couldn't master it. Justin went next. He managed to get up as high as the ceiling, but fell back down again with a bump.

'Your turn, Acacia,' Tabitha said.

Acacia flourished her wand and aimed it towards the ceiling. '*Flying High*,' she said. They all watched as she left the ground and flew around the top of the room, using a swimming motion. When she'd gone round twice, she gently came back to ground level.

They all clapped and cheered.

Matt hugged her, then realised what he was doing. 'Sorry,' he took a step back, 'second nature. Well done.' He moved over to the counter at the back of the room where the coffee equipment lived, and got busy making fresh coffee for the group.

Nate walked over to Tabitha and nodded towards Matt. 'They're hurting. How can we fix it?'

Tabitha studied her niece. Acacia's attention seemed to be on the book Tabitha had given her, but she kept looking over at Matt.

'I've no idea. I'm hoping time will sort it out,' Tabitha said.

*

Matt looked out of the window, watching people in the square, some walking dogs, some laughing and chatting. Instead of making him smile, the scene just made him sad. He felt so alone. His marriage to Acacia was finished. And

Morgan – dashing, attractive clever Morgan – was in love with her. He had hoped Morgan would not act on his feelings. But now? Now, with Milton's death, everything had changed. What sense did it make? Milton had been a brilliant inventor, everyone missed him. And Linus! Matt had watched in amazement as Linus and Savannah had rolled around on the backseat of Savannah's car. Linus a traitor. Matt's world had changed. He'd tried to fit in with the current situation, but it wasn't working. He'd thought he could become a *charmer*, but… watching Acacia, she was naturally brilliant at it. She deserved to be with someone as talented as her. She deserved to be with Morgan.

He'd watched Acacia and Morgan closely the last time they were together. He knew Acacia liked Morgan. He'd hoped it was just friendship. But now she had become a talented *charmer*. She wouldn't come back to him. He just knew it.

Matt felt his mood plummeting further. Milton gone, Linus a spy, Acacia and Tiger living with Peter and Tabitha…

He poked his fork into his beef lasagne and moved it around his plate. Now Acacia wasn't there, he needn't feel guilty about eating meat. But now he didn't want to. He prodded the meat again. No. He didn't want it. He pushed his plate away and took out some of Acacia's Quorn and made a sandwich – how long had it been in the fridge? Probably weeks. He used it anyway.

'Matt!' Justin called up to the flat. No response, so he climbed the stairs and knocked on the door. 'I'm ready to do that stock take if you want to come and man the till?'

Matt opened the door. Justin did a double take. Matt looked like he could fall over any minute.

'Did you get any sleep last night?' Justin asked.

'What?' Matt asked, then took a breath. 'Oh, sorry, Justin. Yes, I think so. We could do the stock check another day.'

'Why don't you come downstairs and help me sort out the display?' Justin said, trying to motivate Matt.

'Display? Oh, no, you can do that. You don't need me.'

'Matt,' Justin said, 'actually I do need you. You're exactly what I need. I can't do everything on my own. I need your help.'

Matt didn't seem to hear him, at least he ignored Justin's remark. Usually a clean and tidy person, it was as though someone had stuck a pin in him and all his energy had leaked out, leaving an unshaven, tired grimy man. Now Matt was the one who didn't want anything to do with magic, and suddenly he realised how Acacia had felt till recently. Now he understood.

Changing the subject, Matt said, 'Acacia and I never ran out of things to say to each other, you know. We talked all the time. Now suddenly we're leading different lives, and when we do see each other, there's nothing to say.'

*

Justin glanced around the flat. Without Acacia cleaning regularly, it looked grubby and unloved. Last night's dishes remained unwashed. He could see Matt needed help.

'I'll be back in a minute, Matt, okay?' Justin said.

Matt chewed absently on his sandwich but gave no reply.

Justin went downstairs and keyed in the number for Matt's grandparents. 'Tara? I hope you don't think I'm interfering, but, could you come over and sort Matt out? He's extremely depressed and the flat is a tip. He's not coming into the bookshop much to help. I don't know what to do.'

'You leave it to me, Justin,' Tara said. 'I'll be there in about fifteen minutes.'

Justin was serving customers when Tara appeared, nodded to him, and climbed the stairs to the flat.

'Hi,' she said to a surprised Matt. 'Going to offer me a coffee?'

Matt ran his hands through his unwashed hair. 'Nana? What are you doing here?'

'I thought it time I paid a visit to my grandson. Is that alright?'

'Yes, of course. Coffee. Erm...' He seemed at a loss.

'This is worse than I thought,' Tara said. 'You've got to pull yourself together, Matt.' She picked up the phone and dialled the doctor's surgery. 'Yes, I need an urgent appointment for my grandson, please. He's suffering from depression. Can we come this afternoon? I'll bring him in. Right. We'll be there.'

'Get yourself in the shower, Matt,' Tara said, 'and put some clean clothes on. I'm taking you to see the doctor. You might need some pills for a while, but it'll be okay. Trust me.'

Matt nodded at Tara, and stumbled into the bathroom.

Tara went to work and washed all the dirty dishes, then got the vacuum cleaner out and cleaned through the flat. She dusted and polished everything in sight, then opened the windows to let in the fresh air.

Matt got out of the shower, dressed, and then sat with his grandmother.

'Just because Acacia's not here at the moment, and I think

that's temporary, doesn't mean there's no one who loves you, Matt. Sam and I love you. You know that. Nate and Morgan love you, and Acacia still loves you, I'd put money on it.'

*

Two hours later, back from the surgery with a prescription for antidepressants and an invitation to dinner with his grandparents three times a week, Matt took a deep breath and walked into the bookshop that he loved so much. He started unpacking boxes from his supplier. He was tired and sad, but the pills would help. And there were people who cared about him and needed him.

Justin placed a cup of hot coffee in front of him. 'Good to have you back, Boss.'

Matt lifted the cup to his mouth and sipped. Wonderful. Real coffee. He'd forgotten how great it tasted. Why had he been drinking that instant stuff? 'Thanks, Justin. And not just for the coffee.'

*

It was the end of the work day, and a tired but more upbeat Matt decided to visit the walled garden. He had hardly been out there since Acacia and Tiger left, and it needed some work. The grassed area was long overdue a cut, and weeds were sprouting in between the flowers and shrubs.

Elizabeth saw Matt sitting on the bench and materialised beside him. 'So, how are things going?'

Matt smiled ruefully. 'A bit better, I suppose, but it'll take a while.'

'Some wounds take longer than others to heal,' Elizabeth said, 'but some are self-inflicted.'

'What do you mean?'

'You and Acacia are meant to be together. You know that.'

'Yes, but she's chosen Morgan hasn't she? What can I do about that?'

'Who says she's chosen Morgan?'

'Well, it's obvious,' Matt said. 'She's left me. And she took Tiger. My Tiger.'

Elizabeth sat at the end of the bench. 'You couldn't be more wrong.'

'What?'

'Acacia had to leave you, Matt. You had that spell on you. You weren't yourself. You were extremely difficult to live with. She couldn't trust you. Tiger couldn't trust you. Because it wasn't really you. Don't you see?'

'But, she likes Morgan a lot. I know she does.'

'Yes, she does like Morgan. But she loves you.'

A spark of hope took root in Matt's brain, but he wouldn't let it spread yet. If Elizabeth was wrong, the pain would be intense. 'You mean, they're not having an affair?'

'They have a strong relationship as friends and family. Nothing more.'

'How do you know that?'

'I've seen the way they are together, and I've seen the way you two used to be together. Morgan and Acacia are close friends. That's it.'

Matt got up and began wandering around the garden. 'I used to love coming out here with Acacia and Tiger. He used to really enjoy chasing butterflies and stuff.'

'You miss your cousin too, don't you.'

'Yes. I miss Morgan almost as much as I miss Acacia and Tiger.'

'Time to do something about that, don't you think?' Elizabeth asked.

'What can I do?'

'Pick up the phone. Call Morgan. Meet him for coffee. Say you're sorry. Then do the same with Acacia.'

Matt inspected the ground, and moved a collection of dead leaves with his shoe. 'I'll think about it.'

'Don't leave it too long,' Elizabeth said. 'There's a big showdown coming, and Acacia and Morgan need to know their relationship with you is sound before that starts.'

Matt nodded. Elizabeth was right. This couldn't wait. He picked up his phone and called Morgan, and they arranged to meet.

Matt turned around to thank Elizabeth, but she was gone. He felt nervous. What would Morgan say?

*

They'd arranged to meet in the coffee shop, and as Matt walked in the door he saw Morgan already sitting there with two big cappuccinos on the table in front of him. The air was filled with people talking and laughing. Someone at the counter was trying to decide between a chocolate brownie and a fruit scone.

Morgan stood and held out his hand for a handshake. Matt's eyes filled. He blinked back the tears and gripped Morgan's hand.

'It's so good to see you, Matt,' Morgan said. 'How are you doing?'

'I'm okay,' Matt said. He gazed at his cousin, and then took a deep breath. 'I'm sorry, Morgan, jealousy got the better of me.'

'Oh, Matt,' Morgan said. 'You had that spell on you. Of course you weren't thinking straight. And by the time the spell was off, you'd gotten used to the idea that Acacia and I were an item. You know my feelings for Acacia, Matt, but Acacia and I could only ever be good friends. You and she are the couple.'

'I've missed you, Cuz,' Matt said.

'I've missed you too,' Morgan said. 'Erm… we've arranged a little get together at my cottage this evening. Just close family and friends. You, Acacia, Tabitha, Peter, Justin, Nate and me. Okay?'

Matt nodded. 'Have you settled into your cottage?'

'I love it, Matt. Why don't you come over to the cottage now? Justin can manage the shop for the rest of the day. What do you think?'

'Okay,' Matt said. He realised he'd finished his coffee. 'Could we have another coffee?'

'Let's have one in my cottage. I have a great cappuccino maker.'

Matt laughed. 'Of course you do!'

Approaching the cottage, Matt saw stout stone walls, clematis growing by the front door, an enclosed back garden. And when Morgan opened the front door, Matt could see the kitchen had been decorated, and modern appliances had been fitted. There was a door into the walled garden at the back, and Matt could see herbs, shrubs, and flowers in round wooden tubs. Morgan showed off his new cappuccino maker, and they took their coffees into the garden. Matt could hear the gentle drone of bees visiting their favourite plants.

By the time the others joined them, Matt and Morgan were back to their old selves, laughing and joking. There was an awkward moment as Acacia came through the door, but Matt got up and hugged her, and then they all started chatting.

'We have a meeting planned for tomorrow evening,' Peter said. 'Is 7pm alright for everyone?'

Matt studied Peter, then turned to face everyone. These were his friends and family, and yet he couldn't do it. 'I've decided not to have anything else to do with magic. After everything that's happened, I really can't face it anymore. I'm sorry.'

Morgan's coffee went down the wrong way, and he sputtered, 'Really, Matt?'

'I'm sorry. Really sorry,' Matt said. 'But I've been through it a bit what with the accident, the spell on me and Justin, the strain between Acacia and me, Milton dying and the shock about Linus. I've got my family back. Well,' he looked at Acacia, 'almost, and I just can't witness any more of this stuff. I hope you understand.'

Peter spoke up. 'Matt, you're healing, that's the important thing. We have enough *charmers* for our task. No need to worry.'

Everyone nodded. Nate patted Matt on the shoulder.

Acacia came over to Matt with two glasses of wine and offered one to him.

He felt a heavy weight lift from his heart. Maybe he and Acacia still had a chance. Waking up every day without her beside him had become increasingly difficult. And Tiger. How he missed Tiger.

Acacia placed her hand over the top of his and pressed gently. She clinked glasses with Matt. 'To possibilities and happy endings.'

THIRTY-NINE

Ameeting had been called at Peter's house to discuss the latest and hopefully last needed plan. The evening felt warm, and the windows were open a smidge to let in the cool air. The garden was protected by a heavy-duty spell. Only named people could enter the garden, and Peter had built a bright red metal mailbox, big enough for small parcels, at the entrance to the driveway to accommodate different postman coming and going. Cold callers and unplanned visitors would never get past the gates. They'd feel sick and turn away.

Everyone was excited, aside from Acacia. She listened as Peter outlined the plan to hold Tabitha out as bait. Her eyes widened as Tabitha laughed at the danger. Acacia turned to Morgan, who smiled at her encouragingly.

'So, I'll organise another meeting where Linus will attend,' Peter said, 'and we'll throw this in about Tabitha foraging for a specific herb in the woods. After all, a herb to put people into a deep sleep would certainly help us, wouldn't it?' He laughed. 'Tabitha will go on Wednesday, we'll hold the meeting including Linus tomorrow night, and that'll give him time to report to Wiladelle. Remember to act surprised at whatever we discuss. You've not heard it before. Right?'

Everyone nodded.

'This is extremely dangerous, surely?' Acacia asked. 'Isn't there any other way?'

'There are lots of variations on this theme, Acacia,' Tabitha said, 'but really, when it comes right down to it, I'm an experienced *charmer* and I should be able to handle Wiladelle. She wants to kill me. Let's give her the opportunity to do so.'

The following evening's meeting was like déjà vu with some information being left out, to trick Linus. Peter, at the end of the meeting, said, 'We should really have a meeting tomorrow with so much to arrange, but Tabitha is going to spend time in the woods searching for a herb that induces deep sleep. It should be really handy. You'll be going there around 6pm, won't you Tabitha?'

Tabitha nodded.

'So the next meeting will be on Friday evening. Is everyone alright with that?' Peter asked.

The group nodded their acceptance.

*

Linus smiled as he inserted his key into the ignition. Tabitha was going into the woods alone foraging. Well, well, well. What a great opportunity. Linus drove over to Ezra's house where Wiladelle visited regularly, and he told Ezra and Savannah the news. They were standing in the hallway, and Linus could see their half-eaten meal on the dining room table. He wondered briefly which one of them was the cook.

Wiladelle materialised when she heard his voice. She started to laugh and couldn't stop. She'd have a crack at Tabitha. 'And this time, I'm going on my own!'

Savannah laughed too, but for some reason Ezra stayed quiet.

Linus got a prick of conscience. He and Tabitha had known each other for a long time. He'd betrayed her. He watched Wiladelle, then Savannah and Ezra. He suddenly felt uncomfortable in their company. He made his excuses and left.

*

Outside Peter's house, Acacia was close to tears. 'You don't have to do this, Tabitha. Please don't do this.'

Tabitha hugged Acacia. 'It'll be fine, sweetie. I'm more than a match for Wiladelle. And you guys will be there to help. I have a good feeling about this, and my feelings are usually right.'

Peter kissed Tabitha, and held her face in his hands. 'I'll be right there. Okay?'

Tabitha nodded, and the three of them got into Peter's silver-grey Vauxhall Corsa. The rest of the group would be in the woods by now. It was only 5pm but they weren't taking any chances.

Peter parked the Vauxhall a good ten minutes' walk away, and once there, Acacia and Peter floated up to the top of a couple of trees and used the *Hide* spell to conceal themselves. The rest of the group were hidden behind trees and shrubs, some using concealing spells.

Tabitha placed her wicker basket on the ground, and

pulled on her grubby gardening gloves. She'd genuinely search for herbs, and then Wiladelle wouldn't suspect anything when she arrived. Tabitha was quite absorbed in her hunt, her basket half full of various woodland flowers together with borage, wild mint and ground elder when she heard Wiladelle's laugh behind her.

'So,' Wiladelle said. 'It's true. You're foraging for herbs all on your lonesome.'

Tabitha stood up, and removed her gardening gloves. 'Hello, Wiladelle. Come for a chat?'

Wiladelle laughed again. 'Right. A chat.' She pulled out her wand and aimed it at Tabitha. 'Time for chatting is over, I think.' She opened her mouth to throw a spell, and Peter's group dropped from the trees, surrounding her.

'A party!' Wiladelle exclaimed, seemingly delighted. 'How nice. Now, why do I get the feeling this is a setup?'

'You're outnumbered, Wiladelle,' Peter said.

'Peter, Peter!' Wiladelle said. 'Will you never learn? I'm more than capable of handling you lot.'

Just then, Eliza, Matt's dead mum, materialised in their midst. Peter's group were surprised as they weren't expecting it, and Wiladelle's mouth opened in astonishment. She hadn't seen her sister since her death. She forced herself to close her mouth, trying to compose herself.

'Hello, sister mine,' Eliza said. 'Thinking of killing more people are you?'

Wiladelle stared at her sister, her usual confident banter gone, and stuttered, 'Where have you been all this time?'

'You're not the only one in our family who likes to learn,' Eliza said. 'There's a lot to study up there. You should go and see.'

'So I've heard,' Wiladelle said. 'What do you want?'

'You killed me because I wasn't aware of your real danger,' Eliza said.

Acacia took a deep breath. So that was the truth of it. Wiladelle had definitely killed Matt's parents.

'We all know what you're capable of now,' Eliza continued. 'But I do believe I'm going to hand this honour over to my daughter-in-law, Acacia.'

Acacia was bemused. How on earth could she deal with Wiladelle?

'You're more than able to do this, Acacia. Remember who you are. Remember your parents. They were brilliant. Or should I say are brilliant? You will be too. Draw on your inner strength. Trust your instincts. Remember Tabitha's training.'

Acacia, bewildered at the huge task she'd been handed, nevertheless scrutinised Eliza. She'd not seen her before. She saw Eliza's nose was the same shape as Matt's. She had the same sort of expression on her face that Matt had when determined to do something. Acacia realised Eliza was more than ready to deal with Wiladelle if she failed.

Acacia turned to Wiladelle, surprised that she hadn't killed them all already. But Wiladelle, it seemed, was frozen in shock, still staring at her sister.

*

The woods were hushed – all of nature seemed to be holding its breath. Acacia, seeing Wiladelle still in shock, used the *Repulse* spell, and Wiladelle sailed across the clearing, her wand in flames.

Wiladelle, now alert once more, glared at Acacia and flung herself upright, aiming her hand at Acacia, ready to kill her, even without her wand.

Acacia's natural instinct at reconciliation warred with her need to get rid of Wiladelle. She reminded herself that Wiladelle had caused complete havoc, pain and loss in the last few months.

Tabitha and Peter, alarmed at Acacia's obvious unwillingness to take the ultimate step, prepared to take action if needed.

But Eliza stepped in front of Acacia. 'It seems my daughter-in-law is having second thoughts about what should be done with you. Let's talk about this, calmly, shall we?'

Wiladelle frowned. 'Talk? You want to talk?'

'Come on, Wiladelle. You know you want to. You were ready to talk when Sylvia and Acacia tried previously, until one of your group set the fighting off.'

'That was different.'

'Different, how?'

'I was intrigued by what Sylvia told me. I wanted to hear more.'

'Well, I can tell you just as much as Sylvia can. What do you want to know?'

Acacia watched Wiladelle closely. The manic Wiladelle had disappeared, to be replaced with the intelligent, curious Wiladelle. Acacia was completely absorbed in the conversation going on between the two sisters.

Peter and Tabitha sat nearby, listening, and Acacia watched the rest of the group sit in a circle surrounding Eliza and Wiladelle. They all wanted to hear what Eliza had to say.

'Looks like you've got quite the audience, Eliza,' Wiladelle waved her hand around at the *charmers* gathered there. 'Tell us then. About the Halls of Learning and anything else you think we'd be interested in knowing.'

Eliza studied her sister. She seemed in earnest. She put her wand on the grass next to her.

Wiladelle laughed. 'My wand has gone, of course, but we all know I can cast any number of spells without it.'

'But will you?'

'We'll see. Talk.'

Eliza described the Halls of Learning, the classical Greek architecture of the building, the fact that there was a copy of every book ever written, even the bad ones, and the library contained sections covering a vast array of subjects, anything from how to bake a cake without using animal produce to early Christian beliefs and everything in between. Eliza told them about the classes that took place there regularly, classes including meditation techniques, Universal Law, martial arts (Wiladelle was surprised at that one), the best way to brew tea and even how to overcome demons. Eliza described the Archangels, their duties, what they looked like. She described the Thrones and Dominions. She explained what happened when people first went to heaven, and how they had the option of experiencing more lives on Earth if they wished. She talked about the warm breezes and the clear streams running through lush meadows full of daisies and cowslips. She told them about the animals in heaven and what their role was in helping mankind experience love and kindness.

'I could go on and on about this, but I won't,' Eliza concluded. 'What do you want to do?'

Wiladelle looked around at the woods and the people

gathered near them. 'I never felt ready to leave Earth,' she said, 'not till now...' She looked over at Acacia. 'Well?'

'You... you want me to use the *Metamorphosis* spell?' Acacia stuttered.

'Why not? Let's see what happens!'

Acacia looked over at Eliza, unsure what to do. Eliza nodded at her. She looked at Tabitha and Peter. They nodded at her too.

Finally, Acacia looked back at Wiladelle. 'Ready?'

*

Acacia used the *Metamorphosis spell*. The whole group, including Wiladelle, watched in awe as an elegant, tall golden angel, with long blond hair and wearing a seamless white robe, appeared in front of Wiladelle. The group watched as Wiladelle's twin personalities warred, the curious, intelligent Wiladelle winning as she held her hand out to the angel.

Just before Wiladelle's feet left the ground, Eliza said, 'You have an interesting journey ahead of you. I'll see you in the Halls of Learning.'

Wiladelle nodded to her sister, excitement lighting up her face, and the group watched her and the angel moving up into the atmosphere until finally they couldn't see them anymore.

*

Acacia approached Eliza. 'Thank you for coming, Eliza. I'll tell Matt you said Wiladelle was responsible for your death, and the death of your husband.'

Eliza frowned, and shook her head. 'A lot of time has passed. I hope Matt can let it go once he knows the facts.'

Nate gazed at Eliza. 'You're still beautiful, and so brave.'

Eliza blew a kiss to Nate and dematerialised.

The group congregated around Acacia, congratulating her on her success.

Tabitha hugged her niece. 'I told you I had a good feeling about this. But I never thought for one moment that Eliza would show up, or that she'd ask you to deal with Wiladelle. How did she know what was happening today?'

Nate shuffled his feet. 'I talk to Eliza now and then, out loud when no one's around. I hadn't realised she heard me, though.'

'Oh, Nate,' Tabitha said. 'You still love her, don't you?'

'Yes. I always will. But I feel I can let her go now. Seeing her again, her coming to help us like that, I feel I can move on.'

Tabitha smiled at him. 'And you have Matt.'

'Yes, she left me a son, our Matt.'

Peter placed a hand on Nate's shoulder, then turned to face his group. 'My place, everyone. Time to open that champagne!'

They all headed to Peter's house, where they downed a good few bottles of bubbly. The confrontation had left them tired, but their desire to celebrate was strong. This had been an epic fight, and at one time they thought they'd lose.

'Time to get back to normal, I think,' Nate said to Acacia.

Acacia smiled. 'Yes, I'll see what can be done to mend some more bridges.'

FORTY

The following morning Acacia sensed the day brimming with possibilities. The blue skies and warm atmosphere seemed to confirm this. She took a deep breath and walked into the bookshop. Matt was placing new books on shelves.

'So, it's over and done,' Matt said. 'Thank goodness for that.'

Acacia walked over to join Matt. 'Yep. The remaining members of The Assembly have disbanded… Did Justin tell you that your mum said Wiladelle had definitely killed your parents?'

Matt nodded. 'Knowing helps.' Matt heard the door open again.

Morgan walked towards them, slightly rakish with an eye that was turning different shades of purple. 'Argument with a tree,' he murmured when he saw their surprised expressions.

'Did that happen last night?' Acacia asked.

'Maybe…'

Morgan turned to Matt. 'You know then? About Wiladelle killing your parents?'

'Well, we thought it was her, didn't we? Now we know we were right.'

'I'm so sorry, Matt,' Morgan said. 'If I could alter things, I would.'

Matt nodded. 'Not your fault, Cuz.'

'Your mum said she hoped you could let it go, Matt, now you know the truth.'

Matt nodded.

Justin wandered over. 'If you guys are going out for coffee, could you bring me back a piece of quiche for my lunch?'

Matt turned to Morgan and Acacia, 'Are we?'

'I'm game if Acacia is,' Morgan said.

'When did I ever turn down the chance of a good coffee?' Acacia asked. She studied Matt, her green eyes questioning, and Matt knew it wasn't about the coffee.

Matt grabbed his Barbour wax jacket and reached for Acacia's hand. He held it firm as they went out of the bookshop.

Acacia squeezed Matt's hand in return. Both felt flutterings in their stomachs.

Morgan smiled. Things would be back to normal soon.

*

Acacia buttoned up her new Seasalt coat. The weather matched her mood. She tried to shrug it off. It was not like she'd never see her aunt again, for goodness sake.

Justin was loading Peter and Tabitha's luggage into Nate's Range Rover. He seemed to be having trouble getting Peter's suitcase in, and Matt went over to help.

'You'll remember to call us when you land in New England?' Acacia asked, hugging her aunt.

'Of course,' Tabitha said, tears in her eyes. 'I'm going to miss you. Remember you promised to visit. If you come near the end of the six month mark, Peter and I can fly back with you.'

'That sounds great,' Acacia said. 'I don't know about leaving Tiger, though.'

'I'd love to have Tiger with me for a while,' Justin said. 'He's ace.'

Acacia smiled at Justin, 'Thanks, Justin.' Then she turned back to Tabitha. 'I'll have the information ready about your getting married in Devon when you come back again, okay?'

'Thanks, sweetie,' Tabitha said, placing her hand on Acacia's shoulder, emerald and diamond ring glinting in the sunlight.

Nate pretended to shield his eyes from the glare of the dazzling stones, laughing. 'That's quite the engagement ring you have there, Tabitha.'

'It's so beautiful,' Acacia said.

'It's perfect,' Tabitha said, kissing Peter.

'Right,' Nate said, 'well, we'd better get going. It's a bit of a trek to Heathrow.'

'I'll just get my jacket,' Justin said. 'It's going to seem strange, living here for six months while you're away.'

'Thanks for doing it, Justin,' Peter said. 'I'm so pleased it won't be empty for six months. We weren't sure how long Acacia would stay, so it's great you've offered.'

Peter turned to Acacia. 'You're very welcome to stay just as long as you want, Acacia, you know that.'

'Thanks, Peter,' Acacia said, blinking back tears.

'Tell him, Peter,' Tabitha said.

'Tell me what?' Justin asked.

Peter seemed rather embarrassed. 'Well, Tabitha and I wondered if you'd like to stay here permanently.'

'Stay here?'

'I've looked into building an annexe, and I can get planning permission no problem.'

'An annexe for me?'

'If you want,' Peter said. 'Tabitha and I may travel back and forth for a bit, and it's quite disruptive for you. This way, you'll have your own permanent home. And you won't have to pay rent ever again.'

'Oh, wow!' Justin said. 'That'd be great. Thanks, Uncle Peter.'

'I'll email you when we get to New England,' Peter said. 'You can get the ball rolling with the paperwork and the builders.'

Tabitha pulled Acacia to one side. 'We figured you only needed to stay temporarily, Acacia, we both think you and Matt will get back together. But if you don't, you can stay here forever if you want, you and Tiger. Okay? We could always convert the barn if you do want to stay permanently, that way you'd have your own space too.'

'Thanks, Tabitha,' Acacia said, brightening. 'That's so kind of you.'

'We both love you,' Tabitha said.

Nate turned to Matt and Acacia. 'I'll call you when I get back to Holsworthy, okay? I'll drop Justin back here and then drive back to Bude.'

'Thanks, Nate,' Matt said. 'Oh, and Nate?'

'Yes, Matt?'

'Don't forget the darts match on Friday!'

'As if,' Nate smiled.

Nate and Justin got in the front of the vehicle, and Tabitha and Peter got in the back.

*

Tabitha had mixed feelings. She was caught between her life in Devon and her life in New England.

She hated leaving her niece, Peter's bungalow and garden, and her new friends, but she felt excited about Peter meeting her American friends and seeing her New England home. They had decisions to make. Would they keep travelling backwards and forwards? Or would they make either New England or Devon their permanent home? She glanced at Peter.

'Whatever we decide,' Peter said quietly, seeming to read her thoughts, 'Justin will have a permanent home. I've done what we said and changed my will. Justin will inherit my place when the time comes. Acacia will be back with Matt soon. I'm sure of it. We don't have to worry about her.'

Nate pulled out of the driveway. Tabitha turned her head and watched Acacia and Matt standing there, looking forlorn. Acacia wiped her eyes. Matt hugged her.

Peter put his hand over Tabitha's and gave it a squeeze. 'We'll be back,' he said.

*

Matt and Acacia went back into the bungalow, and Acacia picked Tiger up and cuddled him.

'I can stay with you for a bit, if you like?' Matt said. 'Samantha's watching the bookshop for us.'

'That would be nice,' Acacia said. 'Tiger is going to miss Tabitha and Peter.'

'He's still got you,' Matt said. He brushed his fringe out of his eyes, and then scrutinised the garden through the window.

Acacia could tell Matt was floundering emotionally, and she visualised Matt alone in the flat. She swallowed. 'I'll make some coffee, shall I?'

She busied herself in the kitchen. 'There's fresh fruit cake in that tin. I made it yesterday,' she said as Matt joined her.

Acacia poured some coffee, and Matt placed some treats near Tiger's scratching post. Tiger's body relaxed, he moved a paw and dragged a treat to his face, nibbling it daintily. He was starting to trust Matt again.

Matt smiled at Acacia. He opened the tin and cut them both a piece.

Whatever happens, Acacia thought, we will always be friends.

*

Ezra was looking at Savannah with new eyes. Suddenly she didn't look so good to him. Yes, she was still attractive, but she had a cruel streak in her that he'd managed to ignore before. Well, not any longer.

Yesterday he'd had an interesting conversation with an old friend, and that old friend had told him that it was possible he was Morgan's father. If that was true, he had some bridges to mend. He admired Morgan. He'd like to get to know him.

'I think it's time you moved back to your own place, don't you?' Ezra asked Savannah.

Savannah opened her mouth in surprise. 'What?'

'Look Savannah, I know you've been seeing Linus. Let's make this easy, eh? Just pack your things and leave. No fuss.'

'Well, well, look how the worm has turned. I'll go now. You can send my stuff on. You know where I live.'

*

Matt was at Peter's place having coffee with Acacia and Tiger. The weather being damp, the gas fireplace was lit, and Matt watched the flickering flames.

'So, what do you think?' Matt asked. He felt uncomfortable having this conversation. Emotions were never his strong point, and asking Acacia to come back to him was an emotional thing. 'Will you and Tiger come home?'

Acacia smiled, but she seemed unsure. She looked over at Tiger. He was sitting in his faux fur pet bed washing his face. He stopped, then trotted over to Acacia and jumped on her lap. Acacia stroked the top of his head.

Tiger rubbed his face against Acacia's hand, then lay down on her lap, stretching his front paws out to reach Matt's arm.

'Oh, is that so?' Acacia asked Tiger.

Matt put his head to one side in question.

'I think Tiger is trying to tell us something,' she said.

Matt reached over with his free hand and touched Tiger's paw.

Tiger seemed to smile at him.

'Seems like he wants us to give it another go,' Matt said quietly.

'You think?' Acacia laughed. 'Well, we could try it and see if we get along. Separate bedrooms at first, of course.'

Matt nodded. He hadn't thought of that. It would be awkward at first. 'So, how about I pick you and Tiger up around six thirty this evening?'

'Okay,' Acacia said, but she still appeared unsure.

'Acacia,' Matt said, 'I know I was a real idiot. That spell didn't help, but… it was everything happening all at once, you know?'

Acacia nodded. 'I know.'

Time to change the subject, Matt thought. 'Morgan tells me he's thinking of living in his Devon cottage permanently and doing ninety-nine per cent of the work online and via the phone.'

Acacia nodded. 'The lady who owned that cottage died and left a cat that is being looked after by a niece. Morgan is being carefully scrutinised by the niece, and if he passes muster, the cat will soon be back in its own home with him. I hope the changes he's made don't annoy the cat too much!'

'He needs a cat,' Matt said. 'They're such great company. I'm pleased for him.'

Acacia smiled, reassured that Matt was back to his old self. 'Okay. We'll be ready at six thirty.'

*

Linus felt lost, adrift on the ocean with no chance of rescue. What had he done? His lust for Savannah had completely taken him over. How stupid could he be? No one in New England would trust him ever again. What should he do?

He packed his case and drove to Heathrow. Where should he go? No point in going back to New England. Maybe he'd try France?

Matt was working in the bookshop, feeling happier than he had for a long time.

'Got time for a quick coffee?' Morgan met him at the door. 'I had a thought I need to share with you.'

'Sure. One moment, though.' Matt went over to Justin and told him the news.

Justin smiled broadly, and clapped Matt on the shoulder.

'What's happened?' Morgan asked as Matt approached him.

Morgan handed Matt a mug of coffee. Matt didn't like to tell Morgan he'd already had three mugs with Acacia. He accepted the coffee, hoping he wouldn't be too hyper with all the caffeine, and sipped absently.

'Acacia and Tiger are moving back in this evening,' Matt said, his eyes shining.

'Oh, Matt, that's brilliant,' Morgan said, genuinely pleased.

'Are you still thinking of making your Devon cottage your full time home?'

'I'm in the middle of arranging things so I can do just that,' Morgan said. 'Actually, there's possible office space in Exeter I've got my eye on, too. I might open another branch there, but I can still do most of my work from home, providing I get a good manager.' Morgan watched Justin as he served customers.

'Well you can keep your eyes off Justin,' Matt laughed, seeing Morgan's expression. 'He's mine.'

'Matt! As if! I was just wondering, though,' Morgan said. 'There's this guy I know who reminds me a lot of Justin. I might give him a call.'

'What's this about you getting a cat?' Matt asked. 'Did the previous cottage owner's niece give you the okay to take her aunt's cat, then?'

'She did,' Morgan said. 'I've met said cat, and we seem to get along fine. I just need to get things set up first. I don't want to bring him back to his old home, with its alterations, and then leave him for long periods. It won't take much longer though. And Sally is pleased to think Henry the cat is going back to his own home. He's ten years old and really doesn't like a lot of change.'

'Sally? Is that the previous owner's niece?'

'Yes,' Morgan said, unable to disguise his feelings, and grinning.

'I see,' Matt said. 'Pretty, is she?'

'She is actually, though that's not the only thing that makes her attractive. She's caring, loves animals, and makes wonderful cakes.' Morgan laughed at the ridiculous statement.

Matt laughed too, 'When can Acacia and I meet her? She sounds like someone we'd like.'

'Early days,' Morgan said, and sighed.

'What was it you wanted to see me about?' Matt asked. 'I really should get back to work.'

'You've got loads of stuff to do now, to get ready for Acacia and Tiger coming home,' Morgan said, placing his mug on the coffee table. 'I'll pop over in a few days' time, okay?'

'Sure,' Matt said, but his mind was already on the upstairs flat. He needed to buy some cat food and litter. He needed to get some fresh fruit and vegetables, and veggie protein food, something exciting but quick to make. He'd pop over to Waitrose and buy something there.

Jett was wandering around the churchyard, feeling lost. He stood in front of some gravestones, reading them.

Sylvia materialised in front of him. 'Hello, Jett.'

'Do I know you?'

'Don't you think it's time you went home?'

'Home? I don't have a home.'

'Yes you do, sweetheart. It's been ready for you for a long time. There are people there waiting for you. Your grandparents, some of your friends. They love you. It's time you left here and moved on.'

'My grandparents?'

'You've been hanging around this town long enough, Jett. Your grandparents passed away years ago. They're waiting for you. Come with me.'

Jett stared at Sylvia. His grandparents were waiting for him? How could that be? How long had he been dead, then? He was dead, right? He frowned in frustration. What was the matter with his brain? It didn't seem to work very well at all.

Sylvia held her hand out to him. He put his hand out to grab hers and found that he could. So, he thought, if both people are spirits they can touch each other. Interesting.

Sylvia held Jett's hand firmly in hers and together they floated upwards. Jett could see faces in the clouds, faces he recognised. He smiled. He was going home.

*

Home. Acacia sighed, pleased to be back in the flat. For her, the feeling of belonging encompassed the flat, the bookshop,

Matt and Tiger. Family, love, security, familiarity. She'd missed it. Peter and Tabitha had been great, and she knew there was a lot to be thankful for. But to be back with Matt, her and Tiger, their belongings around them. Could anything be better?

The icing on the cake was the fact that right now Matt's grandparents were here with them, like old times. There were orange and cream dahlias in vases and homemade chocolate fudge cakes in the tin.

'So, how does it feel to be home?' Tara asked Acacia, sipping her tea.

'It's wonderful,' Acacia said.

Tiger wandered over and jumped on Tara's lap, purring and snuggling before falling asleep.

'He seems happy about it,' Tara smiled.

'Tiger's been a big help,' Acacia said. 'Any awkwardness between Matt and I was smoothed over by Tiger. He's been brilliant.'

Matt and Sam were scrutinising book lists on Matt's laptop. Sam was trying to get Matt to have a specific science section.

'You two!' Tara said. 'Can't you leave that for a bit and come and join us girls?'

'Sure,' Sam said, but he was engrossed in something on the computer. Matt closed the programme, and playfully pushed his granddad over to the sofa where they joined Acacia and Tara.

'You know,' Sam said, sitting on the sofa and helping himself to more cake. 'It's been a really boring summer. I wish something exciting would happen.'

Unseen by Sam, Matt opened and closed his mouth but could find nothing to say. Acacia stifled a giggle.

'How about a holiday in Italy, Sam?' Tara suggested, straight-faced. 'We haven't been there for a long time, and we both love it.'

'Sounds like just the ticket,' Sam said. 'Now,' he turned to Matt, 'what about you two? Any holiday plans?'

Matt looked at Acacia. 'I think we'll finish the work in the walled garden this year.'

'Honestly, you two,' Sam said, 'you never have any excitement in your lives. You should expand your horizons a bit.'

Acacia and Tara burst out laughing. Matt sat there with his mouth open.

Sam appeared puzzled. Why had they reacted like that?

*

Morgan arrived the following morning looking agitated.

'What's up?' Matt asked. 'You said you had something to see me about, and it appears it's worrying you. What's the problem?'

Morgan swallowed. 'I don't know how to approach this, really.'

'Just say it,' Matt said, 'whatever it is.'

'Well, your sister, Sarah, she lives in Lancashire, right?'

'Yes, the Pendle area. Why?'

'It's famous for the Pendle witches – did you know?'

Matt stared at his cousin. What was he getting at? Was she in trouble?

Morgan saw the alarm on his cousin's face. 'Umm, it's just that Sarah is my cousin, obviously, although I've never met her, and I'd like to.'

'Why bring up the witches thing?'

'I just have this feeling,' Morgan said. 'I think we should go and visit her. You and me.'

'Oh, no,' Matt said. 'Please tell me she's not having magical problems up there?'

'I'm sorry, Matt,' Morgan said. 'I know you've decided to have nothing to do with magic, but I don't think we should ignore my intuition.'

CPSIA information can be obtained
at www.ICGtesting.com
Printed in the USA
LVHW021313031222
734485LV00013B/1102

9 781803 135380